All the Right Circles

All the Right Circles

John Russell

RARE BIRD BOOKS

LOS ANGELES, CALIF.

THIS IS A GENUINE RARE BIRD BOOK

Rare Bird Books
453 South Spring Street, Suite 302
Los Angeles, CA 90013
rarebirdbooks.com

For more information, address:
Rare Bird Books Subsidiary Rights Department
453 South Spring Street, Suite 302
Los Angeles, CA 90013

Set in Minion
Printed in the United States

10 9 8 7 6 5 4 3 2 1

Library of Congress Cataloging-in-Publication Data

Names: Russell, John, 1954– author.
Title: All the Right Circles: A Novel / by John Russell.
Description: Los Angeles : Red Bird Books, 2019.
Identifiers: LCCN 2019019674 | ISBN 9781644280423 (hardcover)
Subjects: LCSH: Lawyers—Fiction. | Race relations—Fiction. | Social classes—Fiction.
Classification: LCC PS3568.U76675 A44 2019 | DDC 813/.54—dc23
LC record available at https://lccn.loc.gov/2019019674

For my parents, Peggy and John.

Somewhere is better than anywhere.

Flannery O'Connor

Rabbi, who sinned, this man or his parents,
that he was born blind?

John 9:2

Getting Fancy

A HIGHWAY MAKES A circle around my hometown, dividing it neatly in two. The old families of Raleigh own drafty mansions inside the Beltline, where they walk from house to house and socialize. Everyone else lives outside the Beltline, a sprawling tract filled with folks who drive around in cars and don't know each other. My mother has always liked living out there and being alone in the crowd, but I got tired of it growing up. When I came back from New York, I took a law job and moved downtown. Then Pren and I got married—she's from one of the old families. Over time I've done a personal makeover to fit in with her friends, sporting snappy casual clothes and practicing easy chitchat. I even acquired a drafty mansion.

Still, when I'm questioning whether it's worth doing all I have to do to live inside the Beltline, I take a drive and think about the simpler, early years while touring the cul-de-sacs of my youth. Different people now settle in the former outback, successful types who hustle into town for jobs with a blue-chip outfit. They don't care much for the old ways, and they cheerfully mow down everything to start over, preferring new construction.

Invariably, folks call the new people Yankees, whether they come from Boston or Mumbai. All goes well for them, at first. They're taken in by the mild weather, the chitchat. But sooner or later, when they've crossed over the Beltline, they'll make a mistake—laugh too loud, sound a horn in traffic—and meet a glance, cold as a ready blade, that says *You don't belong, you may not even exist.*

I can still see my mother's college roommate, Mrs. Burnside, scowling at new people years ago, while I loaded her groceries in the Harris Teeter parking lot. She was a nice lady, even though she scowled a lot. The blond, chipper family at whom she scowled, Yankees for sure, had both laughed loudly and beeped. On top of that, they drove off in a BMW wagon, much too showy for the time. I wheeled Mrs. Burnside's cart toward a proper Buick.

"Bless their hearts," she said, gathering her cardigan against the chill of history. "They're like those pointy-eared people—my nephew watches them on the *Star Trek* show?"

"That would be the Vulcans, ma'am."

She smiled grimly and fished in her purse for a quarter. A quarter was real money back in the seventies. Now, in 1997, we're lucky quarters still work in the payphone.

Eventually, old people and new clashed over, well, everything. German automobiles versus American-made, bratwurst versus barbecue, but mostly over how to divide up the money progress brought to town. The new people had progress on their side, so they won.

Change triumphed in the grinding roar of construction cranes and the dispensing of bank notes all around. After a long struggle, suddenly, before our eyes, the Raleigh old-timers knew, inside the Beltline and out, turned into an all-American, suburban, brand-name place.

Most everyone adapted. But a few survivors, like Mrs. Burnside, wandered around traumatized. They couldn't get over it: one day they went into the Harris Teeter to get pimento cheese, and when they came out, their odd, old little city had become like everywhere else.

◆◆◆

WHETHER FROM BOSTON OR Mumbai or just down the road, I cheered the Yankees on, since I used to be one of them, and maybe, deep down, still was. But sometimes I thought this: I'd changed everything—clothes, job, marriage, religion, use of the second-person plural pronoun—all to fit in.

Was fitting in the right thing to do? Mostly, I concluded, it was. Surrendering to progress did not humble the old crowd I'd joined. It made them richer, and gave me the idea I could get rich, too.

Still, sometimes I got anxious, being a fit-in person. It's not about other people. The guys at the Club have been great. It was always me. I was always afraid I'd be exposed as an imposter.

Fear of being an imposter turned to panic last year when I agreed to a divorce with Pren. Among other things, marrying Pren had gotten me into the Capital Country Club. I dreaded that some members, or their wives, would kick me out, but they didn't.

I also had to break up with my girlfriend, Teri Lynn, a surprise. I hadn't planned on getting a girlfriend so soon, and it turned out to be a bad idea, since Teri Lynn happened to be my secretary, and this led to me being featured on television as a sexual harasser. The television story did not help my standing at the Club. But members make allowances. They know that being featured on television in an unfortunate light is a modern professional hazard.

Which leads me to work, and a real-life professional hazard. Some Wall Street guys who buy companies and wreck them have come to town to take over my biggest client, Raleigh's century-old, family-owned newspaper, the *Criterion*. I need to fight these Wall Street villains to save the paper, not to mention my career. I've been making a plan, but it's hard to get motivated, maybe because years ago, in New York, I worked for these Wall Street villains, and they used to be my friends.

Frankly, the problem runs deeper. I'm convinced that after a lifetime of being brave in a fashion, I've become a coward. Although I've tried, I can't seem to lord it over people at the office, enjoy guilt-free sex with lots of women, and do bad, destructive things in the service of a higher good, all of which men of courage have managed routinely throughout history. If it were up to me to take Omaha Beach, or rid the world of Goldfinger, we'd all be speaking German, or, if not that, living under the dominion of a Caribbean madman.

Cowardice is a personality problem I have to work through. Right now, though, I'm doing a favor for my mother.

Nora is holed up in a place called Harmony Hall, which is a cut-rate sanitarium paid for by health insurance. She goes there to stay a month or so when the world overwhelms her, which is about every other year. I try to help out, and usually she gets better quick enough. But this time, special circumstances have prolonged her stay—epic alcohol abuse and a near-fatal car wreck, to be specific.

To help things along, Nora's psychiatrist, Dr. Gardiner, asked me to put together a memory box. Dr. Gardiner thinks Nora needs a memory box to confront her past, but she believes this is nonsense. There is no past, she says; life is only one moment after another.

So, instead of being where I should be—at my office, enjoying my job, exercising power, doing manly, heroic deeds like fighting Wall Street villains—I'm standing in the driveway of my boyhood home, memory box in hand, preparing to go through Nora's underwear drawer. It's 9:30 a.m., and I can smell the last whiff of rush hour exhaust on the Beltline as the great world whirls by.

◆◆◆

STANDING OUTSIDE OUR WOEBEGONE sixties ranch house, which once looked regal to my eight-year-old eyes, the beginning seems a dream.

Nora was born just down the road in Durham, which is like Raleigh, except less so, and you'd think the old crowd inside the Beltline would give us a pass. But in 1964, we had to make our way as flat-out aliens. We did it up right, though, on the way down. We took the Southern Storm from Penn Station, all gleaming and steaming. Leaded coffee pots stood level on every turn, while the folks in the seats rattled around. Nora wore gloves and a fox fur in the dining car, and read aloud to me the train scene from *You Can't Go Home Again*—"Thumpeta, THUMpeta, THUMPETA," she intoned in crescendo during breakfast near Richmond, conducting a symphony of words, dead fox heads bouncing at her chin.

Hearing the racket and thinking Nora was drunk (she had sipped early from the silver flask), a bald black man in a starched white jacket handed me a coloring book meant for little kids. "Southern Serves the South," I read aloud, flipping through pages of locomotives.

"Sure enough does that," he said, patting me on the head, and handing over a box of Crayolas I didn't open. I didn't need crayons. I was eight, and ready for adventure.

When we got to Raleigh, a man named Buddy, who sold houses, drove us outside the Beltline to what he called a "starter neighborhood." Buddy was a regular guy. He didn't care whether you lived inside the Beltline or not. A starter neighborhood sounded just right to us. We were "A-1 starters," Nora said.

Nora picked out our house that afternoon. "Easier than lipstick," she said. "It's a ranch-palace. And not a busybody in sight." On the train, she'd insisted I stop calling her Mom and use her first name, so we'd be friends down here. I didn't think being friends with my mother was a good idea. She still got to tell me what to do, and I still had to hide the silver flask.

Getting the house in Raleigh back in 1964 was a big deal, after the problems we had in New York—Dad leaving us, Nora having to get a new job, the rise of the silver flask. Built new, with shutters, the ranch-palace seemed gigantic after our city apartment, and very colorful, the bricks orange, the yard lime green and pocked with clumpy, deep-red clay turned up by a bulldozer parked down the street.

I drew what the bulldozer looked like, with the Southern Railroad crayons, for Dad and the folks back home in New York, and put the pictures in letters. Long distance got expensive, Nora said.

Having approved the deal, Nora got out her good writing pen, the one she used for her books, and signed a contract with Buddy. He carried our bags inside. We were official Raleighites. I knew we were never going back to New York, even though Nora said we would. *In triumph!* she always said. *We'll return in triumph!*

Buddy stopped by every afternoon to check on us. He apologized for smelling like a bass boat. I'd never met anyone who smelled like a bass boat. Nora made him put on Aqua Velva before he came in. One day, Buddy asked me to go fishing with him, but it was not like he really wanted to. I could tell he wanted to take Nora on a date. Sure enough, he took her to see Elvis and Ann Margaret in *Viva Las Vegas*. Nora ironed one of her big city dresses and put on stockings and high heels. She swayed back and forth humming that song, "Vee-Va Las Vegas…Vee-Va Las Vegas," while she stuck on fake eyelashes. All I got out of it was a babysitter who rolled up her hair with orange juice cans.

The next weekend, Buddy helped us pick out a used woody wagon. Then Nora "sent him packing." That's what she always said when she broke up with a guy.

To beat the August heat, Nora threw our bathing suits into the woody wagon and sped onto the Beltline, which propelled us toward Highway 70 and humid, vacant Atlantic Beach. It was, I thought, like Jones Beach back home in New York, except even hotter, and there weren't any buildings, or trash, or even very many people. What sort of crazy place was this, I thought: a beach all to yourself?

She wore a bathing cap with pink flowers on it and sunglasses perched on top, her head always above the water. She taught me to swim like the famous guerrilla fighter Geronimo, showing me how to paddle through dangerous waters with noiseless tomahawk-chops, and make a war whoop when I came up for air. She admired guerilla fighters, like Geronimo and Che Guevara, and thought she was one too, in the colleges where she taught. At lunchtime, we got fried shrimp and hush puppies from some little shack. It was pretty tasty. I decided I liked this new place.

From that day on, Nora believed—wrongly, it turned out—that the Beltline was not a limit, but a launch pad for A-1 starters like us. From the great circle of the Beltline, you could spin off any which way. "It's a big damn highway to the moon!" she'd declare, gunning the woody wagon, whose false paneling had already started to peel. "Yo, little man, we're at Cape Canaveral!"

In her spare time, she scrutinized the *Criterion*, searching for scandals. She loved a scandal, especially if it involved "fancy guys," as she called the owners of the drafty mansions. The *Criterion* in those days featured a scandal a day, maybe two. Mostly they liked to get grifters—fancy guys who stole money. Along with scandals, Nora liked *incidents*, as she called them. After a while, when people in Raleigh got comfortable with us, she caused incidents, and everyone would get uncomfortable again. We mastered the art of the walk-out, from restaurants or neighborhood cook-outs, usually after she had used the word *racist*.

"Oh well," she'd say, shrugging. "We'll have a peanut butter and banana sandwich back at the ranch-palace. Who needs these racists." She didn't believe anything was more fun than causing an incident, so that the two of us could go home alone and share a peanut butter and banana sandwich.

On slow days for scandals and incidents, she read the *Criterion* to find out why the racists were on top and we weren't. The Beltline's self-conscious grandeur made her suspicious. Four lanes, six lanes—an incredible eight lanes soon—and where were they all going? Who was in, and who was out? Were the Beltline's origins racist? Had the Negroes been screwed over again? The Negroes were always getting screwed over, she told me, especially on highway projects.

"Aha," she said one day, jabbing the newsprint with a ruby fingernail. "Not racists! Grifters!" She read the story out loud, laughing because some fancy guys had bribed a contractor to over-build the road. "Rigged the bids plain as day!" She chuckled. "What chutzpah!"

Fraud she understood, and chutzpah she admired. "What the ruling classes call progress," she intoned in her teaching voice, gesturing over the steering wheel to the asphalt ahead, "is mostly plain old crime." She said things like that in her classes at St. Elizabeth's, a girls' boarding school downtown where she'd gotten a job when we had to leave New York. At St. Elizabeth's, she wasn't supposed to be talking up Marxism, but teaching young women about Shakespeare.

Most of the girls loved her, because she didn't give a damn, and secretly, they wished they didn't. Sometimes one of them would repeat Nora's tales about the ruling class at home, and ruling-class parents would complain. The headmistress, Dr. Poindexter, whom no one saw out in Raleigh without a perfect henna coiffure and double strand of pearls, would call a meeting of the Board of Trustees. Gavel in hand, at the head of a glossed-up antique table some ladies had saved from Sherman, below full-length portraits of Episcopal potentates in their white and scarlet, she refereed testy exchanges about Communism-in-our-Midst.

No doubt Dr. Poindexter could have done without that. She'd heard about Nora as a sassy prodigy at the Women's College in Greensboro. She'd hired her after the trouble in New York. No matter how much hell Nora raised, Dr. Poindexter never considered firing her. She loved that Nora didn't give a damn. She didn't care for her Board of Trustees, fancy guys every one, who half-listened, and then lectured, and then looked at their watches and went back to the office.

All in all, Dr. Poindexter thought she was lucky she had one faculty member who tried to teach the little darlings some reality, although she never said so to the Trustees. From time to time she called Nora into her office and instructed that she "take it easy with the Angela Davis stuff."

Then they'd have a glass of sherry.

Strange Water

D ESPITE HERSELF, NORA GREW attached to the Beltline. She drove us in full circles around it to find St. Elizabeth's. She burned gas to reach a faraway exit for the Winn-Dixie, which had better coupons than the Harris Teeter. She wandered in curlicues to the War Memorial Auditorium, where we saw Rodgers and Hammerstein musicals, which she thought tastefully challenged the white supremacy of the day, and to the piano lessons she made me take so I could learn to be a cultured person.

One weekend, she drove to the neighborhood where the fanciest people inside the Beltline lived, the ones with the lock-jaw drawl she imitated from parent-teacher conferences. She turned on a street with big oak trees and gabled houses set back on grassy hills, with sprinklers that hissed and rotated in arcs of water. I was scared and mad at her, which was sometimes the same feeling—we weren't supposed to be there, and she didn't care. Finally, she cut the headlights and the engine and rolled the woody wagon silently to a stop in front of an old stone house big as a city block. We sat in the dark and ate a peanut butter and banana sandwich and watched the family inside, like it was the *Ed Sullivan Show*.

"Are these people happy?" she whispered. "Their daughter has so many nice objects." I nodded and tried not to think about a police car roaring up lights blazing and us getting arrested. Instead, back in the realm of nice objects, I focused on the ankle-high, star-stamped Chuck Taylor basketball shoes I'd asked for last week.

"Plop, plop, fizz, fizz, oh what a relief it is—not to have nice objects." She broke off a piece of sandwich for me. "How do we get happy, little man? This is the question for our research."

Nora was always going after happiness. She would get happy for weeks, months at a time, so happy we'd go to New York and "seek asylum," as she called it, camping out in friends' old-smelling professor apartments across from Columbia so she could write pages of her book and tear them up while I watched TV. Then we'd go home, and she'd get unhappy and not come out of her room except to teach class. "Got to soldier on," she'd say, and the druggist would deliver strange pills "for energy." I'd hide the silver flask.

Most of the time, though, she just "got through the day." To show her stuff, she put on capri pants and rhinestone sunglasses and drove fast everywhere. In the land of outside-the-Beltline, we were outsiders plus— Nora worked, she didn't have a husband, and she wore capri pants. After years of living in New York, she'd decided to ditch her drawl. I'd never had a drawl, but it wasn't long before I was y'alling it up with the best of them.

The sum of all this foreignness was the charge, hard for a West Side kid like me to take, that we came from—ta da, Jersey! That was way worse than being a plain old Yankee. Somehow Jersey had become Raleigh's special ruin. People condemned us with a single remark: "You do know don't you—they're from New Jersey."

I explained we came from the City, for crying out loud! But I was half from here, too, since Nora was born in Durham, real tobacco-worker Durham, not Duke–Durham, where a lot of people did come from Jersey. I didn't mention that my dad now lived in Jersey. They didn't need to know that.

Explaining only made things worse, because that meant I was nothing really, just some big-mouth Yankee with an attitude. So I stopped explaining. The guys at school ganged up on me anyway. They called Nora a Commie, and then whistled at her from behind the pine trees when she picked me up, packing raw steak for my inevitable black eye. Their whistling gave rise to one of her throaty laughs, and she blew kisses and called them the "Lollipop kids" and waved goodbye with her rhinestone-sparkling cigarette holder. They never got it, and they never figured out she enjoyed being the outsider crashing the gate. I didn't like it as much as she did, but then again, she wasn't the one getting beat up.

◆◆◆

THOSE EARLY TIMES BUBBLED up today, after being buried in the fluoridated amnesia of my refugee childhood. Years of bad home maintenance had turned the brick ranch-palace I remembered into a dull period piece always in need of paint. Our once dead-calm street was now busy enough for speed bumps. The splotchy roof needed replacing. The yard, meanwhile, struggled against the forest primeval. Spider webs circled the porch, canvas furniture rotted. Two stray tabby cats that Nora had befriended wandered through unmolested, eating dishes of kibble I set out. The pines and scrub oaks had uprooted much of the grass, and red clay washed over the drive.

Last year, I persuaded Nora to start using a housecleaning service, an idea she accepted because hiring the can-do cleaning women of E-Z Home uplifted the working class, she said. It was not like hiring a maid, which was something she expected Pren and me to do, something, that is, for the bourgeoisie. Nora still used words like bourgeoisie in casual conversation. Long ago, in the fifties, at real-life coffee houses, I imagine she and her grad school friends regularly pounded Eisenhower, and General Motors for good measure, rounding off the afternoon with a bongo lesson or maybe a rump meeting of the World Federalist Society.

Reflecting on what had to be done to fix up the house, I heard what sounded like an old pickup pull into the driveway. It was Lowry, in the same Ford truck he'd driven the week Buddy stopped coming, to ask if we needed his help with our red-clay front yard. With some effort, Lowry got his big frame out of the truck and bent down to focus on an unruly stand of grass by the street. He'd been coming around more of less ever since Buddy left, taking a break whenever Nora got a new boyfriend who cut the grass.

Lowry tended yards around Raleigh and otherwise looked after living things. I remember he drove around for years with some old lady's parakeet in a cage lined with pages of the *Criterion*. He did so many good deeds like that, I couldn't figure out how he made ends meet from his yard business. At least he no longer rode solo. After he started taking on help, I got on him to form a company—Lowry Seed Ltd. Now, spiffed-up Lowry Seed trucks sporting the name moved at warp speed through the city, piloted by teams of Mexicans. The Mexicans he hired were different new people from the same new people the old people were still trying to get used to.

Lowry wheeled an old Toro from the back of the pickup. He cut stray grass that poked up by the street in a crisp, straight line. Then, throttling down, he pointed to a percolating stream of water I hadn't noticed.

"Jack," he hollered. "Looky here. You got a spring going in your yard! Come on and see this." He bent over to taste.

"Jesus, Lowry, stop drinking that, could have mercury in it."

He laughed and spread his hands over the dirt, making a bed around the fresh stream. Quickly he found loose rocks to make a small culvert. "Jack Callahan, listen to me. Do not be afraid of the Earth."

"Come on, Lowry, what the hell does that even mean? You can't just drink stuff out of the ground."

"Where do you think water comes from?" he said, rising up.

"Look, around here people don't drink strange water. They drink city water. It's a rule."

He laughed again and pointed his Toro up the hill. "That spring's a sign. You need to let me and Juan clear out this patch of scrub pine and start your swimming pool. Nora keeps talking about it."

Nora had always wanted a swimming pool where she could lounge like Betty Grable and read magazines. She imagined me on the patio in Foster Grants, flipping burgers for a crowd of studio hangers-on.

"That's crazy talk. Nobody has swimming pools in this neighborhood."

"Must be the strange water."

Grinning, he walked up the driveway, wiped his hand on his overalls and shook mine, his hammy palm overlapping my downtown grip. Lowry had a solid barrel chest from outdoor work, a round open face, and rich copper skin that some mistook for Italian, or Greek, or Arab. He was, by origin, a Lumbee Indian from the tribal lands south of Raleigh, which made him officially more ancient than the inside-the-Beltline people, not that they noticed. Nora referred to him as chief of the tribe, without any evidence. I regarded him as a chief of a different tribe, an evangelical church up Six Forks Road called Mighty Lamb, where he led choir practice and translated everything into Catholic for the new Mexican people he brought with him.

"So, today's the day," Lowry said, grinning wider. He usually showed up on the days Nora returned from Harmony Hall.

"Well—see—"

"Brought these for the big homecoming." He produced a wrinkled paper bag I guessed held two late-season German Johnson tomatoes, one of his home-garden specialties. He lived out in the country, beyond the outside-Beltline-settlers, on a small farm, with stray dogs and cats, and the occasional chicken.

"Lowry, she's staying in."

He whistled long and slow. "Dang. What happened this time?"

"She took a bottle of Allegra. Dr. Gardiner told me to pack a memory box."

I'd packed some trinkets into the memory box—easy to corral items such as earrings she ordered off the TV, a program from my daughter Robin's middle school graduation—and I really didn't want to do more. Nora had something of a pack-rat problem, and plunging into closets full of manuscript boxes, Broadway show bills, and Hallmark cards from 1967 didn't float my boat. Truth is, I'm a pretty bad caretaker, which is what you call picking up after sick people these days. That makes me a bad son, as well as a bad hero.

To get back on track, what I need to do now is climb up on the hero horse and fight villains at the office. That's how I'll get the money to pay for Nora's swimming pool, not to mention the extra bills from Harmony Hall. Somehow I'll have to find time to brush up on my caretaking. I don't have brothers and sisters, and there's nobody else to do it.

Lowry whistled again. "Allegra? Shoot. Nora doesn't have allergies." He leaned forward and squinted. "But you sure got the yellow eye. Need to take that trip with us to Mexico."

Lowry drove Juan and assorted hangers-on twice a year in a beat-up Cambio to some nowhere Mexican town called Dolores Hidalgo, where their mothers and wives and kids hung around by themselves and cashed gringo money from Raleigh. So, now, I'm invited.

"I don't have time to go to Mexico. I've got a job, and stuff."

"You had time for Juan. His mama wants to cook for you."

Last year, I'd agreed to help Juan get a green card, pro bono. This changed Lowry's attitude toward me. He said I was finally doing useful work. I thought I was doing useful work every day, but it was hard to sell Lowry on that.

First, though, I had to keep Juan from being deported. Answering a summons, we rounded up his papers and rode to the old federal building in Charlotte. He and I sat there for five hours before confronting INS in their natural habitat.

"Juan Hernandez?" Ms. Sanchez, the examiner began, staring at us sitting ramrod-straight in wooden chairs before her regulation metal desk. Juan had dressed in a crisp white shirt Lowry got him from Belk's, and was prepared to charm her with photos of his two sons in altar-boy garb. "Your papers have expired," she declared. "We've arranged for you to leave the country this afternoon."

Juan retorted in Spanish, pointing to me, and she jumped in rapid-fire. Didn't help that my high school language skills had gone useless.

"Officer Sanchez," I interrupted, tapping Juan's arm until he sat back in his chair. "I believe there's been a mistake. As you see, we've redrafted this statement and the papers are in order." I placed the file open in front of her.

"I didn't know Butler and Symmes took immigration cases," she said, noting our letterhead and eyeing my suit. Perhaps I had overdressed.

"We represent Mr. Hernandez, and we'll take all necessary steps to enforce his rights, including going upstairs right now to find a judge."

She stamped the papers. "Enjoy your stay in the United States, Mr. Hernandez," she said, smiling thinly.

We rode back to Raleigh and celebrated with Lowry over a steak dinner. Apparently, though, Lowry thought we needed a proper fiesta. "Lowry, I'm happy to go at it with the INS every once in a while. Nobody has to throw me a party south of the border."

"Jack Callahan, I've got two things to say. First is, you saved Juan from the INS, and that's using your God-given talents to help people, you need to do more of that work."

"Thanks for the advice. What's the second thing?"

"Sorry?"

"You said there were two things."

"The second thing is you could use a fiesta more than anybody I know." He waved vaguely southward. "On the way there we'll stop off for a couple of days and see the Fathers. The Sanctuario is near Dolores. How can you beat that?"

I had no idea what he was talking about. Lowry was always cooking up some scheme for self-improvement, and I figured going to see the Fathers, whoever they were, was more of the same. "Lowry, I've told you a million times, I can't go to Mexico."

"What if I said your life depended on it."

Lowry was always saying my life depended on this or that. I didn't take him seriously.

"I'll think about it, okay?"

"Great! We'll go for Easter. That's when the guys get off." Lowry bent down to collect strange water in a plastic bottle and then straightened. "Stop worrying, you hear? I'm taking this along to the church."

Lowry drove off, the seed truck putt-putting. I got left with two ripe German Johnsons.

Attending to my memory box assignment, I rummaged in Nora's underwear drawer where I found an old sewing kit. Clipped inside sat a photograph of the two of us—she in a dark cloth coat and a tartan scarf, holding my hand, a toddler in a snowsuit in front of Grant's Tomb. As usual, Dad was AWOL, probably taking the picture. The black and white Polaroid had blurred in the middle, giving the scene an antique look, foreign like the name on my birth certificate: Jacob Callahan Gold.

After we arrived in Raleigh and met Buddy, Dr. Poindexter, Mr. Peebles, Mrs. Burnside, Lowry, and the Lollipop Kids, and after I got used to strangely colored things like yellow school buses and red hot dogs, Nora took me to Ballantine's, an old-style cafeteria she thought of as a southern-fried automat. I'd gotten beat up again, and she said I needed a treat. We caught the afternoon sun on the Rebel Terrace, with its twin Colonel Sanders-like marble statues guarding the door.

Attacking her hamburger patty, she speared a sweet pickle slice and cackled, startling an elderly couple beside us who were enjoying the early bird discount.

"Jake," she said, saying my name like she'd never heard it before, and looking at me over her rhinestone spectacles, "I've thought of something fun."

"What?"

"We'll get new names."

"That's dumb. You can't get new names."

She gave me her teacher look. "Open your mind, little man! We're free people!"

I hated it when she said we were free people. That usually meant she was about to cause an incident. I couldn't eat any more mac and cheese.

"So, what's our new name, Mommy?"

"Callahan! Let it ring! And don't say Mommy."

"What about Daddy? Jacob Gold is his name. He's not changing."

She nodded her head slowly. "You're right. But your father won't mind if we do."

"Yes, he will. Nora Gold is your name, and Jacob Gold is my name, like his. And people call me Jake, so they can tell us apart. That's the way it's supposed to be."

"Honey, there's no 'way it's supposed to be.' Your father won't mind if we change our names. To mind, he'd have to think straight, and that's impossible for him right now."

Dad had called. He was getting married to Laura.

"You're being mean."

She sighed and rubbed my hand. "Maybe I'm being a little mean. But I'm allowed. My own mother is mean as a snake. I'm a picnic compared to her. Now another thing we have to do is change that first name of yours. People don't know what to do with Jake. It sounds Jewish."

"But we are Jewish."

"Not anymore. We'll be—Methodists! They're a good bunch."

"How can you stop being Jewish?"

She laughed. "That's a good one."

I didn't think it was funny. I wanted to know.

She pressed on. "Look, lots of people call you Jack already."

"Sometimes Miss Clarke does," I admitted, reluctantly.

"See? That settles it. We'll call you Jack from now on."

"Mommy, I don't want to change my name. I don't care if people think I'm Jewish."

She gripped my forearm, smiling, "I'll get you that beagle puppy…"

Thus, Nora changed me from Jacob Gold the Jew to Jack Callahan the Irishman, all for the price of Sammy the beagle, who lived with us through the summer of eighth grade until he met his end on the grille of a Dodge Dart. Changing our names only intensified rumors that we came from New Jersey.

End Times

I PADDED AROUND THE silent ranch-palace, turning on the kitchen radio for company, and dialing in one of the preachers you listen to down here. *The world is ending!* he said. You could hear it in the drip, drip, drip of the mercury-poisoned spring water, and the putt-putt of Lowry's truck as he drove off to save people. End Times!

But, like all the other radio preachers, this guy didn't say what the End Times meant. Did everybody disappear, like *pow*—in an instant, you're standing in the Harris Teeter checkout line, and then you're in the hereafter? Or, are the End Times more personalized—say, your wife kicks you out of your house, and you start living in a room at the Club, and your biggest client goes under.

Kaboom!

I finished out my memory box work with a book of matches from the West End Café on upper Broadway and an old subway token. I'd ended up following a New York theme: upbeat times; good times; leaving out the manuscript drafts smudged with lipstick and bourbon; stuck in the manic years, 1973, 1985, 1992; and then the depressed years, 1974, 1986, 1993, and so on.

Rather than think of myself as a caretaker, I decided to think of fetching for Nora as a hobby. I don't have other hobbies, except maybe playing the piano. I still play golf pretty well. It takes my mind from work, and my failures, and the Club makes golfers turn off portable phones, which helps everyone relax.

Before my recent reversals of fortune, work had been good to me. About ten years ago, at the ripe young age of thirty-one, I became a partner in the now-huge law firm of Butler and Symmes that gave Officer Sanchez such pause. I'd started there as the junior lawyer to Hugh Symmes—it was his name on the door. Turns out, I was pretty decent at doing stuff right away, sometimes without having to ask. When I got to be a partner, fancy guys who once ignored me didn't anymore. They paid me to set up their deals, say grace over money, and write words that kept the venture capital flowing, or financed hospital bonds, or sold the family tobacco farm. They forgot to mention Jack Callahan was an Irish Jew from New Jersey.

Big clients like Wardie Forrest, who ran the *Criterion*, began to call directly, which was fine with Hugh, though I didn't know why until later. Decades before, the Forrests had begun to go liberal, which at first confused, and then infuriated the conservatives around them. Wardie himself was very liberal, if not personally evolved, and he didn't care what conservatives, or anybody in fact, thought about him. This was a useful trait. Changing the Forrests from Jim Crow segregationists to civil rights crusaders had proved a long and winding road, and Wardie was now the trail boss.

Looking after the *Criterion* for the last century had also proved a long and winding road for Butler and Symmes. Butler and Symmes lawyers acted as the paper's praetorian guard, protecting the newspaper princes from libel charges and politico attacks. Last year, after Hugh's retirement, chief guard duty passed to me.

Inconveniently, Wardie Forrest had picked that moment to borrow money from Victor Broman, the Wall Street guy I once worked for. In my new role as chief of the guard, I warned Wardie not to do it, but he did. Being a newspaper magnate and all, Wardie sometimes didn't follow my advice.

Wardie took money from Victor Broman because Ameribank wouldn't loan him any more. Ameribank had been the Forrests' bank for years, but now, after a thousand or so mergers, it was the biggest bank in the world, and didn't seemed to care much about the Forrests. The bankers in charge basically thought Wardie had gone crazy, fallen under the spell of people in California and the World Wide Web.

Wardie did love the World Wide Web. He thought he could turn his newspaper into an engine for it. When you say "engine" to bankers, they assume it means something that runs on gasoline and makes noise. This isn't what Wardie meant, and when he tried explaining what his "engine" was, it made him sound like a mad scientist, which is not what bankers expect a newspaper magnate to sound like.

But Victor Broman understood what Wardie meant, and so did people in California, who had started calling the World Wide Web the Internet, and were getting very rich from it. Victor Broman would loan money for Wardie's engine.

Broman loaned, and Wardie spent—so far, no engine. Now, Wardie couldn't pay Broman back, and we had big trouble. Losing the *Criterion* would be more than a bad day at the office. It would be my personal End Times. Kaboom!

◆◆◆

ON THAT POINT, LAST night we got an ominous fax from Broman. Your money or your life, it more or less threatened. "They're serious this time," Elaine, my partner, said, calling from the office fax room. "Ferris is coming on the morning plane."

Ferris was Broman's lawyer, and he used to be my friend in New York. "We've had these fire drills before. I don't think he's coming."

"Jack—I've got a bad feeling. What's your schedule in the morning?"

"Need to deal with Nora first thing, then I'll be there. Odds are he's bluffing. But call me."

While rummaging around for Nora's memory box, I channeled Elaine's bad feeling, and sensed things getting nasty at the office. Before I could make a move, Nora's old princess phone rang in the kitchen, bearing news, I thought, from Harmony Hall. I hustled to pick up. "Jack?" a familiar voice said. "Where's Nora? Not home yet?" It wasn't Harmony Hall, but Hugh, my old boss. Calling Nora's princess phone was one way to check on her, or me.

"She's staying in. Took a bottle of Allegra. Gardiner thought she was at risk."

"That's ridiculous. Since when does taking allergy medicine mean you have a plan to kill yourself?"

"I'm not a psychiatrist."

Hugh didn't think much of me these days. He noticed I'd been doing a lot of caretaking. That was outside the realm of acceptable, manly work. Somebody else—a wife, for example—should do the caretaking, and I should focus on hero stuff, like saving the *Criterion*.

"Damn. This is Lowry's doing. I'm gonna have him tailed."

"Don't have Lowry tailed. He drives Nora to Mighty Lamb for AA meetings and then drives her back, that's all."

Lowry had convinced Dr. Gardiner to furlough Nora for AA, and said he'd be her sponsor. This good deed got Hugh agitated. He'd just returned from his own, more executive rehab at the Center, where the firm sent partners who had troubles with their own silver flasks.

"Hugh, I've got to run—feel free to go down to Harmony Hall yourself. I doubt Gardiner will talk to you, but while you're there, you might look in on Nora. She's been asking."

"Sounds like you're having me tailed," Hugh said.

"Nope, absolutely not. Hey, listen, I've really got to go to the office."

"Yes, you do. I'm not one to give advice, but you left Elaine there by herself. The *Criterion*'s on your watch now."

Though retired, Hugh kept sources at the office. What he meant was he didn't give the *Criterion* account to me so I could give it to Elaine.

"And mind yourself with the Bank," he added, by way of not giving advice. Ameribank was also our client. It had become our largest client, mostly because it grew so big and we chased it shamelessly.

I checked my flip phone to see why it wasn't ringing. Turns out, I'd pushed the wrong button and it got stuck on silent. Elaine had left five messages. The last one said: "They're here. No money. What's the plan, Stan?"

Suddenly, I saw the way the End Times would happen for me. Victor Broman takes over the *Criterion*. Headline reads: "Newspaper Eaten Alive by Wall Street Raider." And then, below, "Fake Fancy Guy Fired."

"Better get ready!" the radio preacher said. And then, Lowry: "Your life depends on it!"

A trumpet sounded. Or was it my flip phone? Be a hero, Hugh said, and don't let a girl do your work.

Time Zones

ELAINE MET ME OUTSIDE the twenty-ninth-floor conference room. Brown hair still freshly curled to her shoulders, she was in full battle dress: black suit, silk blouse, and mascara. Flushed at the throat, she tapped her stilettos fast. She had a right to be mad for being left alone with Ferris and his crew. Actually, she'd been mad at me a while now, since she had to help me with the Teri Lynn mess. I was still working my way out of that doghouse.

"Where've you been?" she whispered loudly. "Could you for once pick up your phone?"

"Sorry. Got stuck on silent."

"That happens—to idiots."

"Sorry."

Elaine and I went back all the way to law school. We had a parallel understanding of the fancy guys around us. She liked some of them individually, but didn't like them as a class group, and generally slid under the radar by being a woman, a Yankee, or both.

She'd also been with me during the Broman period in New York, so she understood what we were up against. For part of that time, she was sort of my girlfriend, a history we ignored, except lately, in a negative way, which was part of the problem.

"Want to get the facts, or are you just going to wing it?"

"Facts, please."

"Ferris showed up first thing. Guess somebody in Washington let him out."

I was going to say sorry again, this time for the federal penal system, but thought better of it. I'd been saying sorry a lot lately, mostly to Elaine and Pren, and my daughter Robin, and, oh, to Nora because of the memory box, and to Teri Lynn, because I'd behaved badly, and we had a lawsuit against each other. Saying sorry didn't usually bother me, but lately, it made me feel like an abject, beaten dog.

Leonard Ferris, recently released from the executive cell block at Lewisburg, waved at me goofily from behind the glass windows of our main conference room, which we'd recently fitted with a marble table big enough for Mussolini and a modernist wall painting featuring skinny, frightened people making scary faces on a bridge.

We sought to create anxiety through art and furnishings. It was useful to our craft. Ferris, however, was immune to art and furnishings. He had shed anxiety years ago, having done many bad deeds without a reckoning. Then he went to prison. Funny, I never thought I'd have friends who went to prison.

Elaine and Ferris had bad blood from the old days in New York. I clerked that summer at a Wall Street firm; Ferris was my boss. The two of us worked for Broman, while Elaine watched on in horror. She worked for liberals, suing to give homeless people the right to sleep on street grates.

Back then, Broman had been a lone wolf, a corporate raider who used junk bonds like napalm. Now, decades later, he had become a leader of private equity, which was a polite term for continuing the rape and pillage of his early years, but with respectable people as partners. He'd already gotten rich once with the napalm, and private equity made him rich beyond rich. It'd been a swell ride.

Over the years, I'd helped out when asked, enjoying the whoosh-whoosh of Broman's jet stream and putting away the dough he paid me on the side, which my increasingly fancy lifestyle demanded. Self-exiled in Raleigh, I figured I could keep my hand in and be safe from Victor's bad doings. I was wrong.

"Ugh. Why did you put them in there?" I motioned ahead to the Mus-solini room, where Ferris was already at the courtesy bar, helping himself to one of his daily dozen Diet Cokes. She knew I hated the new decor.

"Only thing not booked up," Elaine said. I didn't believe her. I think she did it deliberately. She eyed me up and down. "Do you want me to deal with Ferris? You look shaky."

"Nora took a bottle of Allegra. They're not letting her out today."

"That's why you're moping around? Antihistamine? What was it last month? Didn't she wander off to Wendy's?"

Elaine had little patience for Nora's Harmony Hall drama. She professed long experience with addicts from her work with the poor.

"She needs to stop playing games and get out of that place," I offered, excusing the recurring mess.

"She doesn't want to get out, Jack. You men all flit around and she gets attention."

"It's not that simple."

She stepped back and eyed me critically. "Does Hugh know?"

"He called this morning at the house hoping she was there. She wasn't so he ended up yelling at me."

"That's how you act when you have a girlfriend, even if you're seventy-five."

Nora was Hugh's girlfriend, a fact people had had to keep secret for the last several decades, since he was also married. Inside the Beltline Nora and Hugh were what you called a non-secret secret. Everybody knew, but nobody talked about it. There were lots of non-secret secrets.

"I'll ask again," Elaine pressed on, gesturing to the room behind. "Do you want me to deal with Ferris?"

"Nope."

"Okay, then. Forget about this morning, can't do anything about it. Breathe," she said. "Now, open." She pushed me through double glass doors into the conference room.

Inside, lounging in the corners, leaning over piles of paper, pouring more sodas from our bar, stood Ferris and his pinstriped accomplices. Surveying the casually corrupt scene, it occurred to me that over the years Broman had moved on from mere self-interested behavior to true evil. I didn't pursue the thought, however, as it required applying moral judgment to the private equity world, an empty, futile gesture.

Also, there was this slippery notion of evil. Was Broman evil like Hitler, or like the Oakland Raiders? If Hitler, one needed to mobilize; if the Oakland Raiders, one could root for another team, perhaps the Securities and Exchange Commission, and, during the course of the long and bloody struggle, be yourself enriched.

Was I crazy to care, to fight for the fancy guys, save the *Criterion*? It'd be easy enough to roll over, cut a deal, and get a few bucks for the Forrests. Maybe that's what Ferris expected. But right now I wasn't feeling it. I was feeling like Humphrey Bogart at the end of *Casablanca*, like John Wayne at *Fort Apache*. Bring it on!

I couldn't help taking it personally. Victor made a show of being the bloodless tycoon, but he wasn't. "Fellas, I'll do your deal, or you do mine, doesn't matter," he would say for effect. But, oh yeah, he kept score. In my case, after that summer gig in New York, Ferris had asked me to become his number two—be on the phone with Broman, be on the plane with Broman, do everything Broman said. It was global, transformational, all the buzz words, sounded great.

I tried hard to fit in. But then, a deal went bad. Moral issues arose, and I left New York to go back to Raleigh. Victor didn't forget that I'd jumped the pirate ship. That would be his G3 jet, which is what pirate capitalists cruise the world in today. Now, of all the gin joints, as Humphrey Bogart himself said, Ferris showed up in mine—Raleigh, the hometown where I'd returned to escape.

Having been on Broman war-parties before, I tried to nonchalantly assess the conference room muscle. "This is bad, bad," I whispered to Elaine. "Ferris brought a full team. Probably more wise guys outside the *Criterion*. Need to grab Wardie."

"I'll put him in your office," she said quickly, clacking off in her war pumps.

Counting from the start, Ward Forrest was the third generation of Forrest men to run the *Criterion*. For five years he'd turned a small profit. Now, technology threatened even that.

This was a generational problem. Back when Hugh ran the praetorian guard, there wasn't an Internet, or private equity. Hugh's biggest problem had been Jesse Helms, or the Great Satan, as he was known around the *Criterion*. Whenever Senator Helms blustered, Hugh would call and give him the what-for. They'd jaw at each other and tell stories about the War.

But today's a different world. Senator Helms is long gone, and Wardie just borrowed big money to bet on the Internet. How was I going to fix that? Tell a story about the War?

"So, what's Ferris saying?" I asked Elaine, who'd reappeared with Wardie's file.

"Here, take a look," she said. "He's been behind for months. It's too late to get a wire out today, so you need to come up with something."

"Great."

"At five, Ferris and the boys are going to walk down the street and take over the building."

"That so? Maybe Jimmy Hoffa will show up."

She laughed. We encouraged humor in crises.

"You talked to our friend Judge Blount?" I asked.

"Of course. I drafted an order. Kai-Jana didn't jump to sign it."

"What did she say?"

"'The Forrests are in big trouble,' and then she laughed and went back into chambers. What the hell?"

For all her time down here, Elaine didn't have a refined ear for the cries and whispers of high-level race relations. Judge Kai-Jana Blount—coming from three generations of civil rights aristocracy—would take a schadenfreude moment in her chambers, channel her own grandfather, Reverend Blount of the NAACP Hall of Fame, and enjoy the difficulties of an old foe. Way before Wardie's time, the Forrests talked up Negro outrages and the perils of race-mixing. In the 1890s, the Blounts fought on Wilmington's bloody streets against a racist mob backed by the *Criterion*. During the forties, the *Criterion* chastised the Reverend Blount for being impolite when demanding his rights. Times are different, but bad memories stick around.

"But did she actually get what was going on, that Victor Broman's involved?" I asked.

"Oh yeah. I went back in there and made sure I told her the whole thing. She asked if Ferris had come down, and I said yes, and then she signed the order."

Thankfully, karma had worked our way. Our law school classmate Kai-Jana remembered Ferris from the old days. At least the order would keep Ferris out of the newspaper office for a while.

But there was another thing: even if Wardie came up with the money later, Broman didn't have to take it. I told Wardie this could happen. Most people who lend money want it back. But some people don't want it back. Some people want your stuff.

If Broman took over the paper, I knew, somehow, everything would turn out to be my fault. It'd be a century of prestige and power down the drain on the Irish Jew's watch.

Leaving Ferris to his plotting, I walked down the hall to find Wardie making calls from my office. He waved from my high-backed swivel chair. A half-dozen pink message slips lay crumpled on the floor.

Although I had no reason to know Wardie growing up, it felt like I did. His image had appeared to me in granite for years. Ward, his first name, sat chiseled on my middle school; Forrest, his last name, graced a gargantuan soccer park and the school of journalism at Chapel Hill. Not much older than me, it was though he rose to his job sua sponte from decades of philanthropy and intrigue. So much finger food and stone work.

"Jack," he said, standing to offer his slow-rhythm handshake. Tousled salt-and-pepper hair had begun to chase away the sailor's blond locks, and he stood slightly stooped from a life of bending down to mask his six-foot-four frame, annotated for all time in the basketball stats of the 1969 Woodberry Forest yearbook. Spurred to travel by his father, he had once circled the world in a small boat, which led him to stoop all the more. At the *Criterion* helm he dressed casually and for command, but today perspiration rimmed his pressed blue Oxford shirt; he stretched, and stifled a yawn, his tan face crinkling at the eyes, as though he wished mightily to be on the inland waterway, staring into sunlight from the captain's chair of his Grady-White. "Where you been, man, on the course?"

"Sorry, came as soon as I could."

"Well, get me the hell out of here. They're making me nervous, just milling around. I think one of them has a gun."

"Wardie, we need to talk. It's bad."

"Look, if it's about being late on the money, I've got it. Every dime."

So why don't you pay on time? I thought but didn't say. Skating to the edge like this had pushed me into yelling at him before, dangerous to do with a headstrong client.

Elaine cleared her throat. "Wardie. We can't do a wire today. It's too late."

He shrugged. "What do they care if it's today or tomorrow? Just get Ferris in here and cut him a check."

"Ferris isn't doing that," I said. "Broman wants the paper."

He snorted. "What! That's crazy. What the hell would he do with it?"

"You tell me. I do know they could go down there in an hour and change the locks."

"You mean Broman can walk in and take over my family business because he won't cash a check until tomorrow? Jesus, Jack. This isn't Russia."

"Nope. More like Vegas. On the good side, Kai-Jana Blount is issuing an order, and that'll hold them off for ten days. But we really need to figure out a way to pay, or else they'll just come back."

He studied the ceiling for a long second, cursed, and then slapped his hand on my desk, rattling more pink slips. "How the hell could you let this happen?" he said, voice rising. "Hugh Symmes would never get beat by these clowns."

I held my breath and walked to the window, which looked over the *Criterion* offices fronting a trash-strewn park with a heroic statue of his morning-coat-bedecked grandfather, Old Man Forrest, finger pointed upward to posterity. Most days Wardie poked fun at Hugh and his backroom way of doing things, the non-secret secrets. But at crunch time, Wardie figured Hugh the Great would just ride in to save the day, like a tale from yesteryear. Hi ho, Silver!

"I mean it Jack, how the hell—"

"Wardie, you need to stop being so reactive," Elaine said firmly, in her alpha-guys-cut-it-out mode. She closed my office door. "The fact is, we're late on the payment. Can't change that." She turned to me, eyes pleading against a blow-up. "Jack, is there a plan? We've got maybe forty-five minutes."

I did some in-out breathing I'd learned in anger management. There was a plan. The End Times summoned heroic acts. At the End Times, all is not gloom and doom. Dragons get cut up by muscular guys in togas.

"Jack, the plan?"

"Got it," I said slowly, exhaling. "We'll go backward in time and bypass this bad moment."

I illustrated by making a curvy motion with my arms.

Elaine sat down heavily in a side chair. "Are you insane?"

"No. Different time zones! We'll take money from San Francisco and give it to New York. It's all good."

"Damn, Jack, that's brilliant," said Wardie, slapping his hand on my desk again. "Can I leave now?"

"Hold on," Elaine said, scowling. "You can't wire money across time zones."

"Not wiring, transferring. We're in the same giant bank. It's a beautiful thing!"

"How do you even know Broman has an account?"

"Don't."

"How do you know the Bank won't get pissed off?"

"Don't."

"There's Kai-Jana's order. Tomorrow—"

"We'll be exactly where we are today."

Wardie was nodding his head. But Elaine? She believed I needed a month at Harmony Hall.

"Jack," she said, "if you piss off the Bank, we'll get fired. I've got a kid to send to college." She jerked open the door and clacked off, muttering.

"You know Elaine, she gets melodramatic," I said to Wardie.

"Yeah, just like my ex-wife. Never got my bold ideas."

I was about to add that the list of people who didn't get Wardie's bold ideas also included every other member of his family, who all wanted their money out of the paper, except his little sister Tatty, who thought everything he did was cool, and whom he was about to call in San Francisco to help supply the missing cash personally.

"Genius is so little appreciated in the moment."

"Absolutely, man."

While Wardie got on the phone, I went next door to dial up Billy Arnold, the city exec for Ameribank, and my golf partner. He was a good guy, and I felt bad about what I was about to do.

"Billy?" I had dialed his car phone, guessing by the hour he was on the way to Pinehurst. "It's Jack."

"Hey, podner, when we gonna hit the little round ball?"

"Soon. Look, I got a favor to ask. It's for Wardie."

"Sure. What's the deal?" Billy and Wardie had grown up riding around in the same powerboats.

"We're trying to get a payment done today, and we've run out of time on the East Coast. Tatty Ward has the money in San Francisco, and we need to get it to Victor Broman in New York. You know—'One Bank, One America.' Great ad, by the way."

Static crackled over the car phone. Maybe Billy was stalling, trying to drive out of range in the Pinehurst sand pits. He felt responsible, he had told me, for Wardie being shut out of the Bank. He'd been overruled by the top brass in Charlotte, something that seldom happens to a city exec. He'd extend himself if he could. But this was a big ask.

"Sorry podner," he said, finally. "Got under a bridge. Jack, you sure this is okay? You've got to be my lawyer here. You're not supposed to wire across time zones."

"Not a wire, man, a transfer. Y'all invented this really cool national bank, remember?"

He laughed. "Yeah, I remember." He fell silent, considering. It was a risk. But Billy was doing more risky things these days. He started meetings now by asking people how they felt, which set an odd tone, since he was supposed to be in charge. He told me over beers at the Members Bar that he'd been thinking about taking a break from his marriage and asked what it was like on the outside. He'd missed golf last month for some strange-sounding man's weekend, where he banged on drums and chanted. He'd lost fifteen pounds and cut his hair really short. Sometimes he didn't even wear a tie to work. I worried about him, but I figured it was his business. Heck, given my record over the last six months, he might think I'd gone a little haywire, too.

"Okay Jack," Billy said, his voice just audible through the static. "If you think this is okay. I know the gal out in San Francisco."

"Thanks, Billy."

"We'd best not talk about this again."

Elaine reappeared, having processed the risk of lost college tuition. She fixed her team smile in place. "Told Ferris about Kai-Jana's order. He went total batshit."

"Good. Don't let it bother you."

"Did you think it would bother me?"

"No. There's more good news."

"You got Billy Arnold to do it, didn't you?"

"Yeah."

"We're all going to get in big trouble."

"No, actually, we're going to save a newspaper."

Winston Churchill might have said something like that, facing down the Jerries. I began to feel heroic stirrings.

Just Like Dad

JACK, THANKS FOR THE card," Ferris said, meeting me and Elaine at the conference room door. He squeezed my arm in a power clinch. "Hope my note got back to you."

"Didn't know what was appropriate," I said, reclaiming my arm. "A cake with a screwdriver?"

"The card was very thoughtful."

Ferris looked more worn and less jolly than I remembered, with wrinkles starting at the eyes and mouth. A machine tan had turned him nearly orange. It occurred to me we were both getting older. Seeing me pause, he decided to step back and case my outfit. "Wrong decade for the classic blue suit, Jack," he said. "Besides, you've got a golf glove in your back pocket."

Ferris and I always sparred over wardrobe. The first time we met, when he interviewed me years ago at law school, he opened with an insult about my stiff new Church cap-toed shoes, purchased by Hugh for the occasion.

"Where'd you get the JLDs?"

"JLDs, sir? What are JLDs?"

"Oh, shit, don't call me *sir*. We're in Cambridge, not—oh, let's see—North Carolina. Duke, no, Chapel Hill? Just like Dad's—that's JLDs. Your shoes. Nobody under fifty wears them."

"Oh. They were a present. Hugh Symmes gave them to me. He's my mentor."

"Let me get this straight. There's some older guy named Symmes in North Carolina buying you fancy English shoes? Something you want to tell me that's not exactly on the old resume, Callahan?"

Cackling, Ferris left for the next room to answer a phone and yell into a speaker at somebody I later learned was Victor Broman. Broman ordered him to "Get on a plane to Juarez and shut Pro-Mex down."

"I've got one question for you, Callahan from North Carolina," he said, returning to his interview seat. "Is your mother Nora Callahan?"

"Yes."

"Author of *E. M. Forster and the Death of England*?"

C'mon, he'd actually read it?

"That's my mom."

"Fantastic. You're hired."

"Wait. There's supposed to be a process. They told us all about it in orientation. This is step one. The campus interview."

"There's no process. They lied. But you need to take the job right now, because I have to go to Juarez."

"Is this really—I mean, are you sure—"

"Look, do you want the job or not? You get a ridiculously high salary." He leaned over and whispered a number.

"I'll take it."

"Great decision, Callahan." He patted me on the back. "A girl from the office will send you papers to sign."

Turned out Ferris had indeed read *E. M. Forster and the Death of England*, Volume I, that is. Nora was still working on Volume II. He'd studied modernism at Yale and gotten confused about the meaning of history. Apparently, Nora straightened things out. Forster proved history didn't matter, she said; all that counted was people mixing together in a great big gloppy mass, connecting. Then World War I messed everything up. She planned to sort out World War I in Volume II. The E. M. Forster Society gave her an award.

But the sorting out had her stuck. World War I proved more awful than expected, and Forster had to deal with a lot of non-secret secrets. She'd been blocked through multiple drafts. Dr. Gardiner didn't know whether being blocked made her depressed, or being depressed made her blocked. The silver flask didn't help.

Ferris started writing her admiring letters, after he got the address from me. Nora especially prized his prison correspondence. "If only Leonard had known Foucault!" she'd said, clutching his robin's-egg-blue stationary to her peignoir. No one on Wall Street called him Leonard.

Today was not a day for Forster, or Foucault. Casually, I retrieved the golf glove he noted and tossed it aside. I tried to imagine I was throwing down a gauntlet. Ferris once played a good game of golf himself, and they used to let you take your clubs to Lewisburg.

"C'mon, Ferris. I wasn't going to say anything, but the turtleneck makes you look like Barry Manilow."

He laughed, but I could see it wounded him.

On a great arc from Juarez to Carolina, Broman had ordered Ferris to do many bad things, and sowing Raleigh with salt was one more. It's not like he especially wanted to destroy us, but it was on the calendar.

"C'mon Jack, Manilow? I live in California now," he said softly. He swayed manically, moisture forming on his advancing pate. "I'm a Dot-Commer. Haven't worn a suit in years."

"I'm sorry, I take it back."

"It's hard to take back hurtful things once you say them."

Ferris employed faux pathos to obscure his bad intentions, which served to make me mad, which was likely his goal. "Can we get back to the deal?" I said, rapping my clenched fists on the table. "Wardie took some calls on Victor's money. He's got it all lined up."

Ferris retrieved a handkerchief and mopped his forehead. "God, I forget how humid it gets down here," he said, slowly, folding the linen. "It's past four o'clock." He pointed to his mountainous Rolex, official timepiece of the foreclosure Olympics. "You're screwed, my friend."

I took a breath and searched for good karma somewhere, fighting a vision of wise guys bashing in the front door to the *Criterion* in less than an hour. "No, not screwed. Your client keeps money in this new nationwide bank, see? Money is zipping into Victor's New York account right now. Or maybe zapping. What is the sound of money moving?"

"Jack, c'mon, this is bad enough, don't embarrass yourself. Time zones! What's happened to you down here?"

"We don't need no stinking time zones! Zip-zap, Ferris. Zip-zap!" I made the sign of bees flying. "Check Victor's account."

"You've got to pay me in Eastern Standard Fucking Time! What are you going to try next month? A wire from Samoa?"

"Zip-zap, Ferris."

"There's no zip-zap! I'm calling the SEC!"

"What a joke. You, Leonard Ferris, notorious ex-con, complaining to the Commission? The Staff would pee themselves. You couldn't even get the words out of your mouth, they'd be laughing so hard."

"Anyone interested in Judge Blount's order?" Elaine interrupted, stepping between us. "I'm sure the room could take a break from all this peeing."

Ferris pursed his lips, shaking his head like a disappointed schoolmaster. "Et tu Elaine," he said, slowly, elongating the Latin. "Once, you inspired me. No more. I hope you sold out high."

She smiled, leaned forward, and whispered into his ear, "Up yours, you worthless Wall Street shitbag."

Ferris laughed and grabbed the handkerchief again to dab at his eyes. "Now I'm feeling the love! That's the Elaine I know! Let's cut the crap, huh, kids? Jack, you can't do this zip-zap shit. We're taking you out." He motioned to his entourage. "Fellas, prepare to occupy."

Six pinstriped wise guys grunted in unison. Ferris snapped his fingers for the paperwork. A fidgety associate sprawled over the marble tabletop, and began stapling pages like he was making a bomb.

"My, but your boy has a lean and hungry look."

"You know how we like 'em, Jack."

"Okay, here's the thing. You're taking the money. You've got no choice. We're all in the same bank, from sea to shining sea. It's on a commercial."

"For the last time, Victor's not going to accept—"

"Oh, for Chrissakes, he's paid! It's in his account! If you try to send the money back, I'm going to tell Victor's partners you gave back their dough! Then I'll sue you. Read Judge Blount's order for starters."

He snatched the order from Elaine and scanned it, face reddening. Stepping in front of her, he ripped the blue-lined embossed pages to pieces and tossed them on the floor. "This is bullshit," he said, kicking at the stricken papers. "The two of you have gone absolutely fucking native down here! You think I care you own some local judge—who, by the way, sounds like Huey Newton's date. I'm tired of this Mayberry crap! We're going in!"

So, they really did want the paper. Well, not on my watch. I nudged Elaine out of the way, sensing a machisma surge. I didn't want her to hit him and ruin things.

"Hope you brought your toothbrush, Ferris," I said. "'Cause, see, this really is Mayberry, and we've got Opie standing by at the courthouse, and one word from me and he'll tell Judge Blount and she'll put your ass in some nasty county jail. You know how that works down here. I mean, when the brothers in the lockup hear your accent, and get a load of your Barry Manilow outfit, I don't know, but I'm thinking *Deliverance*, with Shaft in the title role."

He winced. "You don't have the guts, Callahan."

"Watch me." I flipped open my phone and held it in his face. "See that number? It's the courthouse. It's ringing. Now call Victor and tell him you're pulling out, or you'll be bunking with Shaft."

He stiffened. Then he backed up and waved off the wise guys. "Okay, Jack," he said evenly. "Put that away."

"Good decision." I holstered my flip phone.

He punched up Victor's number and whispered to me between perfectly clenched teeth. "Can't believe you're making a scene in front of these nice southern people. It's so ungentlemanly."

"I'm calling you a cab for the airport."

He shrugged. "Fine. Got to be on the Coast anyway."

◆◆◆

AFTER THEY ALL LEFT, Wardie stopped back at my office. "See you and Robin on the field Sunday?" Robin played in the Raleigh Youth Soccer League, and Wardie was Commissioner.

"We'll be there."

"Good. Um, thanks for getting this done," he said, buttoning his blazer.

"Just trying to help the ball club."

He smiled broadly. "Sorry about, you know, what I said about Hugh. I already apologized to Elaine. You're my lawyer, man. Numero Uno. I want you to know that." He shook my hand again for emphasis. "That Ferris is a total piece of work, huh?"

"Yes, he is. Can I ask you to do one thing?"

"What?"

"Don't talk to Victor Broman anymore. He's going to call you like nothing happened. Just hang up."

As I headed downtown to pick up Robin from practice, the lights of Raleigh's scattered skyline flickered into dusk. Inside the Beltline, Wardie was driving to his big house with the white columns and the historical marker, and maybe thinking about how he almost lost his paper. But, he didn't lose it after all. Paper saved, and I got to be the hero. Isn't that what I always wanted?

On the Outs

SINCE PREN AND I separated, I've been living in a furnished room above the pro shop at the Club. It turns out the Club is very supportive of husbands on the outs. My room is comfortable if small, and the sound of golf carts gently revving up wakes me each morning. With a few books, some photos, and a good chair, I've established a comfortable bachelor domain that requires little maintenance, unlike the immense, heavily mortgaged drafty mansion across the street that I still sort of own.

Pren and I couldn't have bought the house without her family name behind the bid. Bloodworth, no kidding! I married a woman named Pren Bloodworth! Given the purchase power of her impeccable moniker, I ceded the house. But the Club membership is mine by manly right.

Robin visits on weekends, and the Grounds Committee approved converting a storage room into quarters for her. Between visits, I sometimes get lonely, but there are other members around, so I can always have a conversation.

Every day I have to resist calling my ex-girlfriend, Teri Lynn. We had rough patches, but mostly good times, hot tubs, stock car races, clean adult fun, right up until the lawsuit. Elaine warned me, and she was right. Still, it's been hard getting over the old thump-thump of parts.

Looking over the golf course does give a sense of perspective over the peaks and troughs of life, a view from the middle distance. To the south, I get good early morning light and enjoy the unfolding, cathedral-like valley from the first tee to the green below. In the center of the fairway, geese flying north have recently landed on a settlement pond, forming and reforming V shapes and behaving as though they're truly in nature. Though I enjoy the friendly squawking geese, I've thought lately that I should move out of the club to my own condo, and take steps, as Elaine would say.

For meals, I choose from the Club's daily menu. This week the chef's special has been a dry stuffed flounder, and the sommelier's pairing an oaky Sonoma Valley Chardonnay. I eat alone at my usual table by the verandah, read the *Wall Street Journal*, and then go to the smaller ballroom to play Bach exercises on the Baldwin grand. The Baldwin sits under a plastic shroud, unplayed except for special events, or by me at odd hours. I paid to have it tuned myself. Mercifully, few notice when I play—my skill level remains stuck at eighth grade, when I quit taking lessons.

Sometimes the staff closes the doors when the dining room gets full, but not this time. My mediocrity filled the faux Georgian space. After banging for a half hour, I went upstairs and dialed Elaine's number.

"It's me," I said, as her message machine clanked off.

"My life is shit."

"Let me guess. Your son still out?"

"Yes. No. Thank God, I hear him in the driveway."

"You bought Adam a red Fiat. You're going to suffer."

"It's used."

"It's still a red Fiat."

"Why did you call, Jack?"

"Second thoughts about the paper."

"Didn't you show off in front of everybody?"

"It's Billy. I think I took advantage."

"Ah, guilt. Remarkable."

"Oh, come on. I've had guilt before."

I really did feel guilty about using my friendship with Billy to accomplish a risky business end. That sleight of hand, the bold mixture of the personal ask with the professional need, was what fancy guys lived for, and I should have high-fived around the office all day. But it didn't feel right. Billy could get in trouble, and he trusted me.

"Jack, don't waste guilt, it's a precious resource for you. Billy's a grown man."

Elaine was usually right about these things, but I didn't think either one of us would get away clean.

"Anything else bothering you?" She paused. "Did Ballard come by?" Our partner Ballard Starr had charge of the office, and he busied himself by ordering us around. We used to be friends, but now we had a trust problem. He didn't trust me because of sex, and I didn't trust him because of money. Sometimes the bad things got reversed, sex and money, or money and sex.

"Yeah, Ballard came by. Wanted to know how Broman got paid. I explained to him the latest breakthroughs in nationwide banking."

That was wrong. I had actually explained nothing, choosing to tune out. No doubt the bank had called, pissed.

In a Golden Age long ago, Ballard and I had been Hugh's boys, thrown together as up-and-comers at the firm. Ballard's wife, Ginger, was Pren's best friend. At our wedding, everyone assumed Ballard and I went to some Virginia prep school together. It was great cover. The four of us had babies on the same schedule and shared condos and nannies at Atlantic Beach. As Ballard and I advanced in the firm, Pren and Ginger threw themselves into hosting client dinners fit for *Southern Living*, ranging from your basic small patio cookouts to Christmas buffets so large that both the guests and the caterers came in shifts.

For years we did whatever Hugh said, and it always worked out. He kept us guessing, and the money was good. We had fun. But then we grew up, and he grew old, sitting in that big office between us. Now that he was gone, what were we supposed to do?

"Shit, Jack, you've got to tell Wardie to hire another law firm, and I mean today," Ballard said, corralling me again first thing the next morning. Standing in my office doorway, he hitched up his gray chalk-striped pants and flicked a stray ash from a battered blue-and-gold Brooks Brothers tie. I smelled faint tobacco leavings from the cigarette he sneaked in the stairwell before work. "When are you going to make the call?"

I hadn't even opened my briefcase. I counted to ten. "Ballard, where does all this anger come from?"

"You can't help Wardie. The paper's a damn socialist rag."

"You're just noticing?"

"Not the point."

"Who's making you do this?"

He shook his head to dismiss orders from above. "Nobody. Look, I've known Ward Forrest all my life, and he's a nut job. So's Tatty. The family gets it—they're not backing him anymore on that Internet craziness. Do you know some company out there wants to sell you books on your home computer? Jesus Christ."

"Some of those Silicon Valley ideas work out."

"Have you ever bought anything on your home computer?"

"No."

He threw his hands up in triumph. "I hear the sound of millions flushing. Bring out the little white coats. Oh, sorry, bad joke."

People inside the Beltline were always stumbling around the non-secret secret of Nora's nervous breakdowns. They all knew, too, about Nora and Hugh's non-secret secret affair. The tribal chatter didn't bother me, except when somebody went all passive aggressive and then apologized for it.

"You've baked this already, haven't you?" I said. "C'mon, Drac ordered it. That's where this is coming from."

Drac was the head of the firm, based in Charlotte. He was also lead minder for the Bank. He had forced Hugh's retirement to get the top job, and could very well be gunning for me.

Ballard waved away the flatulent whiff of a plot. "Haven't talked to Drac in a week."

"When you do get around to it, tell him I still represent the *Criterion*, as we've done for a hundred years."

"So, you're not going to call Wardie?"

"Nope."

Standing quickly, Ballard stumbled over files by my desk. "I can't believe you'd put the firm at risk for a crazy man."

"Which one?" I shouted after him down the hall.

Selections from the Great Obits

ROBIN MET ME AT Harmony Hall, as she does every Sunday. After visiting Nora, I take Robin to the Soccer Center, and then to supper. We do other scheduled things during the week—carpools, dinner, anger management class, until I flunked out of that. When she was on the traveling soccer team, we spent most weekends together on the road, caravanning. Then there were the muggy nights at practice, me and the mosquitoes watching.

Dropping Robin at Harmony Hall does make a good Sunday for Pren. She can rationalize that she's visited Nora without doing it and deposit Robin without seeing me, thereby making a clean getaway from two unhappy encounters. To her credit, she continues to visit Nora like she and I are still together. At St. Elizabeth's, she'd been one of Nora's best students.

After doing all these good works, Pren can even find time to go by her office and sell more real estate. Pren is managing our messy lives like a pro. I'm not. I'm a daily disaster, doing fatherhood on the run. Case in point, I was late, again. It was already a quarter to one, and there was no way I would have time to properly engage Nora, buy acceptable low-calorie fast food for Robin, and arrive at the Soccer Center by two.

Inside Nora's room, Robin sat on the bed, her legs curled beneath her, posed for a weekend sleepover.

"The Mets won again," she said, reading from the *Times*. "Five to three. Strawberry homered."

I hung back, enjoying them together for a moment, knowing when I walked in the good feeling would vanish. They had grown alike, suddenly. In something like a week, Robin had taken on Nora's vampy dark hair, buttery skin, and hazel eyes. She'd turned fifteen going on twenty-one, with an attitude to match. In reverse, even indisposed, Nora managed to look fifty-five when she was sixty-four. Pudged out by forty, I was the only age-appropriate human in the room.

"You're so late, Dad," Robin said, getting up from the bed.

"What's that on your eyes? You look like a raccoon."

She shook her head at the ceiling before speaking. "It's called eyeliner?"

"You need to take it off. You're going to a soccer game, not some night club."

"No."

"What did you say?"

"Hell no."

"You can't use that language in front of your grandmother. Or, period."

She looked at me and rubbed at her eyes, smudging the eyeliner. Her lower lip quivered. "I'll say any fucking thing I want," she said, tossing the *Times* on the floor. She shook her head and started to say something else, but then gritted her teeth and marched out.

"Well, that was special," I said, picking up the paper with unsteady hands.

"You can't lord it over her, Jack," Nora said evenly.

"What?"

"She wants your approval, she wants her freedom. When I was her age, it was the same."

"When you were her age, you lived in a mill village and ate Spam out of a can. Robin gets anything she wants."

"No, she doesn't."

"Oh, so now it's about the divorce. Thanks a lot."

Nora squinted and looked me up and down. "Sit down. Your color's not good. I don't want you to have a heart attack like your father."

"I'm not going to have a heart attack."

"Breathe slowly and regularly. Slowly and regularly. That's right. Did you bring my smokes?"

Smoking was an acceptable addiction at Harmony Hall. I produced the pack of Virginia Slims, lighting one as she eagerly propped herself up. She held my hand over the match.

Content, she lay back on her pillows, humming the thrilling strings from *Now Voyager*, our favorite movie to see together; she, as always, Bette Davis, in and out of the happy sanatorium; me, who was I today? Hans Conried, the boyfriend? Claude Rains, the doctor? Maybe I played some Bette myself, the misbegotten daughter who lived on Beacon Hill with a bad mommy.

Nora smoked and got happy and I chafed at that. Better she lectured and stayed mad. But, getting mad made her tired and unattractive and, it being Sunday, Hugh might come by. She made up for him from the start years ago, opening our front door in a crackly pleated skirt, her favorite red sweater, and Chanel Number Five in the air. He bent down and shook my hand, and I could smell Listerine and lanoline, the sweat-touched starch of his Brooks Brothers shirt. When he left, she always crawled back into bed and asked me to get her cigarettes.

"Okay," I said, checking the time and flipping through the paper. "Now for a selection from the great obits."

"I don't want that today."

"What?"

It was her favorite thing. Nora regarded the *Times* obituaries highly as writing and kept a collection of her favorites—John Coltrane, Louise Nevelson, Paul de Man, and her incongruous hero Allen Dulles, whom, she told me on good authority, once had his way with the Queen of Greece on a table in his office dressing room at Langley.

"Can't do any more death." She sat up on her plumped pillows, twirling the ends of her long, gray-streaked hair, looking down at the coverlet. "Louise Burnside died." She started to cry.

Of course, I'd forgotten to bring the one obit she wanted. Mrs. Burnside had been sick with cancer for a long time. She'd visited Nora until the end, fellow battlers against different demons. I came upon them last month here in Nora's room, laughing over an old bon mot, Mrs. Burnside perched thin and tall as an egret in a defiant red dress on the edge of the bed, a jaunty green scarf for a headdress. "I'm sorry. Jeez, I was thinking about her today. Loading bags at the Harris Teeter."

"She was the only woman in this town who was ever kind to me."

"I guess you're not counting Dr. Poindexter."

Nora shrugged. "She was my boss."

Mrs. Burnside had invited Nora to her book club when *E.M. Forster and the Death of England* Vol. 1 came out, which upped the wine-fueled conversation. As talk lagged, she told the group how everyone had been so excited at Women's College when Nora published a short story in *Mademoiselle* and got to go to New York on the train.

"At WC, I couldn't play field hockey, and Louise covered for me."

I didn't know how you covered for bad field hockey.

Sometimes Nora and Mrs. Burnside would get dolled up with gloves and clutches and go together to docent tours at the Museum of Art or chorales at Reynolds Coliseum. Then they'd come back to our house, the neighborhood a little louche for Mrs. Burnside, and drink a gin fizz.

"Hugh said he'd take me to the funeral."

Hugh was coming? Probably not. Lowry would take her in the truck.

Hugh kept us all guessing. I used to guess with the best, but some time ago, I started getting things wrong. Worse, I slid backward in basic skills, such as lying for the greater good. This was alarming, because telling the truth often led to low achievement.

"Nora, do you want to get out of here?"

"Of course, dear."

"No, I'm serious."

"Of course. But not now. I'm still on break."

She stretched out her hand for a tissue, and I gave her the box. "What did they say about this morning?"

"You took a bottle of Allegra."

"I thought it would help me sleep."

"This puts you back on Level three. No shampoo or other deadly things. It's regulation."

"I'm not much good at regulations, am I?"

"No. And if you don't learn, you might never get out of here."

Two weeks ago, the problem was a different edible. She wandered off on Wednesday at suppertime, before her scheduled release on a Thursday. I called Lowry, thinking he'd taken her to AA. He found her down the road at Wendy's, eating a chili dog.

"I don't know why I did that," she said, when I reminded her.

"I guess you wanted a chili dog."

She picked up the memory box I'd left on her bed. "Why do you bring me these useless things—your birth certificate?"

"Dr. Gardiner said you have to remember the past. It's part of your treatment."

"What, giving birth to you? He thinks I forgot?" She held the birth certificate in two fingers as though it were an especially interesting artifact from the British Museum.

"He doesn't think you have dementia. He thinks you willfully forget things."

"Gardiner's an idiot. I remember everything. It's a curse."

From the memory pile she produced a yellowed Hallmark invitation with balloons and smiling Howdy-Doody guy beckoning to good times at a summer barbecue. I recognized Aunt Judith's writing. Aunt Judith was my dad's younger sister. "Remember this? I do. One of her barbecues. Almost ruined us. People need to stop with all this remembering."

Actually, I liked going to Aunt Judith's barbecues, in the summers, in New Jersey, when I could spend time with Dad and the new family. I wonder how many of those invitations Nora deep-sixed over the years.

Smiling, she picked up her knitting pile from a basket beside the memory box. She liked her knitting class. They used plastic needles.

"I'm making you a sweater. I should have made sweaters when you were young. Maybe then you'd have liked me better than Judith."

For a while, when Nora taught in the summers at what we called the B-places—Berkeley or Bennington—I'd stay with Dad and his new wife

Laura, and Rachel and Danny, my younger stepsister and brother, in Red Bank, New Jersey. Really, I'd stay with Aunt Judith, who lived down the street. Rachel and Danny were little kids, but there were lots of guys my age, too. We ran around this big neighborhood with woods and a creek. Aunt Judith cooked for everybody from a list of meals she kept in her purse. Sometimes I went with her to the market.

Dad ran the carpet business then. He dressed in bright sports coats and penny loafers and got a new Buick every year. On Mondays, he took me to Sal's for his haircut and shave, and to talk about how the Yankees were doing. On Tuesdays and Thursdays he took me to see customers in the new glass office buildings outside town. I carried satchel swatches around while he told golf stories and wrote down orders.

On Saturdays he drove past the glass buildings to his golf course and taught me to play. We stood in the bottoms, and he hit shag balls, and I chased them down with his old pneumatic caddy.

I could hit pretty well. One day, after all his customers had teed off, he led me to the first hole. "You're ready," he said, and showed me how to line up the driver.

I hit it solid, and, I remember, a little left. "Learn this," he said, huffing and puffing down the fairway. Had to get in the exercise, he'd always say, patting his waistline. "For some guys, golf is a game where you yell fore, shoot six, and write down five." He waited for me to laugh, like he did with his customers when he was selling. "But take it from me, son: tell the truth from the start. It's better."

He didn't have a chance to give many pieces of advice, and I've tried to remember that one, although for me it's easier said than done, telling the truth right away, especially given the demands of my job. I do enjoy my golf, among other reasons because I can be truthful outside the office. It also reminds me of Dad. And people think golf's a silly game.

◆◆◆

I HADN'T SEEN THE New Jersey Golds for over twenty years, so back in the fall I paid a call on Aunt Judith at the family carpet store in Paramus. I wore the suit I take traveling, and the manager at the front had to decide I wasn't from the IRS before he'd call her from the back office. A trim, middle-aged woman with frosted hair and a pensive look emerged; even though it had been years, I thought I recognized her, and knew it positively when she tilted her head, frowning in the visible act of concentration I remembered from Dad.

"Aunt Judith, it's Jake."

She stared at me, and then fell gently back against the wall before recovering and disappearing behind a tile display.

"No, wait," I called after her as she retreated into the office, but before I could say anything more, she reappeared, wearing a pair of glasses.

"Jacob," she said softly, holding her arms out to me. I took her hands like a shy teenager.

"It's really me."

"I know. I had to get my glasses. You gave me a start—I thought you were your father."

"Don't cry. I should have called."

She dabbed with a Kleenex. "You look the way he should have looked."

"What do you mean?"

"Lighter by a hundred pounds. It killed him. My poor Jacob. But look at you. So tall and handsome, and that lawyer suit. Very fancy."

"Aunt Judith, I'm sorry everything's been so messed up."

She hugged me. "I'm calling Rachel."

"She's around?"

"You'll come to dinner at her house. She can go by the market."

I touched her arm and she stopped. "Okay. But first, I want to see Dad's grave."

Aunt Judith drove her new Lexus north on the Turnpike toward the George Washington Bridge. We headed over the Triborough to Queens, where the family mausoleum stood. I had no idea the Golds rated a mausoleum.

"The store must be doing well," I said, stroking the glossy, cream-colored seat.

"It's the company car," she said, waving off with disgust the third-finger obscenity directed at her as she aggressively merged. "I've got to have it to get to the stores. C'mon, take one lane already."

"Stores?"

"We have five now. Jacob liked to concentrate them. Television is expensive."

"You advertise Gold's Carpet World on television?"

"'Let the Golds cover your home.' You haven't heard it? Of course not— the commercials don't run in Carolina. Danny does the TV. At first, he jumped around with a wig like that Crazy Eddie person. Now he's calmer. It was lucky you caught me in Paramus. On Tuesdays I'm in Piscataway."

"How did the business get so big?"

She sighed and slowed reluctantly for a yellow light. "Your father had a picture in his mind about how the stores went. Every display."

"That's how you do a good business."

"What?"

"He saw the stores in his head, like poetry."

She smiled. "Sounds like something he'd say."

"Really?" That pleased me. "Nora never talked about him except to say he couldn't write poems. With some dirty words thrown in."

Judith applied the brakes vigorously and swerved to avoid a meteor-sized pothole. "I will not speak ill of your mother. But, my God, the things that came out of her mouth. Screaming. Then he'd scream back at her."

"About poetry?"

"No. He stopped writing it."

"Because of her?"

"He thought he was no good. Me, I could never understand the good from the bad. And then the rest happened."

"The rest I don't know."

"You were so little."

"All she said was that he left us, and we had to pack up and move south. She never talked about it. What did he do? Have an affair?"

Judith slowed behind a delivery truck and stayed put as cars and liveries passed manically in the outside lane. From the glove box, she retrieved a pack of Chiclets and offered me one. I shook my head.

"Well," she said quietly. "To begin with, he didn't leave her. She left him."

"What?"

"She did something very bad."

This challenged my lifelong belief that we left New York to escape catastrophe. Escaped in the nick of time! We'd have been goners if we stayed. Goners! What could be worse?

"Please tell me what happened."

Judith stared ahead and measured traffic. "Oh well," she said. "Why not, it's all so long ago. Your mother—" She took a deep breath. "—had an affair with her professor at Columbia."

"Wow."

"She said she was going to stop, but she didn't."

"I don't know what to say."

"Either she had to go, or the big shot."

"Of course."

"The dean got her that job in Carolina. It broke Jacob's heart. He never talked about her again."

"But what about me?"

"He wanted you to come live with us. But she cut him off, and you were so far away. I tried to keep up."

"I know."

She rolled to a stop in line for the tollbooth at the Triborough Bridge. I reached for change, but she waved me away and paid the attendant herself.

"The truth is, Jacob, your mother did a bad thing. But it was a blessing. Not for you, maybe. But for them. She was not good for your father."

I didn't know what to say, "I'm sorry" is what came out.

She shrugged. "It's just the past."

Signs for LaGuardia ahead. "I feel like we're going somewhere far away."

"We're coming to the cemetery. Maybe souls fly away easier, being near LaGuardia."

I considered this concept. "Don't know of a religious teaching that takes proximity to airports into account."

She shrugged. "There are lots of souls here, and lots of airplanes."

"That's absolutely true." We both paused to consider the metaphysics.

"So, tell me about your job," she said finally. "Are you in an office with other lawyers?"

"Oh yeah, it's a large firm now."

"Are you rich?"

"We're comfortable."

She held out her hand like mothers do to keep me from going through the windshield as she braked to avoid a speeding taxi, and then accelerated through a cacophony of horns and curses to reach an outside lane. "You sound just like your father," she said calmly, nonplussed by the Grand Central Parkway in chaos. "*We're comfortable,* he'd say. He took care of us all. I miss him very much."

"So do I."

To the right, the old watch factory sat, with its Bulova face peering over the highway, keeping time for everything. The clock hands ticked slightly off the hour, always fast, never quite in sync with the cabs and limos and trucks bearing down on LaGuardia. For years it stood sentinel to my airport anxiety, as I hunted my ticket, weighed the chance that I would be late. The forlorn clock face and dingy granite façade in forties municipal style stood shielded by a barbed-wire-topped fence; highway curbs intruded on the once-ample grounds, now ringed by road trash of rubber and metal. Close on the asphalt stood squat storefronts and a faded hotel, besieged by carbon monoxide and the smell of jet fuel.

"Judith, are we—"

"What?"

"Nothing, I see it." Before us, sitting on a slope beneath old trees, emerged the cemetery. As Judith signaled to turn, I remembered the sight as a landmark, a curiosity on the traveler's landscape. Having passed so many times, I thought of it as a prop, not a real cemetery with real people in it.

"Full fathom five thy father lies," said the spirit to the lost boy, when Nora read the lines to me.

Judith drove through the gate. The groundskeeper let us pass with a nod.

"He knows me," she said. "I bring the flowers."

She parked at the bottom of a small rise. We walked for a few paces and she gestured toward a grove of maples. "Behind the trees," she said.

"Aren't you coming?"

"I'll wait here," she said, unpacking a fresh Chiclet.

60

From the top of the hill, I could see the Grand Central curving below, and to the east the swirling compound of the airport. To the west, the midtown skyline stood above faint haze. I heard one bird, and then another, a mockingbird; and then all drew quiet, and in the midst of the metropolis I felt strangely alone, among trees, among the sleeping. GOLD, the inscription in marble said above the bronze door to the mausoleum. I felt stupid that I couldn't get in; I hadn't asked for a key. How sad, but how typical, that I should come this far and couldn't take the final step. A breeze lifted leaves from the mossy ground, and blew them around gravestones at my feet, and then I noticed the one that completed my errand after all: JACOB GOLD 1930–1981.

Those were the only words, above a Star of David.

Dad never quite fit in, even at the graveyard. Wrote poetry. Married a mad shiksa. Built a rug empire. Died young.

But I remember him laughing, in a chef's apron, turning a hamburger, then peeking underneath and pointing, like he knew the answer to Nora's question, the one about what makes people happy.

I brushed some of the leaves away and moved Judith's flowers from the door of the mausoleum to the gravestone. "Dad, it's Jake. I'm sorry it's taken me so long to get by. Sorry I missed the funeral, and, oh, I'm sorry I was never bar mitzvah, just wanted to get that in. See, I've generally been a fuck-up, not to put too fine a point on it…"

◆◆◆

NORA OFFERED HER CHEEK and I kissed it, getting up to leave Harmony Hall. From the doorway, I could see Lowry's tomatoes sunning in the window.

In the car, Robin flipped the radio to a rap station, volume up. I reached to turn it down, and she groaned.

"What's gotten into you," I said, in a half shout, above the lewd chatter of the artist.

"I'm really sorry, Dad. I shouldn't have dropped the f-bomb on Grandmother."

"I'm talking to your mother about your language. It must be the school." Rather than St. Elizabeth's, we had sent her to Bingham, a leafy,

Mr. Chips-style public school, which featured the top soccer team in the state, as well as the requisite street talk.

She shrugged. "Mom uses curse words back at me."

I doubted it. "Do you care how it makes you sound? It's trashy."

She laughed. "Great. I'm so embarrassed, for our family and all. Like, after my father has sex with his secretary? And it's on television?"

Robin had been especially angry with me since the unfortunate sex incident with Teri Lynn. How could I explain? She was fifteen years old—Robin, not Teri Lynn.

"That's not true," I said, turning into the parking lot at Bruegger's. "And watch the likes."

"Oh, right. Like, which isn't true, like the sex, or like the television?"

I left the motor running in park, contemplating and then rejecting the advice of our anger management counselor to engage at tactical moments on the Teri Lynn question. She was my daughter, I was her father; some things I didn't discuss. Actually, on that point, there was a division between authorities. Her therapist came down on the let's-have-boundaries side, arguing with the anger management counselor, who pushed for no-boundaries Armageddon.

Robin believed that my affair was causing the divorce, which was a natural thing for her to believe, but wrong. As usual, there were many twists and turns, infidelities of multiple sorts over a number of eras—the Era of Good Feeling and No Money, the Era of No Time and Frayed Affections, the Era of Bad Mistakes and Alienation—each of those punctuated with difficulties in managing willful in-laws, alcoholism, lies, and business reversals. But I couldn't really explain all that to Robin.

Somehow, anger management sessions came very easily for her. Somehow, she could dramatize her feelings and be very articulate about her anger at many things, animal, vegetable, and mineral. But when it was my turn to speak, I couldn't say anything.

One thing I could have said, but didn't, was that I was surprised at how easily Robin fit into the inside-the-Beltline world, seamlessly invited to one event after another, welcomed into the houses of the good and the great. I didn't figure on that. I thought she would struggle, like me, even after I so carefully arranged that she wouldn't.

So, I made up struggles for her, life as competition. Work hard at school, be a killer in soccer, fight, fight, fight. Since we were already inside the Beltline, with good dating and mating all around us, and excellent debutante prospects, Pren thought it was all overdone, the eat-or-be-eaten world, and Robin resisted too, setting her perfect jaw just so. She wondered, I could tell, like her Grandma, what do people do to be happy? I wondered, too, but didn't give much time to the question, since somebody had to struggle for one reason or another.

Every time I dropped Robin off after anger management class, Pren asked, "So, did you get mad?"

"Nope. Tried hard."

"It's two hundred and fifty dollars an hour from the joint account. I say let's bag it."

"Look, I'm trying, I'll get it next time."

"Anger's just not your thing," she said, patting me on the arm. "Let's go for some other emotion…"

"Why don't you get a plain bagel with a bottle of water? Ought to be okay on your stomach before the game," I said to Robin, nodding at the 7-Eleven.

She held out her hand and I produced a five-dollar bill. We may have been a bust at anger management, but we had one key father-daughter interaction down pat.

I was working, however incompetently, on my relationship with Robin, but media coverage of the Teri Lynn incident presented a special challenge. Channel Four proved especially vindictive, Brenda Bobelink, the six o'clock news anchor, set on overdrive. The talk at Bingham ran to the phantasmagorical: in addition to a being sexual harasser, I was also, according to gossip, a vampire. For a while, Robin shut down; she couldn't look at me. Eventually, she came back around—actually, she was still coming around, but with a wariness that broke my heart. Sure, I'd fallen off the pedestal, but couldn't I get back up, maybe at a lower level?

Now, she strode out of Bruegger's with her soccer shorts rolled up, and what looked like excellent self-esteem radiated forth.

"How's Algebra II going?" I asked brightly, as she plunked into the seat.

"Flunking."

"How about a tutor—"

"Dad, Asian kids take that class."

"Maybe I should try to get you out of Honors. Do you want me to talk—?"

She groaned and turned up the radio, losing herself in the bang-bang lyrics.

"Do you know what field you're on?" I asked plaintively.

She shrugged and pointed.

The Criterion Fields, where Robin's soccer team played, meandered over acres in the once-vacant northern reaches of the city, now surrounded by cul-de-sacs, convenience stores, and yellow construction cranes. The land had once been the Forrests' farm retreat, and when Wardie's kids took up soccer, he got the idea of a sports park. With the city's blessing, he made from his family's grassy vale a marked collection of deep green fields that stretched toward Virginia, beckoning all comers with the comingled smells of college scholarships and manure.

"There," Robin said, peering through the tire-dust of the parking lot.

"How can you tell?"

"Duh, the slutty red uniforms? Cary Clash? They're the ones, you know," she said, arching her eyebrows in a Nora imitation, punctuating her allusion to a sad Clinton-esque oral sex scandal among fourteen-year-olds at the last Thanksgiving tournament. It had been a nasty business: calming down the security guard, cleaning up the gazebo, notifying parents. "Ask Adam Marchetti what Olivia put up about him on MySpace."

"Jesus," I said softly. She patted my arm.

Although I could barely form the thought, I had to wonder if Robin had oral sex in the gazebo, too? The president had told everyone that it wasn't really sex, but non-sex, and also safe from AIDS, and therefore doubly appealing. She denied it, claiming only the girls from Cary Clash were involved. But maybe she'd fibbed, and maybe she also had oral sex with Adam Marchetti in the red Fiat Elaine bought him. I knew Robin had a crush on Adam. Suddenly, I feared that both my fifteen-year-old daughter

64

and sixty-four-year-old mother had more sex than I did—certainly more non-sex, not counting Teri Lynn in either category. Now there's a topic for anger management.

Seeing me lost in this disturbing reverie, Robin gave a pitying look, and even kissed me on the cheek getting out of the car. I shook my head at her, wondering if things were finally going to get better between us or if she was torturing me with mixed signals.

All this work nurturing Robin's self-esteem had given short shrift to the old-fashioned virtues. Being made to feel grateful for every small thing—well-prepared Jell-O, for example—often led to suitably modest, Ben Franklin-style behavior, a penny saved is a penny earned, etc.

Yet, everybody was doing it, all the parents I knew, building up self-esteem. If blow jobs were getting handed out in the gazebo, you didn't have to worry about self-esteem for the boys. With girls, common parental wisdom said to buy them things. Madison Avenue fostered this default, with billboard-size ads featuring supple preteen models, hair flaring, gaze forward, proclaiming Girl Power in well-cut jeans.

"Jack Callahan, report to Central Station. Callahan to Central Station."

Wardie's loudspeaker voice issued from the soccer official's command post. I made my way through the anthills of maize and azure and crimson-dressed soccer players to the small rise where Central Station stood. Wardie, sporting a safari hat and seersucker shorts, sat among the referees and schedulers in a monogrammed web-backed director's chair, electric bullhorn in hand.

"Tournament time, Jack," he said, motioning me to take the vacant director's chair beside him. "Damn glad we got here."

"Me too, man."

We had worked months to put the oral sex scandal behind us. I'd led grievance meetings and crafted community service disciplinary plans, also useful for college applications. Everyone signed confidentiality statements.

That done, we were back to the wholesome business of the Criterion Cup. Each year, Wardie gave the Criterion Cup to the winning boys and girls team by age-group division of the Capital Federation Soccer League. You can happily lose yourself in the nomenclature of international youth soccer. Robin played on a U-15 Challenge Team—a designation as baffling as freemasonry, but known everywhere.

"You didn't play Robin up this year," Wardie observed critically, consulting his master lists.

"She likes the girls on her team."

"Damn," Wardie said, surveying the referees in their black shorts. "Samsit is late again. What's his problem?" He clicked on the bullhorn. "Mr. Bell, report to Field 29. Immediately."

"Are you short referees?"

He shrugged. "It's just my life, man. Saw Pren, by the way."

"Where?"

"With Ginger, in the Harris Teeter. Why do ITB women dress up to go to the grocery store?"

"Don't know, man."

It was only in our inside-the-Beltline neighborhood—or ITB, as the cognoscenti said—that women got dressed up for the Harris Teeter. You could go to any other market in the city of Raleigh and find women in running clothes, overalls, sans makeup, not a pair of pantyhose in sight, except those wrapped for sale.

"My ex dressed up for the Harris Teeter. Maybe she had something going with the fish guy. Couldn't see it. He always had his hands in a baggie, sloshing around in the shrimp."

"You know Pren. She's not going anywhere without fixing herself up."

"Yeah. And she's single again."

Divorce led us to spend guy time together, taking in the scene, grunting and pointing. It was kind of non-talk therapy. We referred to eligible women laconically, in monosyllables if possible—smart, sexy, pretty, dull, scary. Mostly that last one.

"Wardie, love to chat, but was there something you wanted to tell me?"

"Oh yeah." He took one deep breath, and then another. "Damn, just out with it. It's a hard one, you'll be mad."

"What?"

"I'm getting more money from Victor Broman." He ducked involuntarily.

"Jesus, Wardie—"

"Don't start in on me, Jack. You were right. He called and apologized."

"I didn't tell you he was going to call so you could take more money! I told you so you wouldn't! Jesus."

"I know, I know. He said he was embarrassed, and that Ferris had been—disciplined. That was his word."

"Disciplined?"

"That's what he said. Anyway, he wanted to make up, so he said he'd loan more on the Internet engine. He said we'd take it public in a whole Big Data thing and make a ton of money."

That actually sounded logical, but then, so do some mass murders. "One question, Wardie. What happens when you can't make the next monthly payment?"

He grinned like a fifth grader ad-libbing a book report. Broman the tycoon flattered his industry leadership, while Jack the lawyer warned him of failure. Who was going to win?

"It's the future, Jack. We'll make the numbers work."

Broman had gotten involved with people in California who wanted to collect information on everything, match it all together, and put it out on the World Wide Web, aka Big Data. That's what Wardie meant by the future.

I called it Crazy Idea Two. But Crazy Idea One, buying books over your home computer, had started to take off. Wardie tried to get me to buy the stock, but I passed. Who wanted to go to the trouble of dialing up your computer to buy a book? All those flashing lights and symbols, and the funny whistling noise? What's the matter with going to a bookstore, which, aside from having actual books, was filled with attractive, well-read women, eyeing you as a candidate to buy them lattes?

"So, Broman's really doing this Big Data thing?"

Grinning, Wardie handed over a transcript of Angie Angstrom's latest market report. Everyone referred to her now as "Celebrity Analyst Angie Angstrom." Angie had been on television for a while. Everybody knew she also worked for Victor.

Angie and I had been very good friends for a long time. We met when I was still in law school and she was getting Victor's latte. Then, she had short blonde hair, wore jeans well, and moved like the dancer she had come to New York to be. Now, she'd had surgery for TV that made her face perfect and brought her bosom to the tipping point. Her voice was the same—Minnesota-cum-Vassar—and she worked it into network-neutral for the morning stock shows. On TV, she'd become much like gravity. If she said a company was good, the stock went up; if she said it was bad, the stock went down.

We hear Victor Broman is moving on solid opportunities in the Big Data space, Angie had reported. *We expect him to drive a rapid roll-up of media content providers into an IPO at attractive multiples.*

"See," he said gleefully, holding the transcript. "I faxed it to Tatty this morning."

"Angie doesn't know anything about Big Data."

"Well, she just said it was great on TV."

"Victor Broman tells her what to say."

He shrugged. "Look, we have to be in Victor's deal. Print is dead. He told me the *Times* just went Internet for classifieds. Did you hear that?"

"Nope, missed the headline."

Cries from players contending below blew upward, and a slight breeze ruffled the canopy under which we sat, generals surveying an adolescent army.

"Who the heck is that?" Wardie said, turning away to train his binoculars on a leggy soccer mom in the distance.

♦♦♦

I LOOKED FOR ELAINE at Adam's sideline before the two o'clock matches. I'd already decided not to mention Robin's report of Adam's blow job, or discuss blow jobs in general. Elaine would probably take it the wrong way.

I did have to wonder: how did young guys like Adam get blow jobs? In my day, you had to put in your time and get very lucky. Your first blow job ought to be something special, handled by a professional, or maybe a friend of your mom's, not by a soccer player in a gazebo. Clinton's to blame for this. Blow jobs demystified, nice girls talking about it, nice girls doing it, politicos on TV saying the word fellatio during prime time. Great work all around.

"Isn't Robin playing? Or does she have anxiety issues?" Elaine sat upright in a regulation blue canvas chair, sunglasses and book fixed for the contest, her white pants rolled up to sun in a new pedicure color. The last one she'd called Ramona Red. Smiling, she motioned for me to sit on the stadium blanket at her feet, where she'd laid out celery sticks and apple slices on a Tupperware lid.

Choosing celery, I contemplated how soulful it would be to talk about our kids and not go into the Wardie story. But work was work.

"Have to tell you a Wardie thing."

"Please God, say he's quitting."

"No. More money from Broman."

"But Wardie's broke! I don't understand how capitalism works."

"Let me explain. He's not broke; he's an entrepreneur. There's a big difference. Besides, Angie Angstrom says he's a genius."

"An-gie Ang-strom." She drew out the words slowly, making a face. "Hydrate yourself," she said, producing a bottle of water.

"Something's going on. Time to go see Hugh and try to figure it out."

"He'll preen and gloat." She cocked her head in a patrician, Hugh-like way. Holding Nora's cigarette holder, Hugh could pass for Roosevelt in profile.

"Yeah. But he knows things. He knows the paper, knows Broman, knows the Bank."

She stopped herself before making another crack, probably along the lines of running home to Daddy.

I did run to make Robin's game before halftime.

"You didn't see it, did you?" she said, crumpling her plastic Gatorade on the sideline.

"Got held up," I said, a little breathless.

"The ref is so clueless."

"What happened?"

"Caitlin Gurney pushed me down and pinched my butt. So I asked her if she wanted my phone number."

"Not cute. And?"

"I got carded."

"Jeez, honey."

"I think my elbow hit her nose. There was a lot of blood." She motioned to a towel beside her.

"Is she going for an x-ray?"

"I don't know. It was just a lot of blood and Caitlin was screaming."

She started to cry, and I handed her another towel.

"I'm so bad. Why did I hit her?"

"You're not bad."

"Yes, I am, Daddy."

"Look, I'll go check on the Gurneys. I see them over there."

"No, please. Wait until after the game. Okay?"

"Why? Never mind—all right. Are you hurt? Why aren't you going back in?"

"Remember? I got carded."

She looked forlorn, sitting away from the girls on the team. She started crying again. I sat down beside her on the grass and put my arm around her, and she put her head on my shoulder. "It's all right, honey," I repeated, whispering it until she got quiet. "I love you very much," I said, and I felt her relax.

"I love you, too, Daddy," she said, and I started to cry a little, too. The game ended, and the crowd divided around us. "About that f-bomb. I'm sorry I dropped it on Grandmother," she said, and we both laughed.

She put on her sweats and started packing her bag, and I met the very-mad Gurneys at midfield, Caitlin holding a large sandwich bag of ice to her face. They were on the way to Rex Radiology and had nothing to say. Maybe they'd seen me on TV and thought it logical I'd spawn a prison girl. Arm in arm, fellow renegades, Robin and I marched to the car and drove back inside the Beltline for the handoff to Pren.

Soccer wasn't really my game. When the girls were young, we traveled together, and it was fun—weekend tournaments in Richmond, Greensboro, sometimes Washington, Dad and daughter outings. But then they all got older, and everything turned into somebody's broken nose.

70

Do the Right Thing

THE NEXT DAY I went to see Hugh about the paper. For the Symmes family—meaning all the Hughs, beginning with Hugh's grandfather, Big Hugh, and his father, incongruously named Little Hugh, and then Hugh himself—the paper had always been a family trust, a nearly mystical bond with the Forrest men of their generation. Bonding with the Forrests wasn't about getting rich, or gaining political power—not directly, that is. The Symmes had all the real power they wanted, vetting candidates from dogcatcher to U.S. Senator, whom the *Criterion* then backed. Wags often spoke of a "Symmes Machine." The Hughs always denied the machine part, but any way you cut it, they had more power than any officeholder in town, even the governor, whom they usually picked.

Unlike the Forrests, who ferried back and forth to Washington so much they rented a permanent suite at the Mayflower, the Hughs didn't much like serving in governments. It distracted from operating their non-machine machine. But they would serve, if a president asked. Hugh had served as assistant attorney general in the Justice Department when his Navy buddy Jack Kennedy called him. That mission was never about "ecclesiastical advancement," as Hugh once termed the politician's climb. He relished going to Mississippi, wielding his officer-issue .45 and his Southern accent, and making people do the right thing.

I was still mastering the finer points of doing the right thing. For example, doing the right thing sometimes led you to do a bad thing, and I had trouble with that. I was getting better, though. Witness my lack of moral confusion over time zones. In the past decisions proved easier: when morally confused, Hugh would tell me what to do.

I can still see him at his desk, large hands playing over fading photos of Pinehurst foursomes, a tarnished Phi Beta Kappa key in a scrimshaw bowl, a leather-framed picture of Bobby Kennedy, signed with the thanks of a grateful nation. "Goddammit," he'd roar, laughing madly with the big black phone cradled on his shoulder, exulting as he worked his will, "Goddammit, Frank, you're just going to have to put that money back where it belongs." It was the sound of Hugh making people do the right thing.

The *Criterion* and Hugh made no bones about working together. Everyone knew information passed. Everyone saw the paper promote and ruin people. What your eyes and ears told you was this: if you wanted a job, go meet Hugh Symmes. If you wanted a highway, don't cross Hugh Symmes. If you did, your worst photo would turn up in the *Criterion*, and if you complained, you'd get a call from Hugh himself, asking if you believed in the freedom of the press.

I learned early on that going after grifters, such as the bid-riggers on the Beltline, was important to enforcing the right thing. That didn't mean every grifter "felt the lash," as Hugh put it. The powerful must feel the lash, but selectively, to keep the wary uncertain.

The origins of right-thing-ism eluded me for years. Then, one day, by accident, I stumbled on it, at the unlikely venue of the Club. On Mondays, I settled the weekend's golf bets around the Members Bar. Sometimes, people got testy. One day, a loser reaching for his wallet made a joke about how it was only money, and not "dead black bucks in the Cape Fear River." That brought guffaws from the regulars, and a quick change of subject.

I didn't say anything, figured it was an inside joke, grinned, and pocketed the twenties. Then, I went to the office and asked Hugh, in passing: "What is this stuff about dead black men in the Cape Fear River? When all I'm trying to do is collect the Nassau."

He closed his office door behind us.

"Who was saying that?" he asked.

I mentioned a couple of names in the Members Bar crowd.

"Huh," he said, opening up the butler's closet to pour us bourbon and branch. It was two o'clock in the afternoon. "You really don't get it?"

"I really don't."

He sighed. "I forget your origins. Best sit down." I did. He refreshed his drink. "What you're going to think is wrong."

"I don't think anything yet."

"Good." He paused, head back, muttering to the heavens.

I'd had the Nassau conversation at the Club thinking it was nothing. Now, it was something. Hugh got up and paced the room, drink in hand.

"Hugh, what's all this about?" I said finally.

He took a deep breath. "Back in the nineties—not now, but then, a hundred years ago—the Republicans built up the black vote. They took over in ninety-six. Big Hugh and Old Man Forrest had to do something. It was a leadership problem."

"A leadership problem for who?"

"The Democrats."

"That would be the racist party in those days."

He closed his eyes and nodded. "Suffice to say things got out of hand. It was Wilmington. It was 1898." He glanced conspiratorially around the empty room, and I realized we'd stumbled on a big non-secret secret. "That's what they're throwing in your face at the Club, the sons of bitches."

"I'm sorry, I'm not following this."

"Following what?"

"What happened in Wilmington."

Hugh sipped down his bourbon and branch and poured another. "The old crowd down there—you know who I'm talking about—got out of control. Big Hugh ended up going himself. He rode with Waddell."

I had no idea what it meant to "ride with Waddell," but I went along. "Okay, so, there was some trouble with Big Hugh?"

"Waddell was a madman. He threatened to choke the Cape Fear with black carcasses, totally out of control. The Wilmington Guard, they were just back from Cuba. So was Big Hugh. Old Man Forrest was in charge, see, and he sent Big Hugh down there because of his military experience. But somebody fired a Gatling gun into the crowd, and they all went crazy, waving the Stars and Bars, gunning down blacks in the street. Big Hugh always thought there was a moment there when he could have—I don't know."

"Made them do the right thing?"

"Exactly."

Hugh took a long breath and looked out the window. He poured himself another.

"Next day Big Hugh took the train back to Raleigh and told Old Man Forrest what happened, chapter and verse. But the Old Man didn't write what happened. You see, he was in charge. The battle, as he called it, was a great victory over 'mongrelization of the races.' That's how they explained things, see. It was always *the blacks wanted white women*, that's what you said when you needed to get away with something."

"What battle was he talking about?"

"That's what I mean. There wasn't a battle. They just shot the poor bastards down in the street. The next day Waddell took over the whole town."

"Jesus. And Big Hugh—"

"Never got over it."

"Big Hugh was what, in the Klan?"

Hugh took a final sip and closed up the butler's pantry. "He never said."

I went back to the *Criterion* offices late that afternoon, sat in the morgue until midnight, and read the Wilmington stories, still arranged a century later in neatly clipped files. The articles recorded that some uppity colored men had gotten what they deserved, and now white people of the right kind were back in charge. Nobody counted the bodies.

Instead of going to jail, the Symmes and the Forrests got power and money. Until they became used to being successful criminals, it must have been like living in a funhouse, seeing your ugly self get handsome by a trick of mirrors. Over time, what happened in Wilmington became the greatest of the non-secret secrets. Nobody talked about it, or taught it in school, at least to white kids. I imagined the black kids learned what it meant to ride with Waddell.

As penance, the next generation of Symmes and Forrest men resolved to do good works, and be redeemed. They'd put violence aside and rule by law. In the name of progress, they'd place suitable white men in power and make them do the right thing.

But no amount of good works would raise the bodies in the Cape Fear River, or ease the memory for Hugh even now, who sat in his office, pouring bourbon and branch, his head full of sin. Others had moved on. While the Symmes men brooded in Raleigh, the Forrest men took the train to Washington and advised presidents, sailed on ocean liners, served as ambassadors. The Symmes men worried for their souls. What could erase the stain? Out, out damned spot! When would the mad river leave them in peace?

Although I was not good at brooding, I got the rest of my part straight. Signing up with Hugh meant I was the new right-thing guy, partner to Wardie for the next generation, exact bloodline or not.

But Wardie had tired of Wilmington original sin. When I told him about Hugh's lesson, he yawned and said, "Oh yeah, ask him more about the Gatling gun, you'll be there all night."

It turned out Wardie had thought long and hard about the great non-secret secret, and he took a more here-and-now approach. When I last tipped him on a grifter, this time that a well-connected economic developer repaired his beach house with state money, rather than hold the presses for an auto-da-fé, Wardie said: "So what? Seen that place? Needed a makeover."

"But this is a no-brainer," I'd protested, doing my dynastic duty, but deep down relieved I wasn't going to have to come up with a smoking gun receipt for duct tape.

"Jack, you can't take German investors to a dump. He did us all a service."

Rather than hoist up the grifter, we went to Riley's Bar with *Criterion* reporters and watched the NBA finals.

Wardie cared little about the Gatling gun, but he did want a Pulitzer Prize. Last year, as a strange prelude to the current troubles, he took on the Bank's red-line habit. "They're still doing it plain as day," he said, pumped up from his meeting in Chapel Hill with the Center for Southern Justice. He'd come back with a picture of himself beside the Reverend Sweeney, the newly militant, street-marching leader of the NAACP, and protégé of the

Reverend Blount. "This is what keeps the black man down! Can't even buy a house in a good neighborhood with his own money. It's un-American!"

I urged caution, but he'd have none of it. He invited me to a lunch he organized for the Reverend Sweeney and his editorial board. "I've got a team on this nonstop!" Wardie assured the Reverend. "Charlotte's just the tip of the iceberg, man. Florida, Texas, California. Jesus, it's 1996 and they're still doing this shit?"

Sweeney came dressed in a red-striped robe, and sat Buddha-like listening to a history he already knew backward and forward. At the end, he opened his arms and led a prayer in a sonorous, Sunday-morning baritone. I closed my eyes thinking how dumb it was for Wardie to embarrass the Bank. Then, a year later, I went and sent money across time zones. Dumb and dumber.

"Four-part series starts Monday," Wardie announced, research done. "Don't you even think about tipping off Dalton Griffiths," he said fiercely, seeing the Pulitzer medal far-off in a heavenly haze. "I know how your firm likes to work things." Dalton Griffiths was CEO of Ameribank, and Hugh's friend.

The stories ran, and the Reverend Sweeney marched thousands through uptown Charlotte. Griffiths fumed on the sixtieth floor of Ameribank headquarters, watching the crowds below take his name in vain.

I waited in Hugh's office the next day, scared. "Don't worry," he said calmly when he walked in, waving off my apologies. He folded his *Criterion* open to read the story, replete with pictures of forlorn shotgun houses across the street from gentrifying townhomes in Charlotte's Fourth Ward. "You boys are playing with fire cozying up to the Reverend Sweeney," he said, shaking his head at impetuous youth. "But you did the right thing. I'll go see Dalton."

Hugh met Griffiths for lunch at the Charlotte City Club, and somehow convinced him that instead of being a bad guy, Wardie had shed light on a tough problem Griffiths had mostly fixed. *Make a speech and take the credit*, Hugh suggested, *and fire a couple of regional managers.* Griffiths did both. The Pulitzer Committee listed the series in Honorable Mention.

I came to relish being quasi-heir to a shameful past. It was large, ennobling. Before, none of the Gold/Callahans had a shameful past. None of us had owned slaves, or raped the land, or affixed our heel to the throat of the working class. But now, I, too, had bad history; I, too, could go mad by the dark river. It was all part of being an evolved fancy guy, embracing guilt for privileges and sins, sharing small but meaningful tokens of power with downtrodden brothers and sisters. I, we, Symmes, Forrests, and now at least one Callahan, were all in for redemption.

◆◆◆

FROM THE BOTTOM OF the swept driveway, I spied Hugh pruning his boxwoods, an activity he'd picked up in retirement. He walked up the sloping front yard, which moved from a stand of grass at the street into rhododendrons, quinces, and a hillside of loblolly pines and straw. Mary, his wife, smiled and waved from the porch, holding her handbag. She wore a gold skirt and white blouse; they were probably going out for lunch. I'd had lunch with her the week before. She asked me, as she sometimes did, for financial advice, and helped me not to overreact about Robin's bumpy course to young womanhood. I was a quasi-heir, and she was a quasi-dowager. We kept all that separate from the business.

At noon on Monday, in ordinary time, before retirement, Hugh would have been wrapped in a towel, getting his hair cut in the Men's Health Club of the YMCA. His regular man, Johnson, would entertain him with barber-chair tales of corruption. The mayor would lie nearby in the sauna reading the *Wall Street Journal* and awaiting his turn. Other regulars would be slapped around by blind men giving Vicks massages in side rooms off the steam bath. Nearby, the soft cries of office seekers would rise in rhythm to the whirring of canvas fat belts stroking their pink, hair-speckled bellies in useless, strange exercise. "Jocko," he'd say, "Over here," and he'd arrange his flagship member dress right, while promising Johnson more ACC Tournament tickets.

That was Monday in ordinary time, and Tuesday usually meant bad bean soup in a card room off the Members Bar, with sputtering colored lights that hid the expressions of men who disliked Hugh and made jokes about the Cape Fear River, but feared the lash.

But ordinary time was over. "Hello, Jocko," Hugh said, without looking up from his shears. That was his name for me as a boy. Dressed in corduroys and a beaten tweed hat, he looked the part of a Scottish laird, tall, still un-stooped, with a full, if thinning, head of white hair and sharp blue eyes that brought out his deacon-like smile.

"You're doing some job on those bushes."

He offered the shears. "Go ahead, Jocko, take over."

"No thanks. Won't keep you long. It's about the paper."

"You recall I'm retired."

"The whole thing could go down. I haven't figured out how to fix it."

Hugh chopped away, nonplussed. He gathered a handful of cuttings. "Hear you're living in bachelor quarters."

I followed him toward a Tudor-style wooden gate to the backyard with an armload of green-tipped branches.

"Over the pro shop."

"Ah."

Hugh could do a lot with an "ah." He disapproved. Marriage was for life in the Symmes household, except for that part about how he had been sleeping with my mother for thirty years.

"Here's the dog cart," Hugh said. We emptied the cuttings into a wooden wheelbarrow, and I held the gate open for him, hearing, as we entered the backyard, the low whine of traffic on the Beltline. Hugh had built a high brick wall to suck in the sound waves.

"I decided not to sell the house."

"Great."

"Mary's the one. She doesn't want to give dinner parties anymore. Downsizing, she says."

I filled the dog cart with more trimmings that Hugh had sorted by color in odd, rotting piles. "Where's your mulch pile?"

Hugh motioned to a staked area, where he'd dumped brackish leaves, yellowed grass caught by the mower, curled prunings, and the occasional potting gone to roots. He bent down to study life in the sweet, decaying mass, flushing a chipmunk out as he turned a graying log over with his shears. "Look at that," Hugh said, pointing to the chipmunk hole. "Won't live long there." He grunted and tried rolling the log. "Stuck."

After staring at the stubborn log and the chipmunk hole from his haunches, he stood up stiffly. "You could use some lemonade. That's what we're on now. Coca-Cola after five. Some life, hunh? I'll see if Mary—excuse me for turning my back—ah, she's gone inside. Watch it, that's mud over there."

"I see it."

"You were more upset about selling the house than Tessie. She was coming from California next week to clean out her things, but she canceled."

Their daughter Tessie was a public defender in Los Angeles County. During some long, teenage summers, we lay by the river, argued, and scrambled toward adulthood together at the Symmes house on the River, down from Wilmington. The last time I wrote her, she said she never wanted to set foot in North Carolina again. Ditto for Hugh's son Hubie, her older brother, who had escaped earlier, and ran a fishing boat in the Puget Sound.

"I wasn't upset about the house."

"If I ever do sell, I'll bring you in before it hits the street."

"I just bought a house, Hugh. Moved out of it."

"Oh, I forgot. I apologize. So, how's Nora?"

He knew how she was. "Still progressing."

"Lowry's a bad influence. Did I tell you I'm having him tailed?"

"Still a bad idea."

"Mary's been mad about me firing him. But he's got his nose in everything. I couldn't even control my own yard."

Hugh had fired Lowry, which was why he was cutting his own bushes. Nobody had fired Lowry before—maybe stopped using him, which wasn't the same thing. Hugh had done research claiming that Lowry was the blood descendant of Lowry the Outlaw, who led the Lumbees in guerrilla combat against the Home Guard during the Civil War, which made him a bad dude. I had to look up what the Home Guard was, and turns out they were the bad dudes, so good on Lowry, I guess. Although what could it mean that your grandfather did something bad? Except I was dealing with Hugh.

"He's still over here," Hugh said, not able to let it go. "He drives his truck around, taking Mary to that damn holy-roller church. He knows too much."

"About what?"

Hugh shook his head, as though I were naïve about something. It was a familiar gesture.

"Lowry's not the problem, Hugh."

"The Lumbees aren't even real Indians. The Cherokees despise them, say they're just mixed breeds, even got Chinese in 'em from that old land bridge. I read an article on it."

"Lowry takes Nora to AA. Do you want to sign up for that job?"

"It's not proper."

"Leave him alone."

He smiled again, which meant he'd do as he pleased.

"What did you want to talk about, Jocko?"

"The paper."

"Oh, right. You know what FDR said. If you stand in the road—"

"—ten boulders will come at you, but nine will go in the ditch. It's only the one you have to worry about."

"I've told you that story?"

"Yessir."

"Whenever Old Man Forrest and Big Hugh brought up a problem for the ticket down here, that's what FDR said. Then he'd wave his cigarette holder, meaning it was time for them to leave. All this happened after that trick you pulled last week?"

"Not a trick, just folks getting paid."

"It was a trick. Well played, I grant you." He bowed slightly.

"Thanks. Anyway, Wardie borrowed more from Victor Broman, after I told him not to. Wants to keep building his Internet thingamajig. Except there's no thingamajig, and he can't pay Broman back."

"It's all about Big Data, isn't it?" In retirement Hugh kept up with lot of topics—the Home Guard, Big Data.

"That's the financial page story."

"This is a wrong direction for the modern age. Knowing more things doesn't make you smarter."

"Tell it to Silicon Valley."

"They all should read Marcus Aurelius. Been going through the *Meditations* again. He didn't know much data, but he was very smart."

"Somebody out there no doubt is sticking the *Meditations* into Big Data so you can access it on your home computer."

He shrugged. "I'm very happy not to do that."

"Right."

Hugh put the shears down and squinted at the sun. "I do have a theory on what Broman's up to, call me old and paranoid. I think he's gone political."

"What?"

"If you think about it, Big Data is a new way to buy votes."

"But Broman's never cared about politics." Broman's political attention span before had consisted of reading the first ten pages of *The Fountainhead* and falling asleep.

"Rich people change when they figure out their money doesn't buy everything." Hugh capped a wayward rose head. "Why doesn't goddamn Broman leave us alone? I blame myself, you taking that job."

"It was twenty years ago."

Hugh wiped his brow with the back of a grimy work glove. "Twenty years? You're right—the year he went after Lorrie Bridger."

We kicked at the dirt, shifting awkwardly in on-again, off-again sun, remembering poor, dead Lorrie Bridger, Hugh's friend, and one of Victor Broman's early victims.

"Broman and his crowd used to be happy clipping coupons. But now I see them at these conferences, all huddled together, complaining about their taxes, wanting to know who's in charge."

"So now maybe they want to be in charge."

Hugh cut again at the roses. "Rich people can cause a lot of damage."

"All I know is everything about the paper has turned into a fight. Every day, something new from Ferris. It's over the top, even for them."

"It may not be just them. Think bigger, national."

"What do you mean?"

Hugh flipped the log and flushed out a mass of scattering beetles. "The Volt brothers could be in it. They're into everything these days."

The Volt brothers bankrolled far-right campaigns all over the country, hoping to accumulate enough votes in enough legislatures to gerrymander Congress and outlaw the income tax. They used to be a joke in polite political circles, but not anymore. Could Broman have thrown in with them?

"That would be a big leap."

Hugh shrugged. "I could be wrong. Like I said, call me old and paranoid. But any way you cut it, you're in a war, Jocko. You need to run hot."

Last week I ran hot enough. But maybe we really were in that FDR moment, when one crazy boulder comes right at you.

Mary appeared again at the back door, purse in hand, pointing to her watch. "Sorry you can't stay for lemonade," Hugh said. "Mary wants to go to some lunch talk with the new rector at Christ Church. Apparently, my soul needs work."

"Boy, mine does, too. Tell me if it does any good."

He walked me down the driveway. "I'd help, Jocko. But you wanted the job for yourself."

"Not true."

He held the car door open and smiled in disagreement. "Oh, by the way, Dalton Griffiths called yesterday. He went on about your trick with time zones. You know how he gets."

I didn't but, as usual, Hugh had the last word. We were in a war, he said. Distant mortar sounded.

"You look bad," Elaine said. She moved her briefcase from the chair she was saving at Café Quarto, a neighborhood spot near her townhouse in trendy, singleton Five Points, where we sometimes had lunch to get away from downtown.

"Why does everyone keep saying that?"

"Because you do."

The waiter brought a Diet Coke. "I ordered you a Chicken Caesar," she said.

"I need a drink."

"No, you don't. Here, pull your chair closer."

"Why?"

"So you can hide when Pren and Ginger walk by."

"Oh shit."

Pren passed in red pumps and Lilly Pulitzer. Ginger pushed up her Chanel sunglasses and smiled to the air.

"All clear," Elaine said, patting me on the knee. "They're going into that cute antique store I can't afford."

"Ginger hates me."

"She thinks we're sleeping together. Did you ever—"

"Oh Lord no." I took a long drink of Diet Coke, which had a cooling, if not calming effect.

"Just checking," she said, squinting for signs of perfidy. "So how was Hugh?"

"Paranoid."

"Did he tell you what you needed to know?"

"Told me we were in a war. Told me Griffiths had called him."

"Who's Griffiths?"

"Dalton Griffiths. CEO of Ameribank. Broman's gotten to him."

"Wow."

"You think I should get back, don't you?"

"They can box up your lunch."

I followed her dinged-up minivan through the noonday traffic. She stopped at the light at Five Points and rolled down her window.

"I'm dropping Adam's practice clothes at school."

"Okay, but we need to speed up on Big Data."

"I'm on it."

"Thanks. Call tonight?"

"Hmm. Having dinner with somebody."

Meaning she had a date. The light changed, horns blared, and Elaine sped away.

Blow Jobs Demystified

T HAT AFTERNOON, I HID out in Hugh's old office. Feeling around for his bottle of Maker's Mark, I retrieved that plus some oddities: a crumbling King James Bible; his old .45, wrapped in oilcloth; Big Hugh's medals from the Rough Rider campaign; and, something truly strange, an unexpected guidebook to family dysfunction—*The Rule Against Perpetuities*.

The old leather volume carried the bookplate of Big Hugh himself, who, after duty on San Juan Hill, rode with Waddell, and had a guilty conscience about it. Maybe, at odd hours, he drank bourbon and repeated the ancient lawyer's incantation that drove Symmes men toward their reckoning: "No interest shall vest, unless it must vest, within twenty-one years from the death of any life-in-being."

In English, that means you can try hard, but you can't keep your family's shit together much past three generations. Until I signed up for destiny, it was simply a plot twist I knew from English novels of the eighteenth century.

"Jack, who are you talking to?"

I slammed the book shut. Ballard stood in the door. He would know to find me here. "Nobody. Getting into Hugh's Maker's Mark. Want some?"

He blanched. "Give me that." I handed him the bottle and he tossed it into the trash can. "We heard from Charlotte. Griffiths is on the warpath."

I feigned shock. "Look, Wardie made a timely payment, that's all."

"Not gonna fly. You really fucked it up this time. Victor Broman is after you personally."

◆◆◆

CRISIS CONFIRMED, I WANTED a reality check with Elaine. After worrying through dinner, I dialed her up, even though there was the thing about her having a date.

"Come on, I know you're mad I called."

She had answered the phone in her gruffly distant fashion.

"Not mad at you. Mad at myself."

"You had dinner with?"

"Zal. My high school boyfriend. I kissed him."

"What? You made out with your high school boyfriend?"

"No. Listen carefully. I kissed him in the parking lot of the Glenwood Café, and then he lifted me off the ground and the breath went out of my body. That's not making out."

She'd told me about Sergeant Zal, of the Groton, Connecticut, police force. "He's a cop, Elaine. Probably knows CPR."

"He said he was here on business. You don't think he came down here to take me to dinner? Is that even possible?"

Of course it was. Sergeant Zal wouldn't have police business in Raleigh. But he did have the power to turn on Elaine's time machine. I did not have the power to turn on Elaine's time machine. She got starry-eyed talking about her and Zal's high school hell-raising, not our New York summer of my big deals and her good works. His time machine banished all present worries, such as a son getting blow jobs in a red Fiat, a condo that needed painting, a doctor ex-husband with yet another twenty-five-year-old nurse in tow, or a law partnership that made her defend venal businessmen rather than the noble poor.

"I'm going to our high school reunion next weekend."

"I thought you hated reunions."

"Am I a bad mother to go to my high school reunion when Adam's got SATs?"

"I think Nora took heroin the day of my SATs."

"I feel better, then."

"Wonderful."

"Jack, this is my stuff, you get that."

"I guess."

"I've got something else to tell you anyway."

"Maybe some good news?"

"I saw Teri Lynn Tucker at the Glenwood Café. She's got a new haircut, and she was with a man, younger, wearing a sports jacket. It's very good news."

Elaine, ever the skilled litigator, had diverted us from the Zal Question to the Teri Lynn Question, or from her stuff to mine. It was indeed good news that Teri Lynn was with Another Man, younger, wearing a sports jacket. That meant people would finally stop talking about Teri Lynn and Jack. Instead, people would talk about Teri Lynn and Another Man, younger.

Although, if Elaine was with Zal, and Teri Lynn was with Another Man, who was I with?

Things had gone quiet on the Teri Lynn front. She'd called just once in the last couple of months, out of work, asking for a reference for a job at Belk's. She'd like that, working at Belk's behind the cosmetics counter, spraying the atomizers at strolling ladies, dressing in the latest fashions at employee discount.

Teri Lynn had started out as my secretary, and then became my confidante. I should have known this was dangerous. Turned out she wasn't very good at the first job, and too good at the second.

Without telling Elaine, who would have disapproved, I'd written a cheery, business-like recommendation letter. But another letter could have gone like this: Teri Lynn had sad, yet merry eyes, was great over a gas stove barefoot, inventive in bed, and in a hot tub, and wherever the spirit moved her, and she was full of understanding about the shitty side of life.

When I came in that day and said I'd moved out, handing her, like an idiot on remote control, my scribbled address at the Club, she was calm and sympathetic, like a very good nurse when you showed up in the ER with a nail through your foot. I was too embarrassed to tell anybody else, so it was officially our non-secret secret. Expert on breakups, her sympathy grew daily. "How's that Heartbreak Hotel working for you?" she'd ask breezily as I came in late, mumbling over some slight from Pren's lawyer, or some mommy-placed accusation from Robin. She'd lock the door to my office and dish the latest on her running troubles with Ronnie, who worked as a pit-stop mechanic for a leading stock car racing team. Ronnie, she had said before, had been loyal and sweet, and wanted to marry her.

Sadly, Ronnie changed. He took up with a tramp at the Rockingham Speedway.

"A tramp?" I repeated, feeling better in our shared misery, savoring a term not commonly used outside Frank Sinatra lyrics.

One day she handed me a Tupperware bowl. Inside sat plumped-up biscuits, warm. It was my first experience with warm biscuits, neither Nora nor Pren being familiar with them.

"So how are you really doing?" she asked in her casual, concerned way. "Things get better, you know."

Indeed, I could feel the old thump-thump again, that rising in the gorge, the stiffening of parts. Suddenly, I had feelings for Teri Lynn. She understood everything and wanted nothing. Unlike Elaine, she provided pure sympathy, without a judgment in sight. I trusted her to lead us through the cool, dark woods toward a clear place of classic rock music and relaxed adult fun. I'd had flirtations before, normally with Pren's friends, disenchanted women of her circle who wanted to ride around in the dark and talk. Except in one or two cases, I'd kept things all zipped up. Maybe there had been a couple of what Nora would call "flings"—sex-like behavior in the Mercedes, or somebody's pantry, or the occasional pool house, and once under a pile of coats at the Starr's now suspended Blackbeard's Birthday Party. It was hard to maintain a normal level of inhibition while dressed like Captain Hook.

None of that counted as sex in my ledger-keeping; there was no connection to it, and with all spouses and children either physically or psychically present, the combination of explosive horniness, anxiety, and self-medication made the flings about as fun as naked Thanksgiving at the in-laws.

But now, I had done the move-out from my drafty mansion, and the world was different. Being alone felt good, for a while. There was something about those biscuits and the Tupperware, something exotic and enticing. Maybe it was too much, too soon, this biscuit love, but I couldn't help myself. I was like a junkie, and the biscuits were my junk.

When Teri Lynn delivered biscuits, she looked better than before. Maybe I hadn't noticed. Could her breasts have gotten bigger? They bobbed and weaved, perched against the straining top button of her silk blouse. Her high-toned full legs, lotioned and crossed just so, spoke of an outdoor life, and when she talked, laugh wrinkles matched her hair, newly blonde. I surrendered to the juju and confessed: freedom had turned lonely, raw, too many chitchats at Whole Foods.

I followed her home. She'd said she lived in Garner, but when she turned off the Beltline, we drove into flat, black nowhere. A dirt road opened to a field that bordered a squat white house on blocks.

"It's a modular home?" she said, in the lilting country way that sounded like a question.

She had a pot roast in the oven, a salad in the crisper, and another stack of biscuits on the counter. She opened a Bud Light for herself and a Heineken for me. She must have heard me say it was my favorite.

The pot roast smelled sweetly of wine and carrots. My very soul opened to it.

Briefly, I felt the old anxiety return. She knew things. She answered my phone. What if she—what? Turned me into—Stasi? The KGB? The Bank?

She ladled carrots around the roast. "Are you okay?" she asked, squinting at me over the stove.

"Yeah, I just had a moment."

She shook her head. "I think you have PTSD, like my cousin Tommy. He got it in Iraq."

"I'm sorry to hear that about Tommy."

"All day long somebody's yelling at you. Can't be good for your self-esteem."

"It's not like getting shot at. They pay to yell at me, and money has a lot to do with my self-esteem."

"So just sit there and take it? That's the answer, while your self-esteem drains away?"

"It's my job."

She shook her head. "See, I went to nursing school. Being a nurse, the patients yell at you, but they have cancer and all."

"So why aren't you a nurse?"

"My life just got too disorganized. Big time. Momma gets all over me about it."

"Talk to your mother a lot?"

"Every day. She lives down the road."

Reflexively, I checked the windows.

"Relax," she said, laughing. "Miles down the road."

I put my hands on her shoulders as she stood at the stove. "I love those biscuits."

"Wait until you try the pot roast." She brandished the ladle.

"I need to tell you something, about what we were saying back there. I can't change. I am my fate."

She set the ladle aside. "What does that even mean?"

"I don't know."

"So why'd you say it?"

"Just nervous, I guess."

She laughed. "You're a Pure-T Geek. I don't know why I like you."

"Actually, I don't either."

"Okay, Mr. Fate. I know what I want to do."

"What?"

"Drink another beer in the hot tub."

She motioned to the corner of her deck, and there, sure enough, sat a hot tub, shaded by crepe myrtle bushes and already bubbly. She disappeared and returned with towels.

"Go on in. I'll grab the beer."

"You mean?" I gestured toward the water.

"Yeah. In the water. With your clothes off."

She disappeared toward the kitchen. I piled my clothes in a butterfly chair. The air was damp and warm; crickets and tree frogs chimed in from the darkness. Lowering into the warm water, I could smell the sweet haze of liquefied hog manure settling with the evening dew over the neighboring soybean fields, hear the whirring mechanical arms of the distant irrigators deftly rotating in the dusk.

Teri Lynn returned, padding barefoot on the deck. She held a towel to her chest and posed on tiptoe. She stepped in over the redwood side of the bubbling tub, and I made room for her beside me. She closed her eyes and looked up for me to kiss her, so I did.

"Move up a little bit," she murmured, in a soft commanding voice. "I'm going to do your back."

"But—"

"No. I want to do things. I've been thinking about it."

From behind, she pressed the cold beer against my cheek and giggled. She struck a match, and I smelled a cigarette.

"Smoking is so bad. No, don't look at me. You'll think I'm trashy."

She scrubbed my back with a loofah, and her nipples played a tattoo against me rhythmically as she worked. Presently I could feel the softness between her legs as she stretched out behind me. She hummed and stroked, and stroked and hummed. I leaned my head against her breasts and at once felt full, warm, and aroused, with only clean white noise for thought. Her mouth smelled of beer and cigarettes in an intoxicating way, and I turned to her again, but she pushed me back.

"Stay put, honey. This is so nice. Now lie back. I'm just gonna—oh my Lord!"

We had great sex. She was happy to make me happy, and I was happy to make her happy, and when we did it, I could feel that moment when you're really close.

We kept things separate at the office. Sometimes, though, I took her for early lunches to the Charter Room at the Velvet Cloak. George got the usual table ready, looking up next door at the corner room in the YMCA where Deputy Barney Fife stayed on official trips to Raleigh. If you ever had to make conversation at the Velvet Cloak, it was a good starting point.

On Tuesdays and Fridays, we'd go to her house, and she'd cook. Sometimes I'd have too much to drink and spend the night, which made me feel better about us. I thought about asking to keep a suit there, but

I didn't. I kept one in the car, squished in with the golf clubs in the trunk so I wouldn't look like a traveling salesman.

She seemed experienced in this kind of relationship. She easily kept some parts of her life open and other parts closed. After she told me her mother lived down the road, she never mentioned it again. There was a room in the house she kept closed and locked. Once, I tried to go in, thinking it was the laundry. "My sewing closet," she said, and led me away from the door.

"Whatcha got in there?" I asked, trying to be playful. She changed the subject.

I didn't take her out in Raleigh, and she didn't ask to go. Basically, we just ate, soaked in the hot tub, and had sex.

After a while, we fell into boredom. Teri Lynn drank more, and I did, too. The sex died down. The more she drank, the more she talked about Ronnie and cried. Why did women always talk about their old boyfriends with me? That made us both drink more. To keep things going, we agreed on a road trip. I was thinking haute cuisine, the Inn at Little Washington. But against my better judgment, we drove to North Wilkesboro for a race.

◆◆◆

IT'S STILL HARD TO get North Wilkesboro out of my mind. I'd been living at the Club for a couple of months and spending the odd night at Teri Lynn's, and this road trip felt like the end. Things could hardly have been set up better, or worse for a rough finale. Ronnie's ghost, the nowhere boulevard of our affair—it could have been a French movie about an American backwater starring Jean Seberg as Teri Lynn, and me as a Euro hipster with bad eyeglasses. In the real world, the woman described to me as Teri Lynn's cousin, Betty, loaded us into a beat-up gold Winnebago, and her escort Bill drove, popping pills and emptying beers down the Junior Johnson Highway. I sat in the back with Teri Lynn and Betty, who was also popping pills. I drank tequila. When I woke up, Teri Lynn was massaging my head.

"I do love that curly hair," she said, nipping at the bald spot.

Betty appeared through the bead curtains with salt, a new bottle, and a shot glass. Suddenly I noticed a resemblance I hadn't before. Teri Lynn, in her dangling hairpiece, white tank top, white jeans, and white heels, was a younger version of Betty, who wore the same getup in canary yellow.

"Are you two really cousins?"

Betty laughed. "We sure look it, don't we?"

"What about Bill?"

"He's a maybe cousin."

"You're Pure-T confusing him, stop it."

Betty handed the bottle to Teri Lynn. "Honey, he's drunk, not confused. Let me rub on him a while."

When I woke up again, Teri Lynn was cleaning up around me with a towel.

We parked at the racetrack and walked toward the roar. Teri Lynn took my hand and guided me through the bleachers, past a guard and to grass at the edge of the track.

"Here, drink this," she said, handing me a cold beer. "It'll settle you down."

She teetered to the edge of the grass in her heels and leaned against the fence. I leaned against her. "Smell it," she whispered.

"Smell what?"

"Shh," she said. "It's starting."

She put her arms around me and I felt her heartbeat joined to the whoom-whoom-whoom of the circling engines. My head spun in the industrial haze of burning oil and melting rubber. We leaned together on the fence, breathing the singed air. Minutes, hours passed as we stood in the backdraft, hypnotized by the whirling combat.

"Jeff, Jeff, Jeff, JEFF," she yelled, pulling away from me and tumbling us to the grass.

"Who the hell is Jeff," I shouted.

"Jeff Bo-dine—that's Ronnie's—he's winning the damn race!"

A multitude took up the cry. Chicken bones and beer cans rained down on us. A crowd massed in the infield, and somebody picked me up by the elbows to stand facing a now-empty circle of track. A throng of people at the opposite end gathered before the glistening victor, who held aloft a silver trophy filled with cash.

"Jeff?" I asked.

"Yep," she said. "Jeff."

I marveled at him, standing there like a young god in a jumpsuit, the lord of the fumes and the dust, with a strange, adoring woman on one arm and a trophy cradled in another.

Rock Bottom

SOMETHING ABOUT THE WEEKEND at Wilkesboro told me I'd hit rock bottom. I had changed from a respectable married man with attractive, Christmas card–worthy dependents, and a highly leveraged but nonetheless substantial home to a—a what? A middle-aged boozehound shacked up with his secretary in a Winnebago?

I resolved to tell Teri Lynn it was over. I felt bad because it was more than a fling; I cared about her, maybe even loved her. Still, I shouldn't have started it up.

When she got to work Monday morning, I closed the door behind us and told her we had to stop. Before she could say anything, I added that things would go better if she stopped working for me and started up with Donovan, a capable associate down the hall, who needed an experienced hand.

I pointed out that Donovan was a special hire, our first technology man, lured from Silicon Valley itself. He shunned neckties, sported a retro buzz cut, and wore purple eyeglasses. But I should have known that all this change would upset her.

"You were Pure-T lying when you said you loved me?"

I remembered having told her that in the hot tub as the water drained and her head bubbled acrobatically around my midsection, and, also, after one or two especially tasty meals.

"We have to stop."

"Why? I don't care what people think."

"I'm afraid I've been unfair."

"Honey, this ain't a ballgame."

"But it's complicated. I'm still married, and it's hard for me."

"That's such bullshit." She began to cry again.

"And you still have feelings for Ronnie," I said, reaching for my handkerchief.

She blew her nose and shook her head no, unconvincingly.

"Try working for Donovan and let things sit. Maybe you'll want to go back to nursing school. I could help."

She stood up, red-eyed, folded my handkerchief in fours, and dropped it in the trash can. "I'm a fool," she said. I tried to hug her, or at least engage in a clinch, but she ducked and ran out the door.

At first the plan to hand Teri Lynn over to Donovan worked. She dashed around, organizing. Donovan now arrived at meetings with a properly sectioned Day-Timer. She brought purple silk flowers for his desk, anchored in glass marbles.

The world appeared to right itself. But then, not.

"You sent me to the wrong place, I can't even—" Donovan sputtered.

Teri Lynn sat crying at her desk, mascara flowing in rivulets.

"She sent me to the wrong address for a meeting with the Bank. Somewhere out in the Park. We're probably fired."

She tried to speak, but kept sobbing.

"And, look, she's been writing on stickies or something. Who does that?"

Donovan produced a piece of correspondence on our cream-colored embossed letterhead, with a typo corrected by application of a yellow tab, marked by the word "oops" in her handwriting.

"Teri Lynn? Were you going to send this out?"

Her look confirmed it.

In the old days, Hugh and I simply would have done the right thing: found her a job down the street, produced a check, and said we were very sorry things didn't work out.

But now, Butler and Symmes had an HR department. Tim, our man, arrived the next day from the Washington office tie-less and sporting a Zapata-style mustache to "work up the file," as he put it. I told him Teri Lynn and I had an ill-considered affair, and he wrote that down.

Tim arranged a probation for Teri Lynn that prescribed psychological counseling and Prozac, which I learned then was some kind of legal dope. I pulled in favors and she went from desk to desk, but collapsed finally into disoriented weepiness. The last days were marked by her flirting with a well-muscled young laborer, who cinched Marlboros in his T-shirt sleeves and worked each day without success on the HVAC system.

One day Tim came back from Washington and fired Teri Lynn. Everything had failed, including the Prozac.

Elaine's anger is a many-splendored thing. Sometimes it's to the point, cold and cutting; other times it sputters in rapid-fire fury. On the day Tim fired Teri Lynn, I heard Elaine's door open and then slam, knowing Ballard had related, in his unctuous tone, the sordid denouement.

"You bastard," she said, spitting the word and slamming my office door for good measure. "Were you sleeping with her?"

"I don't know. I mean I don't know how—"

"Screw you, Jack," she exploded. "I'm not getting you out of it this time, understand?" Elaine was an expert in sex problems. She'd stepped in when I'd gotten into scrapes before.

"You're not going to help me?"

"You never stopped, did you? How much is a blow job worth, Jack? You like markets, right? There's a market for blow jobs, and working girls don't sue. Why don't you make things easier on everybody and go to a whore?"

She said the word *whore* with special relish, as though someone were to be burned at the stake. I could see myself slowly roasting while she listed my inadequacies, purifying in the sinner's flame.

"Jesus. You can't make me feel any worse."

"You're not even cute anymore."

"That does make me feel worse."

"All this time, Pren just turned her back. I swear, Jack."

At least Pren didn't lecture me. She did ignore me, but she didn't lecture. And I couldn't very well ask Pren to help me out of a sex problem.

Elaine, on the other hand, had to help. She was my helper. I depended on her not to leave me high and dry. Nora said adieu every day at three thirty when Hugh arrived. Pren had mastered the art of being there and at the same time leaving a long time ago. But Elaine always stuck it out for me. So, of course, I had to screw things up.

"I'm sorry, I really am."

"No, you're not," she said in an arctic tone. "The saddest thing is, you really feel good down there somewhere in your pants. Nailed another one. Congratulations, you pathetic bag of shit."

I'd been meaning to have a talk with Elaine about sex, but one thing or another kept intervening. She had it wrong, understandably wrong, but wrong nonetheless. I did these sex things, which I did feel bad about, to feel free, not out of general lust, or a specific need for blow jobs. I didn't know exactly why it made me feel free—still working on that. I'll have the conversation with her when I've sorted it out.

One of the worst things about the immediate disaster was imagining how jubilant Ballard had been in telling Elaine the news, lingering over details, taking another opportunity to rub her nose in the not-quite equality of the partnership that compelled her, as the lady of the house, to tidy up the mess.

"She sent her panties to Rod by interoffice mail. Did you know that?"

"Who's Rod?" I asked.

"The courier, you idiot. Ballard—" She spit out the syllables and closed her eyes. "He told me about the inter-office panties so I could spread the word that Teri Lynn is a bad girl."

She muttered *bad girl* again under her breath, and violently turned up the thermostat, which she regarded as set too low by policy, another gender slight.

"I don't know what happened. She baked me biscuits. I went with her to a stock car race."

"Can't do it, Jack." She opened the door to leave.

"Please, don't go."

"Won't do it."

"Please. I can't make it through this by myself."

"All you had to do was keep your pants zipped up."

"I'm begging. If I was some homeless guy on the street, you'd help me."

"Get a clue, Jack. You are homeless."

People came and went. I ran to the men's room and threw up. It wasn't hard to do, throwing up, and the sensation after reminded me of Nora's suppositories, the ones she kept in the refrigerator and gave me before Hugh came. I would lie against her slip, her perfume fresh, waiting for the drugs to work. She carried me down the hall back to my room, to my bed, where I was unable to move until the drugs wore off. It was like she'd calmed the devil himself, she said.

To heck with pathetic sex guilt, and to heck with Elaine and her cracks about me not being cute, I thought, swishing the firm's institutional mouthwash and looking around to make sure I was alone. Nothing wrong with Old Jack, or so the mirror says. Still a good lie at six feet. Mostly steady at 195, on bad days pushing 200, could work out more. But then, a healthy paunchiness in the Gilded Age signaled confidence and prosperity. Are we not in a new Gilded Age? Last week's *New Yorker* said so.

Puffiness in the face, that's difficult to mask. Flying, which I do a lot, spreads the sinuses to the Adam's apple. There'll be an article in the *New Yorker* on that soon, saying flying is bad. It'll be whacked by the industry, the author tagged in ticketing and banned to smelly rear seats that don't tilt back, where you listen to the john flush for six hundred nautical miles.

Gilded Age or not, I couldn't do anything about male pattern baldness. It was genetics on the mother's side, Nora's fault again. I'd tried self-dosing massage oils to no avail. Less hair highlighted the generous jutting nose, but I'd made peace with the Gold family honker a long time ago.

Not cute anymore? What the heck was Elaine talking about?

Word about Teri Lynn being fired spread the next day, which made me persona non grata. The support staff put me on deep freeze, and the two young women associates I'd ask to help with research found a way to cancel our morning meeting. Around noon, Willis, the maintenance man, began shouting Teri Lynn's name in the hall outside my office. Security removed him by force. Then, the HVAC broke down completely. All you heard throughout the building were valves clicking and hissing, and no cold air came out, just room-temperature bowel-smelling fumes.

Around two, security removed Teri Lynn's effects from her desk to a long black box and sealed it with yellow tape marked HR and the date. When security cleared out, Ballard popped by for a chat.

"So, Jack," he said, striding into my office and closing the door, "let's talk about your midlife crisis. We'd all hoped it was over."

Ballard developed a peculiar glow that traveled to the curve of his receding crown when he sniffed out an office sex scandal, particularly one pertaining to me. Ballard didn't have sex with Ginger anymore, and no backroom sex with anybody, hence no sex. Dissecting my sex life, and then resenting it, and punishing me for it, was a sex-like thing for Ballard, a searing orgy of the super ego. That day he positively smoldered.

"What do you want, Ballard?"

"Ginger said four women asked about you at the pool the other day."

"Four? Really." The name Ginger set off an old panic alert. I hadn't been completely honest with Elaine about—that. The truth was, I'd had sort-of-totally-deniable sex several times with Ginger. The first time had been in the Mercedes, when I shed my Captain Hook costume after their pirate party. I circled the neighborhood wordlessly horny, looking for a place to park.

"Haven't done it in a car since St. Elizabeth's," she said calmly, balancing in order to pull down her Spanx. She'd dressed as Wendy, with a blonde wig.

Then it was in the butler's pantry, against a broom rack, while Robin was out with her kids on Halloween. And then it was—oops, good, the memory-suppression technique caught the others. Stopped pretty suddenly; maybe she found somebody safer. She'd gotten so distant I feared she'd told Pren, but time passed, and the rule is, after six months, everything gets erased and nothing really happened.

"Ginger told me she was certain Pren was going to divorce you once and for all, but you'd do far better because you have money and status and, what? Good looks? Yes, she really said that, and a Mercedes—you have a range of women of all ages to choose from who want those things. Witness four, count 'em, women at the pool."

"I was with Robin."

"See, that's a positive. Attracts them like Tiffany's ads. You're a caring father, and only with your kid on weekends. Also shows you're not a homo."

"People use the word 'gay' now, Ballard."

Even though I did have good freedom thoughts, and the memory-suppression trap blocked all the pictures, and so nothing really happened, I did feel bad for Ballard about the car sex and pantry sex and other non-remembered sex with Ginger. Nothing Ballard had done deserved that, not even being a shithead for decades.

I suffered for both the remembered and non-remembered sex. Guilt rendered me professionally supine. Yet, while Ballard lorded over me about sex sins, there were plenty of power sins and money sins for him to own up to.

Ballard was always enlisting me in some plot to take money from our other partners, but somehow it never seemed as bad as the sex. They were equal sins in the Bible. Thou shalt not steal, and Thou shalt not commit adultery sat right there together. Some people, the pope for one, thought lending money for profit was stealing—the whole business of the Bank! To stay out of trouble with money, the best strategy was to tell people what you stole quarterly, as I explained to my clients. This quarter we stole this much this way, and a lot more another way, and kept it all to pay ourselves that way. It's all there in the report.

Somehow, sex always seemed worse. Maybe there should be a report for that, too. This year, when compared to last year, showed an increase in screwing across all segments, with a notable uptick in our North Carolina operations.

"Are you enjoying yourself, Ballard? Can we get to the point?"

"Pardon me while I turn my back, as Hugh would say. See if you can find the knife in there somewhere. I was having fun with the four at the pool, but you see I just didn't know that you and Teri Lynn, and her cousin—some reports say her mother, you pervert—were an item, or would that be *items*? You're an English Lit guy, Jack—I just went to the fucking business school. What would that be, item or items?"

I sat immobilized in the guilt-fest. Had I finally lived up to the name motherfucker, too? My phone rang, ignored on the credenza. I tried to think of something wise to say, achieve perspective, the classical middle distance, Canadian geese on the first hole...

"It was just one day, really, at Wilkesboro. It's not like an entire life."

"Know all about Wilkesboro. The Charlotte boys know all about it, too."

"Jesus."

"In a Winnebago. Drinking tequila with the cousin-mother."

"Only one point in time. Over now."

"Nope, not over. Teri Lynn's suing."

"Oh God."

"If you'd told me all this before we fired her, then maybe I could have gotten a release for some dough, but now what I've got is a call from Sid Wheeless, and I don't think it's about a campaign contribution."

"Wheeless? Oh my God." Sid Wheeless was a former partner with a rival firm who'd thrown in with the trial lawyers and gotten rich, which naturally turned his mind toward politics. I'd faced him a couple of times, and it wasn't pleasant. He loved suing the firm's clients. He would love suing me.

"What the hell's the matter with you?" Ballard thundered. "We went through a lot of shit together. And now you go and screw your secretary?"

One has to lie about these things, since the truth makes everything difficult with insurers. This lie seemed particularly stupid, something you'd say to your North Vietnamese captors at gunpoint on TV. I closed my eyes and repeated, slowly:

"Let the record show I deny screwing my secretary."

Ballard nodded, expressionless as Ho Chi Minh.

He put an Incident Report Form for Lloyd's of London on the table. I held it in my hands, marveling—an austere, antique, multi-witnessed English document of Dickensian formality.

"This is a joke, right?"

"Nope," Ballard said. "Sign it."

"Then what?"

He smiled thinly. "My advice is to get the women partners behind you. Word is your girlfriend Teri Lynn is a slut."

Wheeless filed his lawsuit that afternoon. I got a panicked call from the receptionist, who, being new, went gaga when she saw a sheriff. Nothing stops sheriffs from reading the complaints they serve, and this one, a short-coiffed trim woman in a creased tan uniform, looked me over like a wife-beating menace.

"You Callahan?"

"Yes, ma'am."

"You're served."

She thrust the blue-backed folder into my chest and walked off, adding me already in her mind, I guess, to the sex offender rolls.

Ballard sent an email to the Management Committee announcing that he would personally monitor my work product until the matter got resolved. What was that about? Did Lloyd's believe I was sexually unfit to do legal work?

The complaint read like others I'd seen. Wheeless alleged that I demanded sex in exchange for Teri Lynn retaining her job, and, when she refused, the firm fired her along with the HVAC guy, because I was jealous of him.

"It's Mr. Forrest," Delores, my competent and utterly plain new secretary, announced as I sat dumbly holding the foul papers. Delores didn't seem frightened of me, God bless her.

"Hello, Tiger," Wardie said through the voice box. I switched it off and picked up.

"Wardie, I was going to call you."

"I heard everything. How're you doing?"

"Okay, I guess. I don't really know how any of this happened."

"Well, let's see. You got drunk and did a two-bagger with Teri Lynn and the cousin, who some people say is really her mom. Yowzer! Used to happen to Billy Martin and Mickey Mantle all the time. If I knew you wanted a date, we could've all gone out on the boat. I've never really done two before. I mean all the way. I've had two in the sack, but –"

"Not her mother, her cousin. That's what she said."

"You need to own the mother thing, stop sounding so defensive. You didn't kill anybody."

"Damn right. Didn't knock over a liquor store."

"That's the spirit. How are they getting behind you at the firm?"

"They're not."

"So Ballard's acting like a shit. Great. Where's Elaine?"

"Gone."

"Gone where?"

"I don't know. Home."

"I'll call her. She's the one with the balls."

"Thanks."

"Oh yeah. You need to get ready for something from Pren."

"Why?"

"You're a divorce rookie. Trust me on this. Don't worry, I've decided not to cover the story."

"Oh shit. It's a story?"

"Yep. But I'm not covering. Big firm, sex lawsuits, *Sixty Minutes* just had a thing—way overdone."

"Wardie—"

"Stop it, my mind's made up. The Forrests and the Symmes, remember?"

"Yeah."

"You can't do anything about the TV people, though."

"What?"

"Don't worry. Nobody remembers what's on TV the next day. There'll be some pileup on the Beltline and the Ballad of Jack and Teri Lynn will be over. Have to get through the news cycle, that's all. That Wheeless is a jerk-off, isn't he?"

"I thought you couldn't wait to endorse him."

"He's still a jerk-off."

◆◆◆

PREN'S PAPERS ARRIVED THE next day, as Wardie predicted, revised for the late-breaking news. She'd rethought custody, alimony, and child support. You could call it the Teri Lynn dividend.

For the thousandth time, I went over the whole mess. My fault, my fault, my fault! Why couldn't I just get happy? On the plus side, we had a great kid together. Okay, big check mark on that. It ended because of—what? Lusting after money and drafty mansions, many sensitivity errors, no boundaries, tacky car sex, freedom urges, the works. Our marriage counselors talked about origin stories. Apparently, we got each other wrong from the start. I thought she had the perfect family I didn't; she thought I was the rebel she wasn't. Wrong, wrong, wrong!

But then maybe it was plain old sin, Old Scratch at work, conniving with endlessly peeved modern people. The marriage counselors don't deal with sin. End Times!

Cut to the boffo last scene: I drove in early from the airport and, as the Mercedes chugged up the hill to our nearly redone garage (no floorboards, have to punch-list that), I saw Bingo Bricker, deck shoes in hand, beat it out the back.

Courteously, I made way for him to blow past me in his leased Bloodworth Properties Beamer. I had no idea whether he and Pren were actually doing it, or if he was acting from practice, but it certainly had all the look of a guilty afternooner.

Bingo was a family retainer in the Bloodworth's once-a-go-go real estate business that Pren had angrily reentered, having mistakenly believed that she could retire to marriage and motherhood. When her dad and mom checked out and went off to live by a lake in Florida, the business faltered, and she had to push aside her feckless brothers, whose interest in almost any outdoor sport—boating, fishing, hunting, golf, Bocce, horseshoes— had kept them from work. She booted them in one big-sister chat from their little-used desks, to permanent exile in the shiny pickups they washed and polished like Rothschild eggs.

I'd watched all this admiringly, as she charmed the strip mall world with an updated version of the no-nonsense, pave-that-damn-thing-over style of her old man. It occurred to me that her business flair had been wasted organizing carpool lists.

Robin and I got used to takeout food, and I didn't mind that, especially from this new Indian restaurant. Besides, the money Pren brought in was good, and she didn't seem so mad all the time. Maybe she even seemed happy, the work being her free thing, the way sex was mine. *Lieben und arbeiten*, Dr. Freud had said, something else marriage counselors don't quote.

After a while, Pren put Bingo in the front office. This surprised every-body, because his real job was going down to the Legislature and gutting environmental regulations. If you wanted a wetland shrunk or a river muddied up, Bingo was your guy.

Socially, he alternated on a list of Raleigh bachelors brought out to entertain ladies between marriages. Did he and Pren really sleep together? Absurd, I thought. Bingo Bricker with my wife, Pren Callahan? Please. Besides, she was all about the work. But then I caught him beating it out my back door.

I gave her a minute to compose herself.

"Don't say a word," she said, flipping her sandy bob and leaning against the JennAir in another wildly colored Lilly Pulitzer frock. Regular Pilates had given her impressive guns and abs, and her newly cut hair bobbed and weaved as she spoke.

"I was going to ask Bingo if he'd stay for a drink, but he rushed off."

"Don't think I'm going to stand here and be accused by you, after everything, Jack Callahan, oh my gosh."

This was a technique learned by Pren and her friends at their so-called book clubs. Always make him feel bad for something you've done.

"I don't remember accusing you of anything. I just can't believe you'd take up with a redneck. The guy doesn't even wear socks to the Legislature."

"Jack, that's enough," she said, pointing at the door, hand shaking. "I want you the F out of here."

"You want me the F out of here? Can't you even say the word *fuck*?"

"Shut up! I can't believe you'd say that to me."

"If you can do it, sugar, might as well say it."

She threw a can of Progresso green pea soup at my head, but I ducked, and it broke a picture of the two of us and Robin smiling dockside the year before on our vacation in Maine. "I will leave, my dear," I said, trying not to sound like an asshole, giving it my best Clark Gable imitation, even bowing slightly. I picked up the broken frame, shed shards into the trashcan, and stashed the photo in my briefcase.

"I never wanted this house anyway. See if you can get Bingo to pay for it."

She shook her head slowly at the drafty mansion argument, as though it stood for all the arguments between us. "You'll pay for it," she said quietly, flicking back her hair. I never bothered to ask whether she liked it that short.

"I'm going to the Club for now. I'll pick up my things when you're not here, which is most of the time these days. Please tell the truth to Robin about this."

I grabbed the mail from the counter and waved goodbye. It felt absurd waving goodbye, but I didn't know what else to do. I realized some people would say Bingo had done a good turn here, providing an excuse for me not to be the bad guy, even though it felt like I was.

"One more thing," I said, looking back at her and doing a double-take. She was crying by the JennAir. I was going to say something witty, but let it go.

◆◆◆

PREN HAD BEEN AMONG Nora's best students, and when I first saw her at one of Nora's teas, she was full of Virginia Woolf, rooms for women, and all that. She looked great in seventies clothes, bell bottoms and clogs and tube tops, her black hair pulled back with an Indian headband.

"Jack Callahan," she said, holding out her hand.

"You're—"

"Pren Bloodworth. We met at Tessie's party last summer."

"You mean with the melting ducks?"

She laughed and grabbed my arm. "Pitiful old ducks."

Hugh had given Tessie a large debutante party before school started. She'd invited me since we'd gotten to know each other at the Landing, the Symmes retreat on Cape Fear, where Nora enjoyed a writing cabin. I was against debutante parties for political reasons, but I went to them if asked.

As for the Landing, I'd visited there for the odd weekend since I was a kid, and I mean truly odd, after I figured out my mother was screwing her father in the writing cabin. Things with Tessie started out rocky. I should have cut her some slack. Clearly, she didn't know as much as I did about what was going on. She never could figure out why I was there, and for something to say referred to me as the pool boy in front of her private-school friends.

Truth is, I liked Tessie from the get-go. She was a year older, and for high school she went off to Madeira. She was tall like Hugh, had long hair all curled up in a couple of shades of blonde, and always said she was watching her weight, which didn't seem to be a problem. She played an aggressive game of tennis and made that Chrissie Evert noise when she hit backhand. What I liked best, though, was that she read novels instead of *People* magazine and didn't think politics was boring. Eventually, she let me take her, in her dad's venerable blue-hulled Chris-Craft launch, to the sandspit island across the waterway, where I didn't have to be the pool boy.

I felt bad she wasn't clued in to the screwing. But what was I supposed to do? Put it on a billboard?

She had a deep, husky voice, like she was forty and smoking cigarettes, except she didn't. Usually, she wore a modest brown two-piece on the little sand river beach the teenagers shared, and lay face down on her stomach trying to correct her tennis tan before, as she put it, she "had to rock the strapless," whatever that meant.

We learned to coexist in that non-secret secret. We learned to do more on the sandspit island. I turned up at her deb party.

Hugh gave a swell coming-out, sporting a Gatsby theme, which the girls liked for that flapper look. Doug Clark and the Hot Nuts played the high fraternity version of cool, and although my taste in music in those days ran more to heavy metal, I shagged on. Pot smokers gathered in the rhododendrons, and everybody shared. The ice sculptures, however, fared badly in the August heat. Ducks and castles and fountains melted, which gave the food tables a Dresden look, post firebombing. Tessie cried, leaning against Hugh in her yellow satin flapper dress and matching boa.

I felt sorry for her, and helpless. It wasn't her fault the ice sculptures melted, or that her brother hadn't come for the party from the West Coast, or that Mary, her mother, flitted from table to table, head erect, scanning for imperfections. For once, I didn't feel Hugh's critical eyeball. He had his hands full with his A-list family.

That's when I met Pren, although it wasn't a meeting, really. She was lounging on a sofa in a green shimmy and costume tiara, twirling ridiculous red beads. Tessie had talked about her more than once, about how she'd been

107

counselor in Pren's cabin at their summer camp, and said she was smart and different and I'd like her. Maybe she'd said the same thing to Pren, because she seemed to know who I was. Whether she really did or not, she smiled at me so directly across the room that I looked around to see if I was in someone else's way. It was a spiritual moment between strangers.

I had that feeling of not really wanting to be there, but wanting to at the same time, and later I learned she felt the same. We stared at each other for several long seconds before her date returned, a guy named Kennell whom I knew vaguely, to the circle into which old man Bloodworth would sell her for a match, if he could. I studied him as he walked by in his well-cut tux, casual but in control. Kennell was one of the guys Tessie had listed out that her mother and other mothers wanted as sons-in-law. She and her friends had a code word for them: SEMs.

"Oh, that, it's what we say at school," she explained one afternoon, lying on her stomach in the brown two-piece. "Stands for Southern Effeminate Man, the ideal. Wears a barn jacket but never rides, owns a lab that doesn't hunt, polishes a shotgun he never shoots, drives a truck and never hauls anything, impeccable album collection, alphabetized—oh, and most important, perfectly positioned for a six-figure income."

"What does that mean, six-figure income?"

"I don't know exactly, but it's *real* important..."

Some SEM skills I could master, but others not. For example, SEMs were very good at beach-music dancing. I witnessed Kennell pretzel-arm Pren and deftly spin her around as a human top in a way I couldn't possibly copy.

I didn't say a word to Pren that night. Really, all we had done was observe each other. Later, when she and I started dating, we got close to the meaning of that moment. In a deafening beer hall in Chapel Hill the next year—one where you couldn't get but two beers, Bud or Miller, and the bathrooms merged with the keg plumbing to form one ecosystem—Pren said she wanted to escape what I, without knowing, wanted to enter.

Entrances and exits, she said, that was us. I loved that she could make a phrase like that.

But that was all in the future. Later that night, Kennell led her twirling and swirling outside the tent, shagging in the dark to "Carolina Girls"—a smooth but cynical tune. "Carolina girls, sweet southern pearls… California girls are sexy and New York girls are too but Carolina girls got good looks and sweet personality, too…"

I had gone to the wrong high school to know many people. Enright, the inner-city school where I got bused was for outside-the-Beltline kids who wanted high SATs. They made it into what they called a magnet, filling half with kids from the hood, or the "base population" as the school-o-crats said, and the other half with geeks like me. Most of the inside the Beltline kids went to Bingham, which was more button-down then, unless, like Pren, they enrolled at St. Elizabeth's or some other boarding school.

But Hugh had paid for golf lessons, so I knew some of the guys. I'd been captain of the Enright squad. We got to play on this great old abandoned Donald Ross course landlocked by the projects, where you could hear gunfire starting at dusk from the back nine. Of course, the Bingham guys played at the Club. A couple of them were cool enough to introduce me around. So, I went out back with the golfers and smoked more grass, and asked about the girl in the green dress, Pren Bloodworth, who, consensus had it, was strange and moody, but good-looking, and so maybe worth the trouble.

"You think it's karmic, having all these women in your house?" Pren asked, months later, saying the word *Women* with a capitalized swagger, as though having two x chromosomes could make you into a superhuman figure. We were at one of Nora's Women's Lit student teas. She'd been working to transform the tone at St. Elizabeth's from Betty Crocker to Germaine Greer. I'd made a point to come back from Chapel Hill and hang around for tea, maybe because Pren was there.

"Totally karmic. Ask Nora about the time Anne Sexton passed out on the rug."

"Anne Sexton? For real?"

For some time, I'd been having dreams about Pren in which she wasn't wearing clothes. I hoped her dreams mirrored mine. I imagined her thought process, that this boy she might sleep with had a mother who hung with Anne Sexton, and we could accomplish a feminist transference of enlightenment cum penis.

I pointed to a spot on the carpet near the coffee table. "That's where she threw up."

Anne Sexton liked it here with Nora. Drinking, cursing, lipstick, poems. She was the first woman I heard say the word fuck out loud—other than my mother, that is.

"Oh my gosh," Pren said, transfixed. "Right there?"

"Too bad she offed herself."

"Stop, that makes me sad. Do you think it was liberation, from the pain and all?"

"Yeah. Listen, do you still go out with that Pooch guy?"

"Excuse me?"

"Kennell Whitfield."

"I wouldn't say we're going out."

"Did you know he was a SEM?"

"What? You're not supposed to know that. Where did you learn that word?"

"Never mind. What kind of name is Kennell, anyway?"

"It's a family name."

"Which family? The Spaniel family? Beagles maybe?"

She laughed. "Tessie told me you were strange."

"Are you and Tessie Symmes really friends?"

"Since forever. She was my cabin leader at Camp Seafarer."

I got the idea this had been a real bonding experience. "Cool. What does she say about me?"

"Nothing much. She's not ever coming back here, you know."

I still thought about Tessie sometimes, but our Landing summers were over, and, like Pren said, she was adamant about not coming home. And Pren was standing right in front of me. Pren did remind me of her: good-looking and really smart, but you couldn't tell.

"Tessie's very smart, but she tries to hide it."

I thought that remark was an intriguing piece of mind reading.

"She didn't hide it from me," I said. "We talked a lot about Jane Austen. Didn't get to Anne Sexton."

"Tessie's more the Jane Austen type. I think she wants to be a lawyer."

"Like her dad."

"No, not like her dad. She doesn't want anything to do with her dad."

"I know. I wish I could have more to do with my dad, but Nora forbids it."

Pren rolled her eyes. "How do you like Carolina?"

"It's a laugh a minute. Come on over."

"I'm going if I get in. Your mother needs to give me an A. But I do get there sometimes now. I'm—in the Cold Cuts."

She'd said that hesitatingly, knowing that singing in a bluegrass a cappella gig could muddle her rap. And yet, telling me could have been a way to endear herself, and therefore move closer to having sex. "You dress up like Ellie Clampett and sing at frat parties? Sorry, I'm never invited."

"The Cold Cuts are a serious singing group. Some of the girls are training professionally. To go to New York."

"Yeah. So they can date bankers."

She looked down at the Sexton carpet. "I don't know how this could ever work, but for some reason I want you to call me."

I produced a paper napkin and Bic pen to secure the number. "Do you think you ought to ask Nora, you know, maybe in class, what it means culturally that your girl band is named after lunch meat?"

She wrote out her number. "Why do you call Dr. Callahan *Nora*? She's your mother."

"Better get away now!"

"Such a strange boy. On second thought, don't call me. I imagine you have no time to go out. Your mom said you had a poem published."

"Oh God. It's a piece of shit."

"I don't think so. I read it. It's very—emotional."

"Can't believe you found that old magazine."

"Your mother has it out."

"Jesus."

"She read it out loud to us."

"Oh my God."

Pren tossed back her long mane in triumph. I was actually glad for the last humiliation, since she might now think about having dominatrix sex.

"Even though you make fun of everything, it's still kind of interesting to talk to a poet. I'm always with these, you know." She made a flinging motion with her hands.

"Frat guys? Bankers? War criminals?"

"Yes."

◆◆◆

SEEKING A DIGNIFIED END to Teri Lynn's firing day, I sandwiched myself between two couriers and tried to leave the office unobserved. But it was no use. The Channel Five news crew spotted us by the service entrance and gave chase.

"Mr. Callahan—Mr. Callahan—did you fire Teri Lynn Tucker because she stopped having sex with you?" Brenda Bobelink, who until that moment had been a disembodied presence reading the evening news, fairly spit the words. Her cameraman fixed me with a light so bright that I threw up my arm.

"What? That's—that's preposterous."

"Did you assault Miss Tucker in North Wilkesboro?"

"Oh God, no."

"Do you think sexual harassment is a major problem at Butler and Symmes?"

One of the couriers shoved me into a running car, and we hightailed it through yellow lights down Wilmington Street, out of downtown toward the Club. Another news crew sat waiting by the entrance, and so I told the couriers to turn around and drive back to the office. I had nowhere else to go.

I went back to my desk. It was only eight o'clock, and there were plenty of people still at work. All around me, I felt the firm's comforting hum, the churning Xerox machine, the click-click-click of an overtime secretary's Selectric.

"You looked really special on TV, Jack," Elaine said, materializing coolly from the hall, as I sat squinting at the diplomas and ornately gilded law licenses on my wall.

Pren had fussed over framing my licenses and diplomas with the right matte and distressed wood, and had insisted that Maurice, the family decorator, see to their hanging. In the bargain, he'd managed to sell her a Chinese standing screen with a domestic scene for my office. He claimed it was Ming, but I thought was a fifties vintage Hong Kong knockoff of Madame Butterfly, which was not only kitschy, but the wrong country.

This provoked a brief but painful argument, and I felt bad because Pren was proud of me, all promoted and in a new office, and trying to be nice. She took the screen home and draped nightgowns over it in her dressing room.

"The arm in the face was a nice touch, sort of like those really guilty guys on *60 Minutes*."

I tried to focus. Despite her disgust at my weakness, Elaine had arrived to save the day. She stood expectantly in the door, wearing jeans and an Oxford shirt, her hair up and Diet Coke in hand, the way she used to look when we worked on low-income housing cases together in law school.

"Thank you for coming." I tried faking a tone of normalcy. "You don't know—how—how—oh, Jesus." I started to cry.

"Actually, I do." She walked to the credenza and pulled a Kleenex from the box. "Here," she said. The cleaning crew had begun to vacuum the hall, and she waved them away and closed the door.

"I'm such a mess."

"It'll be okay one way or another. Six months from now, kind of a blur. You're not going to prison or anything."

"Just look at this." I handed her Pren's papers. "My marriage is over."

"Your marriage was over in 1990."

I put my face down on the desk and rested for a moment, relaxed, finally, in the knowledge Elaine was going to take charge. "Where's Adam?"

"At home on my computer. Did you eat?"

"No."

She produced a cheese sandwich in wax paper. "I think this will be all right on your stomach."

"I almost threw up on television."

"I could tell."

"I feel so ashamed. I haven't done anything wrong. I mean legally."

"You took a perp walk, Jack. That's what it feels like. If you were a black man, you'd be in jail."

"Lucky me."

"You bet you are. Here's the deal. Thank your smooth-talking friend Wardie for this. I called Ballard and told him I get total control. As for you, you'll do exactly what I say. No press of any kind unless I dial it in. We'll forget about your screen test this afternoon."

"Thank you."

"Stop thanking me. Do you understand the instructions?"

"Yes."

"I got a room for you at the Radisson under a fake name."

"Do I have to?"

"Want Brenda to track you down?"

"What's the name?"

She smiled. "Mr. Jack Zipper."

Kai-Jana to the Rescue

M R. ZIPPER ENDURED TWO restless months as Elaine worked through the case. Courthouse wags joked about wrongful discharge.

"Sid's making me crazy," Elaine said. "I think he's going for a TV trial."

"That couldn't possibly happen, could it?" I said, imagining Brenda in her glory. At this point, I couldn't discount any disaster.

Elaine shrugged. "Sidney Wheeless loves attention," she said, calling him by the full name his old friends used. Sid was for his man-of-the-people politico phase. "He's a good lawyer. And a good man. Don't make a face, he is. Gives a lot of pro bono time down at Central Prison. Going to run for Senate. I keep on telling him to go for the Legislature first, but he wants Washington." She shook her head dreamily. "The thing is, I was filing sex cases before he knew what they were."

Now she and Wheeless shared a secret correspondence, and a professional admiration society.

"I'm so glad."

"Better be. And thank God Kai-Jana won for Superior Court. You finally contributed to her campaign. Just under the wire, I checked."

"That's a relief."

"Yeah, two hundred. You don't remember, do you?"

"Look, I've been okay to her at parties and things recently, haven't I?"

"No."

"Winston and I still play golf at his club—we were out last month."

"Winston is her husband. She's the judge. Try to remember that."

I got on fine with Winston these days. He seemed to be having a rough go with Kai-Jana's political ambitions, and the realization that that was why they were back in North Carolina. He liked it better when they lived in Boston and he could do venture capital.

Winston had ditched his venture capital career to run the bond portfolio at North Carolina Associated, an insurance company in Durham his father-in-law sort of ran. He managed through it all to be a perfect husband and father, shepherding around two adorable girls, still young; we'll see how he does later. He and Kai-Jana had kept their marriage together, unlike Elaine and Roger and Pren and me. Looked like the two of them were on to something.

"Does she really not like me? I've always been nice to her. We're classmates, for Chrissakes."

"She thinks you've become a tool of the ruling class. But I'll take care of it. I'll make you into Alan Alda. No white man will be more sensitive and liberal than you."

Or, she left unsaid, more unlikely to have sex with his young, pretty secretary. "Great. Do I get to wear a vest like Mr. Rogers?"

"You want to get off, don't you?" She patted me on the head gently, like a dull schoolboy.

◆◆◆

IT PLEASED ME TO think of Sid Wheeless as a bumpkin in a shiny suit who advertised on television and took bad cases that settled for nothing. In truth, that never was Sid Wheeless, and certainly not after he caught Norfolk Southern with a screwy crossing gate and pocketed a cool seven million out of the twenty the jury thought was fair. Sid Wheeless could buy and sell any partner at Butler and Symmes. He could have passed for a SEM, but sought power too openly. Cutting a path his own way, he dressed in bespoke suits, fitted at his desk while he fielded calls from the aggrieved. He also led animal conservation safaris to the Serengeti, spoke out at Rotary Club luncheons about civic virtue, and built the finest wine cellar, it was thought, in the Triangle.

"Jack," he said, grinning broadly and extending his manicured and becuffed hand in Judge Blount's anteroom. "Haven't seen you since that old storage tank thing."

"Unbelievable," I muttered to Elaine, who smoothly took my elbow and guided me toward a neutral corner.

Wheeless looked like he'd been done up at a spa. His once shaggy hair now flipped up just so, its lustrous honey color highlighting an all-season tan. My God, he is running, I thought, watching him sidle against the pasty green courthouse wall just under a smiling picture of Bill Clinton, who had won some elections on good hair alone.

Elaine gave him the high sign, and they escaped to another corner for a sidebar. She batted her eyes and borrowed his shoulder for a laugh. Not only did I have to endure this wretched case, but I had to watch Elaine flirt with Wheeless, which, in spite of myself and the circumstances, made me jealous. How dumb was that, being jealous when I was in sex jail for dating and then firing my secretary?

I should give up sex completely, and love, too, as I stink at both. Better to become a monk, join Lowry on his trip to see the Fathers—or, alternatively, concentrate on golf.

"Calm down," Elaine said, having left Wheeless in the corner to coach Teri Lynn. "Sid's just playing. He thinks he can goad you into losing it in front of Kai-Jana."

"Not a chance, baby. I'm Mister Cool, standing here, being cool."

"That's the spirit," she said, patting me again on the head.

"You had lunch with him yesterday, didn't you?"

"Jack. Lunch is good when I'm trying to make things go away. Besides, he's doing something for us."

"What, besides messing with me?"

"You'll just get mad."

"I'm already mad."

"He's helping me research Big Data. I need his network in California."

So now Wheeless was doing Butler and Symmes' legal work, and inventing another excuse to lunch with Elaine. Would this torture never end?

Teri Lynn arrived in a white blouse and dark blue skirt too small for her. Probably on instructions, she wore no makeup. Tugging at her skirt, she smiled tightly at Elaine and me before Wheeless led her away. Kai-Jana motioned us into chambers. She had livened up the oak-paneled sobriety with triple rows of photographs: her grandfather with A. Philip Randolph, Martin Luther King Sr. and Jr., her grandmother with Eleanor Roosevelt, her dad laughing at a café table with Andrew Young. It was a counter-Pantheon to the white-man wall found in the political dens of the Symmes and Forrests. Somewhere on the back credenza were the usual working-mother pictures of herself and Winston in formal garb, and the kids at play.

The judge greeted me benignly, not giving any sign of her current view that I was a tool of the ruling class. Since we went back so far, that did make me mad, and was maybe the reason I'd been rude to her at parties. Kai-Jana worked as hard as any, and had a big dream, as evidenced by the Pantheon, but playing the tool of the ruling class card against me had gotten old. She was the one who now enjoyed the Party's preferment. Hugh said the leadership wanted her to run for attorney general. So why wasn't she a tool of the ruling class?

I needed to put that negative energy aside, though. Kai-Jana could have recused herself from my case, in fact she took some political risk by not doing so. I guess I could get used to her preferred status and new photos, and being ritualistically called out as a tool just because I was white and a man.

As we sat, I pulled slightly at my trousers to reveal the mismatched blue and gray socks Elaine had me wear. I couldn't tell whether Kai-Jana noticed the Alan Alda touch or not.

More importantly, she bore down on the bad guys.

"Mr. Wheeless," she began, looking at her watch, "You don't have a plain old sex case here, do you? You don't think Mr. Callahan straight up demanded sex for typing?"

Wheeless closed his eyes and clasped his hands in a prayerful mode. "Your Honor, my client is in a very vulnerable place right now."

"Oh, please Lord, no, Mr. Wheeless. I have a feeling you're about to go into your jury speech, and I just can't listen to that right before my lunch."

"Your Honor, I feel so passionately about—"

"Look, Counselor, we don't need any more passion. Too much passion in this case already. Facts, that's why we're here. Any additional facts?"

"No, Your Honor, I don't believe—"

"Are you going to drop your sex-for-typing claim, or not?"

"I want to put that in front of the jury."

"Let me be clear. Unless you come up with a fact or two in the next five minutes, I'm going to dismiss that claim right when Ms. Marchetti asks me to."

Elaine nodded slightly. Even though I didn't frequent judges' chambers, I could tell this had been a cracking good meeting so far. Teri Lynn, to her credit, had not made up some story about extorting sex. She received Judge Blount's words impassively, shifting to adjust her skirt and accommodate the odd posture of legs crossed at the ankles.

"There's no written contract here, am I right, Mr. Wheeless?"

"No ma'am. I mean, yes ma'am."

"We're still a right-to-work state, I believe?"

"Yes ma'am. But if you'd look at my brief on current wrongful discharge cases—"

"You mean the ones where I wrote the opinions? I already know what those say."

"We have other claims, Your Honor," Wheeless pressed on. "There are only eight female partners in the entire firm of, I believe over three hundred lawyers, and only one here in Raleigh." He nodded at Elaine, who smiled. "There is a history of sexist behavior toward staff. That incident in the break area—"

"You mean the magazines."

"Yes, Your Honor."

Despite myself, I winced. In the staff break area, *Victoria's Secret* catalogs sat on display, along with similar erotic literature, such as *Cosmopolitan* and *Redbook* magazines. Once, about seven months ago, I looked in there for Teri Lynn to finish some dictation and paused over the *Victoria's Secret* catalog. The so-called Wonder Bra was making its debut. Noting the cat-ate-the-canary expression of the model, I said, "Jeez, a fella's got to be careful with all this false advertising." It was a lame joke; several secretaries giggled, but one newly hired paralegal stalked out, which I took to be a bad sign.

I reported the incident immediately to Human Resources, and they flagged it for the file, with a copy to Lloyd's, which is how Wheeless got the story. HR also removed *Victoria's Secret*, along with *Cosmopolitan* and *Redbook*, which were both currently running how-to columns on preferred methods of oral sex.

"You see from the record, Judge, that Ms. Howell felt so threatened by Mr. Callahan's remark, she left the break room, and—"

"Ms. Howell's not here, Mr. Wheeless. Ms. Tucker is the plaintiff."

"Judge," Elaine broke in, "our filings establish the plaintiff's standards of offense to be quite broad."

"You are referring to the panty episode."

"That stands out."

Judge Blount studied her well-manicured nails, painted vermillion in deep contrast to her dark robes. She wore her hair stylishly angled and with a hint of reddish color. I imagined she might be herself familiar with the *Victoria's Secret* catalog. Indeed, it was a kind of a lingua franca among fancy women of my acquaintance.

Teri Lynn sat silently with a helpless expression. I felt bad for her. Actually, I felt guilty. This whole charade was because I couldn't not have sex with her. My two women friends from law school had their game faces on to keep me out of sex jail and ward off the press. I ended up recklessly throwing Teri Lynn under the HR bus, when all I'd had to do was date somebody else, anybody else, even her cousin-mother who looked like her. Now she was even named in my soon to be ex-wife's revised scandal sheet of a divorce pleading. I'd put everyone out. Elaine was right, I was a shitbag, and what the heck is a blow job worth anyway? Kai-Jana should throw me under the jail.

"I'm frankly unsure what to do with that evidence," Judge Blount said, looking straight at Wheeless.

"I would certainly object—"

"Oh, it's quite relevant, Mr. Wheeless. What I meant was, I find the story hard to believe."

"I can explain, Your Honor," Teri Lynn said, raising up in her chair and fending off Wheeless's restraining hand. "It was a joke, that's all. Now Rod, he was the courier? He kept saying how when he was over at State—now Sid, calm down, it was just a joke. He'd taken off work, and I guess he went and stole girls', uh, underwear? I put some in the office pouch to sort of make fun of him?"

"I see."

"If I'd known it was going to cause folks a problem, I'd have sent them in the mail."

"Them?"

"My tap pants."

Judge Blount rose from her desk, gathering a file in one hand and her purse in the other. "I need to see counsel alone, please," she said. I held the door for Teri Lynn.

We stood in the hallway, awkwardly silent at first.

"Teri Lynn, I'm sorry for what happened, for what I did, or—I don't know—what I didn't do."

"That's just like you, Jack Callahan. You're sorry for something and you don't even know what it is."

"I'm sorry just the same. Also, sorry you can't smoke in here." I took the lighter from her hand and found two wooden chairs for us.

"All I want is to be treated right."

"I know."

She began to cry quietly, and I offered my handkerchief.

"You think I wanted to do this? You think I don't know Sid's out to get y'all?"

"Well, then—"

"I'm broke. I got one cup of tomato soup and a half can of Crisco, and I reckon I'll eat the soup tonight and the Crisco tomorrow and then I won't have anything. I'm trying to get on at Belk's."

"You could have come to me earlier. I've been such a shithead."

"Jack, I don't want your money. What's done is done. I want a job."

"What's happening at Belk's? Why hasn't that come through?"

"Repo man came and took my car last week. I chained the bumper to a tree but he towed it anyway. Tore the bumper flat off."

I had eighty-nine dollars in my wallet, and I rolled the bills up and put them in her purse.

"Jack, I said I don't want your money."

"Hush. Take it."

"You're dumb, but sweet."

"Have you paid your light bill?"

"Second notice."

"How much is it?"

"Sixty-seven dollars and thirty-eight cents."

I wrote out a check for a thousand dollars and handed it to her. She glared at me, but put it in her purse.

Judge Blount bustled forth from her chambers. Elaine and Wheeless whispered in the doorway. He shrugged and they shook hands.

"Come on, Jack," Elaine called.

Teri Lynn winked by means of saying goodbye, and I joined Elaine as she hurried us down the corridor.

"We have a deal."

"Terrific."

"Fifteen thousand."

"What?"

"Kai-Jana really came through."

"I have to give that asshole fifteen thousand dollars?"

"Yes, you do. Think about that next time you want a blow job."

"Shit."

"You did remember to bring a check, right? Or could you not even do that?"

I thumbed through my wallet, but knew the result. "I did bring a check. But I had to use it."

"What are you talking about?"

"Teri Lynn needed some cash."

"You gave her money? Just now?"

"Her light bill's past due. She's eating Crisco out of a can."

"She sued you, Jack. You're paying her fifteen thousand dollars. Now it's fifteen thousand dollars plus a light bill."

"I know. Why did I do that? I'm sorry."

"Go get another check. And don't talk to me anymore. Ever."

◆◆◆

"NORA? I'VE BEEN IN some trouble." After giving Wheeless his odious check, I'd picked up a carton of Virginia Slims and headed to her room at Harmony Hall.

"What in the world?" she said, sitting up. She was surrounded by stacks of library books.

"It's over now—Elaine handled it with Kai-Jana. Are you writing?"

"Look at this," she said excitedly, producing a Xeroxed page. "*The Thunder, Perfect Mind.* Lowry and I read aloud, and I felt the power. I'm a Christian again."

"Terrific."

I had no idea what *The Thunder, Perfect Mind* was. It sounded like a Led Zeppelin album. In any event, she sounded as though she'd crossed over to the sunny side, which occurred periodically, and meant happier days for all.

"That Lowry, he's something."

"His work at Mighty Lamb is world-changing."

When on the sunny side, Nora tended to exaggerate.

"Right. Did he go to the library for you, too?"

"No, Robin did. I'm paying her to be my research assistant. It will give her something to do other than play semi-professional soccer."

Having faked field hockey herself, Nora was unmoved by contemporary arguments that young girls needed to develop teamwork skills by playing sports. She believed in the calm spirit and large vocabulary produced by reading.

"There'll be another Forster volume soon, I guess."

"Leonard hasn't said anything?"

"Ferris and I don't discuss your work."

123

"We read Foucault together when he was in prison. Marvelous. One is so seldom incarcerated."

"Jeez Louise."

"He's a wonderful reader. But I've been blocked, horribly."

"That's over now? Blockage?"

"Yes! I think so! There are so many new things!" She bowed to the book stacks, lemon peignoir floating to her knees. Then she took my hand. "Sit down, dear, and talk to me. What was this trouble you were in?"

"Over now," I repeated, sitting down, but taking my hand back. "It involved this woman at the office who used to be my secretary. We got involved, and she sued the firm, which is why I was on television. It's nothing, really."

"You had an affair with her?"

"No, well, sort of."

"Was it a fling, or are you in love?"

She got so straight-to-the-point when on the sunny side.

"More a fling."

"Are you still in love with Elaine Marchetti? You have a tendency to get confused."

"I'm trying not to be."

"Good. I'm proud of you for trying. Go back to Pren, that's the answer."

I didn't think there was a question. "Pren doesn't want me anymore."

She patted my hand. "Don't give up, honey. Listen to Lowry."

She applied lipstick, smiled broadly, lit a cigarette, and promptly stubbed it out in the seashell she used for an ashtray. I sprayed the room with Glade and helped her settle back in the pillows.

She grabbed my hand again as I stood up to leave. "I'm glad you won your trial. What a stupid thing, suing over sex."

"Thank you. I didn't want you to be worried."

"Mothers worry. From now on, I would appreciate it if you'd please tell me when you're sued, or going to be on television."

Put on the Kneepads

BACK TO PRAETORIAN GUARD duty, I had just finished reading more threats from Ferris when Ballard called. "Jack?" he squawked from his speaker phone.

"Still here."

"Don't move. I've got Drac."

"I was just going to punch out. Can we talk from the car?"

He breathed heavily, and then again, and then again. I was afraid he was having a heart attack.

"No, you've got to get focused," he finally choked out.

Drac had taken over as head of the firm after chasing Hugh out. His jack-booted charm played well with the Bank. Ballard got on with him because they both greeted new ideas with fear. He had taught Ballard the word "focus," which, when invoked as now, simply meant I had to do as told.

"Focus," in the broader sense, commanded us all to shun any form of life-giving energy in favor of billing more hours in a day. Doing away with sex fit in there nicely, as did taking up gunplay as an outlet. Gunplay was Drac's hobby of choice. He had recently bought a plastic gun—a Glock, he informed us. It was easy to get in and out of airports.

After the Teri Lynn business, Drac would happily annihilate me, except that I had big clients, and thus made the firm money. So instead he treated me like an unruly teenager, straining to hold his temper, slowing down his words as though English were not my mother tongue, and gobbling Maalox by the handful.

I grabbed my briefcase and jogged down the hall.

"Drac, he's here," Ballard said. Drac, I should add, was a reference to the famous vampire. Our boss had the same name as Vincent Price, the actor. It was his SAE handle at Duke. Years ago, he could be funny and good company, but there was something about being in charge that made him unpleasant. I had to remember he had marched to the top by becoming a kind of high-level slave to the Bank, which paid him a lot of money, monopolized his time, and terrorized him and his fratty team daily. I used to feel sorry for him, but now he was always threatening to kick me out of the firm, so my sympathy had dried up.

"Callahan," Drac said, voice crackling over the speakerphone, "we need to get some focus on this Bank thing."

"That means you're about to give me an order."

"Are you going to mess with us, Jack? Weren't you just screwing your secretary, and her mother?"

"Over now."

"Glad to hear it."

"Besides, I thought me and you was 'us,' or all of us was 'us.' How could I mess with 'us'? Gets kind of metaphysical."

I could hear the line go mute, as Drac consulted his lackeys about my attitude. This was non-focus indeed: Jack Callahan, a known profligate, was making jokes.

"I'll get to the point," Drac continued, with a show of calm. "The Bank wants you off the *Criterion* deal." The clamor of the mob rose and fell on the distant phone box. "I hear Forrest is broke."

"Not broke."

"That's the word on the Street."

"It's Broman, and he's lying. And the firm's *Criterion* relationship is older than the entire history of Ameribank, even when you add up all the little banks they swallowed."

"Callahan, face it, you jobbed our biggest client. Time zones! Are you kidding me?"

Drac was now shouting. I checked my watch: he'd surpassed ninety-five seconds of relative calm, a new record.

"Tricked that Billy dumb-fuck in Raleigh! He's going to get fucking fired! Now get this through your fucking head! You're going to come to Charlotte, put on the fucking kneepads, and beg Griffiths for your life. Do you fucking understand me?"

Drac used a lot of fucks when he gave orders. I could see how it all came down the chain: Broman squeezed Griffiths, Griffiths squeezed Drac, now Drac squeezed me. Faux outrage at its best.

Drac spun out further, yelling that Raleigh was a "fuckfest" and people were going to pay. Bullard put his head on his desk.

"You know what's really going on?" I shouted back, deciding to have some fun. "We've lost our manhood. We used to be manly, dick-wielding warriors. Now we're just dicks for the Bank, bought and paid for."

I could hear the Charlotte mute button go on again. Ballard paced, or rather did something that looked like the Chicken Dance on *Saturday Night Live*. I made out strained voices in the background, discussing a plan to get rid of me. "Fuck Callahan," the voices said, first in unison and then repeating it one by one, with competitive ardor. "Fuck Callahan, who does he think he is…"

But, majestically, Drac rose to resist the mob.

"Callahan-let's-not-argue," he said, coming back on the line with his best Prozac voice. "You've-got-to-get-out-of-this-deal."

"No."

"Just-go-see-Griffiths. I-can't-believe-I'm-actually-saying-this-but-we'll-hold-your-comp-harmless."

"Hell, no." I considered explaining to him about my role as quasi-heir, but that would have been useless.

Drac picked up the receiver to speak to me alone. "Jack, you and me go way back," he said smoothly. "I'm serious. I'm begging. I've got the kneepads on. This is the Bank. Griffiths thinks you were jerking his chain."

"I hear your concerns," I said slowly, trying to use what I learned in anger management. "But I have to stick with Wardie."

Ballard knew better than to follow me out. I rode down twenty-nine floors with two UPS guys, cursing Drac all the way.

"He's really out to get me this time," I said, reaching Elaine from the car. She was in Groton at her reunion.

"Who?"

"Drac. You sound groggy. Are you asleep? What is that—the TV?"

"I'm taking a nap."

"Oh. Sorry. Drac says Griffiths wants me out of the deal. I'm supposed to go to Charlotte and grovel."

"Be careful with that," she whispered.

"I know. I'm not good at groveling."

"Ow, let me."

"What?"

"Stop that—let me do it."

I had no idea what she was talking about.

Rules of Golf

MAYBE DRAC WAS RIGHT. Maybe Raleigh was a fuckfest, and I'd been flippant and defensive. Drac was right sometimes, when sucking up to the Bank didn't make him crazy and he went off shooting his gun at decorator pillows, his favorite targets. But, then again, I had to remember—without the Bank, this big, lumbering, humorless thing, Drac would be nothing. At least I had my role as quasi-heir.

Elaine returned from Groton on Tuesday morning. She'd taken a cab straight to work, and said nothing about our strange conversation. "Let's play golf," she said, more strangely still, sunglasses fixed, roller bag trailing. She closed my office door behind her.

"What the heck? Golf? How did that reunion work for you? Looks like you need about two weeks' sleep."

"I need to play golf."

I rolled her suitcase to my car. I liked playing golf with women, but Pren stuck to tennis, moving up the Club ladder season by season. Elaine knew how to play golf from Duke—they have a great Robert Trent Jones course—and we snuck away from the office when we could. She dozed against the window as I drove against traffic, toward the Club. I took the back way, through progressively upscale neighborhoods that led finally to the lion-pedestaled entrance. A row of sedate and substantial homes across the street formed a prim guard, like good gray ladies dressed for church.

One, with a high balcony and flecked white brick, once belonged to my father-in-law, and another, with a new slate roof and a mortared stone wall, still belonged to me, sort of.

I turned between the lions and looked back reflexively for Pren's car. There was no sign of it. She was probably out doing her job, selling real estate with Bingo. Since it was Tuesday, the longtime yard man Ike stood raking the already raked yard. He wore dirty-gray twill, buttoned from head to toe, with a broad-brimmed hat and pipe. Unlike Lowry, who embraced modern advances, Ike still preferred a wide-flanged rake to a leaf blower. He squinted at the Mercedes, thinking, no doubt, it needed a wash.

Ike knew my story, and he wasn't surprised. He had viewed me as an interloper from the start. He thought I was craven and insane to leave Pren, the house, the family dream—"broke bad" like his nephew, serving time in Central Prison for selling pot down on Cabarrus Street. I'd done much worse things, but got to live across from the Club. White man's world.

Squinting again, Ike saw Elaine in my car. Aha, the other woman, he no doubt thought. Ike was wrong about that, but right about one thing: I was craven and insane, broke bad for sure.

"Checking for Pren?" Elaine asked matter-of-factly.

"It's like I divorced a continent."

She yawned. "If you took some steps in the process, maybe you wouldn't have these bad feelings."

Elaine's clubs and shoes were in my trunk from the last time we'd played. I pulled up at the bag drop, and Tommy wheeled up a cart to strap us in.

"Tee time, Mr. Callahan?" he asked, knowing I didn't have one.

"Is it a problem?"

"Nope. Ladies Scotch Foursomes this morning. They're in the Grill."

It would be a while before the ladies finished their cantaloupe and honeydew medleys. Elaine and I changed, and I made a call to the office from the Members Bar. She was putting when I returned.

"Ready?" I asked.

She sat down on a bench by the putting green. "I did a bad thing."

"Zal?"

"You think your life's a mess. Shit. Shit. Shit." She dug at the turf with her putter. "I spent two whole nights with him."

"Sounds really bad."

"He's been separated six weeks. What am I doing?"

"You're asking the wrong guy."

"Don't worry about me leaving, Jack. I've got to pay for Adam to go to Duke. Roger, you know what he said, he won't pay for anything more than Carolina."

"What a schmuck."

She sniffed and blew her nose daintily. "I did another horrible thing."

"What?"

"I called Adam last night and said the flight got canceled and he had to get himself up for school. I couldn't tell him—"

"That you were fucking your high school boyfriend?"

Jesus, why did I say that? Stricken, she looked down and retrieved a pack of Marlboro Lights from her purse. She'd stopped smoking five years ago. Her hand was shaking, so I held the match.

"I'm sorry. I have no idea where that came from."

She looked down and started crying.

"I'm really, really sorry. I'm such an idiot."

"I deserve it. I'm a bad mother. I'm a bad law partner."

I felt around her purse for a Kleenex.

"No, you're not," I said, handing over a tissue. "There's only one thing to do now."

"What?"

"Tee off."

Elaine and I played a kind of best ball together, not the usual tournament setup, but an exercise in which we both hit the better shot to the green, then putt two balls. There wasn't any logic to it, but it was our game, a formal exercise to put life into pattern. If it were the Middle Ages, we'd walk a maze.

I pulled out the driver, a magnesium-shafted Callaway that Pren gave me for Christmas. I thought about leaving it behind when I moved my stuff, but it was a good club no matter the source. I swung away, and the ball hung for a second, and then accelerated. It caught the down slope of the fairway, and since we had a dry day, rolled to a pitching wedge of the pin.

"Well, well," Elaine said, shading her eyes, her mood brightening, our golf maze working. "Let the big dogs hunt."

"Thanks."

She put her driver back in the bag. "I don't need to hit."

"Go ahead. You're all-woman, roaring around. You might drive the green."

She shanked into the trees.

"Jack, I really don't know what I'm doing."

"Too fast on the release. Common problem."

"Very funny. I can't get it out of my mind."

"Your mind? That's where it is?"

"Yes. On my mind, Jack. It's men who think with their penis." She put her index finger to her temple to emphasize the point.

"If you say so."

"I thought if we played our golf game, it would go out of my head. But we keep on talking about it."

"So, let's divert. What's the topic?"

"Give me a minute." She walked to the cart and applied lipstick. "Oh, I know. The Great Bylaw Problem."

One of Hugh's projects in his final months with the firm was rewriting the Club's bylaws to get rid of all the racism. As a task, it ranked with the Augean stables.

"Did he ever get them to vote?" Elaine asked.

"You know his views."

She sighed. "Oh yes. 'If you have to have a vote, you don't have a Club.'"

"That's it.

"So how does all the racism get out, then?"

"I think you wake up one day and words are different."

"Doesn't that upset the racists?"

"Well, Hugh wouldn't act unless it was time. It's very mysterious. We need Latin—*Mysterium Convincicum Right Thing Hughissimus*. Something like that."

We confronted the Great Bylaw Problem up close and personal while celebrating one of Elaine's trial victories on behalf of a Japanese client years ago. She asked if we could take the happy fellows, who froze North Carolina shrimp for Tokyo consumption, to the Club, and I, being in a devil-may-care mood, said yes.

It was reckless, Hugh said later. Some busybody called him about our lunch reservation, and he appeared behind us in the dining room, reading the *Wall Street Journal* and eating a bowl of soup at the Members' table. Maybe he packed his .45 just in case there was trouble. Unfazed, our guests from Tokyo sat by the picture window, mesmerized by the green glory of the golf course, unaware that they were dangerous aliens, unwelcome threats to the social order.

"It's hard for me to think of Japanese as not being Caucasian."

"Well, they aren't. And I'm a secret Jew. One of these days they'll find out and I'll get the boot."

"You won't. Your father was Jewish. Big deal. You're not a Jew unless your mother is."

"You think they know that?"

"Sure. The Jew Rule. Standard in all racist Country Club manuals. Besides, you couldn't be a real Jew if you tried. You're a nothing. Nora raised you that way."

"C'mon, she believes in stuff."

"Like what?"

"She believes in Jesus again. Reads feminist Gnostic texts." I had looked up *The Thunder, Perfect Mind*.

"No way Nora Callahan really believes in Jesus."

"Maybe she believes in the power of love."

"Or sex? More likely."

These were old charges, being irreligious and libertine. Lately, I'd been working through some revisionist history. In fact, Nora once believed mightily in Jesus. For years she took me to the earnest Methodist church near our house, where we loudly sang optimistic Wesley hymns with friendly strangers. She scrounged for collection plate dollars. Eventually she lost heart.

Elaine and I disagreed on the meaning of this. I'd say Nora was very religious, but snake-bit by sin. Elaine, being godless and pure, didn't allow for sin and faith to coexist. As for love and sex, a lot of people confused those things, lately including Elaine, and if you believed in Jesus like Nora tried to, maybe it didn't matter in the end.

"Your shot," I said as she stood over her chip.

Elaine could bump and run an eight iron well. She chipped toward the pin, stopping the ball stiff.

"Nice," I said. "I don't need to hit."

We putted out and walked up the steps to the second tee, timing our passage to the off cycle of spitting sprinkler heads.

"You know what I'm going to say, don't you?"

She flinched. "Not what you said back there."

"Nope. I'm sorry. I just thought maybe we could go back to the way things were."

"You're kidding. When?"

"You remember."

She ripped a head cover off her driver. "Gross. I've blocked all that."

"Thanks."

She took two wheelhouse practice swings. "Not going there, Jack."

"Why?"

"We've been through this. Same old, same old. You're too—complicated." She punctuated her pronouncement with an air chop of her driver, which startled the first group of the Ladies Scotch Foursome standing on the tee.

"Complicated?" The word had always made me angry. "That's bullshit."

"You're so complicated, you're almost insane."

"So Zal's not complicated?"

"Simple as a lawn mower."

"This is really pissing me off."

"Shh." Three of the Scotch Foursome whispered in unison from the ladies' tee. A fourth caught her swing at the top and glared.

I waved, smiling broadly.

"Very sorry, ladies—bee sting, yellow jackets everywhere."

"That's exactly what I mean," Elaine whispered. "You can't tell the simple truth to strangers on a golf course."

"Yellow jackets make me complicated?"

"You have affairs."

"Not many, jeez."

"You forget, I've been to this rodeo."

"Aha. Tainted by your bad first marriage. What we need is a blank slate."

"Nope. What you need is to get happy with the way things are with us. You're pretty lucky."

"I'm not seeing it."

"At work, you get me at my best. I'm cheerful, industrious, wear good shoes. You think you want sex? You might for six months, and then you'd go for another blow job and ruin it."

The last members of the Scotch Foursome had taken their second shots, and I hit a three wood behind them into the left rough. Elaine pushed hers right, so we split the difference and dropped in the fairway. It was part of our rules.

"When Ted cheated on me, you found me this job. I was depressed and had no money. You had to drag me away from Legal Aid, and you were right. Now I have a life."

"You're welcome."

"And so when you've had your issues, I've stuck by you, including the Teri Lynn fiasco."

"Thanks, I mean it."

"In two years Adam's leaving, and I'm forty-three years old. Do you know what I'm saying?"

"No. But you're smoking hot right now, if that helps."

"Stop with that. It's pervy. What I need from you now is—"

"What?"

"Friendship."

"Actually, sex would be great, too."

She stopped and put her hands on her hips. "Really? I need your help right now, and you're going to talk about sex? Okay—since you can't think of anything else, let's give the Club ladies a real treat, right there behind that wax myrtle."

She marched off behind the wax myrtle and made a fake show of unbuttoning her top. "Coming?" she said.

One hundred and thirty yards was between a wedge and a nine iron for me, and since the flag showed a bit of wind, I went with the nine. The shot bled a little, but stopped on the fringe.

At least we were putting.

More on Blow Jobs

W HAT'S THE BIG DEAL about a blow job?

Elaine had posed the question. I'd been stumped for an answer.

One could ask President Clinton for his views. As I read in the *Times*, we're to believe he received blow jobs with a cigar as a "prop," whatever that means, in his private bathroom off the Oval Office, courtesy of an intern, Monica Lewinsky. He denied it, his defense resting on an interpretation of the Latin copulative, present tense.

It depends on what the meaning of *is* is, the *Times* reported. Excellent work. That's as good an explanation of the mystery of the blow job as you're going to get.

Clinton got nabbed at the office, the Oval Office no less. Imagine the shock of being done in by your intern. Work had turned dangerous. It used to be the safest place. I was untouchable at work, with Hugh. There were so many safe rooms, you could find one, close the door, and hide out. But in the new world, the world of "is," there were no safe rooms, even for the president.

"You should be gone," Ballard said from the doorway, tapping his watch.

"You, too. We should have retired last year. Taken the staff bonuses and flown to Costa Rica."

"I'm serious. What the hell are you doing here? Doesn't your secretary print out your emails?"

Red-faced, Ballard retreated to Delores's desk and tossed me a plane ticket with my name on it. There was a same-day round-trip to Charlotte leaving in fifty-five minutes.

"Jesus, Jack—you better deliver."

Ballard slammed my door for emphasis, and Delores printed out the morning emails, belatedly. One from Drac directed me to appear for an audience he'd arranged with Griffiths. Griffiths had told a vice president friendly to our firm that he wanted to meet "that Callahan sonofabitch."

What exactly was I supposed to say? I'd already told him I wasn't giving up Wardie. Was I supposed to chat about forgiveness, the mortal sin of greed? Drac would expect groveling.

◆◆◆

HUGH REFUSED FLYING TO Charlotte when you could drive door to door before lunch. *Fly to Charlotte!* he'd thunder. *Nobody could abide such high living!* Still, I did it, a small act of defiance.

Our prop plane lurched into descent. To my left, a man checked a folded suit coat for his next ticket, quickly flicking on his loafers. Across the aisle, a woman folded chewing gum into a page torn from the in-flight magazine and studied her eyes with a pocket mirror.

Swollen feet, puffy eyes, all cured by—blow jobs! Finally, a rationale! Read about it soon in the *New England Journal of Medicine*!

As we approached, the city sprouted from red-flecked hills like a sparkling Erector Set: man-made lakes hard by nuclear towers, freeways careening into mounds of clay, office parks set in bronze and taupe. Blue sky darkened as we passed through low turbulence, and then lightened again when the ground closed. The fuselage vibrated as the pilot hit the flaps, and he deposited us with a drop and a thud.

"Beepers off," the suddenly stern flight attendant said as I exited.

Drac required a beeper to track my movements. "I thought it was off. Really. I don't know how to work it."

She motioned me to the side of the gangway and unclipped the beeper from my belt loop. "See this?" she said, smiling. "Button down, you're turned off. Flick it up, you're turned on."

"Thanks. I get it now."

"Looks like you doctors could learn how to use your toys."

I thought about setting her straight about my profession, but didn't. It would be a cruel blow to discover she flicked my beeper because she thought I was a doctor.

The beeper beeped, and I called from the cab line. "Do you know where you're going?" Ballard demanded.

"Nope. My secret agent package didn't say."

"World Crossroads. Speech starts in twenty minutes—check that, eighteen. Sit at the front and tell security you're CSOB."

"CSOB?"

"Callahan Son-of-a-Bitch."

"Nice."

"Drac came up with it."

"And then what?"

"You know what."

"I'm not groveling."

The line went quiet. I heard voices and static.

"Don't put that mute button on, Ballard."

"Jack. This attitude of yours. You need pills. The firm will pay."

"I'm not taking pills."

"Listen for once. A doctor guy was telling me about these new ones called Xanax. It's great stuff, tranquilizer for your brain. Calms down the sex drive. You'll be more productive."

"Sounds like *Night of the Living Dead*."

"Jack, seriously, I'm worried about you. You're beginning—"

"To act like Hugh?"

"Didn't say that. Don't go getting paranoid."

"Lost my focus already, damn."

Ballard hit the mute button again. "Another call came in from the Bank," he said flatly, coming back on. "Grovel. There's no more chances."

No more chances, the man said. Who knows, Drac could get a twofer: Hugh and me gone in the same fiscal year. Swoosh, swoosh.

Hugh had been a champion of lost focus. Sherman on horseback couldn't make him carry a beeper. His secretary never printed out his emails, since he didn't read them. He did approve of FedEx. He said it reminded him of what the US Mail used to be.

Old but clever, Hugh knew what he rebelled against. Drac wanted him to disappear. He refused. I've tried to disappear, but failed. Ballard has successfully disappeared. He glories in his disappearance. With his gadgets, he can work all the time and convince himself it's normal. He can talk to Drac from his car or on the beach; he can push a button on his IBM and produce instant reports on everyone and everything.

An entire labor movement fought to free workers from this shit. I took to reading Marx in the bathroom. Maybe somebody will find my copy of *Das Kapital* by the john, and that will be enough to put me away.

Banks Either Grow or Die

I SIGHTED AMERIBANK'S POINTY tower, which helps me locate World Crossroads, where the great man would soon speak. Charlotte people liked to build things and name them World this or that, to the amusement of the old crowd in Raleigh, but I thought it was cool. I mean, if you could name a local stock car race the World 600 and turn NASCAR into a zillion-dollar business, what's to laugh about?

Setting out on foot, I walked through the Ameribank lobby, marble pointing the eye and spirit to the financial heavens. Hugh once told me that if you wanted to understand Griffiths, you had to get real Presbyterian. "Dalton thinks God is always revealing a path that leads upward to greater greatness," he whispered before a board meeting. I got the feeling that more than once Hugh had put Griffiths' piety to use, much like Churchill played "Onward Christian Soldiers" on the decks of His Majesty's destroyers to pump up Roosevelt for the Lend-Lease.

Sure enough, WPA-like murals swept ever upward, portraying that old-time Presbyterian destiny, crops and cloth turned to money, farmers and workers marching toward heaven, all to bless the purposeful mass of blue and gray-clad bankers crowding ahead.

I had to ask how to get to World Crossroads. A security guard in sunglasses pointed to a billboard at the entrance across a cobbled pedestrian mall. Once in, a bespectacled lady event official handed over a nametag and hustled me to a seat.

The great man himself sat by the podium, head bowed. Then he rose.

"Banks either grow or die," Griffiths began, addressing the darkened hall, his suit a paler gray than regulation, his figured tie a darker blue, a crispness to his button-down Oxford shirt that suggested sensible laundering. He held half reading glasses that clacked for emphasis against the podium, his shadow intruded on the bullet points of a slideshow.

"Gazelles in the heart of Africa wake up knowing they must outrun the fastest lion to survive. The fastest lion knows he must outrun a gazelle to eat. We outrun our competitors. If it's our destiny to eat one along the way, so be it."

An aide scurried, trying to scroll through the slides. Griffiths waved him off.

"Forget my speech, gentlemen. Nothing has changed in banking in the thirty-six years I've been in it. You've still got three risks: credit risk, interest rate risk, and liquidity risk. You make money one dollar at a time. You only lend money to men who pay it back.

"But this isn't banking as usual, gentlemen. This is a battle for the future. In 1930, Chase Manhattan Bank had three billion dollars. In the whole city of Charlotte, we had one hundred and fifty million dollars. Now we've got six hundred and eighty-one billion dollars and Chase is gone. Eaten.

"Gazelles and lions!"

His fist came down hard on the podium, and a colored graphic showing projected growth rates in mid-Atlantic metro areas wobbled like jelly.

"'When they take this Marine home to die, I want them to say I knew the arena,' as Theodore Roosevelt said. Been there with men who fought and bled and died. And unless you're willing to make the ultimate sacrifice for your bank, gentlemen, you're all going to be playing a lot of golf very soon, by God."

He stalked from the stage, rustling the curtain bearing the World Crossroads seal, leaving behind handlers who busied themselves securing the forgotten PowerPoint. Bankers in Izods and blazers strolled into the daylight, blinked their eyes, and punched up flip phones, nonplussed at another Griffiths performance.

"What now?" I said to Elaine. She had called to keep me on task. "Griffiths took off."

"Where are you?"

"World Crossroads."

"Is that a shrine?"

"It does have a kind of spiritualism, like the beginning of *Triumph of the Will*. Foreboding camera shots, then the chanting, and finally the Fuhrer comes out."

"That's not how *Triumph of the Will* starts. You made up another movie. Will you try to keep your mind on what you're doing?"

"I was going to check in with a VP or something, but all I see are a couple of muscle guys. They'll probably beat me up."

"Nobody's going to beat you up. Ask someone in a uniform how to get to Griffiths' office."

"Just like that? Seems very direct."

"Go for it. He's probably sitting there waiting for you, throwing a grenade around."

Griffiths was known for his stash of grenades. He gave them out at staff parties.

I asked a nearby security guard how to get to the executive floors, thinking he'd handcuff me as a nutcase if I asked for Griffiths directly. He pointed to the last elevator bank. I entered with two dudes carrying fruit cups, each wearing paisley braces, one with a ruddy complexion and the other pale. As instructed, I punched the button for the sixty-second floor.

"Not going to happen," said the ruddy one.

"Sorry?"

"You've got to have the pass key."

"Oh, right, darn that pass key."

Suddenly the cabin shuddered, gathered momentum, and shot upward at G-force speed.

The pale one groaned and started punching buttons. Then they both turned and looked at me accusingly. "You did this, didn't you?" the ruddy one said.

"Did what?"

"We've just been rerouted to C-Suite One. That never happens."

We glided to the top, and I blew out my stopped-up ears airline style. The door opened and I stepped out fast. A pleasantly trim older woman with cleverly tinged blondish-gray hair smiled at me. She wore a peach pantsuit and carried a Brooks Brothers bag in one hand, and what appeared to be the vaunted pass key in another. It was a curious presentation for Griffiths' outer office, but there was something familiar about her, and she smiled as though she knew me.

"I'm Jack Callahan," I said. "To see Mr. Griffiths? Is this his office?"

She held out her hand. "You're Hugh's young man. Your darling mother did a reading at our home."

I realized it was Mrs. Griffiths. "Oh. Right. Mrs. Griffiths. It was for—?"

"The Mint Museum. Call me Dolly. Would you please give these to Dalt? I forgot."

Dolly handed me six rolled handkerchiefs from the Brooks Brothers bag.

"I'm sorry about that poor Forrest boy. I've known him since he was born."

"We're doing what we can."

She patted my arm. "Go in there and be yourself. Dalt hates faking." She smiled and stepped into the elevator, waving as it closed.

Was Dolly an ally? Perked up, I knocked on Griffiths' door.

"Dolly, where are those damn—"

I held out the handkerchiefs. "These, sir?"

"Who the hell are you?"

"Jack Callahan. Butler and Symmes."

"You're late." He waved a chastising finger.

"Sorry, sir."

"What the hell are you doing with my handkerchiefs?"

"Mrs. Griffiths gave them to me."

He glowered as though I'd mugged her, inspecting me up and down.

I'd watched Griffiths in action from afar at board meetings, while playing second chair to Hugh. I'd seen him bull his way through with a gruff but jolly attitude, professing to know every man worth knowing, whether from prep school, college at the proper latitude, starter neighborhood in Manhattan, or military service in a suitably inconvenient place. He made it clear, in his Marine officer's take-that-hill manner, that he ran the world with his buddies and would do more or less whatever he wanted.

"Sit down, Callahan," he said, motioning for his handkerchiefs. "Let's get down to it. We're both busy men. You've made a damn mess."

"Yes, sir. I mean, I'm sorry, sir. I was solving a payment problem."

"For years I've been trying to get into Broman's deals. Now I have to explain this to him?"

What he didn't know was that Broman had paid me a finder's fee to connect with the Bank two years ago. Griffiths' aides made him think doing deals with Broman was his idea, which was their job.

"With all due respect, sir, there's not much to explain. We arranged for the Forrests to make a payment out of a San Francisco account. If Broman—"

Griffiths slammed his hand down on the burnished desktop, rattling manila folders and a hand grenade. "Don't bullshit me, son. Who do you think you're dealing with?"

"The CEO of Ameribank?"

"Damn right. And don't forget it."

"I won't, sir."

He chuckled. "You can tell a Harvard man, but you can't tell him much, eh Callahan?"

"That's what they say, sir."

"I've got the whole file on you." He motioned to a beaten-up wooden file cabinet with a spirea fern draped over it. "You missed a mortgage payment in 1992. How the hell does a Harvard man miss a mortgage payment?"

"If I remember, sir, we were at the beach, and—"

"At the beach!" He wiped droplets of spittle from his chin with a new handkerchief. "Do you see this?" He grabbed the hand grenade and tossed it in my direction. I lunged and caught it. "That's what I mean, Callahan. Right there. A Marine trusts a Marine."

"I get that, sir. But why did you throw a grenade at me?"

"Because you have no honor."

I put the hand grenade back on its perch. "With all due respect, sir, I disagree."

"You sold Hugh Symmes down the river, didn't you?"

"No, I didn't do that."

"Like hell. I understand you fellas are running a business, but you've got to live with your ethics."

"Sir—"

"Hugh Symmes is a friend of mine."

"Mine, too."

"But Vincent Price is a good man. You're lucky he's around, or we'd be shopping."

"Yes, sir, it's an honor to serve with Vincent."

"Do you know who Broman called after you pulled your stunt?"

"No, sir."

He fixed an index finger to his chest. "Me. I'm the man on the line."

"I'm sorry about that."

"This is my bank, not yours."

"I realize that, sir."

"You don't act like it! You act like it's your bank! Getting Billy Arnold to make that transfer! You smart-ass son of a bitch! I'm going to have to fire him."

"Sir, it's not his fault."

"You didn't think about the unit, did you? Not one bit."

"No, sir, I mean yes, sir, I tried—"

"You did your thing, like some hippie in a suit. Where's your damn earring—take it off for this meeting?" He leaned back in his chair and folded another handkerchief, placing it just so in his jacket pocket. "I don't think you're sorry at all. You think you're a real smart guy, don't you?"

"Not today, sir."

"Who is your client here?"

"Actually, it's the *Criterion*."

"Like hell!" He smacked his hand on the desk. "Y'all work for us." He gestured to the five floors of our offices below.

"It's—it's a complicated situation, sir."

146

He smacked his hand again, shaking the desk grenade. "Complicated! That's you all over, isn't it? I'm getting to know you now. 'Complicated.'" He said it the last time in a dainty voice. "A Marine trusts a Marine, Callahan. There is no 'complicated.'"

"I understand, sir. But I'm not a Marine."

"Thank God."

"May I speak freely, sir?"

"Speak your damn mind, son. That's what you're here for."

"Remembering your speech, sir, you talked about gazelles and lions, and the law of the jungle. You suggested the need to do bad things in order to achieve a good result—in this case, one animal killing another to eat. The alternative was playing a lot of golf, which didn't sound bad, really, except it meant that you'd been eaten."

"Humph. I don't push my beliefs, Callahan. If you're a member of the Elect, you're led to do some tough things, but that's in the Divine Plan."

"I see your point, sir. But Victor Broman doesn't believe in the Divine Plan, just his plan."

"You don't think Victor Broman believes in the Divine Plan?"

"No. You recall the Bridger Industries deal."

"Junk bond stuff. The eighties. Milken and his crowd."

"Sir, Victor Broman did that deal."

He rose from his chair, red-faced.

"I loved Lorrie Bridger like a brother. We had one hundred and seven million dollars out to him."

"One hundred and eight million."

"Excuse me?"

"One hundred and eight million, six hundred eighty-four thousand, to be exact. I closed them out."

"You were on the Bridger deal?"

"Yes, sir. Broman recruited me when I was still in law school. He knows me, and he wants me off the Forrest deal. He can't fire me himself, so he wants you to do it, through your relationship with our firm."

Griffiths rocked slowly in his high leather chair, and then nodded as though ticking off the things I'd said. "I'm careful with my bank, son," he said, quietly. "I've got a whole diligence file on Victor Broman." He motioned again to the wooden cabinet. "Worked it up myself."

"Sir, it's not about being careful. I'll bet that file doesn't say a word about Bridger Industries. He deep-sixed it. Poof."

Griffiths stared into my eyes for a long moment, and I forced myself not to look away. "So, you worked for Broman and knew Lorrie Bridger. That was a long time ago, and you're a young man."

"Sir, I'm destined to be on the Forrest deal. I won't resign."

He nodded his head, and turned slowly to look out the window. Planes preparing to land lined up on the horizon, wings blinking in a purple sky. "I respect that," he said, turning slowly to face me. "And you misunderstand. I don't want you off the deal."

"But I thought—"

"If you're destined to fix this mess, you better get to work. Clock's ticking." He opened a file on his desk and started reading. I figured that was my clue to leave.

Parris Island of the Mind

"How DID IT GO?" Elaine asked, putting me on speaker. I could hear in the background the *tick tick tick* of her computer.

"I'm now a Marine."

"Excuse me?"

"A Marine trusts a Marine. It's civilization's highest value."

"Really? Did he give you a hand grenade?"

"Threw it at me."

"Why?"

"I have no honor. Also, I wasn't thinking about the unit. He had a point."

"So, you liked him? Before, you compared him to Hitler."

"I did like him, sort of. We discussed predestination."

"Oh my God. Did you grovel?"

"A little. But we're still on the deal."

"Drac will be so disappointed."

Groveling was a skill I'd polished over time, starting with my legal education. I hadn't carried a gun at Harvard, like a Marine, but after I had fun at Carolina, for law school Hugh arranged a Parris Island of the mind.

Ignorant of his larger plan that I return as the quasi-heir but dutiful to the task at hand, I reported to Cambridge in August of 1977, finding my way to Professor Alfred Monroe's amphitheater-like classroom in Langdell Hall and the high-altitude seat directed by his name chart. Monroe had been Hugh's roommate in law school. He now served as chief drill master at Parris Island North, and he'd cooked up a fine first-day hazing.

"Mr. Callahan," Monroe said, in his network-perfect accent, "I see you hail from the State of North Carolina. The facts of *Strong v. Elwood*, please."

My new classmates averted their eyes. I felt like I was on a movie set, and I remembered a couple of films that played this very scene. Hollywood versions never turned out well for the student. I sought relief vainly along the walls of Monroe's amphitheater, where portraits of blank-faced English judges sat, wigged and robed.

"There was a woman, and she was walking—"

"Stand up, Mr. Callahan."

"Yes, sir. She was walking across a field, and Elwood scared her."

"How did he do that?"

"I don't know."

"Think."

"He must have said something."

Monroe had ignored hands that shot up. Presently, he chose one.

"Yes—Miss Blount, also of the State of North Carolina. Carry on."

"The situation here is plain," said Kai-Jana, then known as Connie. "This is a black man in the South who talked to a white woman walking alone, and the sheriff went after him. There's no crime here."

"Miss Blount, the case resulted in conviction affirmed on appeal."

"Means nothing," she replied, as laughter echoed against the vaulted ceiling. "All those judges were white men elected in a county where black people couldn't vote."

Groans and hissing grew to high volume. Monroe stared at me, waited a few seconds, and then waved the hissing away.

"Stand up, Mr. Callahan."

"Sorry, sir."

"Do you care to argue with Miss Blount that the outcome in *Strong* is a result of race prejudice?"

"Seems like a bad case, sir."

"Is what you'll say in your Supreme Court argument as your state's attorney general?"

I looked again in vain to the English judges staring down, locking in on one who seemed proud of a fruity blue garter.

"I don't know the law of assault well enough to give a good answer. It's the first day of class, sir."

Monroe moved from behind his podium and advanced up the aisle, stopping in his blazered magnificence at nose level with me. "The law surprises, Mr. Callahan. Best remember that."

"Yes, sir."

"We're still waiting for your answer."

"I don't know the answer, sir."

"Use your native wit, Mr. Callahan. Admissions thought you had some."

The clock ticked dumbly, and outside the open doors unburdened classmates laughed on their happy errands. A physical dread buckled my knees, rising to my chest and vocal cords. Scenes of my past life appeared dimly, as though it were the end.

"Professor Monroe—excuse me, Mr. Monroe?"

He turned to see a woman in front waving both arms.

"Mr. Monroe," she pushed on. "Are you going to call on women? This is a case about women."

"Miss, let's see, Miss Mar—Marchetti. Not from North Carolina. Connecticut, thank God, a civilized place."

"It's Ms. Marchetti."

"My apologies."

Elaine stood, tugging slightly at her open blouse tucked into faded black jeans. She appeared to be wearing pointy-toed alligator cowboy boots.

"The woman in this case has been silenced. All of you are addressing the problem of this man and a racial verdict. But this woman Strong has a right to walk without being harassed by a man. What if Elwood were a very big man and she was small? If he approached her and said something inappropriate, he could put her in fear for her immediate physical safety, which is the definition of assault. It's her subjective perception that should count, applied to the standard of a reasonable woman, *not* a reasonable man, or the desexed reasonable person. We must hear women's voices."

Connie/Kai-Jana rose and pointed, angrily. "Elaine, look what you're defending."

"Connie, I'm defending a woman's right to be heard. Men of color must hear women's voices. And women must hear men of color."

Murmurs of approval contended with scattered boos. Monroe retreated to the podium and flipped through the casebook that bore his name. All he'd tried to do was break in a kid Hugh Symmes sent along, and then these crazy girls had to ruin it. The Law School was going to hell.

Later, I saw Elaine in the library, and tried some friendly conversation. She dismissed my compliment to her cowboy boots. I tried thanking her for taking heat off me with Monroe. She got offended.

"You think I spoke out to help you?" she said, savagely biting an apple as we waited to have our book bags x-rayed.

"Not at all. I'm trying to say thank you for getting me out of a spot."

"'Out of a spot'? Are we on the BBC?"

"Heavens no. Upper-class twit accents. Awful."

"Let me be clear. My class participation has absolutely nothing to do with you. And you were wrong about *Strong v. Elwood* anyway."

"Wrong about what?"

"It was a race case."

Elaine and Connie/Kai-Jana both worked after class at the legal services center in Dorchester, representing poor tenants in housing disputes. I signed up, too.

"What does he add to the struggle?" I overheard Connie/Kai-Jana say while I made coffee in our battered collective urn, the whoop-whoop of police sirens sounding a midnight serenade. "He's so one of them. Not even a smart one."

"Connie, stop it. He's your basic corporate guy. But nice, you know, southern."

"Honey, I know southern white boys. They're not so nice."

"I did go to Duke, remember?"

"Right, and my aunt cleaned your dorm."

I thought Elaine and Connie/Kai-Jana were both really attractive, especially when they got after each other. Eventually, Elaine and I became involved, but at first I had Connie/Kai-Jana on the brain.

Tall with broad shoulders and slim hands that rested often on her hips, she tensed from head to toe when outraged, which was daily. She also came from Durham, but with different baggage, maybe because she'd been shipped off to some New England prep school and then Brown. I wanted to talk to her about home, but she didn't bite; in fact, any conversation beyond correct-familiar hit a wall. Maybe it was the fact that she had a serious boyfriend, or maybe it was just that I was white.

I'd dated a black girl back in high school, Vanessa, who played second violin in the orchestra. She made All-State, and I held her case during concerts. She had a great figure she didn't care about and wore her hair in long ringlets. On stage, she squinted at the score because she hated wearing glasses, and she cried listening to the Schumann Quintets, which made me cry, too. Eventually, her braces made kissing difficult, and dusk became a limiting factor, since she wouldn't go out with me in Raleigh at night. She broke up with me outside the Rialto Cinema downtown before an afternoon showing of *Annie Hall*. At least I didn't have to pay for the tickets.

After the rough beginning, Connie/Kai-Jana and I fell back on a circling behavior, because we both knew the other was pretending. I wasn't the high frat guy I pretended to be, and she wasn't a radical street chick. Her dad was the senior vice president for underwriting at North Carolina Associated in Durham. Her grandfather was the famous Reverend Blount, who appeared often on PBS, discussing the skinny-tie period of the Civil Rights movement.

As the semester wore on, Connie/Kai-Jana had the lefties to her apartment for proper soul food: fried chicken and okra.

"I decided not to do the collards," she said, bustling about in a genuine apron.

"I know. Smells up the apartment for days." Grandma Callahan would cook up a mess of them the few times Nora and I visited East Durham.

I spied on Connie/Kai-Jana's bookshelf a picture of her in full deb regalia for the AKA Ball in fancy black Durham. Her marshal was Winston, the boyfriend. Winston and I had met in Cambridge and bonded over a couple of beers while Connie/Kai-Jana and Elaine were duking it out over some cause.

Winston had graduated Morehouse and done a year at Columbia Business School. He looked really uncomfortable in the beret Connie/Kai-Jana made him sport around Harvard Square.

"What do you want to do when you get out?" I asked him above the barroom din.

"Join a VC firm."

"Cool. Which one?"

"Don't know. Interviewing." He'd stashed the beret in the booth. "You think this is bullshit, don't you? Please say yes." He motioned toward Connie/Kai-Jana and Elaine, who had moved to dishing on an unacceptably moderate Democrat of the male persuasion who didn't want to imprison executives for bad accounting.

"Totally."

"Good, just checking. Hey, you're a Carolina guy. Why did Dean go to Four Corners with seven minutes left? I mean, really."

Somehow, Connie/Kai-Jana found out about the Callahans of East Durham, and the Irish/Jew confusion, and developed less of an attitude. She also seemed to get along with Pren, which was weird.

We came to observe a non-aggression pact. On dates, as a gesture, I asked Pren not to wear her espadrilles when we all went out. I noted, too, that Winston started leaving his beret behind.

Then the name issue came to a head. The summer after our first year, Connie went to Johannesburg to organize students in Soweto. The police had killed Steve Biko, and it was "just a matter of time," she said, before revolution hit the streets. She had to go to South Africa, no matter what the danger. She barely escaped. She came back calling herself Kai-Jana, which was the name of a woman who organized with her and had gotten killed.

"Her mother told me Kai-Jana meant 'girl-child of heaven,'" she said. "One second we were laughing about her boyfriend, and then somebody threw a bomb in the window and she was dead."

"Must have been unbelievably hard."

"I wrapped my shirt around her head, I didn't know what to do. The ambulance made it but she'd passed."

We were standing outside class on the first day back, and I didn't know what else to say, so I held the door for her and we took our seats in the welcome-back hubbub. Later, I told her that going to South Africa and taking that woman's name was a real stand-up thing, and I was proud of her.

She teared up a little bit. "Thank you," she said quietly.

Elaine and I took her out for Chinese in Central Square that night, and by the end of dinner she was back to her wisecracking self. "Ya'll aren't going to that party, are you?" she said, after we walked Elaine to the train station and headed up Massachusetts Avenue.

That party was the annual Southern Ball at the Crane mansion in Ipswich, put on by guys with a drawl at the business school. There were bands in two ballrooms and a lot of cavorting around in antebellum costume. Last year, Pren had taken two months to figure out what she was going to wear. It was a big scene, but, truth be told, sort of nauseating. The British expats did love it a lot. They sometimes cross-dressed as Scarlett.

"What? It's just a dance."

"It's disgusting, like a minstrel show, except you're in whiteface."

Game, set, and match.

"What am I going to tell Pren?"

"Say we'll all go into Boston for dinner, and I'll get Winston to come up, and we can get Elaine to take what's his name."

"Roger. Okay, you win."

She actually did a victory dance on the sidewalk.

After a rough start, we ended up being pretty good friends. Somehow it went bad when I started working for Hugh. She had no use for the Symmes family. To make things worse, she blamed me for getting Elaine to quit legal aid and join the firm, thus turning her to the dark side.

But all of that was down the road. At first, we were all just trying to survive school and manage our lives. When Winston scored his VC job in Boston and announced he was moving in, Connie/Kai-Jana ran off to South Africa. Elaine's boyfriend Roger accused her of going incommunicado, which she yelled at him about over the phone because he was in his second year of medical school in Durham, and pretty incommunicado himself.

And then there was Pren. Let's say we had a hard time managing expectations.

Still, everybody tried. Winston rode the Beanpot Special from New York on Fridays. Elaine and I practiced airline commuting, sharing a cab to Logan on our weekend getaways to the Raleigh-Durham airport. Pren graduated early and started in her dad's real estate office, and also in the Junior League. She didn't travel north very much. She thought Boston very cold, even when it wasn't.

◆◆◆

BACK IN DORCHESTER, I became a dutiful study-buddy of the workaday left. Much to the collective's surprise, I developed a knack for deciphering Torbruk Dane, a professor whose vague and contradictory lectures made us pine for the cobalt clear, horse's-ass manner of Monroe. Dane easily believed in nothing, and life with Nora had prepared me well for that.

"You guys read the Grand Central case? What the hell, right?"

He walked to the blackboard, gray-streaked ponytail bouncing behind him.

"Let's see. A generates Not-A, B, Not-B, and so on. In other words, everything's both right and wrong at the same time. Do you agree, Ms. Marchetti?"

"Oh shit."

"Excuse me?"

"I'm sorry, when I read it last night it all seemed pretty clear. Justice Brennan said that developers couldn't build over Grand Central Terminal—"

"Uh-uh, not getting away with that! Hey kids, let's all check our Mickey watches! If it's Tuesday, you're in my class, not Monroe's! So, you have to actually think!" Anxious laughter followed him up the aisle, as he strutted Monroe-style, chest out, lips pursed. "Ms. Marchetti, you're still on. The decision is nonsense. Order one idea from Column A, one idea from Column B, one from Column C, and voila—Grand Central is saved! But, intellectually, it's a what—a cheeseburger! Cheeseburger, cheeseburger, ha!

Hurrah for Justice Brennan, and Mrs. Onassis, God help us! Hurrah for liberals cranking their Edsels! Vroom vroom!"

He cocked his head at Elaine as a Cocker Spaniel might, expecting a treat. "So, anything to add Ms. Marchetti? Or are we sleepwalking through history today?"

Dane rejected seating charts as tools of the ruling class, so I got to sit next to Elaine whenever I wanted. Quickly, I scrawled a note: *Criticize Hayek.* Laying into Hayek could divert Dane from his craziness.

She gave a panicked look, but took to the game. "Von Hayek is wrong."

"What in the world are you talking about?"

"Hayek, no Von," I whispered, looking straight ahead.

"Hayek—Hayek believes that property is freedom—and money is good, and vice-versa. But that's wrong! Everybody should enjoy property, like, for example, walking across Grand Central and seeing the funny constellations on the ceiling. And the clock in the middle, don't forget that. So you've got a right to enjoy Grand Central as a thing, without the money."

Dane paused, nodding and tapping his forefinger to his forehead. "Very good, Ms. Marchetti," he said quietly. "Hayek is a farce, Brennan, too. My God, Brennan! But Brennan is *powerful,* a great presence. Sometimes the father, I mean the parent, sometimes the child. . ."

"Jack, jeez—how did you know Hayek would get him going?" Elaine asked after class.

"Because Nora took me to meetings of the Modern Language Association."

◆◆◆

In February, Hugh arrived.

"I asked Alfred to dinner and told him we'd both be coming," Hugh said, as he ducked his head to enter the cubicle that stood for a room in my retro Bauhaus dormitory.

"We're eating with Professor Monroe?"

"Don't look like you've been read a death sentence." He was poking through my closet. "Do you have a coat and tie in here somewhere?"

Hugh had made a reservation at Locke-Ober, which he prized mainly for its dark wood and unchanging menu. In Hugh's day, women weren't allowed in most of it, which caused him to start when a pinstriped lady bustled past.

"A group of them lay down by the coat check—oh, might've been ten years ago," Professor Monroe said, noting Hugh's wonderment. "Couldn't stand not having their scrod at the bar."

"Well, you know what the cabbie said."

They chuckled in an old-boy way, remembering an off-color ditty that today would be a punch line on a primetime sitcom. *Lady to cabdriver: Can you tell me where I can get scrod?*

Monroe grimaced at the menu. "For pity's sake, Hugh, we have good restaurants now."

"I thought Jack needed to see Lockes."

Monroe sighed. "I suppose. Mr. Callahan, you're enjoying the Law School?"

"Yes, sir, immensely."

"Alfred," Hugh broke in, "why did you drag out that old *Strong* case? It's over the top even for you. Fifty years ago, my friend."

I could have gone through the floor. But Monroe, agreeably sedated by Bordeaux, didn't care. "Don't worry, Hugh. Had to do something for young Callahan. He bore up manfully. Admitted to knowing nothing."

Hugh raised his glass in my direction. "To Jack. And knowing nothing."

Monroe drained his and poured another. "Didn't your father argue *Strong*?" he added, raising an eyebrow in Hugh's direction.

Hugh stared evenly ahead, meeting Monroe's puckish gaze. The chemistry between two old roommates rekindled, and I had a glimpse of early right-thing-ism. "You know he did. Jocko," Hugh continued smoothly, "Little Hugh handled *Elwood* pro bono, since the state wouldn't pay in those days."

"Still doesn't, right?" Monroe, I noticed, didn't do a double take at the family nickname for Hugh's father, Little Hugh. He must have gone down to Raleigh on break.

"Men of color must hear women's voices," I intoned.

"Come again?" Hugh said.

Monroe huffed. "You have no idea what we put up with now. A girl named Elaine Marchetti saved Mr. Callahan with feminist nonsense."

"I didn't think it was nonsense, sir. Elaine Marchetti's one of the best."

"Hmm. I hear she's with that ragtag bunch defending the rent deadbeats."

"You mean the Dorchester Project? I think that's good work, sir. Do it myself. Those poor tenants get ripped off. Some don't even speak English."

Silence enveloped the table, and Hugh couldn't stop grinning.

"I take it you and Miss Marchetti are now experts in operating low-income housing," Monroe said evenly.

"Not me, sir. But she moved around a lot growing up. She knows landlord tricks first-hand."

"Your answer to the gross injustice of paying rent is to drive small landlords out of business? You might ask your friend Torbruk Dane what his rentals have been."

"Professor Dane?"

"He owns four tenements. Suppose you wouldn't call them that. Section 8 housing is the polite term. Terrific tax shelter."

"Professor Dane? That's not—"

"How he teaches you? At some delusional level he believes what he's saying, but rents send his children to St. Marks, on the sly of course."

"You have no secrets, Alfred—or do you?" Hugh said. A waiter in starched shirt and bow tie stood at the ready, slightly bowed. The room had filled with quick-talking, gray-suited men of Boston checking well-worn menu cards for anything new, and comforted in finding nothing. Outside, evening fell, and busboys lit candlewicks table by table.

"No secrets for us plain Boston folk," Monroe said. "You keep enough secrets for us all down in Raleigh."

"Touché," Hugh said, tipping his glass.

"And don't worry, I wouldn't dream of dampening young Callahan's political ardor. Surely he can take up where you left off."

"Where who left off?" I asked.

"Hugh was going to be governor, or senator. Now I hear he just picks them out."

Styrofoam Boxes

HUGH AND I MET the next morning for coffee in the Square. Dinner had gone well, he said, and Professor Monroe was going to write a recommendation for Dudley and Price, which was the Wall Street firm Hugh had picked for my summer job. Hugh whistled up Dunster Street. I dreaded the whistle. Audrey Hepburn would be getting more out of this: admirers bursting into song, fur collars, champagne at the Savoy. Come to think of it, I was getting the benefit of very expensive law lessons, a little Rain-in-Spain from the songmasters themselves, not to mention Just-Like-Dad shoes.

Sure enough, after torturing me in class some more, Monroe wrote the recommendation that bagged the prized interview, which turned out to be my first meeting with Ferris. In preparation, Hugh took me to J. Press to buy a gray herringbone suit, and to Church's for the aforementioned JLDs.

"Shoes make the man," Hugh insisted, maybe the only time this century that proved true.

I would have thought a cummerbund or monocle would make the man. Edward VI, who wore both cummerbund and monocle, gave each of his mistresses a watch in the form of a brooch. Reportedly, the mistresses gathered annually in the same box to enjoy the Royal Ascot race.

Would things be different if I hadn't donned the herringbone suit, laced up the shoes, and caught Ferris on the way to Juarez? Sometimes you just put on the uniform and take what comes.

◆◆◆

When I showed up at Dudley and Price the day after exams, there was, as Ferris promised, plenty of work, most of it generated by Broman, who was making a pile buying stuff with junk bonds.

Ferris turned out to be major domo for the shell-shocked staff, who hadn't eaten a meal from anything but a Styrofoam box for days. Soon after I found a desk, he handed me a stack of papers to mark. That afternoon, a lady showed up with a ticket for me to eat cracked crab on a cruise around the Battery, but Ferris said no. I was on the Broman team, and there would be no cracked crab for me. He hinted at greater rewards.

Ferris had come to the law late, by choice, not by fate, like me. He had begun a PhD in English at Berkeley, and then canned it because there weren't any jobs. It didn't matter anyway, he said, because all the best people now believed literature to be incomprehensible.

Economics, on the other hand, was just arithmetic, knowable as breakfast. He taught himself economics by reading the *Wall Street Journal*. Its applied forms—raiding public companies with debt, for example—paid well. Literature used to have the advantage of truth, Ferris admitted, but no longer; and being on the Broman buyout team brought the prestige once enjoyed by literary cults, like Bloomsbury.

"My dad told me I was nuts going to graduate school," he said over one of the Styrofoam lunches. "Then he died."

"Gosh, I'm—I'm sorry."

He shrugged. "Dad had a heart attack on the floor of the Exchange making a hostile tender offer for Woolworths. Victor said he was there when they carried him out."

"Wow."

"Yeah, I was on the Coast. Came back East and never even picked up my shit. Woolworths—can you imagine?"

It was unclear which thing I was supposed to have difficulty imagining: bidding for Woolworth's, or dying for it.

Oddly, I loved the work. We were always pulling something over on the world. Some hapless white-bread CEO teed up first thing at Pine Valley,

161

thinking he ran his company—then the market opened, and by the time he made the turn, poof, all gone!

Soon, Ferris began coming early to the bullpen—the open hall where the summer lawyers worked—and yelling *Callahan! Now!* And I hopped to it. It was the Broman Team calling, and I was, Ferris said, the number one draft pick. I never asked why. Was it because he liked Nora's book?

"You're on the Bridger deal, I hear," Hugh repeated, as a means of catching his breath. He'd come up on the morning plane, and we hiked to lunch at Mabry's. I didn't tell him only has-beens went there anymore. The real crowd skipped food, did a couple of lines at lunch, and played racquetball to chill out.

"Can't really talk about that," I said, looking for something quick on the menu.

It was the Bridger deal that brought him up. An old North Carolina textile firm was on the block for the usual reasons, too many Asian sweatshops to fight, too little cash. Pren's sorority sister Brandy Bridger, who was an heiress to the mess, worked in midtown for Manny Hanny as a trainee. When Pren came up, I dragged out an associate for Brandy, and we found a place to drink filled with single people dressed to the nines, like us.

"The Bank is nervous. I called Lorrie Bridger."

"You know him?" That would be Brandy's dad. There was a bulls-eye with his face on it in Ferris's office.

Hugh nodded. "Yes. He had a hard time in the War. Jap POW camp. Came back to run the company."

"Friend of yours?"

He shrugged. "Jocko, you need to be careful. Is Broman involving you?"

"I can't talk about it."

He drummed away with those fingers. "I don't want you to be used. Dudley and Price has been a great blue-chip firm over the years. Now they're doing, I don't know—"

"Hostile takeovers? Bad things?"

"Not judging anyone's work here, Jocko."

Like hell. "Want to know about the deal, Hugh? Okay, I'll tell you. I'll, ah, hire you for this lunch." I laid a dollar bill on the table. Ferris taught me that.

He didn't pick up the dollar.

I described how we secured the assets of Bridger Industries with junk bonds, leaving out how I used my down-home accent to wheedle favors from county clerks of court. Ferris and I flew on short notice to Charlotte and rented cars to spy on factory sites in little towns up and down I-85, flying back on the last plane to plot some more.

"Are you signing, Jocko?"

"What do you mean?"

"Opinions."

Ferris had given me opinions to sign, offhandedly. It was flattering, and I'd perfected a flashy signature.

"Do you say you're a lawyer over the phone?"

Ferris had told me to do that; it saved explaining.

"I can't talk to you about this anymore."

He shook his head. "One more question. Is Bridger losing money?"

"Not technically."

"What does that mean?"

"The company's worth way more dead than alive."

"Ah. So Broman would sell off the assets of a profitable company?" He snapped his fingers. "Just like that?"

"Sure. How else can he finance the bonds to take it over?"

Hugh looked around the room of the steakhouse he remembered, fixing a puzzled gaze on diners nibbling at rabbit food and talking on portable phones. "Help me here. Why do the deal?"

"The arbitrage, obviously. Look, in Fairington these old guys keep a damn park for their employees! A lake! A nine-hole golf course any employee can use! They need to sell that stuff. And their charitable contributions. Unbelievable! You couldn't imagine what they're giving to hospitals and scout troops. They use the stockholders' money like a piggy bank for the whole town! You can't run a public company like that."

Hugh sank back in his chair and toyed with his second martini. I wondered if he'd go for his third, like the old Jimmy Carter cliché. I sipped at a Pellegrino and glanced at the watch he'd given me. Twenty-two minutes before the team met again.

"Broman's going to buy this company with cheap debt. He's going to tear up Fairington to pay everybody back. Why? Is this the right thing to do, son?"

He only called me son when he was mad. I yawned, not from boredom, but because I hadn't any sleep for two days. I refused to take the free blow.

"The right thing is above my pay grade. The fees are great—oh, and if we want to compete with the Japanese, we've got to get rid of the fat."

Hugh rolled his eyes. He'd already done in the Japanese once.

"What are they teaching you up at Cambridge, anyway?" he asked.

"They're teaching me the law doesn't make any sense. Isn't that what they taught you?"

"No, they didn't."

Hugh paid the bill. We walked up Wall Street toward Trinity Church. The walk winded him, and he suddenly looked old. I hadn't remembered ever thinking he was old. But he turned sixty soon. I didn't see sixty-year-olds working at Dudley and Price.

"I thought you had a meeting uptown," I said.

"Through for the day," he said huskily. "Nora asked me to tell you she's coming up next week. She said not to worry, she'll stay with friends." He paused and grabbed my arm firmly. "Look, Jocko, whether you think so or not, you need to be careful."

I didn't like him grabbing me, and I jerked back my arm, but I nodded yes before jogging back to the office.

◆◆◆

ON OUR SECRETARY'S DESK sat stacks of federal express packages. It was eighteen hours to D-Day. When the bell rang tomorrow, Broman would assault Bridger stock.

"We're all done," said Ferris.

"But it's—Wednesday?"

"No. Tuesday. Get some sleep. I'll mop up."

"You haven't slept, either."

"I make the big bucks, Callahan. Go home."

I grabbed clothes piled in my office, caught an empty express elevator, and stumbled into the subway entrance below the building. At the third-floor apartment on West Twelfth Street where I now lived, I ate two bowls of cereal and fell asleep on the couch. The brownstone belonged to Broman, and Ferris had arranged for me to bunk there, without any mention of rent.

"Yo, deal man," Elaine said, rubbing my shoulder. She spent a lot of time now on West Twelfth Street.

I sat up. "What time is it?"

"Eight o'clock, deal must be over."

"Sort of. Something smells great."

She laughed. "Clam sauce. Don't worry, it's from Dino's. I didn't cook it or anything."

Elaine sat across from me, drinking a glass of wine and smoking a cigarette, shoes off and legs tucked under her dress, which I had financed, over a half-hearted objection, on sale at Saks. "You should take a bath."

"I smell bad, huh?"

She wrinkled her nose. "I'll run a tub."

Elaine had introduced me to fancy bubble bath, which she claimed to be her only classist indulgence. They must have bubble bath in Nicaragua, where she had done a summer internship that turned into a year. NEE-ca-RAG-U-A she said, so everyone got she was a pinko. I lay in Danny Ortega's fancy suds, and she brought me a Heineken.

"You want the paper?"

"Anything happen today?"

"Donald Trump got a new girlfriend. What a shocker."

Elaine's hair had gone lighter. Now it was almost blonde. She also wore more, or different, makeup. Stylish outfits showed up in her wardrobe, along with boxes of strappy Italian shoes. Curvaceous toe cleavage was apparently acceptable for lady lawyers fighting City Hall.

Elaine was becoming Manhattanized, a process in which I was already advanced, thanks to Nora. Looking back, I recognized those window-shopping weekends in the city as an education in taste, with the added benefit of learning subways cold. Nora never spent money on cabs. She thought buses lacked adventure. We either walked or took the train.

By wandering around and taking advantage, I learned how to eat cannoli, to enjoy German cinema, to live well rent-free, courtesy of a rich knave. What a deal, and as a New Yorker by birth, I wasn't ashamed. Only a few blocks separated the rent-controlled Village pied-à-terre of Mayor Koch and my own well-priced digs.

"You seem down."

"Had lunch with Hugh. He fears I'm immoral and in danger. Maybe in reverse order. He doesn't like Broman."

"What? The savior of capitalism in our time?" Broman had enjoyed his first cover on *Fortune* magazine. Tie askew, he had elaborated on Schumpeter and the practical uses of creative destruction. Ferris wrote it up for him.

"He hates the Bridger deal. This old North Carolina family could lose out. Bad form. He thinks I'm going to get in trouble."

"Are you?"

"I'm doing a summer job he picked out for me."

She left muttering, and returned with more wine. "Forget about those stupid Big Daddy speeches. It's not like the great Hugh Symmes helps the poor or anything."

"Yeah! Big Daddy! Mendacity!"

"At a moral level, all of these deals are the same. White males fight. Testosterone. Screaming. It's all immoral."

"Yeah, you tell 'em. Love that view from the left-field bleachers."

She frowned. "Why are you belittling me?"

"Sorry, lame joke. I'm sorry, okay?"

"This is hard for me, what you do. But I care about you, and I want you to do what you want, not what somebody else wants."

"I know."

We had conversations where we hurt each other like people do in love. She had broken up with Dr. Roger. "Not the first time," she'd said, pointing a finger at him, or at me, or at both of us. "But it better be the last."

I had broken up with Pren in my mind.

Elaine exited while I drained the bath. "I'm helping you get free of this Hugh person so you can live your life," she said through the door.

"Thanks. Really. Sorry for being a schmuck."

It began at the opera. The night before, there'd been tears over Roger. She let slip she'd never been to the opera, and so I cashed in a fully funded summer associate Dream Night at the Met, courtesy of the firm. She disclaimed date status.

The Met put on its final *Aida* of the year, and we got the firm's seats in orchestra. Nora had standing room for the original Leontune Price production, with elephants and pyramids hauled around by hydraulic lift to show the rise and fall of civilizations. "It was going to be hideous, grand, or both," she'd say, waving a cigarette holder as the wand of Isis. "And it was very grand, believe me..."

"Egyptian maidens don't wear much," Elaine said, downing her first-act champagne.

"You're not either. Just thought I'd point that out."

She blushed and plunked down her glass. "What do you mean? This is what you wear to the opera."

"Sure. In the movies. I should have sprung for a tiara."

"You don't like how I look?"

"You look fantastic. I just don't see how everything stays up."

"It's got hooks. To be clear, I'm not sleeping with you."

A Bad Necktie Party

I HAD A FANTASY, and it went like this: Elaine and I would get married in New York. I'd do deals, she'd do good works. In the city, we'd be cheerful outsiders with well-adjusted kids who thrived on unconditional love but were high achievers anyway. We'd buy a weekend place in the Catskills, and Nora could visit for short periods. She'd make no self-involved emotional demands, just entertain literary people who came for the weekend. With lots of money and good domestic help, we'd create the dream family.

But, reality lurked. In addition to me working for criminals, Dr. Roger still hung around. Over the Fourth, in an effort to "sort things out platonically," Elaine took off to the Berkshires with him for some bird-watching and the Philharmonic. Now that's a rocking good time.

I took a hall pass for old-man Bloodworth's sixtieth birthday. The clan gathered at the plantation house across from the Club, done to a fare-the-well by decorators who had convinced Mrs. Bloodworth to paint their 1920s mansion Chinese red.

Seeing Pren in Raleigh, or anywhere except New York, kept her and Elaine out of the same zip code, which made it possible to have sex with them both guilt-free. It worked okay for a while, but then doubts arose.

For example, during this trip to Raleigh, a disturbing question popped up: Did I want Pren for her money?

Wanting Pren for her social status as a Bloodworth didn't seem so bad. That was just getting into a club. And I really did love her, I guess. But the money, that bothered me. Was she prettier because she was rich?

I'd never thought about it, until my lack of money presented itself nakedly in New York, in the stares of thin, black-skirted women walking past carrying handbags costing more than a Buick. Working for Broman, I discovered, would fix the poverty part, but it carried risks.

Nora always treated the quest for dollars as something other people did. As a professor with a kid and no husband, she adopted a cheerful penny-pinching style. She bought me no-name basketball shoes, not Chuck Taylors. We ate out at Ballantines for the Early Bird Special. We saw movie matinees to save fifty cents. The biggest perk of our Methodist church membership was free summer camp with limp spaghetti and the Lord.

After she and Hugh took up, she sometimes discovered a "piece of money." Eureka! We burned it on more trips to the city, where we rode in cabs!

Coming from Nora-land, I was amazed not only at Broman's largesse, but at the ease with which the Bloodworths skated through the material world. Hungry? Go to the Club and charge it. Eat any old thing you want and remember not to tip, they get it all at Christmas. Left your golf shoes at school? Buy another pair; you always need an extra. And come with us on our trip to Bermuda, there's nothing to do there unless you're with people.

It's not that the Bloodworths were stinking rich, but they had entered a zone where they need not match what came in with what went out. It was a nice zone, and I enjoyed my time there, while it lasted.

"That's a great one, Jack," Mr. Bloodworth said, rolling sideways with a belly laugh at the yellow and green tie I'd given him, before tossing it on the pile with other garish cravats. Mrs. Bloodworth had organized a bad tie party for his birthday. "Gonna save every damn one of these. Watch out, Jack, they'll be coming your way soon."

This knowing remark caused a mild frisson among female handicappers in the crowd. When would Pren and I marry? The buzz buzzed. She did look terrific, all brown, with a smart short haircut and her own smart black skirt, her legs smooth and creamed. Sex-deprived, we drove out for a tumble in the driveway of a neighborhood tear-down, and arrived refreshed for the cake cutting.

"Hugh Symmes told me you like it up there in Boston," Mr. Bloodworth said. "Too damn cold for me. There's one damn thing going for it, though. Not many of your damn Yaboos up there. Boston's one town where you've got to look out for your Irish more than your damn Yaboos."

As sometimes happened, Mr. Bloodworth had strung together so many objectionable non-sequiturs I had no reply. A reply wasn't the point. It was his birthday, and he wanted to hear himself talk racist nonsense. Having done so, he clapped me on the back and moved on through the room. He had not spoken to Hugh about me, because Hugh would cross the street rather than speak to him. They disagreed over the rights of the "Yaboos," a term coined by Mr. Bloodworth and his friends, and used when they wanted to say the N-word and couldn't. Saying the N-word was preferable in my mind, rather than be both racist and evasive.

I struggled to say nothing. On top of that, he had dissed the Irish!

More amazing than the fact I put up with him was the fact he put up with me. Raised on the other side of the tracks by an artsy liberal woman polite Raleigh shunned as Hugh Symmes' Friday-night girl, with no money, no manners, and no father, here he was promising me bad ties, giving me the run of his palazzo, and entertaining me with his best racist humor. Why?

Mr. Bloodworth's welcome wagon rolled on a mission. He presumed Hugh groomed me as quasi-heir, and the prize, Butler and Symmes, was a choice bauble. There would be fresh money to divide up, and Big Law, finally, on his side. That was no small point. He needed Big Law to obtain real estate cheaply and develop it freely, and he didn't want to budget for any Do the Right Thing lectures.

"Does your Dad think I'm a lock for Butler and Symmes?" I asked Pren. We picked up stray bottles while the rented tents came down.

"He thinks you're going there, or to Wall Street, and you've already said you don't want that, right, honey?"

She said the last part purposefully, smiling gently, her arm on my shoulder, looking into my eyes for indecision. She handled me like the old man: a touch, a suggestion. It could be that he put up with me because he loved her. She was always taking the glass out of his hand and leading him to a better place, away from that Yaboo-land in his mind. With me she steered away from Broman-land, and Nora resentment-land, and outsider-land. She had radar for the bad places and how to keep the brooding man-creature clear. Steering, steering—Pren was so good at it.

"I thought your old man said Hugh was a communist."

"That's the bourbon talking, honey. Mom said last night you're Hugh's protégé. She only uses French when it's big."

I could hear Mrs. Bloodworth, Emily, saying that. Always made up, always wearing layers of blouses and jackets and pleats with a brooch meant to be noticed, always organized with ornately penned tasks in notebooks, and always shaping the domestic future. She would linger over the words: *Hugh's protégé.*

Hugh had put on the full court press. Introducing me properly to Raleigh's old-boy set, he took me into the dark hold of the Oracle Club, modest in tone, where generations broke bread over questions such as who would chair the Terpsichorean, a group of younger men charged with picking the season's debutantes.

"They do go on," Hugh said. We slipped out early.

Then there was the MacIlhenny Fishing Club, at the headwaters of the Neuse, dammed by the Corps of Engineers. We walked in shoulder to shoulder. Blood of the blood I was, bastard or not. Damn, I wanted them to like me.

I told Nora I was invited to a smoker there, and her eyes grew misty. "The MacIlhenny," she said, conjuring in the tone Scottish rapids, stout men attired in Abercrombie and Fitch, cooks and batmen and guides pitching camp, serving champagne and the trout head-on. I did present myself ready to fish, replete with a vest of many pockets.

"No one's fishing," Hugh said as he eyed my getup. He wore regulation burnt-orange pants and Weejuns.

"Nora thought there'd be fishing. The name and all."

"Your mother is a romantic."

We alighted at a cinderblock clubhouse. The fireproof hall had been rebuilt over the ruins of a cedar shake lodge, burned in the thirties by socialite wives wielding gasoline and torches. Reasons for the arson never emerged, but I could imagine. Non-secret secrets abounded.

Current old boys posted the membership list by a swinging screen door that served as the front entrance. "Jeez," I said, recognizing names from history, imagining mine there. "Why are dead guys on the list?"

"We list every man who's ever been a member," Hugh said. "Current men are denoted by asterisk."

"An asterisk proves you're alive?"

"There are exactly one hundred living members. On death, we add a man."

I ate another high-cholesterol meal, amply lubricated, with much of the same asterisked, semi-ambulatory crowd that populated the Oracle. A formidable roast pig stared ahead, barbecued in the Club's own grillworks, which consisted of half a fifty-gallon drum enclosing a truck axle that rotated slowly over charcoal; fried chicken, scalloped oysters, coleslaw, Brunswick stew, tomatoes and okra, hush puppies and banana pudding. Members announced guests in a discreet mumble. At nine, two gentlemen began snoring, and dinner broke up.

"So how was MacIlhenny?" Pren asked as she drove me to the airport.

"Dazzling. Tony Bennett sang, and then we played baccarat."

She laughed. "Daddy never talks about it to Mom. Says it's very secret."

I wasn't surprised. These clubs enabled men of Raleigh to escape their wives. It was like a bowling league for fancy guys. Now that I knew the non-secret secret, I wasn't going to spoil it. They had taken me in.

But Hugh looked like he was going through the motions. Quiet came over him as we drove from one fancy-guy appointment to another. They were his flock; he had to break bread and make them Do the Right Thing. But why feel responsible for all those asterisks, so pink-faced and tipsy, so oblivious, so unmarked by the bodies in the Cape Fear River? I could tell his friends bored him. A man who loved the company of women, my mother especially, he wandered restless in the clammy humidor of his male retreats.

"I did this for Nora," he said in the car, after MacIlhenny. "She thinks you need to be introduced."

◆◆◆

172

SATURDAY MORNING BACK ON West Twelfth Street, after the Bad Tie Party, I slept next to Elaine, who'd been glad to see me and showed it. Bird-watching in the Berkshires hadn't gone well.

She breathed regularly, softly, her hand on my chest. Then she sat up. "Somebody's at the door," she whispered. She pulled on her camisole.

"I don't hear anything." Then came a knock.

"Somebody's here, Jack."

I pulled a towel around me. "It's probably that kooky guy across the hall wanting Coffeemate."

I unlatched the chain, the deadbolt, the security rod, and cracked the door to peer at a familiar eyeball peering back. "Nora?"

"Were you in the shower, dear? I knocked five times."

She stood there in a blue summer shirtdress, hair back with globes of sunglasses stuck on top for emphasis, holding her battered train case and teetering on pointy shoes. She trembled a little and struggled with her handbag while wiping a tear.

"Nora, it's really not—"

She shook her head violently. "I couldn't stay with Miriam another minute. The woman is selling Amway, for God's sake. Not that I don't feel for her. Poetry's not a good living, and Wednesday Nathan left her for a graduate student. Aren't you going to let me in?"

I propped the door open, and Nora handed me her train case, which I barely handled while keeping a towel in front of my privates. She looked me up and down as though appraising stock, and I stood paralyzed, caught between Nora in the hall and Elaine in the bedroom. "Nora," I said sharply, suddenly angry, "what the hell—"

She raised her hand to stop me.

"Miriam, poor thing," she continued. "I couldn't go five minutes without her selling me toothpaste. She's wants to be chief of her pyramid, or some other madness. I think she's gone stark raving."

"Nora, you can't—"

"Do you want to wait until she stabs somebody on the subway? I say nip it in the bud. I feel sorry for her because of Nathan, but my God, what does she expect? She let herself go—she looks like Grandma Moses, and he's in front of ten adoring Barnard girls, teaching them Rossetti. He's weak, but all men are weak. I said, 'When did he leave?' and she said, 'I kicked the bastard out.' I asked her why she did that. To preserve her self-respect, she said. Self-respect? The woman is selling Amway! She has some god-awful tape of the president of Amway playing all the time. After thirty years of marriage, I told her she could stare down some young girl in a miniskirt and take Nathan back. Better that than Amway."

She stood smiling and tapping her foot, waiting for me to stop feeling put out.

"Miriam didn't take it well," I guessed. She bustled past me to the living room.

"She said I was undermining her. I said, 'Miriam, undermining is not the half of it. You need to be re-excavated.'"

"So, here you are."

She sat down on the sofa and lit a cigarette. She couldn't stay, but I couldn't tell her that. I scrambled to find the old lead-glass ashtray Elaine had bought in the Village.

"I should've called, darling, I'm sorry. But I was so hurt, I just had to come right over. A nice young Hispanic man let me in."

"Nora, this isn't the best time. I've got to go out to the Island."

"Madness I can take, but I can't stand her negative energy. Suffocated! And that Amway jerk talking about how Jesus made him rich."

"Aren't the Dorfmans Jewish?"

"Of course they are. It's all negative energy."

"Is she getting therapy?"

"Miriam has a book of therapists. For her, it's like taking antibiotics for twenty years. There's no effect anymore. She doesn't need therapy, she needs a kick in the behind."

"Nora, let me explain something to you. I—we—I've got to go to Easthampton to a client's house. It's Victor Broman."

"A house party? In Easthampton? My little boy!"

"You're welcome to stay here, but I have to go."

"Couldn't you go later?"

"I'm already late. Most of the guests showed up last night."

I could see tears forming. She took a Kleenex from her purse.

"Why don't I make you some tea?" I said, resigned. How much would it take to get her to leave? Thankfully the pot, an old metal one of hers, came quickly to a boil.

"Before Miriam had children, you were her baby. She'd hold you all afternoon when I had to teach. They were my best friends. When we left, Nathan drove us to Penn Station. He gave me fifty dollars, and I never paid him back."

I poured the tea and sat down beside her. She leaned against my chest and rested her head on my heart, her breathing becoming slower as my heart pounded faster. "When you were little, I'd put your head on my heart, and you'd stop crying when you felt the beat. Now my big grown son can do the same for his old mother. Here, give me a kiss."

Elaine stood in the hall, her day bag packed. She tossed me a bathrobe. "Put it on, Jack. You'll catch your death." Then she strode by, hand outstretched. "Good morning, Professor Callahan. I'm Elaine Marchetti. Jack has told me so much about you."

A Hundred Self-Portraits

Overwhelmed by son-guilt and date-anxiety, I barely heard the conversation between Nora and Elaine. At last Nora left, train case in hand.

Short on time, Elaine and I cabbed to Grand Central for the 11:40 to Easthampton. "Here, you take the facing seat," I said, catching my breath as we settled in.

"No, I like this one."

"You get sick facing backward."

"Jack, stop fussing. I'm not your mother."

I hoisted our duffels onto the overhead rack, and we lurched toward sunlight. By making the 11:40, we'd catch the last jitney from Easthampton station.

"What just happened?"

Elaine had already started "Talk of the Town."

"Sorry?"

"How did we get out, instead of doing what Nora wants?"

"I told her it was important to go to this closing party, and we needed to leave as soon as you got dressed. Then I gave her the extra key and told her I'd put fresh sheets on the bed, and she was welcome to stay. She said she didn't know about Broman's party because you never tell her anything, and thanks anyway, she'd check into a hotel. Then she left, and here we are."

I sat, stunned. "Did she say anything, you know—"

"About us sleeping together? No."

"It's terrible, the two of you meeting this way."

"She's the one who showed up unannounced."

"Did she get a taxi? She can't afford taxis."

"Really? If she hocked the Furstenberg dress or the Ferragamo shoes, she could buy one."

"She likes clothes."

"I do, too." She stuffed the *New Yorker* into her bag. "Going for air."

"There's no air. It's the Long Island Railroad," I said, trying to be funny, but it sounded desperate. She stood up, took pity, sat down, and retrieved her magazine.

At Easthampton we found the jitney, which turned out to be a Range Rover driven by Dan, an overly tanned senior associate who worked with Ferris in the LA office. Dan stayed irritated with me, wrong this, wrong that. This was his final kiddie run, he said huffily at the curb, eyeballing Elaine's outfit.

Ferris met us at the driveway, worn at the gills, from the look of him having boozed since breakfast. He sported a wrinkled white Izod and vivid plaid shorts that slung dangerously low. Dan plunked the keys into Ferris's outstretched hand, whispered something, and strode away.

"Damn glad you're here, Callahan," Ferris said. He leered at Elaine. "Damn glad you brought the great white liberal chick. Answer me as a tax-payer, Elaine: when you corn-hole the Corporation Counsel of the city of New York on bag-lady law, does he scream, or is it just a lot of whimpering?"

She wrinkled her nose as he planted a kiss on her cheek. "Could you be more disgusting?" she asked, pushing him away and declining his proffered beer.

"Begging the liberal's pardon, we haven't stopped drinking from last night. Victor flew the team in on the bus."

"Sorry we couldn't make it earlier," I said. "Had to take care of things in the City."

"I bet," he said lasciviously. "Look, Victor's never invited a summer clerk to a closing party before. Try not to fuck up, okay?"

"I won't."

"I meant it when I said you did good."

"Thanks."

"Okay, here's the drill. Croquet on the lawn, and later Rinkley's bringing his boat over for windsurfing. You're playing tennis with Mrs. Rinkley, first name Rita, very important. Bunking with the Rinkleys, too, and Dan's bringing your stuff over."

Rinkley was senior partner on the Broman account. That made him technically Ferris's boss. Ferris said that when Broman moved in, the Rinkleys had him for cocktails. Broman reciprocated with the entirety of his legal business. Now, Ferris did all the work but deferred to Rinkley, who got most of the money. Where do you go to learn this stuff?

"Let's look around," I said to Elaine.

"Shouldn't you warm up for tennis?" Ferris said.

Elaine stared at him, pursing her lips.

"I'm fine without warming up," I said.

He shrugged. "Just don't be late. Oh shit, is that my beeper?"

"I really can't stand him," Elaine muttered as Ferris stumbled off to find a phone.

"He's sleep-deprived."

"He's drunk."

To my surprise, Elaine proved to be a way above average partner in the significant other scene. She had an aptitude for charming older men honed by years of training in jovial backyards from San Diego to Norfolk to Groton, as her Navy family hit the high spots of the military-industrial complex. At school, she hid her upbringing amid talk of trips to Nicaragua and work for the poor. Far from being alienated from her Reagan-voting parents, she spoke to them regularly, and especially treasured calls from her father, who had moved from diving in submarines under Admiral Rickover's command, to making them at General Dynamics, to retirement at Pompano Beach.

"Your dad's in the Navy, you're in the Navy," she said, when I got her to talk about it one night. "We moved six times in ten years. I remember where we lived by the toys I got. The places got better. By the time I was in high school, Dad worked at General Dynamics and we lived in Connecticut."

"Nice."

"Not really. It was nice for the rich kids."

"But you went to Groton."

"Because my mom worked as a secretary there. Don't make it something it wasn't. I never had the right clothes. They made me go to speech class."

"You got a scholarship to Duke."

"Another place I didn't have the right clothes."

We walked down the driveway beside white stone walls and the jutting geometry of Broman's pill-box, carved from a green hill sloping to the water. On either side stood older, shingled houses, each flanked by a stand of hedge.

"It looks like hat boxes stuck together," Elaine said.

"I kind of like it. Very bold."

"Like chalk on a blackboard."

"He didn't build it. Some flash-in-the-pan guy ran out of money, and Victor picked it up cheap."

"Sounds like his life."

Strollers strolled the tiered patios, and loungers lounged in self-conscious choreography, the women dressed in flowered frocks and the men in Bermuda shorts, baring legs rubbed white by the city.

"I don't get a pool by the ocean," Elaine said, shading her eyes. The sound and smell of surf strayed over a seawall separating the grounds from the beach.

"It's a rich person thing."

We walked through a large piazza leading to the house. Caterers unloaded iced trays of fruit and crab legs; vested waiters carried frosted sangria pitchers. A steel band played from one overlook while roadies readied another.

"Staff outnumber the guests," I said, stepping past a technician.

"Yeah. It's a rich person thing."

I followed Elaine through an open door into the main house. A marble floor unfolded in a long curve that never lost the ocean view, ending at a room that seemed like a library. On the many shelves sat few books, and none that looked like they'd ever been opened.

"You're kidding," she whispered, pointing at a painting over one of the fireplaces.

"That's famous, right?"

"It's Ingres—Countess Something-or-Other. Supposed to be in the Frick."

"Comtesse d'Haussonville. She is in the Frick."

We turned to see a barefoot woman with short blonde hair and jeans. She caught my eye and smiled. She was angular and attractive, and I must have been staring because Elaine cleared her throat.

"Watch this," the barefoot woman said, moving on tiptoe. She opened a panel and the painting disappeared over one fireplace and reappeared over another.

"Don't be alarmed," she said. She wiped one hand on her jeans and stuck it in my direction. "I'm Angie Angstrom. I move Victor's paintings around. They're all virtuals. He's cornering the market on virtual art."

"I'm Jack—"

"Callahan. And you're Elaine Marchetti. Looking for Victor?"

"Actually—"

"He's in the study. Follow me."

"I told you to sell yesterday." Broman's calm, nasal voice carried from the next room. "You know what happens when you don't sell your sugar futures on time, Ed? You get twenty cars of Havana Pure dumped in your front yard."

"Victor?" Angie called. "It's Jack and Elaine. They made it."

Broman turned slowly with his whole body, as if his neck and torso moved in concert. He faced us across a glass desk; behind him, through the sound-proofed windows, we saw partiers below and breaking surf beyond.

"Callahan," he said slowly, measuring the syllables. He looked as though he'd been old for a while, hollow around the face and eyes. He gave off a lemony smell, and his thin hair, brushed back, turned orange in the light. He looked intensely into my eyes for a moment, and then looked away, flaring his nostrils as if moved by a forceful, quick thought. Then he stood and turned his whole body again, gesturing for us to sit. Standing, he appeared smaller, bones bigger than flesh. He wore a cream-colored turtleneck and trousers, which I thought wrong given the heat of the day, until I noticed the room was refrigerator-cold.

"I hate hot weather," he said, as Elaine sat arms crossed in her low chair. "Summer's the worst. I bought the house because you can see everything. It's all glass. Built by some German architect. Is Callahan your real name?"

"My mother's name. I was born Jacob Gold."

"I thought so," he said matter-of-factly, shrugging. "You're a smart kid, lots of chutzpah. I want you to keep working for me."

I jumped in my seat, as though his invitation were a command. I wanted to say yes, but I felt Elaine tense beside me. "Mr. Broman, I've got to go back to school."

He turned and waved grandly at the ocean. "Everybody's got to do something. I've got to fly to LA on Tuesday. You know Lorrie Bridger. We've still got a ways to go with him."

"I thought we closed."

"Oh, sure. That's the beginning. We're trying to be friends. But we have problems."

"I guess I can do some work, but—"

"It wasn't Lorrie Bridger you knew, it was his daughter. Right?"

"Brandy. We were in college together."

"She works in the business?"

"She actually works in the City, for Manny Hanny."

"See? You're always telling me something new."

"Trying, sir."

"This girl, she drives a nice car?"

Actually, Brandy was the only one of our crowd who kept a car in the city, since parking by the month cost about as much as another apartment. "Sure, you know, a small BMW maybe, three hundred series."

Slowly, he sat back down at his desk. "Pardon me," he said, as he wrote something in a ledger book.

"Jack, don't do this," Elaine whispered.

"I'll pay you two hundred dollars an hour for your time, plus expenses and a bonus of thirty-five thousand dollars, which should cover your tuition next year after taxes," Broman said mildly, putting his ledger aside. "Use the apartment when you're in the city. All I ask is that you do exactly what I tell you when I tell you."

He produced a battered long-form account book and wrote a check for $35,000. "Here," he said. "You're too proud to keep taking money from Hugh Symmes."

I sat back, speechless as he slid the check to the edge of the table. I'd never seen a check for $35,000 before. It was more than Nora made in a whole year, and Broman wrote it like he was sending out for ice cream.

I cradled the yellow legal tender embossed with Chase Manhattan, the Rockefeller brand, gently like a museum object. "Do you know Hugh?"

He shrugged. "Life is an educated guess, Callahan, or Gold, or whoever you are. Everybody knows Hugh Symmes. Real classy, high-type guy. War hero. Served in the Kennedy Administration, always saying the right thing. Look, I respect that. Don't have time for it, but I respect it. Give yourself a break, kid. Take the money."

I folded the check and put it in my wallet.

"You don't approve, Elaine," Broman said, smiling.

"No."

"Fair enough. Some people think I'm too direct. Why do you work for homeless bums?"

"Somebody needs to. Why don't you write a check like that to the Homeless Foundation?"

"Not writing a check for bums."

This would normally be Elaine's cue to discuss the emptying of New York's mental institutions and the start of the crisis, but today she smiled sharply and declined the opening.

"That's a shame. The support of someone like you could do a lot of good."

He reached for his ledger book. "How much do they pay you?"

"That's none of your business."

He shrugged. "Whatever, it's not enough. Here's ten thousand dollars to beef up your salary, or you can give it to the bums."

She tore the check in pieces on his desk. "I don't want your money."

"You want money for the homeless," Broman said, as he carefully swept the paper into a metal trash can. "Ten thousand dollars buys a lot of hot meals."

"I'll take the money if you make it out to the Foundation."

"Too easy. You have to choose. But I warn you: ten thousand dollars is a lot of money, and law school is expensive. Your parents are probably paying. But parents get sick. I had to quit law school when my father died. Somebody had to run the store. If I'd had ten thousand dollars, I could have finished and been a smart kid like you. The Brooklyn College of Law. I was making good marks."

"What kind of store?" Elaine asked.

"Novelties. My father was very smart about the neighborhood. But I sold the store and bought another store and another one."

"And then textile mills?"

He shrugged. "They're all the same. All novelties of one sort or another. It's the buying and selling that gives them meaning. The stores, the sugar futures, the textile mills, the checks I wrote you, the conversation we had, it's all knowledge. Eventually we'll buy and sell each other perfectly. Not yet," he chuckled, writing another check. "Someday."

"I'm financially independent of my parents," Elaine said, as she put the check in her purse. "This is going to the homeless."

"Like I said, your choice." Broman clasped his hands together. "I'm having so much fun. We're all going to be friends. Let's have wine and look at paintings. Angie?"

Elaine gasped as Angie Angstrom stepped out of the far corner, where she'd been lurking.

"Don't be upset," Broman said. "Friends don't have secrets."

"Maybe the Rembrandts?" Angie said, revealing a computer keyboard from the center console.

"Perfect. Rembrandt never could figure himself out, did a hundred self-portraits, Angie's going to buy the virtuals. Markets are great, aren't they?"

It's Not a Fault When You
Hit Him in the Butt

"JACK, YOU PLAY DOUBLES."

I had left Elaine folding and unfolding her check in a chair overlooking the surf, and I hurried toward my match, stopping at the verandah overlooking the courts to mark the voice of Rita Rinkley, whom I had met once at a firm cocktail party in a worn-out room at the Waldorf. Dressed there in black sheath and pearls, she had presented differently than in the white-and-green scalloped tennis dress she wore today. She held a hugely oversized racket in one hand and shaded her brow with the other, her pose affecting a calculated nonchalance that went well with her tanned, oiled, and appealing, if slightly settled, figure. Naturally, she looked more herself on an Easthampton tennis court than talking over a band at the Waldorf.

Is this Pren in twenty years? I wondered, preparing to compliment her on the day and suggest she looked well. Panicked, I remembered this was what I signed up for, intrigue and all. Pren loved intrigue. You could grow up in the Bloodworth house thinking intrigue twenty-four hours a day. And there stood Rita, ready with a racket, happy to teach me doubles.

"Jack?" Mrs. Rinkley called again, laughing. "Coming?"

"Yes ma'am. I, uh, don't have a racket."

She waved her hand dismissively. "Plenty of rackets. They're in the Garden Tub. We'll play Australian while you get your clothes on."

Soon clothed and racketed, I observed the closing volley of an Australian point, played intently by Mrs. Dunnavant, who was a tax partner's wife, and Mrs. Roth, the much younger wife of a litigator, on one side, and Mrs. Rinkley alone on the other. As often happened in Australian doubles, the odd player took the game.

"Jack, you're all mine," said Mrs. Rinkley, as she dabbed her brow with a towel and pushed her frosted blonde-gray hair farther beneath her visor. "I'll serve first."

I lined up on the net side while Mrs. Rinkley practiced tosses. Concentrating on whether to guard against Mrs. Roth's passing shot to my left, or go aggressively to mid-court like a real man, I was caught unaware by the sting of Mrs. Rinkley's Wilson spiral catching me square in the backside.

"Ouch," Mrs. Dunnavant said, doubling in laughter as I retrieved the ball.

"Fault," called Mrs. Roth, joining in the merriment.

I debated whether or not to massage my wounded buttocks, but decided not to, relying on the sports rule against easing blows near the groin in mixed company.

"I'm all right," I called, tossing the ball back to Mrs. Rinkley.

"Don't mind them," she said, "They're silly."

I turned to face the net again, and the second serve arrived at butt on cue.

"Stop that, Rita," shouted Mrs. Dunnavant. "You're going to hurt him."

"Jack, are you hurt?" Mrs. Rinkley called.

"I don't think so."

"It's not a fault when you hit him in the butt," Mrs. Rinkley said.

"It is too," said Mrs. Dunnavant. "You hit it there because that's where you were looking. Now stop stalling."

"We don't have much time, anyway," said Mrs. Roth, in a knowing tone that provoked stony glances from the older sirens.

"Love fifteen," said Mrs. Rinkley, as I stood astride the ad court, bracing for another rocket.

But it never came. Preempting Mrs. Rinkley's toss, halting her well coiled back-swing, was the sound of crunching gravel on the driveway and the arrival of a taxi from town. The ladies giggled and gathered at the net. As the car rounded the slow curve toward the courts, I spied Nora's profile. She waved first at the tennis set, then the croquet players, her smile fixed, her shoulders set, her hand moving in three-quarter revolutions like Queen Elizabeth.

"Surprise!" shouted Mrs. Rinkley.

"Oh—jeez, Nora, no, no."

"She made good time," said Mrs. Dunnavant.

"Mrs. Rinkley, how did this, I mean how did she—"

"It's nothing, dear. Your mother called this morning and said there'd been some mix-up and could she drop by this afternoon! It's wonderful. Victor loves writers."

So Broman knew she'd be coming. Somehow, she'd been able to insinuate herself into this crowd, my crowd. It was the continuation of an old game, tennis by other means.

Nora alighted from the taxi and surveyed the calm green scene, hand to brow, as an attendant paid the driver and handled her bag. Her gaze stopped on Elaine. Nora waved and said something, and Elaine pointed in my direction.

I needed to face this smash-up like a man. Elaine had let slip the words Broman, and Easthampton, and that was enough for a veteran event assassin like Nora.

Mrs. Rinkley, Mrs. Dunnavant, and Mrs. Roth walked to greet her, and I waited on the court to resume our match. There was nothing I could do for Nora that others hadn't done.

◆◆◆

SOME DAYS LATER, I saw Nora in the city. Her behavior had been terrible, and I wanted an explanation.

We met at Café des Artistes, where she was known. She was still managing to write essays for *The New York Review of Books* on the end of various things—modernism, manhood, processed food. The maître d' showed me to a banquette, in a romantic corner of the back room, likely because he thought Nora had set up a flirtatious lunch with a young editor.

The weekend at Easthampton had showcased her talent for accumulating admirers. While there, she played croquet with Ferris, had iced coffee with Mrs. Dunnavant and Rita Rinkley on the porch, and then sat as dinner partner to Broman himself. When not explaining sugar contracts, he played straight man to her bon mots, and she led conversation at the long outside table over burnt chicken, raw steak, and grilled corn on the cob. Eventually, Nora got caught up in her own talk and forgot to remind people she was my mother. Elaine and I sat quietly as she did her best Phyllis Schlafly imitation—"Let me paste my hair up"—and announced her list of contrarian feminist tastes—"Lawrence is a bad boy, but who can resist him"—while airing the vastness of her financial naiveté. We escaped before Broman's Broadway ringer started the show tunes, and walked undetected to the Rinkleys', tiptoeing upstairs like teenagers sneaking in late.

"Did you keep the ten thousand?" I asked Elaine as we got in bed.

"That wasn't the worst thing," she said, wrapping herself mummy-like in a sheet.

It was hard to think of a bad ten-thousand-dollar check.

"What was the worst thing?" I tried to massage her shoulders, but she twisted away.

"That awful Rinkley woman presuming Nora and I were friends. 'I'm going to laugh until I cry,' she'd say, and squeeze my wrist."

"Why was that so bad?"

"Clanking around with those junky bracelets? I hated it. It was so—Hawaiian."

"Hawaiian?"

"I can't explain. I'm a mess."

"No, you're not. I love you."

"Oh my God. Don't say that."

"I love you."

"I'm going to sleep."

Why did I say I loved her? Pren was the only woman I should say that to. I spoke out of panic. Nora screwed up everything. She had spooked Elaine and messed up the weekend where we could try being a couple, finally.

I tugged at her camisole, but she barricaded herself with a pillow. We spent a miserable night, not sleeping and not talking. Tired from feeling awful, the next morning we avoided the main house, except to get coffee and a paper. We walked to the Beach Club and silently baked, listening to waves and squawking seabirds.

"Should I read the weddings?"

I liked reading wedding stories in the *Times*, which sounded quirky and WASP-laden, and always included who'd been divorced.

"No."

I read them anyway.

"You realize she's staying over," Elaine said, interrupting the genealogy of one Dabney Cranston, whose great-grandfather formed Cranston Mills of Cranston, now likely brought to its knees by Broman.

"How do you know that?"

"My new best friend, Rita Rinkley. She left a note asking if I wanted to stay, too. I said I had to get back to work, in case she forgot."

"Rita was just trying to be nice."

"She's awful."

"Here, this is a good one. Father's corporate VP of Chemical Bank, reception on a yacht in the harbor—"

"They're going to tour the old Guggenheim estate. Jack, your mother just met these people."

"That's Nora. I tried to warn you. You've got to sort of, I don't know."

"Very helpful."

I wanted Nora gone, the whole idea of her. For a moment I fancied her dead, done in by a queer disease whose symptoms were cravings for literary fame and other people's money.

In another life, I would have grabbed Elaine and bellowed Brando-like that I loved her, bought strong Spanish wine, had drunk boho sex on the floor, and gone to glory as the best boyfriend ever, the guy who stood down Vic Broman and Mommy, too. But I didn't. Broman's elf-like hand darted over a checkbook, Rita Rinkley's scalloped tennis dress wrinkled like a new sail, and Nora the Destroyer rode up in a yellow cab.

So, after the weekend and a bad exit by Elaine, who said she had friends to see in Groton, I waited for Nora at Café des Artistes. I bet Hugh would pay for lunch. I tried not to be depressed that Elaine had fled, but my own panic set in. I wanted to take the train to Groton one minute, but the next I couldn't even call. Mine was a curious incapacity, like searching for a lost child and being the lost child at the same time.

A hubbub of waiters and the throaty laugh I knew so well announced Nora's arrival. She took the wall seat I had left for her, knowing she liked to face out. My consolation was the loopy mural on the wall ahead, depicting naked nymphs fleeing a satyr. Strangely, the nymphs all had the face of the same girl, with blonde curls and startled eyes, a look that says *Catch me, please*. Maybe she was the girlfriend. Maybe she was the mother…

"Did you order?" Nora asked, taking her seat.

"Waited. Ordered you a glass of Chardonnay."

"Wonderful." She peered at me. "Darling, you look awful. What's the matter?"

"It's just work. Got to get back soon."

"Oh, yes. The law. Very serious. Are you sorry you've done it?"

"No."

"Do you like this—group?"

"Yeah. We're doing great stuff. LBOs, mostly."

"LBO sounds like a car."

"It's not."

"And Elaine, does she like this group?" Nora sipped her wine, and batted her eyes.

"Elaine is realistic. She thinks the firm is cutthroat. And her politics are different. But, she knows the drill."

"Rita was saying to me how these days the young men come and go. She gets to know them and then they leave."

"It's an up-or-out system."

"Like tenure." She shook her head. "The jealousy, the power to humiliate, they will hang you, hang you, hang you."

"The academic world is nothing like law."

With her small closed fist poised over the banquette, she looked for a moment like Nikita Khrushchev preparing to bury her tormentors. Then she changed course. "You're right, dear. Hugh did say that partnership at Wall Street companies was very chancy, but at Butler and Symmes—"

"I know the differences, Nora."

"I was just trying to be helpful."

"Nora, why did you follow us to Broman's?"

She frowned, disappointed. She had probably rehearsed further points from Hugh. "I didn't follow you, sweetie. I called Rita Rinkley on a hunch. She used to work in publishing."

"You're not friends with these people. Now it's Rita this and that."

She shrugged. "I called her and was very frank, mother to mother."

"So she invited you, a perfect stranger, for the weekend?"

"She thought it was awful that I came to New York to see my son and couldn't. She also needed a dinner partner for Victor. She looks after him."

"Oh my God, you didn't—"

"Of course not, dear. He's got some rough edges."

Nora sipped her wine and peered ahead, waiting for the next sally. She seemed to enjoy arguing with me, as though receiving a spanking she roundly deserved.

The lunch marked a change in our relationship, an expansion of her arsenal. Now she used more than anger and withdrawal, tears and illness: she employed active feminine wiles.

"You didn't even come to New York to see me. You came to see the Dorfmans. You just wanted me around, a slave to your schedule—that's right, don't look at me like that. And for Christ's sake, it's Wednesday! You stayed there two more days—"

"At Rita's invitation."

"Touring the Guggenheim estate?"

"And shopping."

"What?"

"Rita's bored, honey. We know the same people. She worked in publishing, did I tell you that?"

"Nora, stop. These are my friends, not yours. Oh my God, what am I saying? They're not my friends. Ray Rinkley will be my boss. And Rita is his wife. Stay away from them."

"Jack, I would never—"

"I said stay the hell away from them."

Her eyes grew wider, and she dabbed a napkin at the edge of her lipstick. "Whatever you say, dear."

"And how could you have embarrassed Elaine that way?"

"What way?"

"You're kidding. At my apartment for starters, and at Broman's. She and I—we're, we're together."

Nora shrugged. "Elaine doesn't seem to get embarrassed."

Maybe it was the heat of battle, but suddenly I felt angry at Elaine, too. How could she leave me alone? Now I sat knee-to-elbow fighting Nora by myself.

"That's catty, Mother. She's never done anything to you."

"I meant it as a compliment. I knew there was something between you. I wasn't surprised."

"So you followed us to Broman's?"

"Jack, believe me, sweetie, I don't have any interest in your little dates. I'm certain you have lots of girls around."

She said the last with a caustic turn of the wrist, as though filleting a mackerel.

"I do not have *lots of girls*," I practically shouted back. The waiter at the next table averted his eyes, but the diners didn't. "I don't have lots of girls," I repeated quietly, leaning forward as Nora speared arugula. "I've had a great time this summer with Elaine. She's terrific with the partners. She chats them up, she supports me."

"She's cute as a button. I can tell she's very popular."

"Cute as a button?" I took a gulp of water to calm myself. "She's not cute as a button. She's a very serious professional woman and definitely not cute as a button."

"I was trying to be nice."

"And 'popular'? What the hell does that mean?"

"It means men like her."

"Where do you get off criticizing? Good God, there you sat, batting your eyes at Victor Broman. You never stop, do you?"

"I'm sorry I embarrass you."

"It's too much, Nora. The drama, the horning in, Jesus, I mean, look at you. You're wearing a hat. It's New York. We're in a restaurant."

She crossed her long, bare arms. "Jack, this is a beautiful hat. You need to open your mind."

"Are you going for Myrna Loy? People are staring."

She pulled the long pin from her hat and removed it to the table, her black hair falling with a toss of her head. "There," she said. "Better?"

"Much. Thank you."

"Jack, this girl worries me. You need a woman who'll take care of things while you stumble along—someone who will make sure you wear clothes that match, cook so you'll eat, maybe raise a child or two."

"Like you, right?"

"No, sweetie, not like me."

I enjoyed Nora's discomfort. What she said was not what she meant. What she meant was that Elaine threatened the grand plan. I could hear the humming of engines, the mobilization of troops, the grim rendering of orders.

"It hasn't been easy, being your mother. But we've done great together. We made our own little family, the two of us. I'm proud of you."

"Thanks."

"I do believe you've gotten yourself in a situation that's—fraught."

"You mean with Pren."

"Yes."

"I haven't promised to marry anybody."

She sat back on the banquette and shook her head. "Pren thinks you're engaged. I have some experience here, and if you're involved with two women, you need to be honest. If you never take my advice about anything else, take it on this."

I had no idea how she could even say those words. "It's not something I want to decide right now."

She tore savagely at her baguette. "You've become a man. Congratulations."

The waiter filled her wine glass again, and she sipped. "Do you love her?"

What right had she to ask? Was there anywhere I could go without Nora following, interrogating, managing? The vast army gathered, trotting forth, arms presented, bayonets fixed.

"Yes, Mother. I love Elaine Marchetti more than anybody I've ever loved."

She winced as though I'd struck her. Mechanically, she began to put on her hat and pin her hair, and then she stopped and began to cry.

"Nora, I'm sorry." I gave her my handkerchief.

She waved it away and got up from the banquette, purse in hand.

"Does Madame wish to?" The waiter stood by, making himself available with a Gallic gesture.

"No. She'll be back."

I sank down into the brocade chair, feeling bad about what I'd said. Some minutes later, Nora returned with no tears and freshened lipstick.

"Nora, I—"

She held up her hand to stop me. "Don't," she said crisply. "Hugh will call about the Landing. It's in two weeks. He's going to ask about coming to his firm."

"I know."

She handed me a Bloomingdale's bag with a wrapped present inside. "Please see Rita Rinkley gets this. It's a hostess gift."

"A what?"

"A napkin holder for her patio. She was very kind."

No Sex for SEMS

THE DRAMA OF THAT New York summer continued at the Landing. Hugh's shore home still stood solid, perched above the Cape Fear south of Wilmington and much history. A ramshackle, hurricane-tested single story, the main house sat below ancient, sprawling trees. The writing cabin and a small boathouse descended to a slender river beach, which gave way to oyster shells and mud. Across the river perched the sandspit island, and the ocean beyond. Ripe fish smell hung over everything, connecting the bric-a-brac.

Driving the shell–filled road to the main house, I remembered Hugh and Nora fighting the night when I first came as a boy, their dark voices carrying over the marsh.

"You're drunk, you nasty—get off me…" Nora shouted, her voice trailing into muddled words and sobs.

"Damned if I'm gonna…" Hugh joined in deep-liquor tones.

Then something crashed, and the light from the cabin went out, and they went quiet. I thought about going down there with a golf club. But what would I say, brandishing a four iron—*Hugh, get off my mother!*

And you, Nora, put some clothes on! Naked and drunk, smoking a cigarette, is not a good look.

By the way, Hugh, may I borrow the Chris-Craft? Some friends from Raleigh turned up to water ski.

Seemed overly dramatic, that scene, and I never played it out. I did peer in on the mess other summer nights, but I figured they'd clean up. They were the adults, after all.

Starting out, Hugh assigned me Big Hugh's front bedroom in the main house, which had the best view. Later, I later took his graciousness to be a show of power, the *droit de seigneur*.

I didn't get stuck on the *droit de seigneur* at first. Coming with Nora on weekends, the two of us, and then Hugh, wandering the shore, crabbing on the tides, reading on the breeze-soaked porch that wrapped the whole of the main house. I thought the Landing was magical, Shangri-La incarnate.

Enjoying the view that first time from Big Hugh's claw-foot bed, I surveyed the waterway at sunrise, when you could sit with your coffee and count the shrimp boats and barges and cabin cruisers chugging into Wilmington. It was a grand view indeed. Decades later, summoned to vet office-seekers over a weekend, and again enjoying the claw-foot bed, I wondered whether the house and the view were a reward to Big Hugh from Wilmington grandees for putting down those uppity Negroes in 1898. After all, what's some choice real estate when the honor of the white race is at stake?

Once, when we were in college, I snuck back into this room with Pren, and we made out with gusto, banishing for a second the *droit de seigneur*, old sounds of drunk parent sex in the artist–slave quarters below. She lay under me and closed her eyes, and locked her legs around me, rocking to the sound of a tug pushing in the twilight on the sound. We lost our protection in the bed stuffs. Pren got embarrassed, then obsessed. "Oh my gosh, you've got to find—the thing," she repeated, wide-eyed, digging her nails in my arm.

"Ouch, okay I'll go back and look, it's not a big deal," I said, thinking she saw in her mind a scarlet A marked next time on the pillowcases.

I deconstructed the mattresses, but couldn't find a trace. Pren left convinced that Mary, a scary wife in her mind, would salvage it, preserved as a weapon against our future social advance. I figured Mary had bigger fish to fry than whether two young people who weren't married had great sex in Big Hugh's bed. It occurred to me that I could have lost the rubber psychologically sort of on purpose, to reverse the *droit de seigneur*. I figured, too, that if Mary found spent latex in the master bed, Pren and I wouldn't be blamed. I imagined sex at the Landing wasn't her favorite topic.

The semi-Yalta conference Hugh had called this time around promised none of the old fish-camp charm. A portentous air blew through the open porches and set the empty rockers moving to a ghost rhythm. In the sitting room off the main porch, Hugh had made Nora a surprise mantle-shrine— her chapter from *Women Edwardians*, a laminated page from *New York Review of Books*, the galleys from *Death of England*, all flanked by plastic holly and tallow candles.

There was an English country-house patina to the presentation that Nora would feel entitled to enjoy. What a month for her—the conquest at Broman's, now back at the Landing. Which inappropriate man to sleep with next? Was there a chance she had snuck into Broman's bedroom between trips to Saks? What a bad thought.

Hugh installed himself in Big Hugh's room, and I bunked down the hall. Nora played house alone in her writing cabin by the water. Here, the homage to art and sex, or sex and art, fully flourished. Hugh had redone the cabin as Nora's studio: kitchen, bedroom, a study with brick-faced wall, fireplace, camp stove, and Stickley appointments too elegant to be spare. An expensive marriage of Town and Country and the Arts and Crafts movement decorated their Potemkin village boudoir.

He'd gone down in the night; I stayed up to take note. Silence prevailed, no need for a four iron. I woke at first light and took coffee on the porch. I was anxious for the day, and tried to get calm listening to puttering boats. Whatever Hugh and Nora were doing, I was through being embarrassed, through recalling old slights.

◆◆◆

STILL, BEFORE THE BUSINESS we had to do, there was another memory down by the river to confront, sweet and painful, the realest one of all.

After the first couple of summers when we were in high school, Tessie started to like me a little, and she made up a story for her friends. She still said I was the summer pool boy, but she made me into a scholarship exchange student from the East End of London. Apparently, I had a good ear for languages and had lost my Cockney accent. I suppose she couldn't have just said I went to Enright.

Over time, I'd grown comfortable on the grounds, running the Chris-Craft, strapping on the slalom ski, skimming out the pool, perusing Hugh's library of moldy bestsellers. The summer before college Hugh offered me a proper job, and I lived in a back room. I worked in the fields behind the big house with Simmons, a local black man who had his own farm and worked Hugh's property on the side. I followed him around, staking tomatoes, hoeing rows of corn and beans, trying to be a vegetable farmer. I washed down the dock and cleaned the boats on my own.

"Guess I turned out to be the pool boy after all," I said, when Tessie drove up after her college freshman year let out. She went to Claremont McKenna in California.

She stayed long hours in her bedroom, still decorated with shells in a frame and photos from summers at Camp Seafarer, where she'd met Pren. In the late morning, she'd come out alone to sun on the river beach. She'd gotten thin and melancholy. Often, she slept the day away on a towel. Between chores, I'd come down and read in a chair at the other end of the sand. Some days I heard her arguing with Mary, over undone tasks for the debutante ball and parties she hated. That's the only reason she came back, she said, to get ready for the debutante ball, except she wasn't.

Sometimes, I caught her looking in my direction, and then directly at me, and then crying. Finally, one morning, I closed my book and faced her. "Do you want to talk?" I asked.

She got up, folded her towel, and walked back to the house. I figured she didn't. Then she reappeared with a wrap skirt over her bathing suit, holding a six-pack.

"Drive us in the Chris-Craft to the island. Should be pretty over there."

I revved up the motor boat, and she leaned back in the stern, hair flying. Eventually she smiled, or maybe the wind on her face just made it look like she did.

"You're hanging out here because you have to do your debutante ball?"

"I'm the Assistant Leader of the Figure."

"I have no idea what that means."

She sniffled a little and laughed. "That's the best news ever."

"Okay then, another topic—why did you go to college in California?"

"Farthest away from this fucking place I could get."

"What's not to like? You're the princess of Raleigh. You have this great house on the river, private island, nice boat some guy keeps up for you?"

She shaded her eyes as I maneuvered to a pontoon dock. I grabbed the six-pack as she jumped out.

"My family's total shit," she said without expression. "My brother left me with these monsters. He lives in Seattle. He just told me he's not coming back for my debut. That's the only reason I was doing the fucking thing."

Her brother Hubie had skedaddled to the Pacific Northwest to run fishing boats rather than join the family firm after graduating law school at Chapel Hill. Hugh kept a picture of him, his Japanese-American wife, and two cheerful kids on the bookcase, but he didn't talk about them.

She waited for me to put down a towel on a spot of sand behind a dune on the ocean side of the island. Sea oats waved undisturbed, and the beach was almost pink with shells. There wasn't a soul, just us and the Atlantic, stretching all the way to Africa. I opened a beer for her, and she drank leaning back, slipping off her cover-up and crossing her legs.

She finished off the first and motioned for another. "My mother does it with your father," she said.

"I think you've got that backward."

She laughed. "You're right. Your mother, my father."

"I've known that for a while."

She winced. "Not me. My mother broke the news last month, since she couldn't stand it that I was actually happy. Talk about a fucked-up conversation."

"Is that why you look at me like I'm a criminal now?"

"I don't look at you like you're a criminal. I look at you because I'm trying to figure out what it is in her, and whether maybe it's in you."

"That's weird."

"No, it's actually not."

"I'm sorry."

"Why? You haven't done anything. I get the scene here now. My dad gets to make you his son, you know, since Hubie hates him, and you can hang out with Simmons, who's really his slave, and your mother—"

She started crying, and then hit the sand with her fists.

"Here," I said, giving her another towel. She flung it over the dune.

"My dad is such a shit."

She started crying again and leaned against my shoulder. We lay down on the towel and she went to sleep. When she slept, her face got all peaceful, and she kind of smiled, and I kissed her, and she kissed me back. Her lips were full and beery, and she sighed when I lay on top of her, looking away when I kissed her breasts. After a while, she sat up and took off her bikini top, then sat back and breathed deeply as I held her breasts in my hand and kissed her nipples, hard in my mouth. She lay down again on my chest and opened her legs when I touched her, and then took in her breath and pulled me on top of her, and then shook her head, and pushed me off, put on her cover-up, and grabbed up the extra beer before running off to the boat.

I walked after her and stood by while she sat in the back, shading her eyes. She gestured across the river; I untied the line and started us off to shore.

"How long does it take for that to go down?" she said, laughing as we got underway. She pointed to my crotch.

I put a towel around myself. "Depends."

"I'm sorry, I couldn't. It's my problem, not yours."

"Maybe I'll just go swimming, then."

"No, you won't, you'll do it yourself."

"I don't know how."

She laughed. "You're really funny."

"Always trying."

She looked under the seats. "Have you seen my hat?"

I produced her Carolina ball cap and she tucked her hair through in a ponytail, which made her look less severe, although with her hair pulled back, she looked disturbingly like Hugh.

"Your hat's freaking me out."

"Why?"

"It makes you look like your dad. I can't take that mental image now."

She doubled over laughing and took off the hat, letting her hair blow around her shoulders.

"Are you really a Jew? Everybody says so."

"You're a good conversationalist, do people tell you that?"

"No, never."

On the Jewish question, normally I would be offended by her directness, and reference to "everybody says so"—whoever those people were—and by the query itself, which always borders on an accusation and has historically led to pogroms. Pogroms aside, it's just bad manners. I didn't ask her to confirm the rumor she was Episcopalian. But since we'd talked about the non-secret secret of our parents' affair, what's a little religion?

"My dad is. I don't know what that makes me."

She shaded her eyes as the house at the Landing came back into view. "It must be nice not knowing what you are."

I turned the Chris-Craft into the current and edged in to the dock. "Tessie, could be you're over-thinking here. You can't help what your father does, and I stopped trying with Nora. This is a cool place, and nobody has to do anything for money, and you're going back to college in California. What's a couple of parties? I'm sorry your brother's not coming, but how could your life suck, really?"

"You're so right," she said, her voice bitterly sarcastic.

"I think you're cool, and pretty, and smart, and you're a good person, so why don't you take it easy on yourself? I promise not to bother you anymore."

I took her hand to get out of the boat, and she led me back to the little river beach down the hill. "I need to ask you a question," she said, as we resumed our positions in opposing beach chairs.

"What?"

"Have you ever had sex?"

Surprised, I considered my answer. I had always lied about this before. "Nope. Never all the way. Girls have helped with the, uh, *situation*, but that's it."

She nodded, digesting this piece of incredibly personal and humiliating information. "I'm sorry about what happened, unfair, totally, and about—that." She pointed again to my crotch, which had subsided. "I was probably acting out."

"I understand. I get mad, too."

"But that's not what I was feeling on the beach."

"What were you feeling?"

"I haven't had sex either, and I need to before the stupid debutante ball."

"Absolutely, totally, I get that."

"You are a younger man, and all. And you're definitely not a SEM." She had cracked herself up earlier illustrating the SEM concept by using her assistant marshal, Connor, as an example. There would be no sex with Connor, no sex for SEMs at all on her watch.

I was glad to fill in. We met every afternoon at four thirty by the dock. Tessie brought beer, and I fired up the Chris-Craft to what became our pristine private sandspit, untouched by history or sin. We did it on towels, in the boat, in the water, frontward and backward, enough so we learned how to make each other feel good. She had this place where I put my hand while I was inside her that made her yell, and it didn't matter, there was nobody but us. She gave me my first blow job, learning as she went, and then she gave me the next twenty or so, which she also found out made it possible to do the thing she liked most over and over. It was great being the younger man.

We had to be careful on the weekends when Nora and Hugh showed up, and I thought we were. But one Saturday when we were on the main lawn of the big house throwing the Frisbee around in our bathing suits, laughing and drinking the beer we weren't taking to the island, I saw Nora studying us, smoking a cigarette and leaning against the pillar of her quarters. She must have been taking a break from E. M. Forster.

The next day Nora, not Tessie, met me at the dock at four thirty. I stood there, feeling stupid holding a cooler.

"Thought you'd be heading back to Raleigh by now," I said, putting down the cooler and adding a gallon of gas to the boat. I already knew she'd done something to Tessie, and I was shaking. I was so mad, wanting her to own up.

"Tessie's gone back to get ready for the deb ball, then off to Seattle to visit her brother, and then straight to Claremont McKenna—good school, by the way."

"What the hell did you do?"

"She left this morning. She asked me to give you this letter."

Nora turned on her heels and started to walk up the hill.

"What did you do, you bitch!" I yelled after her.

"What did you say?"

"You fuck her father! How dare you mess with her?"

Nora looked at the ground, and then the sky, and then started to say something, and stopped herself. She walked up the hill quickly to her car.

"Find your own way back to Raleigh," she said, driving off.

It was a mercy killing, she figured. I imagined what she'd say, coming on like Medusa with a cigarette, stay away from my son! Don't you know this is incest! He's as good as your brother now, oh, but you have a real brother, did you ever sleep with him? Maybe back behind the pool house where you throw up your food—yes, I see it. You can't fool me, honey, I've done it all, and, believe me, you don't want to do it all, you want to put on that white dress you've starved yourself into and then get on back to California before I tell your father, and your mother, too, don't think I wouldn't...

It was all terror and bluff, and she would never tell Hugh, or speak a word to Mary, how bizarre would that be. But Tessie didn't know, she wasn't used to the crazy like I was.

Tessie's letter confirmed everything. She didn't have to say any more, but she did: she said she loved me. I called her right then at her house in Raleigh and told her I loved her, too. She cried, and I cried, but she had to do the debutante ball, and then go back to California.

I couldn't believe she was gone, and it was hard for me to stay there by the river alone, with the boat tied to the dock, the tide heading to the sandspit, and the sound of her laugh in the wind. She sent an invitation to me care of the Landing to her debutante party with the melting ducks, writing my name in a bold firm hand, but I could tell in the family drama it was over between us. We wrote letters back and forth, and I met her in Raleigh at Christmas, and after that a few times when we could make up a reason. After a while she was able to laugh at Nora's Medusa scene. There were no more summers.

◆◆◆

THE DAY OF RECKONING with Hugh dawned hot, heat rising on the stone steps from the big house to the cabin. "Sleep well?" Nora asked, not bothering to look up from frying bacon. She stood barefoot at the stove in a yellow shift, a cigarette going beside the grease pan. "Thought I'd cook you great big men some breakfast."

Hugh pushed through the screen door with his shoulder, laden with tomatoes from the garden. Nora smiled at him and commandeered one, washing and quartering and dicing for her omelet.

"What are you humming?" Hugh asked, brushing past her.

"Violetta."

"Dying?"

"Dancing."

They both laughed and so I laughed, too. They gazed at each other, he from the metal kitchen table, and she over her shoulder at him, and for a moment I wasn't there at all. Then Nora turned off the faucet and faced her omelet, leaving Hugh to face me.

"No paper until ten on Saturdays, Jack."

"Heard the scores already. Braves won in the ninth."

"What about the Birds?"

"Yankees in ten."

"Damn."

Although Hugh tried to be enthusiastic for the Braves as the south's best hope, his heart still resided with the Orioles.

"Watch out, it's hot," Nora said, angling between us to serve up our omelet. She sat down and sipped coffee.

"Aren't you having eggs?" I asked.

"I nibbled already."

Hugh and I ate and Nora watched, humming the ballroom scene of *La Traviata* until Hugh looked up at the ceiling.

"What?"

"You're making me nervous."

"*La Traviata*?"

"That. And you're just sitting there—watching."

"I like to watch my men eat," she said. "Such handsome men."

Hugh looked at me and shrugged as though to reference one of the old saws about the feminine sublime. "Jack, let's have a walk."

We washed the dishes. I tried to keep from humming the opera, but it slipped, leading Hugh to clear his throat in a menacing fashion. Nora picked her way barefoot from the kitchen across the thistle-laden yard, a slow hot breeze and the call of a bobwhite signaling morning's full march. She wore a simple black maillot and a Panama hat, with her hair loose around her shoulders. Smiling back at us, she put on a gauzy white beach wrap and stepped into the Chris-Craft for her morning swim. With a single tug, she started the engine and set out to the island.

Hugh watched from the kitchen window. "How did Nora get that opera bug?" he asked as she disappeared from sight. "Not much of that going around in East Durham."

He bit off the last words. To Hugh, Nora was not only the moody beauty of his dreams; she was also the bright bad girl from East Durham, a place well-bred Raleighites regarded as dirty and exotic, dangerous as a Shanghai sin shop.

"She started in college," I said. "Randall Jarrell and all that. Used to take him records in the hospital."

"Hmm." He shut off the faucet and shook his hands. "Meet you on the porch in five minutes."

Hugh would take the time to shave. We'd see no one on our walk. But this was a man who donned a sports coat and tie on Sunday, even if he wasn't going to church. One Sunday, Nora told me, he put on a tie to pick up film at Eckerd's.

I did enjoy throwing Randall Jarrell in his face, a man worthy of his jealousy, and famously dead.

"I hear you finished out strong with Rinkley," he said, emerging in khakis and the high boots he wore to inspect the grounds. He grabbed his walking stick, the better to fend off copperheads.

"Yeah, it was great."

"You keep busy in London?"

"They work really hard there—at your desk until nine or ten."

"No theater, no pubs?"

"Lots of work. They put me on privatizing Scotland's utilities. The Queen took shares."

"You don't say. Will she hike the light bills in Glasgow?"

Hugh bent over a stalk of Better Boy tomatoes. On the next row grew the season's last blueberries, and across the farm road a crew raised a new house. Over the years, Hugh had parceled out lots to friends for vacation houses, to ward off development. Like his firm, he wanted the Landing to persevere—to remain tended, but not manicured, on the water but of the land, civilized with old books and Coca-Cola in bottles. Heck, the place even had an artist-slave cabin. Could there be a better modern man's plantation?

"I've always encouraged you to spread your wings, Jocko."

"Yep."

He bent to examine the lower stalk of a parched corn stalk. "Don't know why we keep trying with corn. You and Simmons didn't have any luck."

"Maybe we aren't real farmers."

He tossed the ears to the ground. In the fall the doves would descend for them, and I'd shoot with him halfheartedly, preferring, really, to eat the bluefish running in the crisp ocean beyond.

"Are you upset about something?" Hugh asked, squinting over his glasses.

"I don't eat this much for breakfast, usually."

"I did want to say that I didn't know anything about your mother going out to Broman's. I upbraided her for that, don't you worry."

"Thanks for the apology."

He looked at me strangely and pointed down a row of soybeans with his stick.

"Let's talk about business," he said. "I'm mad at Rinkley."

"Why?"

"I told him to work you hard and send you back. Now, looks like he wants to hire you. Says Victor Broman asked a favor. Number one draft pick, he said. Didn't even sound ashamed."

I stopped in my tracks and laughed, or choked, or both. Suddenly, amazingly, it was all coming together.

"We didn't get you down to the firm, because you had your time in London. Things haven't changed much; we're doing more for the Bank."

"I—I heard that."

"Jocko, you know I want you at the firm. Tessie's not coming back, and Hubie's out of state. I need family people around me. Dammit, let's get this thing settled."

He stopped and looked me in the eye as he said it, and then turned to a tomato stake. Butler and Symmes he presented as he would a roadster to the prodigal son. But there was a clamminess to his offer, as moist as the salt air. *I need family people around me*, I realized then I was one of the "family people." Maybe there was a separate table for us at gatherings. He trembled, as I said nothing, stabbing at the ground with his stick.

"Thank you," I said, remembering my manners.

"We're part of history, Jack. Hell, we are history."

"I appreciate that. What would it be like if I took the job with Dudley and Price for a couple of years and then came down?"

New York paid way more. And Broman would let me stay in the Village townhouse, although that could prove morally expensive. At least there I could think.

Hugh set his jaw and squinted into the sun. "Morning's half over," he said, wiping perspiration from his forehead. My prospects had proved a strain on us all.

We walked, and he looked on me sadly, an innocent, a new sacrifice to the soiled Wall Street. "Morning's half over," he repeated. "Your mother will be back." He turned quickly toward the house.

"Staying in New York two, maybe three years, I'd learn cutting-edge stuff, then I'd be more valuable, see —"

"Cutting-edge? What the hell is that? Sell the Queen some shares? Hell, I did bond deals up there on a handshake. Now they're chasing around trash like Broman!"

"You've taught me how to act. I think I'll be okay."

"I'm going to tell you straight out. If you go with Broman, it'll be the biggest mistake of your life."

"I don't see it that way."

"Just give me a reason."

"Well, the markets—"

"The markets!" he roared. "Markets are an excuse for a man to do whatever he wants!"

"I don't know what you're talking about."

"I'm offering you the future."

"You don't think Wall Street's about the future."

"We're on a mission! Broman will fly you around on a plane to nowhere."

"Maybe I don't get the mission thing."

"Make up your mind fast," Hugh said flatly, head bowed. "If you don't want the job, I'll give it to somebody else."

We both turned to the water, to the putter of Nora's returning boat.

Be Careful Down There

IRETURNED TO NEW York, to the brownstone, to think. I called Elaine's parents in Pompano Beach, but her mother said to me, coolly I thought, that she had returned to Cambridge early to work on the *Women's Law Journal*. That didn't sound like Elaine. I suspected she had gone back early to be with Dr. Roger, who had transferred his medical studies to BU. I called her Cambridge apartment and talked to the machine.

As always, Hugh left me anxious. My well-thought-out plan of taking time in New York he rejected as immoral. I had a summons to do great things, righting wrongs.

Hugh demanded a decision, but two more years of school lay ahead. Why now?

I called Ferris at his office.

"What's going on?" he asked.

I explained, leaving out details about my summons to history. I figured he'd just laugh.

"Symmes is an asshole," Ferris said. "The offer is you work for him and make dogshit money the rest of your life?"

"I do get his clients when he dies."

"And a swell office, with the cow pasture view."

"No cow pastures in Raleigh. It's a city."

"Sure. Look, the capital markets are going crazy, man. It's stupid money! What does Symmes have going down there—Bridger, guys like that? That stuff is going away, man. Mexico, China, gone. And Victor loves you. It's sick."

"Wait a minute. There's the Bank, and the newspaper—"

Ferris cackled. "You're on dope, man. Victor's a Master of the Universe. He's the guy you want to work for, not the people he's buying and selling. They just disappear. Shit, I need to get you out more."

Ferris was making sense in his obscene way. I even detected personal concern. "Thanks for the advice."

"No problem."

"Can I still work this year?"

"Offer's open," he said, not missing a beat. "Use the apartment whenever. Need you on Bridger, and there's other stuff."

"Thanks."

"Hey, Jack, not to get into your shit, but where's Elaine on this? She usually keeps your shit together."

I explained things.

"Too bad," he said. "Everybody liked her. But look, I'll send Angie over. She'll grill you a steak."

Everybody liked Angie, too. I wondered, though, if she'd really want to grill me a steak, or would it be like moving the Rembrandts.

♦♦♦

OVER DINNER AND A good chat—Angie grilled an excellent steak—I decided to continue with Broman. I sent back Hugh's tuition check, with a letter saying I was grateful for the offer but couldn't commit. He didn't reply.

That fall I split weeks between New York and Cambridge. I showed up for enough classes to get my gentleman's B, and I saw Elaine a couple of times. My hunch about her taking up with Dr. Roger again proved correct.

Angie grilled steaks regularly on West Twelfth Street, and I learned about her life. During high school, she'd gotten the boot from Minnesota by her drunk father, and lived in the city with a cousin while trying to get into the Joffrey. She washed out there, but danced around town. The next year, when an acceptance letter from Vassar found her cold-water flat in Chelsea, she had to scramble to pass a high school test to enroll. Enchanted, they gave her a full scholarship.

"How much does Nora drink?" Angie asked one day, exercising her pliés from the bedpost. It had started to get heavy again. The night before, I'd cried in frustration, because the Highway Patrol had picked Nora up and I wasn't there. She called Hugh from jail.

Not put off by tears, Angie sang me a lullaby. "I'm not going anywhere, babe," she said.

The next night, Angie grabbed up the wine glasses I'd set out and took them to the kitchen. No more wine for the weekend. "Holy moly," she said, stashing the bottles. "Nora and Dad would get along great. He never hit you if you'd already passed out."

At work, Ferris had me feeding details on Lorrie Bridger, and Brandy, too, who'd moved back to join the business. He wanted to know how they spent money, and especially loved the new Christmas mink for the misses I heard about from Pren. All of it made me feel creepy, but Ferris assured me it was all part of the law, Broman style.

I grew to feel like a mate on the Broman pirate ship. Angie stayed in good humor as I learned my way around deck. "Jack," she'd say sharply when I complained about a dirty, impossible task just ordered up, her flat Midwestern voice growing flatter, pointing a spatula at me for emphasis: "You listen. You do what Victor says, or he'll throw you in the East River."

It became a joke, that he'd throw me in the East River.

Before every Bridger board meeting, I fly-specked files for Ferris, looking for money going to the family. I never asked what he did with the information. I think I already knew.

I noted in the sparse language of the May minutes that Bridger had resigned, and Victor stepped in as chairman. If I'd bothered to think, I'd have recognized the slow-motion crash I helped engineer. Taking money from the cash box to buy your wife's mink and your kid's car was wrong, but at least you should get to pay the money back, not get fired from the company your father founded.

For Victor to bully Lorrie Bridger over this was silly. Bridger should have laughed him out of town. But Bridger couldn't play the game. The shame of using company money became worse than the fact. As Ferris said, when we tried to put it all together, it was like one bad thing told in front of the board brought up all the other bad things he'd done since childhood, maybe up to and including the Japanese POW camp.

"Bridger should have paid back the money and banged the gavel," Ferris said over drinks in New York, months after the funeral, when I'd speak to him again. "Just banged the gavel. I told Victor we'd have nothing, and Victor laughed at me. Victor was right."

For Bridger to defend his reputation was to ruin it, like talking about a non-secret secret. All Broman had to do was accuse Bridger of something, anything. A car and a mink would do. Broman did four worse things every day before lunch. He didn't care about a car and a mink. What he really cared about was that his new partner Bridger refused to move the cotton mills to Mexico and plow up the employee park. Bridger had the nerve to think his company was more than assets. Using cash to sometimes help people was the "crime," and Victor felt oddly empowered, virtuous in a parallel universe of greed, in using whatever means to stop these travesties, this "waste in a public company," as he so pompously pronounced the words.

"What a tragedy," Victor said later, over the phone, in full damage-control mode. "The things people do for money. My God, Jack, nothing's personal. But you can't know people."

But he did know people, and people like Bridger in particular, and I could tell he wasn't shocked. He'd set it up perfectly. I wrote the briefs, Ferris argued the case, and Victor lowered the boom.

I did my job without thought to the consequences. It was easy to cash checks, send Ferris gossip, and eat Angie's steaks.

I was in New York after May exams, huddled over company ledgers, when Pren called crying and said Lorrie Bridger had shot himself in the mouth, sitting in his bathtub. He used his own officer-issue .45.

"Where are you?" she said, sobbing into my answering machine. "Mr. Bridger is dead. Brandy found him. She's going to pieces. I'm going down there."

I took the next flight from LaGuardia to Charlotte, navigated my rental car from memory to Fairington, past the empty downtown to the fading mansions of the now-bankrupt textile men, the last one, Lorrie Bridger, getting laid out for his funeral.

Mechanically, I turned toward the railroad tracks and the old plant buildings I had scouted for Broman's takeover, which now stood marked for demolition. From the parking lot half full of Chevy and Ford trucks, I could see the second shift was still working. Cotton strands wafted over the old crushed asphalt, and an armed guard stood at the locked gate.

An armed guard, like the peasants would riot. Pure Victor.

"Thank the Lord you're here," Pren said, putting aside her drying towel in the Patterson's high-ceilinged kitchen. Casseroles and gelatins already overflowed for the funeral visitors tomorrow. She held my face in her hands. "The bathroom's full of blood. It's down in the tiles. I had to scrub it off her hands. She just sat there holding him."

"Where is she?"

"On Darvon. Mrs. Bridger can't come down."

Pren had kept house and served food to mourners and guests for a day and a half. Brandy was her St. Elizabeth's classmate and Tri-Delt sister. I remembered coming here in college and swimming in the brick pool while Mr. Bridger made hamburgers and drank a Miller beer, wearing a loud Hawaiian shirt and laughing when Brandy kidded him about it. We were all so young, the girls looked great in their bikinis, and I could play thirty-six holes of golf and drink beer all night and do it again the next day.

I couldn't sit in the house. I stayed outside, out of view. Thankfully, I was able to head off Victor when he arrived in his rented Lincoln Town Car.

"I've come to pay my respects," he said. Ferris stood behind him, staring at the ground.

"Get out of here," I said. "Get back on your plane."

Victor held Ferris back as he started toward me. "No," Broman said, measuring the scene. "This is emotional for Jack. He's right—these are his people. We should leave."

I later made it my business to confirm that Lorrie Bridger was an honest man. He had turned down jobs in investment banking to save his family business. I could have told him, after looking at the numbers the way Ferris had taught me, that he should've given up on Fairington and sent the jobs to Mexico. But he didn't. Instead, he borrowed money from Victor.

"You've been cleaning all night, haven't you?" I asked Pren as we stood in the kitchen.

"Brandy would do it for me," Pren said, scrubbing the scrubbed-clean sink counter again.

"You've got to stop."

I took the sponge away and led her by the hand to the back porch, where the smell of jonquils and hydrangea held sway. We walked by the swimming pool and sat in wrought-iron chairs. A single large towel with a monogrammed B lay draped on a lounge beside us. This was a well-tended garden I had ruined forever.

"How did this happen?" she asked, red-eyed.

She looked at me, wounded and questioning. I was a little afraid of her that moment, and I'd never been afraid of her before. My instinct was to shrug it off and push on, but I just sat there.

"Things were good, weren't they?" she continued, demanding that I answer. "All the jobs got saved. Brandy came back from New York to join the company. That's right, isn't it?" Of course, no one knew about Ferris presenting the case to the board, accusing Bridger of the twin crimes of embezzlement and generosity. Everyone in town knew Bridger spread his money around. They thought it was a good thing. They didn't know you could die for it.

What I wanted to tell Pren was that I did bad, but that I'd figured Bridger would have somebody like me telling him Victor was full of shit, which he was. That was the way the law worked. You took your best shot and you didn't worry about it, because there was always somebody just as good shooting back.

"It wasn't so simple. Bridger and Victor Broman fought. He accused Bridger of stealing from the company. Bridger wouldn't quit."

She steadied herself against the patio table.

"Don't tell me anything else." She closed her eyes.

"Do you want me to take you back to Raleigh?"

"Brandy came home for lunch every day. She heard the shot and dropped the plates on the table. She knew right away what it was. 'Daddy's dead,' she said."

"I'm so sorry."

She held my arm for support as we went back to the kitchen. "Don't ever take me up there to live with those people," she said. "I trust you to do what's best for our family. I'll go if you want me to, but please don't make me."

I learned it wasn't so easy to be happy. My rebellion had already cost one life. They never would have gotten Bridger without me.

That night Pren and I set a date for after graduation. Then I called Hugh to ask him to take me back. He was very understanding. He said again that Lorrie Bridger had a hard time in the War, and what happened was not my fault. A tuition check came for my last year, but I didn't cash it.

For months, I didn't return Victor Broman's calls. Ferris came knocking on my door in Cambridge, yelling at me to let him in. I didn't. Explaining it all to Elaine was hard. She wasn't impressed. White guys fighting over money, it's all the same. We said goodbye over coffee in Harvard Square the weekend before commencement. She'd already said goodbye to me a while back, I could tell.

Confused and down, I called Kai-Jana. She usually offered good advice. She and Winston had set their own date for a big wedding in Durham, and they'd rented an apartment in Boston. She'd gotten a job clerking for a federal judge, and Winston had gotten on with his dream venture capital firm.

"I'd let it go, Jack," she said, arranging herself on a metal chair at a sidewalk café on Brattle Street. "Elaine—I mean, you know this, right?— she's going to marry Roger."

"I know. I guess I'm just behind on this marriage stuff."

"Really? You're going to marry Pren in August, right?"

"I guess."

"Well, I've got the invitation."

"Yeah, I am."

"Great. And I'm marrying Winston. So why don't we all stay on plan, okay?"

"Easy for you to say. You and Winston have a perfect life."

"C'mon, you don't know. He loves it here, he doesn't want to go back home, but after the clerkship, I need to get back."

As time wore on in Cambridge, Kai-Jana, always quiet about her personal life, had become direct about political ambition. Ivy League college, Harvard, South Africa under fire, federal clerkship, then, do battle back home.

"Well, I'll see you there. Starting at Butler and Symmes next month."

She put down her coffee cup and sat back, a quizzical look on her face. "Wait a minute. What firm did you say?"

"The firm in Raleigh I've been back and forth on—Butler and Symmes."

"Guess I haven't been paying attention. You're going to work for Hugh Symmes?" She said the words as though it were a death sentence.

"Sounds like you have an opinion."

She tapped a dirge on the table and sighed, as though deciding whether to share with a white boy something from that close-to-the-vest Blount family file.

"My great-grandfather was run out of Wilmington at gunpoint by Symmes. We left with nothing but the clothes on our back."

I spread my palms wide on the table and thought about what to say. The rap on Hugh was always that he was way too liberal, vindictive even. Now I was hearing, for the first time, that the family's earlier gene pool ran the other way.

I decided, not for the last time, to take a pass on defending Hugh.

"I guess I'm ignorant of the history. I'm sorry. Looks like the Blounts ended up doing okay."

"Yeah, if you call not voting anymore and shuffling out of the way on sidewalks and getting that smelly rear car on the train doing okay. Oh, and I forgot, having to listen to ignorant crackers telling us getting lynched was for our own good."

"It's been a long time. Progress happened, right?"

"Not enough, and no thanks to Symmes. My great-grandfather ran the Freedmen Bank, and my great-grandmother had the most beautiful carriage in Wilmington. Four-in-hand. They'd dress up for ladies' day and go down-town to shop. Symmes smashed up the carriage and threw it on a bonfire."

"I think I'm working for a different guy."

"Just tell me this: what did they do wrong? They did everything right."

She had such pain on her face, and I didn't know exactly what she meant, or what to say.

"I'm sorry."

"The crackers could burn us out, but they couldn't take away God. They never mess with God, did you know that?"

"I didn't, but I'll take your word."

"We moved to Durham, where we worked for the Dukes, and my grandfather studied to be a preacher. They got used to not having pretty things."

I was going to point out that Grandpa Callahan worked for the Dukes, too, but it didn't seem to fit the mood. "Kai-Jana, I really don't know anything about this."

"Of course you don't. You're perfect for Hugh Symmes—a blank slate. What did you call yourself, the Irish Jew from New Jersey?"

"I just wanted us to have coffee."

"How'd you get yourself in this mess, working for Symmes?"

"It's a long story, and it has to do with my mother."

She held up her hand. "Your mother, Jack? I need to go." She stood up and fumbled around for her purse. I handed it to her.

She started to walk away, to disappear down Brattle Street into the end-of-school crowds, and then stopped and came back, and stood in front of me, face to face, hands on hips. "Promise me you'll be careful down there?"

"I'm always careful."

"No, listen to me. You have no idea what you're getting into. Promise you won't turn into one of them."

"Okay, I won't."

I promised her without knowing what she meant, and without understanding the story she told until years later, when I put it together with the greatest non-secret secret. By then, much had changed, for her and for me.

Anger Management

JACK, I'M AT SOCCER. Where are you?"

I shifted mental gears to Wardie, while scoring the elusive twenty-four down of the *Times* crossword puzzle. He was using his casual tone, which meant trouble.

"Cleaning up paperwork."

"Robin looks good today. She should play up."

"I know, you've told me."

"Is she on varsity at Bingham?"

"Yep. Fast crowd. Called last night locked out of the house. Sounded like she'd been drinking."

"Uh-oh. Where was Pren?"

"Good question. Robin said the team was staying at the Warren girl's house, but she got sick and came home."

"What'd you do?"

"Took her back to the Club to sleep it off."

"She's fifteen?"

"Yep. Said it was her first time. Not convinced."

"You came down on her?"

"She said not to worry, she's not going to get drunk, run off the Beltline, and end up at Harmony Hall like Grandma."

"Ouch."

"I'm going to talk to Pren about sending her to a shrink. Anger management's not doing it. What do you think?"

"I'm a pill man myself. Prozac."

"Never seen that work."

"Oh, it works. You'll have to lock her up in her room for a couple of years. But she'll complain less."

Having exhausted parenting advice, Wardie came back to business, that bigger loan Broman had offered.

"Like I said, Wardie, he wants to make sure you go bankrupt this go-round."

"Didn't sound like it."

"Next time he calls, why don't you tell him to fuck himself."

"Good line—think of that this morning?" Wardie paused, and I could hear him light a forbidden cigarette. "Nothing is more important than a red wheelbarrow," he said, exhaling.

"What?"

"You know, William Carlos Williams."

"I recognize it."

"The newspaper, Jack, it's my red wheelbarrow."

Apparently, Wardie read poems when at loose ends. People surprise you.

◆◆◆

"Jack, why are you here?" Elaine met me in the doorway of her condo in cutoff jeans and a sleeveless sweatshirt.

"Wardie's into red wheelbarrows."

"I won't ask."

She closed the door and stepped onto the porch, waving at an older gentleman one door down who was leaf-blowing his driveway.

"Mr. Curtis, you don't have to blow your driveway," she said firmly. "Maintenance does that."

He cupped a hand behind his ear, but there was no chance of hearing over the noise. She waved again, and he blew on.

"The old guy's going to keep doing that. Probably the closest he gets—"

"To what?"

"Oh, nothing."

"You were about to say a blow job, weren't you? Don't lie to me."

"I was, but I didn't."

"Disgusting. And what's this?" She held up a receipt from Tire King.

"Oh, yeah. I got you those tires. The Michelins?"

"After I forbid it?"

"Elaine. You needed new tires."

"Nope. I'm also not going to let Adam go to the Dean Dome."

"It's just basketball."

"No Dean Dome!"

"I'm trying to help."

"Watch this." She balled up the receipt and tossed it over her shoulder in the direction of Mr. Curtis.

The week before, I had mistakenly offered Adam tickets to the Carolina-Wake Forest basketball game. Elaine disapproved.

"Sorry. Should have asked."

"Listen to me. We are not your family. Do not do for us."

"I'm not doing."

"Yes, you are. I will not participate in codependency."

"Are tires codependent?"

"Jack, you want something more out of our relationship than what's there. It's a problem."

"Sorry."

Mr. Curtis had dropped the leaf blower and was coiling the power cord as he eavesdropped.

"It's good you came over. I've been meaning to tell you something." She motioned that I sit. "Promise not to judge me."

"I promise. What is it?"

She took a deep breath. "I'm dating Sid Wheeless." She winced when she said it.

So the high school boyfriend was a warm-up act. I stood up and stretched, for effect. "Your life, your decision."

"That's all you've got to say?"

I wanted to say how stupid it was to date a loser like Wheeless. He was a showoff in court, good-looking and rich, and about to become a US Senator, but otherwise, a total failure. My mouth, though, couldn't say his vile name, so rather than sputter around, I let it go. After a bit of standing there and saying nothing, I left for the office.

◆◆◆

HUGH AND I STARTED out working at his ornate Venetian partner desk, old-style. I sat across from him, taking notes while his speakerphone blared, and he vetted office-seekers for the paper. When he was not in Washington or Palm Beach, Major Forrest often dropped by to get gossip. He didn't mind the meter running while he dealt the dirt, since he knew Hugh, being his lawyer, couldn't repeat what he said.

I hated most things about being an associate in a law firm, one of the worst good jobs ever. It featured long hours, anxiety, and constant blame. But there was a grand style to working with Hugh. Most days we ended by enjoying a bourbon and branch from the butler's pantry. Hugh thought he could control liquor, the way he controlled everything else.

I was, in effect, his private secretary, learning his voice so I could ghostwrite his letters. On weekends, he loaned me to clients for golf. In the spring and fall came Democratic Party retreats at the Landing, in which Pren gloried, fixing this and fluffing that.

When Robin went to kindergarten, Pren went back to work at Bloodworth Properties. She announced it one day, and went the next.

She also decided, without telling me, not to eat going forward. She figured I shouldn't either. I ended up drinking strange-colored fruit shakes for breakfast, and for supper eating salads with "protein," which is what you used to call meat. I went to the Club for lunch and ate what I pleased.

Pren starting back to work meant our house took on a different organization. I was used to domestic chaos, having grown up with Nora, so disorder wasn't a problem for me. Robin's social calendar presented the largest challenge. To get Robin around Raleigh, Pren organized carpools on phone trees that looked like the Periodic Table of the Elements.

Work lifted Pren's mood a notch, which led to more sex for a while. Meanwhile, the real estate market popped, and for a while she looked like a genius.

That's when she brought Bingo to the front office. They must have had some kind of soulmate thing going on from the start. Looking back, I guess I wasn't as supportive as I should have been, probably could have expressed my true feelings about our family needing more attention, but I thought we were doing a good job just meeting the schedule every day and keeping the house from looking like barbarians lived there. As for Bingo, he wasn't exactly Mr. Sensitivity, but it's easy being the other guy. What was going to happen to him when Harris Teeter spelled Robin "Robyn" on the birthday cake? Nothing.

Turned out we needed the money Pren made. This shocked me, the constant needing of money. I guess I'd been naïve. I'd thought the Bloodworths were flat-out rich, permanently fixed in the economic universe. But there was no "permanently fixed" in real estate. Also, and I should have picked up on this earlier, the Bloodworths as a family felt like country cousins in the ITB set. Several decades ago the Bloodworths had moved, as many Raleighites did, from smaller towns in the eastern plantation belt, and Mrs. Bloodworth, clutching at her cashmere, would talk a blue streak about how she was forever slighted at the Capitol Country Club. This provoked an eye roll from Pren, but the history left even in her a remnant of the inferiority blues. Part of the Symmes mystique was social, and connection to me as Hugh's quasi-heir had some perverse cachet.

Maybe the rich really are different, I began to think, and the aspiring rich more so. Maybe having money and desiring more made them all crazy. Maybe growing up poor was better. Having no money made comparisons for Nora and me impossible. A victim of her upbringing, poor Pren drove us to move from house to house, until we got the mansion in front of the Club. It was a quest, not for the Holy Grail, but for the Holy Master Suite.

Pren's dad, who knew a hard-driver when he saw one, gave her responsibility for commercial development. She worked longer hours and traveled more, to county commissioner meetings up and down I-95 and bank offices in Charlotte. We dialed into the nanny network, then the au pair network, seeking out Raleigh college students and Norwegian girls for Robin, and not finding perfection anywhere.

For quality time, Pren took Robin to strip mall groundbreakings. Mayors spoke, dirt turned, and Pren framed pictures of Robin holding a tiny ceremonial shovel in the company of local dignitaries. Trying to hold up the cultural end, I sought out museum openings for those special father-daughter moments.

Speaking of psycho rich people, Ferris called once a month. I figured I was on his Day Timer. Eventually, as he predicted, people forgot about Lorrie Bridger's suicide. Broman put Bridger Industries into a Wall Street merger-orgy of failing textile mills. He found himself on the cover of *Fortune* again, as the CEO of something called Global Cloth. Global Cloth was "waiting for NAFTA," he quipped.

Not to be left out of big dealmaking, one day at our normally soporific partner lunch, Hugh announced our first firm merger. He hadn't gotten around to telling me. Butler and Symmes remained the name of the merged firm, he said, and the Charlotte group joining had our values at heart. Next came deals in Atlanta and Dallas and New York, and finally San Francisco.

It was all about Dalton Griffiths and the Bank. Chasing the Bank across America meant buying airline tickets in ten-thousand-mile voucher books and doing business from airline clubs. At the new mega-firm, committees now decided what Hugh used to decide, which came as a surprise to him. In order to remember each other's names, we took retreats, where consultants led us to the New Paradigm, whatever that was at any given time.

I didn't think things got any better for us when we merged than for Bridger Industries, now a remnant of Global Cloth. I complained, but nobody listened to me. We were disrupting, transforming, changing the world.

After the mergers, Hugh drank more. His new partners complained. Still, he cared little to maneuver in the vast contraption he'd made, believing that nobody could harm him. But rivals turned his winning personality into a risk—long client lunches showed lack of focus; refusing to learn computers elderly stubbornness, maybe dementia; the drinking, well, it was on premises, and unseemly, not to mention a liability, and just how much did he drink, anyway? My job was to prevent something truly bad from happening. On a good day, I accomplished half a dozen face-saving tasks.

While sober, Hugh had seen to it that I escaped associate-dom and became a partner. "Congratulations," he said on the big day, handing me a cigar.

I loved being a partner, seeing my name added to the plaque in the lobby with the others, fancy guys all. I loved the cut-glass obelisk they gave me as a token, the business cards that appeared on my desk, the stationery with my name embossed.

Pren fancied the glory less. Her business now bringing in cash, she policed the checkbook, looking for big dollars from me.

"Aren't you supposed to get more money? Shelley wants to show us that house."

I looked around our sunken living room in the young professional two-story we had just bought and tried to become urgent about the next move up. But I couldn't.

"Honey, you need to tell Shelley we're not in the market."

"But you made partner."

"Maybe next year."

Doors slammed. I figured she could use some anger management.

Her mood improved when bonuses came out. I'll admit to some hubris when I brought home the fat kill. We had sex for the first time since Labor Day. I had come to count by national holidays.

I tried to make another new house work. "Maybe if Robin went to the perfectly good public school around the corner, the one supported by our high taxes, we could save more. Not to mention she'd meet other girls."

"Jack, we're not giving up St. Thomas. That's final. Daddy can advance the tuition."

"I'm not taking money from your old man."

"Then talk to Hugh. He owes us."

What did Hugh owe us, exactly? Pren had a strong idea, eyes flaring, back straight, head turned just so, remembering all the country-cousin slights. Hugh owed us a drafty mansion across from the Club.

Maybe things would have been different if we'd had another child. But she shouldn't yet, they said, and we didn't want to adopt. Then her anxiety got bad, and she took pills, and she traveled more, and Robin needed all her available time, and there we were. She cut her hair, and worried about wrinkles, and worked harder.

Things got worse for Hugh, and thus for me, when his father died. Little Hugh went delirious in his last days at The Meadows, yelling about dead black men in the Cape Fear, which transformed horribly in his mind to the River Jordan, red with blood. Hugh sat there, holding his hand, as he had done for Big Hugh, who'd had it worse, screaming about how the Gatling gun kept firing, firing. Hugh felt the terror, too, as a premonition. How long before the river came for him?

All of us went to his funeral. Little Hugh was partner emeritus, still listed on the letterhead. He hadn't seen a client for twenty years. Hugh wept through the homily at Christ Church; he wept graveside at Oakwood Cemetery, where Little laid down beside Big and a thousand dead Confederate soldiers. Mary stood heroically by Hugh in her black finery, and Nora stood behind the funeral tent in her black hat, dabbing at tears as the priest hurried through the liturgy. I wondered whether she cried for Hugh, or because she had to stand back there.

After the funeral, Hugh did no work for a year. He spent the days speaking laconically on the phone, squinting at stock tables in the *Wall Street Journal*, writing thank-you notes on his monogrammed cards. I took care of business the best I could.

Bad Energy

"SHIT." ELAINE DROPPED HER briefcase on the floor beside the partner desk. "Why are you moping around?"

"Little Hugh, dead black men, the year of no work."

"Snap out of it."

That's what I used to say to her during the early days, when she moved back to Durham with Dr. Roger and young Adam in tow. They did everything at full speed then. Dr. Roger, fresh from his residency at Mass General, took a job at Duke researching one muscle in the heart, as well as nurses of the cardio wing. Elaine signed on to the national Dukakis campaign, going door to door in Iowa on the weekends, and then flying the red-eye back to run Greater Piedmont Legal Aid. A harried handyman tried to keep their row house on the border of Durham's gentrified no-man's-land habitable.

At that time Pren wasn't working, and we lived without as much chaos. Most meals happened, and we showed up to appointments. In Durham, Elaine and Roger kept a doctor's schedule on lawyer time, with a little boy stuck in the middle. Things came apart for them before us.

"How's Sid these days?"

"Fine. Had dinner last night."

"Have you guys—"

"It's none of your business."

"—seen the new Woody Allen movie?"

"No."

Her eyes strayed to Nora's picture on Hugh's desk: Nora leaning on the shingled cabin wall at the Landing, hair long and held by a leopard-skin band, her eyes upturned in dusky light. "Can't stand that thing," she said, whisking it from the desktop.

"Hugh's favorite."

He'd kept the picture in a drawer, setting it out from time to time, playing a game of secret solitaire with Nora his respectable mate, sharing a respectable life.

I never pined for them to be my actual parents. I had a father, after all. Once I understood sex, I believed it was mainly about that. I'd see them through the window in the cabin, and all I could think was how happy they seemed, and how ridiculous people you knew looked making love, especially when one of them was your mother.

They ran away not to a place, but to each other. Maybe running away somewhere is what we do. Tessie runs away to California, I run away from New York, Elaine runs away from Durham, I run away again from Pren. And then Elaine runs away toward Wheeless, after a brief stop at Zal. Nora runs away from her mistakes, and Hugh runs away from something somebody did a hundred years ago. Everybody runs around and around forever. Snap out of it, Elaine said. How do you do that?

"Get ready." She pulled her chair alongside mine. "I have excellent news."

"You found something on Broman."

She smiled the Mona Lisa smile, and produced a manila envelope.

Why would you want an old newspaper, Hugh had asked once, and then answered his own question: *One doesn't make sense, but how about a lot of newspapers! Amalgamated Words!*

Maybe you want a lot of newspapers to get information on everybody. You need a way to sort it—Wardie's engine, for example—and a name—Big Data—for investors to clue in on. Maybe Wardie really was an Internet genius, and Broman was private equity man of the year.

"I got what you wanted. You're not going to like how."

"How?"

"Sidney called some people, and they got lucky with court filings. You were right. Broman's buying newspapers."

"Sid called plaintiff lawyers?"

She shrugged. "He says it's a perfect leak. You can turn the Bank."

I opened the door to capture light from the outside hall. It was getting dark, and I hadn't ordered power for after hours.

"Where's the proof?"

She tossed the manila envelope on the bear-claw desk. "Take a look."

I opened the clasp. Every page said CONFIDENTIAL SEC.

"Jesus. We can't use this."

"Hey, you scammed the Bank over time zones."

"That was a clever maneuver. This is stealing."

"Jack, look at Broman's partners. They're all there."

I scanned down the telefax-faint signatures. "That guy, Peter—"

"Robeson. Head of the Yorktown Foundation. And Robert Readwell, Tecumseh League. Look at the bottom two."

"No way."

Enter the Volt brothers. Hugh had called it—again.

She sat down, crossed her legs, and stared at me for effect. Ronald and Donald Volt, right there on the page.

They weren't investing with Broman for their IRA accounts. Despite a horn-rimmed, aw-shucks manner, the Volt brothers conspired to take over the country. Once again, Hugh had been right. National politics, he had said, was Broman's motive—the biggest takeover ever.

"I've been wondering, since I guess we need to get ready for the Volt brothers to start telling us what's what. How do Libertarians make a government? They don't believe in government."

"Is that a joke?" Elaine asked.

"No, I'm serious. What do they do if they win?"

"Well, they don't want the whole country. They just want enough states to put together something like the old Confederacy. It's a smash-things-up theory."

"Like Batman villains."

"If it helps you to think of the Volt brothers as Batman villains, you go for it."

I put the SEC documents back in the envelope. "We can't use this."

She shrugged. "It makes Broman radioactive to the Bank. You win, Jack. You're the hero. Isn't that what it's all about?"

She left, having delivered the goods. I stared at the envelope for a long time, and then put it in my briefcase. Dammit, I probably owed Wheeless a legal fee for his work.

I didn't have to think. I knew what to do. I'd had marvelous training. Hell, I was the best student in the class. Look, Ma! No hands! I could leak but not leak, tell all and deny everything. As for right and wrong, as Elaine reminded me, I'd already scammed the Bank once. And now Broman made cause with the Volt brothers. He deserved any bad thing that could happen to him.

The Grand Intervenor

I WAS GOING TO have to figure out what to do with the stolen papers by myself, because Hugh retired; or, more precisely, we took Hugh for his intervention last year and made him quit. Looking back, that bad act accelerated other bad events: Nora's crash, Drac's reign, my cowardice, Wardie's doom. Our jerry-built order went haywire, relationships fraying one by one.

It was Drac's idea, the intervention. He'd done it before, to get rid of the older partners, maybe rehearsing for Hugh all along. He was matter-of-fact the day he drove from Charlotte to do it. "Meet us at the house," he said, like we were lining up a fraternity road trip. "Ballard rides with you."

He made it sound like it was all about money. "We're taking care of your points in Charlotte," he said. "It's a thank you for your leadership."

Drac had gone officially nuts. When we ran short in the bonus pool, he ranted and threatened, screaming in the Pinehurst cottage where the management committee met to decide who gets what. "I need more fucking money!" he yelled, waving around his Glock.

"Idi Amin here we come," I muttered to Ballard.

"Shh," Ballard said, eyes straight ahead. "He'll point it over here."

Earlier that morning, he'd blown apart some of his favorite decorator pillows and an oriental ottoman. Ballard called High Point to deliver replacements, and I policed the room for stray shells.

Though revealed as a gun-toting money hound, Drac now believed he had exposed someone worse than himself. Hugh was a bona-fide adulterer, and a liberal to boot, just like the feckless president. So much can be accomplished by stamping out sex.

Although what Drac really despised was connection. Bad, impersonal sex was okay, like the strippers he approved on expense accounts for the black-tie parties we threw at roadside clubs for Ameribank VPs. But human connection made you soft, and risked supplanting the supremacy of money. And, in that department, Hugh had erred big time. He committed adultery with zest, and had no thought of obtaining money from it. From there, the rot spread.

Drac had dragooned Tetley, a tax man, to audit Hugh's sins. After Tetley recited from his list of skipped appointments, bewildered bankers, dinners under the influence, Drac presented the coup de grace: "There's hotels, with your mother," he said, looking at me squarely, at the climax of our last tense meeting on Hugh. We'd met in my office and he sat at my desk. "I haven't pursued that."

"Thank you," I said, with as earnest a look as I could muster.

"I don't know how the two of you put up with it," he went on dolefully, looking from Ballard to me as if we were wayward schoolboys. "It was just a matter of time. Screwing, drinking. The failure to keep good time sheets."

"Hugh's not had a breakdown. Nothing you said adds up to needing an intervention," I insisted. "We can call it off, handle your list informally. Hotels are news to me—"

"I'm done with informal," he interrupted. "This is going on the record."

"Drac, you can't do this. It'll kill him. I won't be any part of it."

Drac slammed his fist on my desk. "You listen to me, Callahan. We're going over to his house and you're going to put him in your car and take him. You need to stop being a pussy for the first time in your life! The man has had a thirty-year adulterous relationship with your mother. Your own mother, for Christ's sake! Have you no self-respect? Thirty years. Everybody in Raleigh knew. It's only us chickens in Charlotte who didn't. We merge and suddenly it all comes out. Symmes and Nora Callahan, Lord have mercy! Thirty years with your own mother! And he swears to me there's nothing in the closet. You better be damn glad we don't go back down I-85 and stick you with this godawful mess! You better not try to stop this thing. Especially after that damn deal I had to cut for you and Ballard—"

Ballard waved at Drac to stop, but he carried on in full voice, veins bulging at the neck, a locomotive of organizational fury.

"He hasn't even told you about the deal? Best friends, right? You guys kill me! Well, here it is: you two divide up Symmes' accounts. You take the newspaper, all the tech stuff, he's got the list. And from now on, we bill the Bank totally from Charlotte. Two hundred and twenty-five points a year for each of you from Symmes, and the rest goes to the pot. He can be of counsel if he doesn't cause trouble. A hundred a year for him to sit on his ass! But if it ends this shit, it's worth it."

I remember being unable to move, planted there behind the drawn shades and premature afternoon dusk of my west-window office, where so often at this hour Hugh had dropped by to share some choice news, perhaps how Senator Helms had shown the Robert Mapplethorpe photographs to yet another skeptical journalist. "Shocked, I tell you, shocked," he would go on, imitating the senator's famously pinched delivery, before slipping away for a cocktail with Nora.

I sat dumb before Drac the Intervenor, not because I was outraged by his brazenness, or shocked by the payoff—which I was—but silenced instead by official mention of the non-secret secret: that Nora and Hugh were lovers, adulterers, as he put it. It occurred to me that no one had said those words before.

Drac loaded his briefcase before my incapacity, and I had to think he was aware of the effect, the calculated power of summary for which our profession is famous. Indecent though it was, the brutal words had the power of bullets among the decorator pillows. Hugh and Nora had committed adultery for thirty years, which made possible my position in life; and now, in an elegant turn, their demise made me money.

Drac prattled on about how Charlotte supported our raises, yet we had to understand that our personal lives appalled the new Christian millionaires the firm wanted as clients. Why, for business, Drac himself had switched from Myers Park Presbyterian to Piedmont Redeemer, an evangelical congregation that first met in an idle skating rink, and now convened in an upswept steel-and-glass arena where buses deposited worshippers for three Sunday services, each broadcast over cable.

The change caused trouble for his family, Drac said, but everyone understood the sacrifice to get new clients who would pay for private school tuition, fuel the German automobiles, and so on. And having gone to that trouble, what did he find? Our competitors told these devout owners of stock-car syndicates and trucking enterprises and high-end fast-food franchises that we, Butler and Symmes, were led by a married man who had fornicated with a brazen woman for thirty years, and whose bastard son sat beside him in Raleigh on Beelzebub's throne!

"Now do you think we got any business over there at Piedmont? Shit, we got crucified. Excuse my language."

I marveled at the vision of Drac's country club brood, hectored about fire and brimstone, for the greater glory of—what?

"Seriously, Jack? You're laughing? You're making way too much money out of this to laugh," Drac spat out, reddening.

"You're absolutely right."

"Got your own fucking problems, Callahan. All kinds of rumors. But I figured you out. You've got what they call 'relationship need.' There's consultants for that."

"We don't need consultants," Ballard said. "It's under control."

"You're getting a consultant, Ballard! Raleigh is sick!"

"I don't believe Raleigh is sick," Ballard said.

"You're getting a consultant, or I'll fire you both!"

"Whatever you say."

"From now on, y'all will come to work, bill time, and go home. No fucking! Understand?"

"This is complete bullshit," I said. "All of it is an excuse for you to be king."

Drac and I stood face to face, he shaking and breathing heavily, clenching and unclenching his fists. Thank God he wasn't packing.

He squinted, and I squinted back, remembering Nora on our back porch, bourbon in hand, crickets chorusing in the springtime dusk, reading aloud *The Tempest* for next day's class. It was always the finale for her senior girls, she and the Bard breaking their wands together. "O brave new world," she drawled, "that has such people in it."

Now Drac starred as Caliban, dressed in a suit, ruling the Island our home, having listened to a TV sermon and taken Psych 101.

After a moment, Ballard took Drac by the arm and led him to the door. "Why don't you wait for us outside," he said.

"Goddammit—"

"Jack and I need a minute."

Drac turned away, muttering, and pushed past us, followed by Tetley, who had sat through the speeches clutching his folders.

"Jack, calm down."

"So, you two worked everything out. Great—Pren can buy that house across from the Club."

"We're not getting a consultant."

"Who cares? This intervention's totally fucked. Why don't you just borrow the Glock and shoot him?"

Ballard closed the door. "I fought it, you fought it."

"Not hard enough," I said. I realized then we were really going to take him. Did I stop fighting because I knew there'd be money in it for me?

Ballard sat down heavily on my sofa. "The alternative is worse."

"What alternative?"

Ballard shook his head. "Drac will call a vote and kick him out."

"What?"

"He'll use the hotel bills with Nora."

"It was a mistake. Hugh can just pay them back."

"I know."

"It's ludicrous. Drac doesn't have the votes. We can persuade enough people."

"The new bank partners give him a majority. We talked about this."

He handed me my keys.

"I can't do it."

"Yes, you can. The intervention might kill him, but being kicked out would be worse."

◆◆◆

MARY MET US AT the door, hair teased up, dressed in a blue and gold Chanel jacket.

"Jack? What a surprise," she said warmly. "I'll get Hugh."

The tap of her high heels on the marble foyer faded as she reached the carpeted stairs, climbing past photos and parchment framed on fleur-de-lis wallpaper. The grandfather clock by the balustrade struck the half hour, startling Drac and Tetley, who dropped his files in a Louis Quinze chair.

"Pick up that shit," Drac said.

Tetley gathered up his papers.

"Can't do it," I said, turning toward the door.

Ballard caught me and held my shoulders, glancing toward Drac and Tetley, who had moved to the front porch, I suppose to guard against escape.

"This was happening one way or another. You can't save him."

And why should you, was the unspoken question.

"But the money—it's a bribe, pure and simple."

Ballard spun me around. "Now you listen," he barked. "I'm your last friend here. Drac will trust us only if he's bought us."

"Great."

"Pull yourself together. We'll live to fight another day. It's what he would want."

Hugh appeared at the head of the stairs, hair combed back, tuxedo jacket slung over his arm. "Jack? Ballard? Mary and I are heading out."

"Oracle tonight," Ballard whispered. "I forgot."

I had an urge to dash down the hall and through the kitchen, making a rear escape into the alley and the side street beyond. I could probably be at the Landing before anyone noticed.

But Drac and Tetley fidgeted in the shadows on the porch, and Ballard cleared his throat expectantly. I plunged ahead. "Hugh, we need to talk."

"They don't hold dinner."

He searched my expression for a clue, then frowned and handed his jacket to Mary. "All right. What?"

"The partners decided…Drac told us an hour ago…we're driving you to Greensboro."

"Why? Did I mis-schedule? I'm not on the Management Committee anymore."

His hand slid down the banister, and Mary steadied him.

"Drac booked you at the Center."

"What? My God—an intervention?"

"I didn't want this."

"I'm not going to that place."

"The alternative is a vote to kick you out."

"Let them vote. I've got nothing to hide."

"Drac has—numbers."

"I don't believe it."

Ballard stepped beside me. "Hugh, he has the votes."

"Any of our people?"

"No."

"Well, that's it then. We'll walk out, start over. You boys can run things."

"Hugh, stop it." Ballard's tone cut through the twilight. "The rent's due, payroll on Wednesday. We can't walk out."

"No, we could make it. Who's with me?"

I felt the test of his darting blue eyes, as I had many times before.

"Jack?" he asked.

"It's not doable Hugh. We're beat."

"But I'm not crazy."

I thought of saying *No, you're not crazy, Drac just wants to bury the legend.* But he knew that already.

"It's the cards we're dealt."

Mary put her hand on his shoulder. "The Center's only four weeks, dear. I'll pick you up, and we'll go to Monk and Jane's house at Morehead. I've got your bag packed."

How long had Mary known? Maybe she hadn't been hard to enlist.

Ballard handed Hugh his jacket. "Here. Jack's got his car."

Mary carried the overnight bag, with tags for prestige airline clubs. I wondered if the Center gave you a bag tag.

"I'll call in the morning." She stood on her tiptoes and kissed him on the cheek.

Hugh buttoned the tux jacket and smiled wanly. Mary took his arm and led him to the door.

"Better call the pro shop and cancel my tee time," he called back to her, as Ballard led us out. "They're strict this time of year."

Old Patrick

WHAT'S GOING TO HAPPEN?" Hugh said, staring down yellow highway lines as I dodged tire parts. He'd been drinking from his own silver flask, a battered job with Deke initials.

"I'll bet Ballard knows," I said.

Ballard leaned forward from the backseat and placed his hand on Hugh's shoulder.

"You're going to rest. Meet executives from all over the country, men like you, taking a break."

Eventually Hugh nodded off and began to mumble. "Can't count the niggers," he said softly, brushing at his mouth with his hand. "River's high."

Ballard started from the backseat, but I waved him off. Once again Hugh was back there: his grandfather's vision, his father's nightmare, his own boozy dream. He held his ears against the Gatling gun. *Rat-tat-tat! Rat-tat-tat! Rat-tat-tat!* "River's high, river's high," he called out louder, and began to weep.

Hugh had tended to Big Hugh, at the end a pale thin face against white sheets. After a while of holding his hand, the shouting stopped.

Then he tended to Little Hugh, when the nightmares came. Hugh held his hand, too, until the end.

Now it came for him. Was I supposed to hold his hand?

"Drac's right. Hugh's fucking insane," Ballard said.

"Nope. He's just asleep."

"He can't say that stuff."

"What? That there's dead black men floating in the Cape Fear River? There are, you know."

"Jesus, you're insane, too."

Highway crews had cut on klieg lights to work as traffic careened around them. Workers steered streams of cement from whirring mixers, stirred tar above gas fires.

"Going for food. Nothing like an intervention to work up the old appetite."

I exited on the next ramp.

"How about McDonald's?" I asked, surveying the roadside list. "At the end of the day, McDonald's still offers the best product."

We drove through the takeout. Hugh revived and ate a double cheeseburger. Mayonnaise dribbled from his chin, and his hands shook as I gave him a napkin. I pulled into a 7-Eleven and bought a six-pack of Budweiser. Figured he could use a road pop.

"Get rid of your silver flask and try the King of Beers," I said, twisting open a lukewarm bottle. "You're not going to get anything to drink for a while."

He tossed the overflowing bottle out the window, and it smacked against the asphalt.

"Here—throw out the rest. Maybe you should have done that ten years ago."

Trembling, he flung the bottles out the window. The car behind us sped past, and we suffered the stares of a country family dressed for Wednesday night church.

"Jesus, Jack," Ballard said. "What are you doing?"

"Ask Hugh, he's the one tossing out a six-pack."

"You're not thinking about—"

"Escape? What, we all go to Mexico and jump off a cliff? Want to go to Mexico, Hugh?"

"You're driving the car," Hugh said, struggling to breathe evenly.

"Good answer. See? Not crazy. We don't have to go to the Center. But, shucks, guess what? Can't lose our deposit. That would be wasting the firm's money."

"You're the boss, Jack. I guess that's what you wanted."

"Nope, that's where you're wrong. Drac's the boss. The highlight of his life is taking over your law firm."

Hugh put his head in his hands. "I don't care about that."

We turned off the highway to an old two-lane road into Greensboro. A black farmer cautiously steered a tractor. Hand-fixed older cars meandered down the blacktop. At the industrial edge of town poked up corroded oil tanks, a thin metallic creek, and rows of shotgun houses beside a long-closed mill.

Across the face of a lone billboard leered Richard Petty in a cowboy hat, his black eyes bearing down on the drivers below. "Take a BC Powder," he urged, "and come back strong." Green dump trucks turned toward the county landfill and the rank plain of the municipal sewage plant beyond.

Killing time, I turned on Battleground, the name of the road that led to the town's military park, where I'd been once with Nora. People who didn't know Nora beyond general scholarly celebrity invited her to give a historico-literary address on the Revolutionary War battle fought there. We arrived late, as usual. It's especially rude to be late for a speech you're giving, but Nora did it all the time. I tried setting her clocks ten minutes ahead, but it didn't help.

"One mile from here," she intoned, speaking in front of a Depression-era marble statue of a Revolutionary general on horseback, "stands an old Quaker community. The women of New Garden Meeting bandaged the wounded that day in 1781. The women nursed American and British soldiers alike, sick with infection and cold. The women buried the dead. The women cleaned up, as women always do."

She gestured forlornly at the battlefield, lined with reenactors in folding chairs. "They were just boys from Philadelphia and Boston, Bristol and York. They should have played cards and talked about their sweethearts."

She had choked herself up, and paused for a Kleenex. The reenactors chafed in their red and blue homespun. A couple of guys got up and started to swab out souped-up cannons. The mayor checked his watch and scowled, waiting for Nora to make a proper speech.

Which she never did. But she did rouse herself, to lambast imperial wars, Wall Street acquisitiveness, the oppression of native peoples, the subjugation of women everywhere, evils all caused by the patriarchy, which was responsible for the dead boys.

"What a useless Revolution! Slave drivers and stock-jobbers. What was wrong with being British subjects? Damn testosterone. We should have cleaved to Queen Victoria! She would have gotten rid of slavery, and not killed another million!"

She gave these speeches all over North America. Hugh called it the Old Patrick collection. Was it weird that afterward she spread her legs for his pleasure (if I can be so crude about my own mother) at whatever local hotel he had booked?

I wondered how it went down when she did an Old Patrick on Hugh. She probably didn't. Somehow it was all right for him to make war against people of color, to kill as many Japs as he could. He could mark the faraway tom-toms, don his battle-fatigues, and be in Tojo's face without hearing any claptrap about rights. He could tee off when he pleased, smoke a cigar when he wanted, not care about his bank balance, and refuse, even, to work a personal computer.

Without second thought, for a long time, he simply possessed: houses, cars, yard boys, women, Big Berthas, and no one gave a damn. Then he got sloppy. How could he have imagined that everything crashes down not because Nixon trashed the gold standard, but because somebody says you're crazy?

Hugh and his friends had beaten everyone who counted, but they couldn't police the empire. How did the end come for the Romans? For the British? Too many loaves for Macedonia, a bad bargain with the Caliph; believe in Christ and go soft, believe in navies and lose the air. No glory, no calories, no sex.

On that last point, nobody could afford Hugh and Nora anymore. They disappeared in a big-band tune, a *Reader's Digest* essay, a bed at the Landing. Elsewhere, the battle raged. Markets closed in New York, opened in Tokyo; the gatekeepers slept in London before turning on computer screens. In Los Angeles, a warrior strapped himself in at midnight to call Frankfurt as Wall Street opened.

In a world of dueling spreadsheets, who cared about the indulgent heartache of two old lovers? Turned out everybody did. Now the game was up, and Hugh was my prisoner. Somebody else would have to buy Nora's hats.

"Take the back way?" Drac met us under the portico. Tetley stood behind a woman and a bearded man, who looked to be in charge.

"I know a shortcut."

He opened Hugh's car door and grinned. "Jack Callahan, you know every damn shortcut there is."

Hugh stood before the welcome brigade, clutching his bag in front of him as a boy might when arriving at boarding school.

"This is Dr. Wishener," Drac said. "The director."

Wishener stepped forward and grasped Hugh's right hand with both of his. He looked into Hugh's beaten face with an earnestness that seemed rehearsed. "Hugh," he said. "Welcome to our fellowship. We call ourselves the Center. We want to be your center now, at this time in your journey."

I took Hugh's bag. "Where does he go?"

Wishener stepped aside, motioning for us to follow the woman. She led us to a registration desk, where Hugh checked his wallet, his pocket change, and, oddly, his suspenders and cummerbund. It turned out the woman was his doctor. "You stop here," she said briskly, taking Hugh's bag from me and leading him by the arm down a long, half-lit corridor.

◆◆◆

I DROVE STRAIGHT BACK to Raleigh, while Ballard nodded off in the passenger seat. Adrenaline sped me along, and I deposited Ballard at his house without offering to retrieve his car. I had to tell Nora.

Lights in every window burned as I approached. She met me at the door, hair pulled back and cigarette in hand.

"Where is he?" she demanded, swaying toward me, bourbon her fragrance of the evening.

"Mother, I really—"

"Where is he?"

"At the Center."

She drew in her breath, and whispered his name ruefully. "You're supposed to take care of him."

"Apparently, I failed."

"You killed him," she said.

"That's overly dramatic bullshit."

She slapped me with a practiced hand, hard enough to put me on my heels. Before I could stop her, she snatched her keys and purse and ran to her Volvo station wagon, gunning it in reverse, and then screeching full barrel toward the Beltline. She'd done this before, putting on the crazy. She drove round and round, drunk and fast, thinking it would lead to somewhere better. Whenever she got stopped, Hugh had gotten her out of it. Now I'd left him at the Center.

I wanted to call 911, but I didn't think you could report an accident that hadn't happened yet. I called anyway. "There's a woman in a Volvo station wagon driving around the Beltline wanting to have a crash," I said in a foolish, lilting voice to the doom-listener on the other side.

"Stay on the line, please," she said, and then, after a moment: "If you're family, go to Rex Hospital."

When I got there, I heard from the trooper that she drove off a curve near Wake Forest Road, spun down the bank, and hit a tree broadside.

I called Lowry on the way. He got to the ER before me and sat in the waiting room on a vacant corner sofa, praying, palms open.

A nurse waved us into a conference room, with a table and two hard chairs. A doctor arrived, in his scrubs, from the operating room. He had blood on his gloves, which he threw in the waste basket.

"You're Jack Callahan?" he said, looking at Lowry and settling on me.

I nodded.

"Your mother has a skull fracture. She went through the windshield and landed by a tree. Luckily, she didn't hit that, too."

"Is she—"

"We operated to relieve swelling on the brain. She hasn't woken up, and she might be in a coma, we can't tell right now. But if she is, we will need to put her on a breathing machine."

"Oh God."

"Do you know if she has instructions?"

"I don't think so."

He reached over and patted my arm. "We're using all our efforts."

The doctor left, and Lowry led me back into the waiting room.

"On your knees," Lowry ordered.

I knelt.

"Father," he said, holding my hand. "Deliver Nora and her family from this trial. Thy will be done."

"Is that it?" I asked.

"You can try some on your own."

"I don't know how."

"Yes, you do."

"You know I don't believe in this stuff."

He hugged me, in a quick motion that took me by surprise. He held me in a clinch, smelling of sweet rye grass. Then he stepped back and smiled. "Believe and be strong. I'll come back. There will be more tests. This is the first."

I didn't know what he meant by that, or what he meant for me to do exactly, but I tried praying quietly, to myself. Everything felt so upended, like the sturdy Volvo, down a Beltline hill, smashed on a tree.

As much as I sometimes couldn't abide Nora, I didn't know what I would do without her. She had gone to her coma place. "Swim like Geronimo," I could hear her say to me, at a strange new beach. "Swim like Geronimo," I said back to her, down in the water, and then up, until you make it to shore.

I did more praying, aloud this time, and tried to believe, as Lowry instructed. I said the Lord's Prayer over and over, like I saw Catholics do in the movies. "Thy Kingdom come, thy will be done, on Earth as it is Heaven." You get the idea something good could come of it.

Lowry came back and sat the next day with me in the ICU. We massaged Nora's hands like they said to do. Robin came, too, Pren dropping her off to bring a nightgown from the house.

"I need my grandma," she repeated, distraught, her eyes darting from the hall to the room, and to the propped-up steel bed where Nora lay among tubes and bandages, "Grandma can't die." Even owing to shock and the hour, she looked lost, like a different girl from the month before, in deliberately torn jeans, a too revealing top, streaked hair pushed back, and dark circles under her eyes as though she hadn't slept in a long time.

"Be cheerful, honey. She can probably hear," I said, trying to be encouraging. "Come here and sit by the bed."

"Why did you let her get in the car?" she said sharply, stepping back. "You were standing right there, Mom said. What are you trying to do, kill her?"

Lowry took her by the arm and led her outside, whispering animatedly, shaking his head as she tried to interrupt. It was the first time I'd ever seen him mad.

"I'm sorry, Daddy," Robin said minutes later, as Lowry stood nodding in the doorway. She'd brushed her hair, and had put a sweater on over the top. "I'm just scared," she whispered, hugging me.

"It's okay. Everybody's doing their best. Hey, Nora's going to be okay."

Except maybe she wasn't. On the third day, the doctors got real quiet. At six, they started talking about a feeding tube. One of the nurses started crying, and I figured they all thought she wouldn't make it out. Maybe Nora heard all that, because before they came back with the tube, she opened one eye, and then another, and then grabbed my hand. "Hi there," she said, looking up, her face round and pink like a baby's.

"Have a good swim, Geronimo?"

She smiled from ear to ear.

She started right out talking. Felt better than she had in years, she said, purged all the way through. Apparently, when you're in a coma, you get sober, and you don't even have to go through the DTs.

◆◆◆

During that horrible week, sometimes I'd pick up the phone and Mary Symmes would be on the line. She asked matter-of-factly about Nora. "Does she move her fingers?" "Do her eyes follow light?"

It sounded as though she knew about comas.

When I asked about Hugh, she was equally matter-of-fact. "He's grown a beard, they don't shave him. They're trying electric shock, the milder form."

Electric shock? I found the conversations strange. I told Lowry, who didn't.

"You two are closest to Nora and Hugh."

Maybe Lowry was behind the chats. Anyhow, I began to look forward to the calls. I wondered if Mary felt triumph. Nora had sinned, now she was paying. Nora had fun, now she had pain. Hugh was boss, now they hooked him to jumper cables. Now he needed her.

In our new confidence, I told Mary about talks I had with Dr. Gardiner, whom I had just met; how he presented, in his sangfroid manner, the same pictures of Nora's brain day after day, a medical Hamlet holding Yorick's skull. I marveled at his statistics. Eighty percent of patients with damage here, forty percent of patients with damage there, and so on. It was always too early, and the cases each so different. How bravely he embraced his powerlessness. All the equipment, all the training, the impressive laundry bill for all his white coats, and he could do nothing for Nora but watch. Mary listened and asked questions when I paused, until there was no more to talk about.

"What do you tell Hugh?" I asked.

"I tell him he should pray for her."

"Does he?"

"They keep him so flattened out. He barely knows what I'm saying."

"I'm sorry."

"There's nothing anyone can do, dear. You listen to Dr. Gardiner. He treated that poor Nichols boy who got hit by the car just down from the Club. He'd be about your age now. Janey said he looked like an angel already, lying there. Dr. Gardiner told Janey it would've been easier to treat if somebody had just shot him in the head, then they could've gotten the bullet out. With this, everything seems ruined. But time heals one way or another."

Ruined. This was the word I seized upon. It was a perfect word. By taking Hugh to the Center, I had ruined everything.

When Nora had recovered enough to go to Harmony Hall, I met with Gardiner to sign the papers. It occurred to me that I had delivered both her and Hugh to the loony bin.

The next week, Mary asked me to lunch in the Charter Room. The invitation surprised me, but I accepted, although not without worry. The Velvet Cloak was a tawdry place, and she knew I frequented it. She deplored my missteps with Teri Lynn. I feared she wanted to confront me somehow, now that we were on close terms.

George the doorman met us, his sideburns longer than they should have been, green Eisenhower jacket needing a dry clean.

"Afternoon, Mr. Callahan," he said, popping a Pez, bowing slightly to Mary. "Mrs. Symmes," he said.

"Mrs. Symmes and I are at the Charter Room."

"Yessir. I have your regular table."

I cringed, but Mary wasn't in a hectoring mood. "George and I are old friends," she said brightly. "He's Greek, you know."

As George showed us ahead, Mary assessed the lobby's worn Queen Anne chairs, faded to yellowness from gold, flanking chipped leaf side tables beneath filmy windows and wallpaper with a tobacco-and-cotton pattern both shopworn and garish.

"Some years ago, the Garden Club met here every third Tuesday, isn't that right, George?" Mary said.

"Yes, ma'am."

"But that was before the legislators started living here. I imagine that meant—all this," she said, nodding toward the worn furnishings and moral rot, generally.

"Yes, ma'am." George coughed again, in advance of another Pez. He presented our menus.

Mary ordered a Cobb salad, and glanced at me over half-lenses while nibbling at it, listening patiently to my small talk and updates on Nora. I felt like she was trying to find an entrance to make a point. Finally, I just asked.

"Mary, is there something on your mind?"

"There is." She nibbled more. "It's hard for me to discuss." She drew her jacket around her shoulders. There was a leaky draft from the air conditioning.

"Have I done something to offend you, because if I have—"

She waved her hand to dismiss that thought, and diverted her gaze to a small envelope she removed from her handbag. She placed it between us, hands trembling. Suddenly worried, I had a fantastic fear it was old photographs of me and Teri Lynn. Had I been followed?

"I feel we're friends," she said. "I hope you don't mind if I ask for help." Daintily, she removed skin from a chicken slice.

"Of course not."

She smiled and leaned back in her chair, fanning herself with the envelope. For a moment she stared at it, breathing heavily as though composing herself inf the face of danger.

"I have difficulty believing people lie. I was raised to believe that men of a certain background are good, and don't seek advantage. When I was at St. Elizabeth's, they taught us that. And, also, that you were never to complain."

She pushed the envelope in my direction. I opened it to find the firm's letterhead, and read the first line about how Drac had halved Hugh's monthly payout. Either mathematics or the law had reached a new low, maybe both.

"This is outrageous, Mary. It wasn't the agreement."

She brightened for a moment. "So, it's a mistake."

"No, they lied." I explained the deal, and she nodded at the main points.

"That's what Ballard told me. I thought it for the best, to get Hugh away from them. I don't talk about money well."

"I don't talk about anything better."

She laughed, covering her mouth with her napkin. "In my world, that's a bad thing to be proud of. But you've been successful."

"Thank you, I think."

"Oh, it's a compliment. My husband's difficult, and you've managed his practice well for us all."

"I appreciate you saying that."

"Truly, I mean it. He's preoccupied, self-centered, stubborn, heedless of others. But he's also a very good man."

"It's been my honor. Now, may I help with this?"

"I can't be poor right now."

"I understand."

"Will there be a fight with that man, Drac?"

"One more in a long series. I'll take care of it."

She shook her head. "I was afraid, in fact convinced, that you were in it with him."

"Why?"

"You bought the Crimshaw house, in front of the Club. I couldn't help but think, forgive me, that you used our money."

The Crimshaw house—the name of the original owners—was how she referred to Pren's dream manse. I guess she figured we'd be short-timers.

"The Crimshaw house is Pren's project. But to be honest, part of the deal was that Ballard and I got more money, and I hate what Drac did. Don't worry, I'll fix it."

She shook her head. "There's so much conniving. I don't want any part of the firm now. It used to be such a good and honest place. I remember when the wives were all friends."

I needed a number. I didn't want to embarrass her. She looked at me expectantly. "What I want you to do," I said finally, leaning forward, "is write down on the back of this card the amount of money you'll need every month. I won't look at it until I get back to the office."

I gave her my pen, and she wrote down the number in a firm hand.

◆◆◆

NORA TOOK TIME TO get better. When she was asleep, I said resentful things to her, since she couldn't hear. But I also said good things. She hadn't been a tidy mother, but we always had food, and she hounded me every day into doing schoolwork well. I didn't want to be an orphan, and she didn't want to leave me. We traded roles for a while, parent and child. As she improved, she had to learn things over, walking properly, remembering names, where she lived. One day she asked for her car keys, to go to Montaldo's.

"Nora, you wrecked your car," I said in the calming tone I used when she got fumbly about the past.

"That's impossible, I need a new blouse," she said.

"We can't go to Montaldo's now."

"Was anyone hurt?"

"Just you."

After some weeks, she sounded no more scattered than usual, and I knew she was going to be okay. A composed mental state would always be a relative thing for Nora.

Sieg Heil, Baby

Since Elaine delivered the goods on Broman, I had to face the fact that he'd thrown in with the Volt brothers and get back to hero-ing, although I didn't much feel like it. Who knows why Broman did what he did: money, power, a new thrill? Talk about conniving. Victor was the primo conniver. He called, tempted, and taunted because—he always had! He'd give you money for your life!

I decided to try a stand-down call. It was traditional practice, in the blood sport of deal-making, to arrange a stand-down call; that is, to see if your adversary would settle for something other than a duel to the death. We were fighting over an old family business, why not go with tradition?

I dialed Victor's home phone, the one on his plane. Ferris answered.

"Opie? That you? Called a couple of times at your Club."

"Put Victor on."

"Is this a stand-down call? Like in days gone by?"

"Yep."

He sighed. "So old school. Love working together. Oh, that's right, we trained you."

The line carried that pinging noise from being tethered to a satellite. Talking properly around satellites required skill.

"Jack?" Victor said, dodging a ping. "Are you in Nashville?"

"Raleigh."

"Wherever. Look, we'll pick you up. I've got to make a stop in Chicago. We'll have dinner and drop Angie in New York, and then we can talk on the way to the Coast."

Instead of taking my stand-down call, he'd organized an afternoon on the jet for us. But I was used to being treated like I worked for him. "Victor, we need to get straight on the *Criterion*. There's developments."

He whispered offline, and then came back through a flurry of pings. "Stay put in Raleigh, Jack. We'll pick you up at Million-Aires."

I called Andrew, the steward at the Million-Aires hangar, and asked when Victor would be landing. "Mr. Callahan?" he asked back, verifying my clearance. "He's landing at three thirty-five. We'll leave your code at the gate."

I was supposed to watch Robin in a rivalry game against Chapel Hill High, but I called her cell and left a message saying that I wouldn't show. Didn't like that, but had no choice. Another game had commenced.

Victor's newly refurbished 727 touched down on the minute. He had traded in the G3. The new plane dwarfed leaner Lears and Gulfstreams at either side of the runway.

"Everybody has a G3 now," Victor said as I climbed on board. "And you can't even get on the list for a G5. All the Arabs."

"I hear you. That's a big problem."

"Always thought this seven twenty-seven would be a good investment. Got it when we foreclosed on that airline with the funny-colored planes."

"Braniff?"

"Yeah. This one was purple. Had to tow it away at gunpoint. Helluva time getting the paint off."

Andrew opened the fuselage door and poked his head inside. "Any luggage, Mr. Callahan?"

"Just a briefcase. I've got it."

Ferris dozed in the back cabin, while Victor sat forward in his captain's chair watching the Bloomberg. Smiling amidships sat Angie, her television script open on the coffee table. She made room for me on the couch.

Angie had added another tuck at the cheekbones since I'd seen her last month. That, combined with her newly spillover breasts, zero-gravity hips, and reddish TV hair, meant that she had an almost entirely different body from the original.

She held up her arms, kissed me hello, and looked back toward Ferris, who sat alone with a drink, leaning against the polished teak bar. "Worried about him," she whispered. "It's like he got beat with a hose. You heard Roy moved out."

Right there, I collected several pieces of information. First, the name of his lover. Second, his lover was a guy. And third, they'd been living together. Oh, and fourth, they'd broken up.

"Hadn't heard. I'm sorry. How long were they together?"

"Almost two years. Prison was hard for them."

"Victor was okay with him, and, you know, Roy?"

"Victor made it happen."

I glanced back at Ferris. He looked round, and feral, and sad. Was that the years or the breakup? I tried to remember the brush-cut charm, his I'll-take-care-of-you-kid braggadocio. At work, he seemed bored by his own menace. A deal to him now boiled down to a series of threats. Maybe that's how things turned out with Roy, too. *I'm leaving, no I'm leaving*, until somebody left.

"Something for you, Mr. Callahan? Meursault? Perrier?" Andrew offered.

"Water's good."

"Are you going with us to LA?" Angie asked. She closed her script and leaned back for takeoff.

"Yeah. I thought we were dropping you in New York."

"Going to LA instead. I can do the show in Burbank."

The plane lurched upward, climbed fast, and banked sharply before leveling off.

"Sit here, Jack," Victor said when we hit cruising altitude. He pivoted painfully from his Bloomberg and motioned me aft.

I took the sofa opposite. Victor seemed frailer, his large head virtually locked into the seat rest. Nattily turned out in a cream turtleneck, camel slacks, and brushed velvet Guccis, his orange hair pomaded, he smelled faintly, behind his cologne, of old age. It occurred to me I had no idea how old he really was.

"Lookit, Jack. We need to finish up in Raleigh. I need Ferris in San Diego, and you're driving him nuts. All of this after you set us up with Ameribank and took fees. I don't understand you. This is not a good thing."

San Diego? I tried not to react. It was a rare mistake for Victor. Maybe he was getting old. San Diego was the other Volt brothers deal, the California caper, Elaine's SEC treasure trove. He paused, for a moment off rhythm, as though he sensed the unforced error. Then he leaned forward to play through.

"Jack, stop stalling."

"Victor—"

"Don't argue. I want this over."

"Fine. Leave Ward Forrest alone."

"He came to me for money."

"It's not a fair fight."

"Did he tell you I gave him another eight million for the Engine?"

"Yeah. So you can take him out easier."

Broman shrugged. "I want him to produce."

Andrew brought out pâté and good Meursault. We nibbled in silence. Soon, the Mississippi passed beneath. The market closed, and Victor turned off his Bloomberg.

"End of quarter," he said. "Lots of people on the sidelines."

"About the Bank, Victor. It's true I planted the idea of putting you into debt deals. It took me six months to work it. In the end, Griffiths thought it was his idea."

"You were well paid."

"The first deals were good. Win-win. Now—"

"The Bank's owed money from way back. We'll pay them out first, still win-win."

"And then—"

"We take over the paper, you work for me again, still win-win."

He crossed his hands Buddha-like in his lap, and stared ahead. He never liked to lose, and it'd be jolly fun to have me on the new and improved pirate ship.

But there was this funny thing about pirate ships: the only way you get off is by walking the plank.

Victor shifted in the captain's chair and pulled a vial of pills from a polished teak cabinet. He measured out three with a shaking hand.

"Are you okay, Victor? Can I get you something?"

He shook his head and gulped down the pills. "Angie will take care of it." I saw her watching from the back.

"I need to ask a question."

"Sure."

"What do you have against Forrest?"

"Nothing."

"Not buying it. You see him, and it's like a red flag with a bull. Like Lorrie Bridger."

"My God, you're still bringing that up?"

"It sticks in my mind."

With a shaking hand, he took two more pills from the open cabinet, set them at the tip of his tongue, and swallowed with Perrier from a leaded glass. He closed his eyes as rivulets traced down his chin.

"Bridger and Forrest. Carelessness. It's the worst sin."

"Worse than murder?"

He shrugged. "Less carelessness, less murder."

To change the subject, he handed me a glossy flier with art on it. "I'm buying a wing at the Metropolitan Museum for my mother. Let the white-shoe boys stew over that."

"You could have done a room."

"Nah. That's for cheapskates. I'm naming it the Bertha Broman Wing. Mesoamerican art. I didn't know what the hell that was, Angie told me. It's the damn Aztecs! They drank blood!"

He laughed and began to cough. Andrew brought more Perrier.

"Now I need to ask you a question," he said, putting down his glass.

"What?"

"Are you going to stand down on this deal?"

"No chance."

"That's a riot. You've got nothing."

"Really?" I leaned closer. "This deal looks a lot like the one in San Diego, the one you were just talking about. In fact, I bet it's the same list of partners. The Volt brothers? Little you do surprises me, but that does."

Broman's eyes narrowed, and he breathed out slowly, like an old lizard. "This isn't about politics. This is business."

"I doubt that. But, hey, it doesn't matter. The Volt brothers will spook the Bank. *Sieg Heil*, baby. Griffiths will never go for it."

Broman had to know now that I'd seen the SEC documents. He set his face hard. It was a look I knew well, a dangerous, vengeful look, and I started to feel prickly heat at the back of my neck, as though I needed to swat a biting insect.

"You don't think I take those political people seriously," he said, shifting to his breezy, what-are-you-worried-about tone. "I don't care who's in the government. All of them are the same: big egos, no brains."

"You used to think that, Victor, but now you've drunk the Kool-Aid. Probably gone to some Volt brothers conference at Jackson Hole, where they put up a PowerPoint about how you need to drown the government in a bathtub."

"Don't know what you're talking about. Never met the Volt brothers."

"Tell it to Dalton Griffiths. You can't hand over the *Criterion* to right-wing crazies. You've gone too far."

Victor banged his veined hand against the seat rest so hard he flinched. "Why are you against me, Jack? It's a nothing deal, a favor to some guys."

Ah, finally, the truth.

"Silly me, Victor. My client gets hosed, the country goes to hell, and it's all about you doing a favor for Nazis."

"Don't worry boss," Ferris said quickly from the back, forestalling a profane outburst. He sat up from the couch, yawned, and tossed aside his airplane blanket. "Jack will never use what he has on the Volt brothers. He could lose his license."

"Spoken like a guy who doesn't have one."

"So, what? After you lose yours, we can travel the world together not practicing law. Nobody cares, by the way."

"Oh, people care, Ferris. They all wonder what you did."

Victor smiled and leaned back in the captain's chair, enjoying a dream of the old days. His boys fighting. Angie keying up the Rembrandts. The soundless sea outside his picture window. Maybe it was an agreeable hell, this dream, something he could settle for, a conga line of financiers circling to razzmatazz that never stops, ordering single malt scotch that never comes, grabbing for a girl in red sequins who always finds another lap. He could dance there forever, and make penance to ease the pain: how about a gallery for cannibals at the Metropolitan?

"Angie," Ferris called sharply. "You better take him."

Quickly, Angie disengaged Victor's captain's chair and rolled it down the aisle past me and Ferris, and through drawn curtains. I could hear Victor's breathing slow, and then he moaned a calm, low moan, in rhythm to a hissing oxygen machine.

"It comes over him late in the day," Ferris said.

"What did they do to him?"

"He's got a zirconium spine. Cleveland Clinic."

"Is he in pain?"

"More like sadness. Angie's the only one he'll let near him."

Two limousines met the plane at Victor's private Orange County airport. Victor and Ferris huddled, and then took the first, motioning for Angie and me to take the second.

"You haven't called," she said, arranging herself beside me in the back.

"I've had this work thing."

She turned and smiled her coquette's smile, made cockeyed by surgery; but, there it was, her coquette smile, circa 1980. "You're single again, I hear."

"More or less."

She looked up for a kiss, but I didn't. She patted me on the knee.

"Victor would've taken care of us."

"Maybe for a while, then, kaboom!"

I remembered West Twelfth Street, the brownstone apartment once reserved for me, the building now deeded to Angie. I felt the allure of her newly configured self, the expertly appointed body, celebrity-hood worth many millions.

"Do what he wants," she whispered. "It's easier."

"I don't want to talk about him."

She sat back and put on fresh lipstick. "I'm trying to help the two of you get through this."

"Why don't you help yourself?"

She sighed, "How?"

"To start with, stop pumping his stocks. You know it's all lies."

"But if I say a thing on TV, it's true for a second. That's fame, not lying."

"You'll go to jail."

"I don't want to go to jail."

"Then retire. Teach art history."

"I can't. I'm afraid if I quit, he'll throw me in the East River, and then I really will be dead."

The limo turned onto the firm gravel of Victor's estate road, up the canyon to the top where Rancho del Rey stood.

"I have to get him settled," she whispered, as the driver opened our door. "Then I'll be in my room, the one at the end."

From the top of the ridge, with a good moon, I saw the Pacific breakers cresting miles beyond against a curving shore. Stars shined dully above the horizon, and below, lights in crescendo north to Los Angeles. In the morning, Victor's horses would run in the meadow, perfect full-chested Arabians kept for one of his daughters by one of his wives. Through the piazza, down a worn marble hall, stood my room, done in somber Spanish décor, with gold fixtures in the bath and a conquistador's bed—but I wouldn't use it, in favor of the one at the end of the hall where Angie stayed, arranged by Victor for my convenience.

From Victor's point of view, if you wanted Jack Callahan to do something, first get him laid. Let the Queen of the Pirates do her thing—that's what Broman and Ferris thought. Poor Jack Callahan, he has that *weakness*.

But did he have to? Angie and I could both use a warm body. But that's really all it was, and Victor was scheming to get me off track. Jack Callahan has a weakness for the ladies? Not tonight.

"Driver, I need to get to LAX for the red-eye."

I saw the red end of Ferris's Italian cigarillo on the near porch. He'd been watching my deliberations.

"Bad move, Jack. LAX is two hours away."

"Not staying the night."

"Angie will be disappointed."

"No, she won't." I sat down beside him. He offered me a drag on the cigarillo. "Listen, I'm sorry about you and Roy."

He took a slow puff and flicked ash into the drive. "You knew?"

"Angie told me."

He shrugged. "I guess it's not a secret."

"Well, like I said, I'm sorry."

He laughed softly. "Thanks. You'd like him—southern like you, younger, a real smartass. I miss him."

"Yeah, been there recently myself." He looked at me quizzically.

Before I could get into the Teri Lynn story, the limo started up, and headlights framed us. "Look," I said, shielding my eyes, "When you're in town, maybe you could bring a friend over. We could hang out."

He glanced up, amused. "Me and my boyfriend meet you and Elaine at your Club?"

"We wouldn't go to the Club."

"Let me think about that one." He stood up and stuck out his hand. "See you soon, when Forrest runs out of money."

"Very funny. Hey, listen—did you know about the Volt brothers?"

He shook his head no. Ferris wasn't a Volt brothers kind of guy.

I got into the limo, and remembered suddenly how much I hated the red-eye. Reading my mind, Ferris gestured again at the room down the hall, where Angie waited. Then he waved and tossed his spent cigarillo toward the tumbling surf below, as though the last twenty years hadn't happened.

Nut-Cutting Time

I'M TRYING TO GET this. He flew to New York, and then here, and then back to New York, and then to California for dinner?"

"No, straight to California. Angie did her show from LA. The point is—"

"And you came back on the red-eye?"

The logistics of Victor's jet fascinated Wardie. I was afraid soon he'd want a jet himself, which would lead to a difficult conversation about how he couldn't afford one, and then some champion fancy-guy pouting.

What we needed to discuss was a topic I'd never imagined having to bring up: losing the *Criterion* to the Volt brothers.

"There's some important Broman news."

"What, other than if I don't pay on time he'll screw me?"

"It's something else." I took a deep breath. "We found out through some sources that Broman is partnering with the Volt brothers. If Broman takes over the paper, it will likely be with them."

Wardie sat down heavily in his office chair. He put his face in his hands and sat perfectly still. "I need to understand this," he said quietly. "The Volt brothers could own the *Criterion*?"

"Yes."

"Why didn't you tell me?"

"Just found out."

"That's why you didn't want me to take the extra eight million?"

"I don't want you to take Broman's money, period."

He paced, whispering to himself. Slowly, he closed the office door with his name on it to the clatter of the newsroom.

"We've got to finish the Engine. We're close to the patent."

"You're bleeding cash every month."

"You've got to get me more time."

"I don't know how."

"Then figure it out. It's what our families do. The Symmes and the Forrests. It's nut-cutting time."

Nut-cutting time—a farm expression known to every good southern boy. I bet that's what Big Hugh said to Old Man Forrest, when he rode back from Wilmington.

End Times!

◆◆◆

NORA SAT UP IN bed and twirled her hair. I'd finished the Sunday obituaries. "You seem preoccupied, dear," she said, squinting to inspect me.

"I got some bad news."

"What?"

"The Bank fired Billy Arnold. It's my fault."

On top of everything else, Griffiths had kept his word about firing Billy, another casualty on my conscience. Grounds: unauthorized use of customer accounts. Made it sound like he was embezzling.

"I imagine the Bank fires people all the time."

"This is different. I got Billy to do something risky to help Wardie Forrest. The president of the Bank—"

"Dolly Griffiths' husband."

"Yes—he told me Billy was going to get fired for it. I didn't believe him. What's Billy going to do now? He's never worked anywhere else."

She arranged the *Times Book Review* on top. She didn't seem worried.

"I think Lowry is already working on it."

"You knew about this?"

"I hear they're making a new bank. It will be for the people."

"What people?"

"Dear, there are higher purposes at work. Start listening to the universe."

Being in a coma had opened Nora to the universe, apparently. She now had visions, often involving Lowry. She believed him to be a time traveler at work in Raleigh, saving clueless white people from themselves.

"Is Raleigh the new Lost Colony?" Sir Walter Raleigh was a character in one of her visions.

"Make fun if you wish. But you're at the center of Lowry's energy."

Her vision featured Lowry as the Lumbee chief who led the original Lost Colony—Sir Walter Raleigh's people—to safety in 1588. Queen Elizabeth had the Spanish Armada to deal with, so Lowry got the call.

"'We are all one,' is what he said to the settlers."

"Please don't tell that story to Dr. Gardiner."

"I won't, dear. I don't want to cause trouble."

◆◆◆

AT NORA'S HOUSE, I caught up with Lowry while he and Juan were working with a construction crew on the swimming pool. Lowry suggested it as the confidence-builder needed to coax Nora out of Harmony Hall.

"Besides," Lowry had said. "I can hook up that spring."

Lowry usually started out with something crazy, and then brought the purpose in view. On that score, I have to say the pool worked. He had cleared most of the lot and added a new driveway, which made an L shape around the back that nestled in the pool: totally retro, kidney-shaped, with a low diving board. They painted the bottom a metallic gray, with dolphins along the side, and had up two-by-six wooden molds for the concrete deck. He was adding patio doors and a screen porch off the old kitchen, which opened the back to the deck. The effect reoriented the whole house to the back, and woods, and away from the busy front street and the Beltline.

"Jeez, Lowry, the place looks brand new," I said, trying to ballpark the cost in my head.

"That's the point, Jack, making it new. How are we doing on the junk?"

The junk, as Lowry called it, were the memorabilia accumulated in the house since 1964, which Lowry had discovered in the makeover. Years of *Life* magazines, obituaries, and the ever-present Broadway show bills beckoned.

The junk made its way to the dump. I left seven versions of *Death of England,* Volume II, tied up in banker boxes.

"She's going to freak," I said.

"No, she won't. Don't tell her it's gone."

Lowry came down on Nora's side in the confront-your-past question. He wanted the past gone, thrown out with the junk, and had it out with Gardiner on the point, actually raising his voice. I guess he figured he could weigh in, since he took her to AA and all.

"You have to live your life in the present," Lowry had said firmly, when I asked him why Nora didn't have to go through the memory box anymore. Gardiner had called to ask whether he could strike Lowry from the approved Harmony Hall guest list, for medical reasons. I told him he had to be kidding; Lowry should be running the place.

"Got one more thing I want to do," Lowry said.

"What's that?"

"Your old room. I want to take out that long window and connect a deck to the pool area." He waved his arms expansively. "It was Juan's idea, opens the whole side."

So now Juan was my architect. He waved at us and pointed to the room, then paced the perimeter of the new deck.

"Sure, Lowry, you and Juan go ahead. It probably helps the resale value."

"I was thinking it made for a better house."

"That, too."

He grinned and clomped off through the red dirt.

"Oh, Jack, one more thing," he said, turning back.

"Don't tell me, another wing?"

He laughed. "No. Check your messages. I saw Kai-Jana Blount and she said she was trying to get you. It's important."

◆◆◆

KAI-JANA HAD INDEED CALLED, inviting me to coffee at exactly 10:40 a.m., which was in fifteen minutes. Her schedule ran this way, because she had just announced for attorney general in the special election. The incumbent had to resign, since Wardie had caught him with call girls.

She picked Café Quarto, which she knew was my favorite, and I imagined coffee would have to do with me giving her money. A phone call could have handled that, but it's always nice to be asked in person.

Elaine had called earlier in the week to discuss Kai-Jana and her destiny to rule, alongside other right-thinking women. We also touched on money for Sid's Senate campaign, which Elaine now apparently ran, as girlfriend-in-charge. She'd called from the plane, dodging pings like a pro. They were jetting to the Coast to see Hollywood donors. Sid's campaign had acquired a Lear jet. I didn't have the heart to tell Wardie.

Kai-Jana sat in the corner, checking her messages on a new state-of-the-art Blackberry. "Jack," she said, rising for an air kiss. "Lipstick, sorry. Thanks for coming. Everything's short notice these days."

I hadn't seen her out of judge's robes for a while. She'd been to the gym, and sported a trim, athletic look, toned-up arms in view as she removed her jacket. She'd kept the red-tinged short haircut, which set off her short-waisted cherry suit, and a pair of swanky heels with shiny black bottoms like I'd seen movie stars wear on talk shows. Must be the fundraising outfit.

"You look great," I said, sitting down across from her, but at an angle so that she could case the room and be seen. Hugh always sat that way, courtesy to the candidate.

"Oh stop. I'm giving a speech at the Raleigh Women's Club."

"Going to tell them they're tools of the ruling class?"

She laughed. "Nope, more like women standing together."

"Good move. Listen, I'm happy to max out for you, don't need to waste valuable face time on little old me—just give my cell to your finance person. Although I'm always glad to have coffee at my favorite place."

She leaned across the table and looked furtively for spies, perhaps the tattooed barista, or the college students doing their homework. "It's not that, but, really, thank you. I'll get that note to Chip, he'll call." She paused to write in her date book.

"Okay, if not money, then what?"

She sighed and briefly closed her eyes. "I need a big favor from you."

"Really?"

"I need you to arrange a fundraiser for me."

263

"Oh, okay. You want me to get you a fundraiser? Really? It's not my thing, but I can set you up. All you need in this town is a big house, and a caterer, and free booze, and you can't keep the power whores away. Really, there's a whole bunch of people you and I both know and can't stand who like doing that shit. I can hook you up. Happy to sign on to a list later, but I really don't—"

She put her hand briefly over mine as though to quiet me down. It occurred to me that I was saying objectionable things really fast. The truth is, I was out of sorts with her, off rhythm. Maybe I hadn't really processed the Teri Lynn thing. We'd never spoken of it. I couldn't exactly thank her. Neither could I thank her for Broman. Technically, she still had that case as a judge. And though I don't go looking for bad motives, some other, more suspicious person might detect the whiff of a quid pro quo in the usual please and thank you.

She kept her hand on mine, cool and relaxed, as though I were one of her kids. "Is everything okay?"

I leaned back and took a couple of deep breaths, like they taught in anger management. "Sorry. I think I'm embarrassed by the Teri Lynn stuff, and the position you were in, you know. I don't know what to say."

She held up her hand. "Don't need to go there. It's done, past, you made it out."

"You're so right. Thanks."

"We're in today, Eastern Standard Fucking Time, as your friend Ferris said recently. Elaine gave me the play by play. Some scene. I think I missed out, not going into private practice."

I laughed, the best laugh I'd had in weeks. She had me. She was going to be a good candidate.

"Okay, so what kind of fundraiser? You must be thinking of something in particular. Chip can line up the usual stuff in his sleep."

She nodded, and then closed her eyes. "This is really hard for me."

"I'll just put it right out there. I can't get Mick Jagger to play."

She laughed, and then tried again.

"Okay. I need you to ask Hugh Symmes to put on a fundraiser for me at his house."

She sat back, having said it. I saw before us a tapestry unspool—the Blounts, proud, ruined warriors, vowing to have their day against the Symmes Machine and the bland-faced white men who killed their friends and burned them out of Wilmington, and then covered it up; Kai-Jana, the hope of the third generation, her daddy's brilliant girl, part freedom fighter, part judge, part wife and working mom, now called to run the gauntlet of a statewide race a little before she's ready, and far from the friendly wards of Durham, elbow to elbow against seasoned white men who would take her out if they could.

And that was only the first round, the Democratic primary. She'd face real race-baiters in the general, Republicans schooled by Helms and company. They wouldn't need to ride with Waddell; they'd run television ads about the ACLU and a burning flag, and sex offenders in your neighborhood, and a bad picture of Kai-Jana in her college afro beside a black man convicted of murder whom she wouldn't let the state put to death.

So, what did my friend now need in the worst way? The blessing of Hugh Symmes and the endorsement of the *Criterion*.

The Symmes Machine had been in the repair shop for a while, and Hugh was holed up at the Landing, recovering from the Center, something Kai-Jana didn't know. What she hoped for, though, I could deliver. I'd vouch for her, Hugh would go along, and Wardie would endorse. The early fundraiser at the Symmes house would preempt the field. Well played, Your Honor.

"Must have been a hard thing to ask."

"Doing a lot of hard things."

"What would the Reverend Blount say about asking Hugh Symmes for a favor?"

She bowed her head. Clearly, she'd thought about it. "My grandfather always said life is for the living. That's you and me, Jack."

Another great answer. This was going to be fun.

"Okay, we'll put together the deal. I'll work it through Mary."

"Mary?"

"Hugh's wife. She runs the fundraisers. She'll probably be at the Raleigh Women's Club today. Walk up and say hey to her. I'll call later."

"Perfect. Jack, thank you."

"Glad to be on the team."

"One more thing."

"There's more?"

"I want you to introduce me."

"What? You don't want that. There are better people, what about—"

"Jack, you crack me up sometimes. There are no better people. You're Jack Callahan, Butler and Symmes partner, defending the *Criterion* in the fight of its life. Over coffee, you snapped your fingers, and I get a fundraiser at the home of the most powerful Democrat in the state."

"You make it sound like a bigger deal than it is."

"Jack, face facts. You move in all the right circles."

A Momentary Release of Chemicals

"HELLO, DADDY? I'M CHECKING in like you told me," Robin said brightly, cracking open the door of my room at the Club. I had taken my briefcase fully loaded for the weekend, and had just begun to dip in.

It was my turn to be on parent duty, Pren having gone to Wrightsville Beach, I assumed with Bingo. Robin's behavior, like Wardie's financial condition, had deteriorated over the last months, caused, or worsened, I feared, by Pren and I hardening into the divorce. Adverse television coverage didn't help. Trying to cope, Pren and I had adopted cooperative parenting techniques to combat sneaking out, alarming wardrobe choices, and suspected drinking. We demanded a strict curfew, check-in routine for nights out, and a bed-time breath test. Still, when one of us travelled, she played divide and conquer like a pro.

Some of Robin's older friends were driving now, and they went out on the town as much as high school sophomores could. Under pressure, I needed to take quick stock of Robin's get-up, which had changed radically even in a week. Since I last saw her on Wednesday, her hair had gone to electric yellow streaks, which contrasted with a new rock-star leather outfit, all black. Her top missed her skirt by several inches, and I caught sight of a belly button ring, a startling addition.

"What's that?" I said, glancing at her midriff.

"Mom said I could do it."

"No way."

"She said she was going to get one."

"Ridiculous. Take that thing off now. You look like a gypsy."

She stared and tossed her yellow mane. Outside, I saw a Chevy Blazer filled with girls I had known since little girlhood, who had somehow made themselves unrecognizable in similar ways, orange hair, green hair, colors not found in nature; rings hooked to places rings shouldn't be—noses, eyebrows, tongues even, which provoked more questions, such as, how does one eat with a tongue-ring? The occasional flower peeked from under a sleeve, or at the ankle, tattooed in technicolor. Pren had expressly forbidden tattoos—but had she glossed over the body piercing discussion?

"I can't take it off. I'd have to have surgery."

I was unfamiliar with the portability of belly button rings, whether you actually had to have surgery to remove them, or whether they clipped on and off, like earrings. I was mad that Pren and I weren't dealing with Robin together right now, but whose fault was that?

"I don't know about surgery—but you need to get that off before you go anywhere in public."

"My curfew's two o'clock," she said, ignoring me, "and I'll check in."

"It's midnight, and you can't—"

"My mom said –"

"You're not going anywhere," I yelled, suddenly seeing red. I grabbed her arm as she turned to clack down the steps.

"Ow, you're hurting me."

"Come back into this house, now!"

"This isn't a house!" she yelled back. "This is the Club!"

Her friends laughed and pointed at us from the Chevy Blazer, music at full volume, cigarette smoke seeping from the cracked windows.

"Temporary quarters. I'm working with Lowry to fix up the ranch-palace. Now get in here, dammit."

"Let go my arm! You can't grab me! It's abuse. I'll call Social Services!"

I let go. My hand had left marks, and she rubbed her arm, staring at the finger trails.

She was right about one thing. The Club wasn't a house.

The drama of how Robin's calm and sheltered life took a downward turn wasn't her drama. She shouldn't have to live in the grand devolution, the history of Nora and Hugh, and the Cape Fear River, and Drac and Ballard and dead Lorrie Bridger, and Ferris and Broman dodging pings in space. She was our beautiful daughter, Pren's and mine, and the last year had been a mess. Nora almost died on the Beltline, and then fought off the silver flask; Pren and I blundered through divorce; I bobbled around in a hot tub with Teri Lynn, somehow on television for Robin to watch, while she got up at dawn to play soccer and try to grow up. I could always say a year was a short time, and next year we'll have worked through, but Robin couldn't. For her a year was forever.

The girls beeped the horn, and she rubbed her arm and waved back at them. Then they made some hooting sound and pumped their arms in unison. "My mom said I could spend the night at Kim's and stay out until two o'clock," she said. "You can call Kim's mom."

"Kim who?"

She wrote a number on a scrap of paper from her purse. "Here," she said. "She's a soccer mom. The team's having a sleepover."

I folded the scrap of paper, helpless at the sleepover alibi, which would allow her to do anything she wanted. "You better not be going to that club downtown. You're fifteen."

"No one drinks. We just dance."

"You're not—who's that driving?"

The driver waved at me—Melissa, maybe, from the team? She tugged at Chanel bubble sunglasses enmeshed in her hair.

"I'm going now."

"You're positive your mother checks out on this?"

"My mom's gone to the beach. Why don't you call her there?"

We had a rule about calling on the off weekend. She'd probably ducked out to a party with Bingo.

"You come by here in the morning," I said, as evenly as I could. "Nine o'clock sharp."

"Ten-four, Chief," she said, saluting.

On the weekends I used to worry about the banks being closed and Wardie running out of money. Now, I have to worry about Robin gallivanting in Raleigh dressed like a tart. To keep busy, I spread out papers on my small desk below the window overlooking the first tee, and tried to concentrate on spreadsheets. Maybe everything would turn out after all. Maybe Wardie wouldn't run out of money. Maybe the Chevy Blazer girls would call Adam Marchetti and his friends, and get some high school boy protection in the downtown bars, or wherever they were really going. I dialed Robin at hour intervals, getting her singsong answering message every time. I'd resisted dialing more.

As I reached for the cell phone again, it rang in my hand. Robin's number, finally.

"Honey?"

"It's—Mister Callahan, can you hear me?"

I recognized Adam Marchetti's voice against a background of static and radio noise.

"Adam? Is that you? Where's Robin? Put her on, please."

"She's, she was—oh shit. I took her to Rex, she's—"

"Rex Hospital?"

"Yeah, I—"

"Slow down. What happened?"

"She was drinking a lot. Then she fell. Some guy was, I don't know."

"Say what happened."

"She fell off the balcony. She wasn't waking up. I don't know. I went over when I saw her on the ground. It was some frat party at State. I picked her up and took her to Emergency. Just go to the hospital Mr. Callahan. I did the best I could." He started crying.

I tried to talk, but I couldn't, and then I resolved to get words out slowly, putting out of my mind the godawful picture of Robin lying on the ground, and then hoping that this wasn't real, a dream, not really Adam, not really Robin.

"Adam, it's going to be okay," I found myself saying, scared it wasn't true.

I ran to the car barefoot, and drove as fast to Rex as I could, sitting on the horn through red lights. I parked in a doctor's private lot and threw on golf shoes from the trunk.

"I'm Jack Callahan. My daughter got checked in here. Is she all right?"

The triage nurse eyed me over her glasses, then reached for a file. "Her brother brought her in a half hour ago. Said you had the insurance card."

"Where's the doctor? How is she?"

"She's under care right now. Here, give me your insurance card. I'll call the attending."

Fifteen minutes later, no attending, but an orderly appeared. "You Mr. Callahan?" he asked, depositing an empty wheelchair by the door.

I nodded.

"Follow me." He led me through the jammed waiting room, and I got confused thinking for a second I had come for Nora, that the police had called me; but no, it wasn't that night, I was here for Robin, and it had been Adam on the phone.

"Friday night," the orderly said, gesturing to the waiting room throng.

"Did you see my daughter?"

He stared at the floor and nodded.

"Boy brought her in from the wreck. Didn't wait for the ambulance."

"But there wasn't a wreck."

He shrugged. "I prayed for her, man. Pretty young girl like that. Look to Jesus, all I can say."

He left me to sit on a vinyl chair in a greenish hallway, flanked by examination rooms with patients in checked gowns and anxious relatives talking softly.

I recognized the hallway as the place I spent the night of Nora's accident. I'd almost gotten the fluorescent lights out of my mind.

"I came as soon as I heard."

"Lowry?"

He sat down in the vinyl chair beside me, and reached into his pocket. "Here," he said, putting a small amulet into my hand. It was a cross with beads. I gripped it tightly.

"Pray," he said, motioning that I should get on my knees. He did, too, as we had for Nora. My prayer mumbled into nothingness, but Lowry went on.

"Father, save Robin, a sheep in your flock," he concluded. "Guide Ibrahim in his arts. Amen." He stood up and gripped my shoulder. "I've got to go for others. You can handle this."

"Lowry, please—"

"Pray. The channel's open."

He disappeared down the hallway.

I gripped the amulet and bowed my head. Then I tried praying, if you can call bargaining amateurishly with God a prayer. Eventually, I said I was sorry for my entire life, and offered to die in Robin's place. When I looked up, a doctor stood by, waiting for me to stop mumbling.

"I am Ibrahim." He held a chart with Robin's name on it.

"I'm sorry," I said, standing up. "I was—"

"Praying, I know. Continue. Praying is a good thing."

"Will she be all right?"

He motioned to a side room, where we sat on straight chairs. "Your daughter was conscious briefly when she arrived," he said, "but she's been unconscious since. She has trauma to the head and back that we're assessing."

"Is she in a coma?"

"I don't know."

"Why?"

"Because she also has a blood alcohol level that could cause the same symptoms."

"How high?"

"Point two-five."

"Good God."

"I need to ask if your daughter uses drugs."

"She's fifteen years old."

Ibrahim nodded and wrote something down.

"I want to see her."

Ibrahim led me to a small room down the hall. Robin lay prone in a head and back brace. There were bruises and scrapes on her cheek.

"At first, we thought it was a car wreck, but now I believe she fell from a significant height—a balcony, maybe."

Lightly, I took her hand, as the doctor had instructed with Nora. It was cold. I pressed her fingers.

"She has no reflex," I said.

He got a folding chair from the hall, and I sat down.

"Doctor," a nurse called, signaling from the doorway. Ibrahim read from a clipboard, whispered, and hurried away.

"Her breathing is shallow, but I don't want her on a respirator. I want her to fight through."

"Could she die?"

He pursed his lips and began to answer, but the nurse interrupted with a torn computer printout. He tapped it with his finger and smiled grimly.

"Oxycotin—a new painkiller. My belief is she fell at a party, and someone gave her this to mask the pain. It mixes badly with alcohol."

Gently, he wiped from her lip a trace of powder I hadn't noticed.

"What's that?" I asked, alarmed, thinking it was cocaine. She lay still, her tinselly hair around her head looking like crate packing for a doll.

"The other drug." He rubbed it rapidly between his fingers and smelled it. "Adderall. Your daughter takes it for ADD?"

"No."

"Then from her friends."

Satisfied with his drug sleuthing, Ibrahim consulted with the nurse, who hurried down the hall.

"I will tell you something, Mr. Callahan, about a decision I made. I see from the forms that you are a lawyer, so I speak at some risk, but like you, I am a father. I believe there are two possibilities. One, she has depressed function because of alcohol and drug intake, or two, because of trauma to the head. In the latter case, I would begin treatment immediately, but I think we wait."

He paused to invite comment, but I had none. "I have to put this in your hands, Doctor," I said.

"Stay beside her. Lowry says you're a good father. She'll know you're here."

Outside, a loudspeaker voice crackled in hospital code, and Ibrahim and the nurse disappeared. I took Robin's hand and stroked to the rhythm of her breathing. When she was being born, just down the hall, I could see breath ebbing and flowing on the fetal monitor while I stroked Pren's hand against the strength of her contractions.

Robin's birth had been violent, but wonderful. I looked forward to a table full of children, a magic family, with me as the good father, a mixture of King Arthur and Dr. Spock. Things didn't work out as planned.

Two hours passed before Robin stirred. It was 3:24 a.m. "Daddy," she whispered.

Her voice was clear and calm. I started crying, and then recovered enough to speak. "Thank you, God," I said.

"What?" she said dreamily.

"I'm here, honey."

She smiled and grimaced. "I had sex with a boy."

"Shh. Don't tell me that. Can you move your legs?"

She wiggled her toes and moved her legs up and down in the brace. "Ow," she said. "My back really hurts."

"You were drinking and you took a pill. Do you remember somebody giving that to you?"

"I just had a beer, I don't—"

"Do you remember falling?"

"No—did somebody put something in my drink?"

"I don't know sweetie, maybe. Thank God you're okay. We'll talk about the drinking and the pills later."

"But that guy, it was only one time. He was from Ohio. I told Mom it was for a school project."

I sighed and rubbed her hand, and tried to remember to ask Ibrahim if they'd checked her. "How did you meet a boy from Ohio?"

"On the Internet. They're soccer guys. I don't want to do it with anyone around here."

I held her hand tighter. "You mean—you found this boy on email? And you met him at a frat party?"

She tried to laugh, but could only cough a little. "No, Daddy, it's hard to explain."

"Sweetie, you're only fifteen—"

"Sixteen."

In a panic, I recalculated her birthday. "Not for two weeks. You can't be having sex!"

"You had sex with your secretary and it was on television."

"Honey, that was a horrible mistake."

"Duh. I used to call her, and she'd bring out a note for my school, and give me five dollars when you forgot, and she called me sugar. I thought she was nice. And you were having sex?"

Robin felt betrayed, when it had nothing to do with her. But of course it did. I couldn't get angry at Robin, who was actually making sense, and just back with clarity from the edge of the great beyond.

"Honey," I said finally. "I'm sorry about all that. I wish I could take it back. Sex is bad, period. I've been having sex for a long time, and I can tell you that after some momentary release of chemicals, nothing good happens. Sex confuses people and leads to sadness. Our family is cursed by it. So, don't have sex, ever, okay?"

She dozed again and smiled dreamily. "Daddy," she said, "I don't want you to think I'm bad. I don't have sex with Adam Marchetti. He's like my brother. But I want to, he's so hot."

"Well, there you go. See, doesn't that feel better, not having sex with Adam?" I was going to add that I don't have sex with his mother, but thought better of it.

She tried to turn in the bed, but grimaced, and I helped settle her. I tried not to think about the sex conversation, or the alcohol conversation, or the drug conversation.

She stirred. "Daddy?"

"What, honey, where's the pain? I'm going to get the nurse—"

"I don't want to be like Grandma."

"What?"

"She told me she wanted to die."

"Honey, she doesn't want to die. She says stuff sometimes."

"It scared me. I don't want to feel like that."

I held her hand with both of mine. "You won't, I promise. I'm on the job."

I kissed her on the forehead, and she smiled and dozed off, and I called down the hall for Ibrahim. He came at a trot and checked her pulse and breathing rate with a stethoscope and pricked her fingers and toes. I made a note to write the CEO of Rex about Dr. Ibrahim and his good work. Then he called for the nurse and waited while she set up a new IV. He checked Robin's signs, took her pulse by hand, and nodded. "I want her to have a CT scan and MRI when she wakes up. Four kids from this frat party last night." He patted me on the arm. "She's lucky, and strong."

Lucky. Strong. The Callahans were lucky and strong, like Dr. Ibrahim said. Maybe we pressed the lucky part these days.

Lowry reappeared. "She's okay?"

I nodded, and tried to give him the amulet.

He smiled ruefully and handed it back. "Better keep it."

After checking to make sure Robin was sleeping easily, I stumbled through the still-full ER to the parking lot, where my cell phone would work. It was four thirty, and I needed to call Pren, rule or no rule.

"It's Jack."

"Where's Robin?"

"Listen to me. She's okay. But it's been a long night. She had a lot to drink and fell off a balcony. Somebody probably slipped her a mickey. But she's awake, she'll be getting x-rays. I talked to her. She's okay."

Pren started crying. "Where was she?"

"We're at Rex."

"Was she at that frat party?"

"Yep."

"Hold on."

I could hear whispering in the background, and a radio.

"I can't cut this thing off," she said. She started crying again. "I've had it. Can't do any more."

"You don't need to come. I've got things covered."

"I'm coming, Jack. I leave town for one night."

"Get Bingo to drive. You're too upset."

Pren got to Rex from the beach in the same two hours it took to get the MRI done. Ibrahim was finishing up a punchy discussion of how to treat compressed discs when she arrived and pushed past us to Robin's bedside.

"Are you okay?" Pren whispered, flicking back her new bangs to bend over the bed.

"Ow," Robin said, as Pren rubbed her hand.

"Is that what you were wearing?"

Because Robin had been strapped in the head brace, she hadn't changed to a hospital gown. Her blouse and short skirt were streaked with blood and IV fluid, and her hair was still matted from last night.

"Pren," I said, "this is Dr. Ibrahim. Why don't you let him give you the story. I'll wait outside."

Down the corridor, I saw our orderly wheel a man I recognized into an exam room. It was Earl, the downtown drunk who slept amid brown paper bags of swill in front of my law office. Loudly, Earl sang an old hymn. "Throw out the lifeline, throw out the lifeline, Jesus is calling to me," he repeated, head thrown back, eyes upward.

"Quiet down, Earl," said the orderly. "Folks trying to sleep."

I stood in the door to the exam room as the orderly gently laid Earl on the reclining bed. Earl calmed as his head hit the pillow, and he was asleep at once.

"Your daughter beat old Earl," the orderly said.

"Excuse me?"

"He only blew point two-three."

Earl snored, blowing his strands of dingy beard. His rancid clothes soon overwhelmed the antiseptic hospital smell. The orderly gently removed Earl's worn-out brogans and stiff socks, and washed his feet with a cloth from the basin.

"Old Earl, he comes in here about every other night."

"What's your name? I'm Jack Callahan."

"I know you. I'm Anthony."

"Thanks for your help tonight, Anthony." I made a note to write the CEO about Anthony, too.

"No problem. Glad your daughter made it. You need to keep her off the street, man. Young girl like that."

"You're right. I'm going to do a better job."

Daylight now shone through the thinned-out waiting area. I nearly ran into Bingo shuffling through the automatic doors.

"Jack," he said. "I was—"

"Parking the car?"

"Yeah."

He stood for a second, trying to decide whether to shake my hand. To relieve him of the decision, I stuck both hands in my pockets.

"Tough night," he said.

"Tough year."

He smiled and lit a Camel with an old sterling lighter. "Want one?" he said, offering the pack.

"Nope. Don't do that."

"Sure."

"Look, Bingo. Thanks for driving Pren."

"Don't worry about it. Glad the kid's okay."

Her name is Robin. Robin Bloodworth Callahan, I was about to say. But I didn't. He drove groggy from Wrightsville Beach, so who was I to get an attitude?

Pren appeared with a whoosh through the automatic doors and stood between us, arms crossed, her face a study in criticism. She glanced at Bingo's cigarette, and I figured that was an issue.

Bingo put it out on the sidewalk. "Why don't you two go to the cafeteria and have a cup of coffee," he said, looking first at Pren, then at me. "I'll read a magazine."

I had to give the guy credit. Of course, he was more experienced in fractured families than Pren or me, since he had scattered children in several major southeastern cities. Now, he could smoke a cigarette in peace.

Pren and I picked our way through depressing off-white corridors, reading color-coded signs to the cafeteria. I half-remembered the direction from past stays, including Robin's birth, a shared event neither of us mentioned.

I was conscious of not touching her, as in the past I would naturally take her arm or guide her into an elevator. She walked with her arms crossed, eyes ahead.

I got Pren coffee, black, and added cream and sugar for me. Lately, I'd quit caffeine, but this seemed like a good time for an exception.

"You spoke to Ibrahim?" I asked after a while.

She nodded. "Tried to talk to Robin, but she was out, or pretending."

Not pretending, I thought. "What did Ibrahim say?"

She shrugged. "They'll keep her overnight. She's got to be seen for her back, that's it."

"Pretty good, all things considered."

She glowered, but declined to renew her standing criticism that I always called a glass half full. I didn't think it was a fault. Somebody had to hold up a little sunshine.

"How could you let her go to that frat party? I told her under no circumstances."

"Now, wait a minute. I didn't even know there was a party. Why didn't you warn me?"

"She's with you, and suddenly no supervision."

"She said she was going over to that soccer girl's house for a sleepover. There wasn't any talk about a party."

"You don't even know her name."

"Who?"

"Kim Whitcomb."

"Who's that?"

"The girl having the sleepover. I called Spunky on the way. Robin never showed."

I figured Spunky was the mom at the other end of the telephone number Robin handed me.

Pren started to cry again, and I got a couple of napkins. I uncoiled her clenched fist and took her hand across the table. She'd bitten down her buffed fingernails, the way she did in college.

"Our little girl almost died," she said quietly, still trying to believe it.

"But she didn't."

She smiled wanly. "Always Jack the brave."

"Trying," I said.

Pren stifled a yawn and withdrew her hand. "What is Ibrahim, Pakistani?"

"Maybe, I don't know. He's a good doctor. He saved her life."

"C'mon, Jack, stop making this stuff up. He's just some foreign doctor they threw at us."

"That's not right."

"I need to go." She stood up and stretched and applied lipstick. Then her face darkened, and she sat down again.

"What's the matter?" I asked, reaching for another Kleenex.

"I'm scared," Pren said. "Drugs? Alcohol? Falling off—a balcony?"

She'd left out the Ohio boy and sex—Robin hadn't told her, I guess—but otherwise I was on board. "I'm scared, too. But I've been up all night and I've got an idea."

"You? An idea?"

Honestly, I'd been thinking about changes for Robin, and I hadn't planned on having the conversation now, but the moment seemed ripe. "I think we should take her out of Bingham and send her to Enright. No social pressure, casual soccer, serious academics, maybe some better influences."

"And you went there."

"A long time ago."

She paused for a second, thinking, and started to say something, and then sat back instead and thought some more. "Not bad, Jack," she said finally, with a touch of amazement in her voice. "But, have you thought of this? It might throw her in closer with the Marchetti boy."

"Adam's not a problem."

"He's wild."

"They're not doing it, if that's what you're concerned about. She told me."

"Really? What else did she tell you?"

I considered giving up the Ohio boy, but decided against it. "Nothing much."

I could tell she didn't believe me. She stood up and stretched again. "Enright, huh?"

"Really, I thought you wouldn't go for it."

"Well, we can't send her off, she's too wild. And St. Elizabeth's, same old, same old."

"That's what I figured."

"Let me think about it."

She applied more lipstick, and we retraced our steps through the hospital, back toward the emergency entrance. We got lost, though, and stood at a hallway crossroads, trying to decipher numbers and arrows in different colors. Too tired to make sense of it, we leaned against the wall for a moment to rest.

"I need to ask you a question," she said.

"Okay."

"Was I a bad wife? Didn't you get what you wanted?"

"Do you want to talk about this now?"

"The evening's pretty much shot."

"I don't know what I wanted. That's the truth."

"Hah. Perfect. My girlfriends called it. It was too much for you, living inside the Beltline. Ginger said so, before we got married. She said I had to get ready, you were going to do something dumb and bail. But I was in love. Stupid. I could've married anybody. Last year we got everything we wanted. We bought the Crimshaw house; I was looking at that cute place in Morehead. Robin was happy, doing great. I remember thinking what a good year it'd been. And you couldn't handle it. You don't have the guts. You gave up and went right back there."

"Where?"

"Wherever you go."

We reached the automatic doors, and with a whoosh Pren was gone, heading for Bingo who lounged on a bench reading the *Criterion* sports page, nursing another Camel.

I'd messed up. Now she had a new guy to train.

I called Elaine from the parking lot.

"Jack? Are you okay? What time is it?"

"Six thirty."

"You don't sound good. Have you been up all night?"

"Robin fell off of a fraternity house balcony. She almost died."

"What? Oh my God."

"She's okay. But it was awful. We're at Rex."

"Pren there?"

"She and Bingo just left."

"What can I do?"

"Nothing, thanks. Listen, is Adam home?"

"He's in bed…he wasn't, was he?"

"Just tell him Robin's okay."

♦♦♦

I SPENT THE WEEKEND waiting for Ibrahim to release Robin, and get her checked out of the hospital. Thankfully she recovered quickly, and except for a very sore back carried no lingering effects. She'd have to take physical therapy for compressed discs, but could walk without a lot of pain, and ease back into soccer before the end of the season.

She grabbed some clothes and books from the house, and spent Sunday night with me at the Club. Over dinner we discussed her new situation.

"You're too young to drink at all now, and maybe ever, your grandmother's an alcoholic, so was her father. You've got the bad genes—it affects you too much."

"Dad, that's ridiculous, a guy put something in my drink."

"On that point, if you ever drink again, never drink anything somebody mixes for you at a party, drink one beer you open yourself—but that's way off in the future, you're only fifteen–"

"Sixteen."

"In two weeks."

We paused while she put away the rest of her rib-eye and started into ice cream and chocolate sauce. The hospital stay had spurred her appetite. She had managed to find a modest blue dress and sandals, and rinse the yellow streaks from her hair. I hadn't asked about the fate of the belly ring, nor brought up the boy from Ohio. Diners oblivious to Friday's near-disaster smiled and nodded at us, a picture of father-daughter comity, as they made their way past to sit at tables on the verandah, cool and inviting as silky twilight settled over the course beyond. The bar hummed, glasses clanked, and liquor poured freely all around us. It seemed an odd place to preach temperance.

"I don't think you should come back to the Club for a while, for sure not to spend the night. I can pick you up at school and we can hang out, and I'll visit across the street some. I think that's better."

She shrugged. "Whatever. It's not like I'm going to be having any fun."

282

Pren and I had agreed on her being grounded for two months, and taking counselling, life skills they called it. Made me wonder if there's life skills out there for me.

"Two months of school and PT for your back, plus counselling, and things will be back to normal."

"What about my license?"

She was eligible for her license when she turned sixteen, I'd planned to take her for the driving test. "Can't get your license when you're grounded. Have to wait."

She groaned. "It's not fair."

"That's the breaks, my dear. Nobody made you fall off a balcony."

Dollars and Sense

MEANWHILE, WARDIE'S CASH RAN shorter by the day, without consideration for my family problems. Trying to forestall calamity, Wardie called a standing Monday meeting to cut expenses in real time, and I burrowed into the payroll. But no matter how many jobs went missing, or how much we negotiated down the price of newsprint, the arithmetic advanced relentlessly. Trying to keep things light, I devised a spreadsheet game to project when we'd flat run out of cash. Sadly, I hit it on the nose. As promised, Ferris wasted no time the day his wire didn't come through.

"Yippee! Pack your bags. We're going to Charlotte!" he said.

"Paper's in Raleigh, remember?"

"Saves time. Figured we'd have one great big bankruptcy party and invite the Bank. I see your office is right below Griffiths' suite."

Ferris had done his homework this time. If I didn't know him so well, I would have gotten mad. "You can't roll Griffiths. He won't go for your bullshit."

He laughed. "Look, Jack, nobody wants to cause a problem with the Bank, right? Figured if we're all there, we could get some financing done. Maybe we can avoid bankruptcy, it's so yesterday. We're open to another deal structure."

"Meaning, you'd buy Wardie out for nothing."

"Not nothing. Something."

"Well, here's the thing. You've got a Volt brothers problem. No matter how you cut it, he's not giving his paper to them."

"Jack, I swear, I didn't know about the Volt brothers. First time I heard about it was on the plane."

"Doesn't matter. You just got out of jail, and now you're turning the country over to Nazis. How much money can Victor pay you to be a total asshole?"

"You use the word Nazi a lot, Jack. It's annoying. There's no analogy in modern society to National Socialism in Germany. The word simply serves as a placeholder for you to describe things you don't like."

"Keep telling yourself that. It's bullshit."

◆◆◆

WARDIE AND I HAD to go to Plan B, or by now, C or D. I called him when Ferris hung up, but neither he nor his secretary answered. He'd probably left for the day—we had Kai-Jana's fundraiser in an hour. We could enjoy that, and then I'd have to tell him the bad news.

Kai-Jana's fundraiser hummed along, over-subscribed with the good and the great. As I'd predicted, Mary had volunteered the house and the list, and, in fact, had taken on the planning herself. She had gotten Hugh's approval to sponsor. He himself was away at the Landing, continuing to recuperate, Mary said, from his stay at the Center, although by now that was months ago. Whether that meant he was backsliding on the sauce, coping with a new depression, or something else entirely, I didn't know and Mary wasn't saying. For today, Hugh's absence left host responsibilities to me.

I shaved again in the firm's men's room, and left for the Symmes house. It was already five o'clock when I got there, and Lowry—having been rehired by Mary—was at the bottom of the driveway, explaining parking arrangements to the volunteer valet force. He held out his hand for my keys, and then looked at his watch and motioned me up the hill. Mary had reengaged Lowry over Hugh's objection, on a wifely protest that he alone could keep up the yard. The grounds glistened, park-like. You could eat off the grass.

"Sorry, sorry," I said to Mary, giving her a kiss on the cheek as she oversaw the caterer's placement of hors d'oeuvres in the dining room.

"Take charge of the candidate," she said. "I'll do the welcome and introduce you. The governor's coming at six."

"Is he speaking?"

"He can only stay fifteen minutes."

She stood back from the hors d'oeuvres, smiling in a slim black dress and simple gold brooch. She'd scored a coup with the governor, convincing him to appear long enough to imprint his imprimatur, when he had another engagement booked.

"Good job on that."

"They think I'm not to be crossed. Comes in handy."

Mary had gone all out, and when I asked her about it, she'd remembered to me Reverend Blount, or, more particularly, Reverend Blount's wife. "Sarah Alice and my mother served on committees together, public health mostly, ridding neighborhoods of flies. The women had to talk to each other back then, because the men didn't."

"You mean during Jim Crow."

"She's a talented young woman, we're glad to help her."

"Did Hugh say anything about the vetting?"

"He got her confused with Sarah Alice." She shook her head. "I don't know whether to laugh or cry."

I kept an eye out for Kai-Jana. She appeared with her finance man Chip in tow, as the first guests were walking up the driveway. I gave Kai-Jana a kiss on the cheek. Chip shook my hand and reached for the acceptance printout at the nametag desk. "Jeez," he said, after a quick scan. "Everybody's coming."

"Why don't you look out for the governor. I'll show Kai-Jana the room."

She was already shaking hands, and I gently commandeered her elbow and led her to the living room, which had been arranged with extra chairs for her speech. "There's a podium by the fireplace, and it's miked, but I don't think you'll need it. Sometimes people like to speak from the stairs in the front hall, and you've got a big crowd today."

"It'll do fine," she said, eyeing the podium. She studied photos three deep over the far wall, a small history of Symmes governor-and-senator-making, interspersed with inscribed portraits of Democratic presidents from Wilson to Clinton. I'd looked at that wall a hundred times, and never noticed something I noticed today: all the photos featured white men, except one where a young Symmes lady doused the bow of a Navy ship with champagne.

"I know what you're thinking," I said.

She turned from the wall to face me. "Jack, I need to say something to you in a very nice way."

"What's that?"

"Don't ever think you know what I'm thinking."

The governor, trailing his entourage, charged across to greet us, his gray-topped, wiry figure and voracious energy commanding the room. "Judge Blount," he said, grabbing both her elbows and dragging her forward for a kiss. "I can only stay for fifteen minutes."

"You should lead off the speeches," she said brightly, disengaging.

"Oh no, this is your night, Jack you're taking care of her?"

"Yes, sir."

He leaned closely in to Kai-Jana again, and I could see her imbibe a large dose of his signature Clubman cologne as she stepped back. "The sons of bitches are out to get you," he whispered loudly. "But you're with the right people now, the Symmes and the Forrests. It'll be ugly for a while, but they'll take care of you. You can tell Chip to call my office for some help."

He said "help" in the country way—"hep"—which meant he was serious.

"What a piece of work," I said, as Kai-Jana escaped from the governor's departing clinch.

"And what's with coming for fifteen minutes?" she said, as she watched him exit in a flurry of snorts and handshakes.

"You want that. He made a point of talking cheek to cheek and then leaving you the room. Everybody saw you together."

"Which sons of bitches was he talking about?"

"Changes from day to day."

Chip gave us the high sign. "Mrs. Symmes says to start. Need to get people inside."

I led Kai-Jana to the head of the room. "Where's Winston?" I asked, realizing I hadn't seen him.

"Not coming," she said, smiling and looking ahead. "Says he doesn't like these things."

"Oh." I figured there'd be trouble in paradise sooner or later.

"My friends," Mary began, to the sound of glasses tinkling for silence. "Hugh and I are so happy you've come to our home. Hugh's sorry he can't be with us, he sends his very best…"

I surveyed the crowd. Chip was right—everybody came. It was a room full of money. Leaning in one corner against the grand piano, I spied Wardie, a glass of Merlot in his hand and a grin on his face, watching the new guard meet the old, the Symmes and the Forrests making book once again. I'd soon have to spoil his good mood.

"…and now, to introduce Judge Blount, her dear friend, and mine, and someone so important to Raleigh. You all know him: Jack Callahan."

Kai-Jana turned to me and applauded, and laughed, thinking—what? As she ordered, I dared not speculate. I reached for the speech in my coat pocket, and was glad I'd taken the time to write one. People might remember this.

◆◆◆

"GREAT TALK," WARDIE SAID, when I dialed him later that night.

"Yeah, I thought Kai-Jana was on. Doesn't have to work on her stump speech."

"No, man, I meant yours. That bit about South Africa? I was ready to put her on the ticket."

I wasn't above enjoying flattery, but that wasn't why we were talking.

"Yeah, thanks, but I'm sorry, I need to change the subject. Ferris called, and we'll get a letter for the missed wire. You know the one. He wants a meeting in Charlotte." We'd strategized about what to do if the payments came up short.

"Same agenda as last time?"

"Except they're better prepared."

He sighed. "Do we really have to do this in Charlotte?"

"He gets to call the meeting."

Going through the last spreadsheets, it was clear we'd have to rely on Tatty's good graces again. When Wardie called her last week, and floated the possibility, she said she wouldn't do a loan, but would take rock-bottom stock. I always thought Tatty's highest and best use was transcendental meditation, but her business instincts proved shrewd. By my back of the envelope, if the *Criterion* survived, she'd own half, and Wardie would be in business for real with his little sister.

"I'll get going on Tatty. Good for you getting me to call her last week. How are you handling the Volt brothers?"

We had gone over the pros and cons of outing the SEC file or confronting Griffiths directly with the takeover. Both had risks.

"You and I still have to decide. As of yesterday, Elaine and Wheeless want to leak, but the Griffiths option is more direct."

I heard Wardie give a direction to his assistant that involved dozens of Krispy Kreme doughnuts. "Sorry," he said, "breakfast for the night crew. Okay, I'll make this easy for you. Hit Griffiths directly. Wheeless is a trial lawyer; he thinks all he has to do is give a reporter some manila envelope and it's an instant front-page story, but the *Observer* would have to do a deep dive on this. Besides, as we all know, Griffiths is no shrinking violet about what he reads in a newspaper. You're going to have to get in his grill, Hugh Symmes style."

"Thanks."

"That's why we pay you an enormous amount of money."

I was about to tell him it wasn't all that enormous, and point out, as Ferris had done gleefully several times, that I was ethically challenged to get in Griffiths' grill. But, I was the quasi-heir, so what's a little risk between friends?

"Elaine and I need to set up a Raleigh plan. They'll drop a team on site."

"Would an unruly demonstration help?"

"Really?"

He chuckled. "Just asking. What time you picking me up tomorrow?"

"Seven sharp."

"Ouch. By the way, Elaine called yesterday—not on this. Money for Wheeless. When did people start saying 'Elaine and Wheeless' like it was a thing?"

I rang off without commenting. Elaine and Wheeless were a thing, more irritating even than expected. They'd skipped Kai-Jana's fundraiser, which was fine with me, because they'd be sucking money down there, too. It looked more and more like Wheeless and Kai-Jana would be leading the 1998 ticket together, the Symmes Machine and the *Criterion* clicking away. Just one big happy family.

Easing Into Judgment Day

R EMEMBER, YOU CAN PROBABLY still make a deal with them," I said to Wardie as we loaded up. I'd told him what Ferris had said about a "different structure."

It was a bad, seductive idea. But I had to bring it up.

He winced, either at the suggestion, or the pain of folding his tall frame into my Benz. "Hell, Jack, we're close on the patent, and if they gave me value, I might take a buyout, but you see there's this one little thing. I don't want my paper run by the Volts."

"Me neither. But Broman could still offer you stupid money, more than value, and hot-box you with it. They do stuff like that."

"Hmm. That's how he got rich, giving people stupid money?"

"No. That's what he does now that he's so rich it doesn't matter."

"Oh. Hey, can we latte up at the corner?"

Drinking good coffee was part of the plan. We had to ease into Judgment Day.

"Tell me again about how you flew all the way out there and then back on the red-eye?" he asked, still fascinated by jets.

"It was either the red-eye or spend the night playing gin rummy with Ferris."

"I thought Angie was there."

"She had to give Broman his lithium."

"Fast crowd."

He brought up Angie as a matter of course. He assumed I'd slept with her, which was what everybody assumed. I felt really good about not having slept with her, like I'd climbed a mountain of self-control. Part of me, though, missed the momentary release of chemicals.

We stopped outside Statesville for a leak and more fluids, switching this time to Diet Coke in cans that came out sweating. Only 9:00 a.m. and heat shimmered from the asphalt.

"Okay, Wardie, let's go through this one more time. You might be able to sell to the Nazis. Or, you can run out of money and lose everything to the Nazis. Or you and Tatty can beat the Nazis and skate by."

He nodded. "I vote for skating by."

I banked right off the interstate for the circling approach to Charlotte, fixing on the imperial dome of Ameribank and our offices below. Wardie looked at me wide-eyed, grinning, like he was ready for the firing squad.

"It's really going down, isn't it?"

"Yep."

"Suppose Tatty backs out this time. She won't, but just suppose."

"Ferris puts you in bankruptcy."

"Sends in the goons?"

"Yes, goons. Elaine's on that. But I get the feeling Ferris doesn't want to go that way."

"Deep down he's a pussy, right?"

"No, don't get fooled. He's not a pussy, but he doesn't want this to turn into a big, public thing. Broman doesn't like news cameras."

"So, we can call their bluff."

"Maybe. And maybe Griffiths will do the right thing. We've got cards to play, just not money, dang it all. Money makes things so much easier."

"I know. I'll call Tatty again when we get there."

We parked in the firm's deck and headed up the elevator to the fiftieth floor. Wardie stowed his suitcase in the closet. Surviving to stay overnight would be a victory.

"They're in the front conference room, Mr. Callahan." Cherry, our Charlotte receptionist, pointed to us a large, glassed-in fishbowl, even more ostentatious than the Mussolini Room in Raleigh. It featured companion art, twin murals of Munch-like shocked people crossing a bridge—bankrupts contemplating suicide, the joke went.

"Jesus," Wardie muttered as he surveyed the swarm of money men ahead; each had ceremoniously doffed his suit jacket, filled his Butler and Symmes coffee cup, and sat in his appointed chair, waiting for another debtor's execution. There was hardly any blood at these bankruptcy meetings. Wardie's scourging would be an advance from the scaffolds of Ludgate Prison, the banging of drums by the King's Guard, and the screaming of a gin-soaked mob.

"Cherry, could you see about our rooms at the Marriott?"

"Yes sir, Mr. Callahan."

"Wardie—are you all right?" He looked sick.

I led him by the arm to the lobby. I realized I hadn't prepared him for how large and black-suited the meeting would be. "Everything's going to be okay. It's just a room. It's just people. Walk down to the gents' while I get them talking."

Ferris had showed up in executioner's garb, wearing his trademark sharkskin suit. He busied himself unloading a briefcase and whispering to his posse. Then, catching my eye, he actually twirled, modeling. "We are in the hallowed halls of Ameribank," he said, pointing upward. "Thought I'd go old school."

"Very spiffy." I held up my hands. "Look—no papers. You brought enough for everybody."

"I'd introduce you around, but you know the boys, right?" He nodded slightly toward the milling crowd, and then to the picture window and the skyline. "Nice town, Charlotte. Looks like Dallas. In the sixties."

"It grows on you."

"Surprised you're here. Thought I'd be mopping up with the B Team."

"Like I'd take the day off?"

"As I noted, we're in the hallowed halls of Ameribank. I can smell the incense. And just look at all the marble and paintings and things!"

"So what?"

"Well, I was shocked to learn that Ameribank is your firm's largest client, and Forrest owes them money from way back. What a pickle! Your firm is on both sides of a bankruptcy."

"Hey, unlike you, nobody here has gone to jail. And Ward Forrest is not bankrupt."

"I think all that's going to change very soon. I'm Ameri-banking on it!" He laughed and then coughed, and I was glad he'd choked on it.

Wardie appeared, looking refreshed. He took a deep breath and surveyed the documents stacked on the table. I maneuvered around the pile and led Wardie back outside.

"You didn't miss anything. Why don't you go ahead and get Tatty on the line? We need to organize her early."

"I just tried," he said dreamily. "She told me she'd be by the phone all day long. But—she's not there!"

"What?"

"She's not at her apartment."

"So, where? Is it Fashion Week in Paris?"

"No, that's April."

Truthfully, I had little faith in round two with Tatty. But I'd had little faith in round one, and been proved wrong. "You go back to the gents' and try until you find her."

I dialed Elaine from the landline in the secure phone booth by the main conference room. That phone booth we conveniently equipped with a one-way mirror, which I used to keep an eye on Ferris.

"Hi. It's me—what's going on?"

She sighed. "The usual gangster stuff. They have three rental vans out front. Looks like eight dudes."

"So, what're you wearing?"

"I'm not telling you what I'm wearing."

"Come on."

"The black dress with the ivory buttons."

"You look great in that."

"Jack, you called the *Observer*, right? They're on the story with the Bank, right?"

"Elaine. We've been over this. The better chance is with Griffiths."

"I can't believe it."

"Listen, Drac's here, gotta go."

Ferris stood talking with Drac at the door to the conference room. I didn't think he was promoting firm unity.

"Callahan, I was just speaking to Leonard Ferris," Drac said brightly, as though he'd just met the new, popular boy in class.

"Didn't know you guys knew each other."

"Oh yeah. Leonard and I worked on a Morgan Stanley deal—oh, three years ago. You remember it, Jack."

"Didn't think you were on that."

Drac glowered, irritated I wouldn't indulge his man crush. "Leonard was asking about the Bank. You've been over the history, haven't you?"

"I don't recall having a conversation about the Bank," I said, meeting Ferris's mock-puzzled gaze. It was clear he didn't know Drac from Adam's house cat.

Ferris shrugged. "Look, fellas. I just went over the file last night, and I don't know all the details. But I've got to tell you, I was shocked when I found out you guys were on both sides of the table."

Drac looked in my direction for an answer.

"Table? Sides? You mean like the Paris Peace Talks? That's way too metaphysical for me," I said.

Drac rolled his eyes. "Leonard, ah—what Jack means is, we can't trace any involvement on this deal. Whatever the Bank did with Victor Broman, they set up themselves."

"No matter how you cut it, you people are on both sides of this. Some things you do down here are cute. You marry your cousins. Always liked that. The kids don't have chins, but, what the hell, the weddings are great, everybody knows each other. But this—this is outrageous." He held a faded Xerox of Wardie's last loan in front of him. "This is unprofessional. Hugh Symmes would never stand for what you're doing."

I tried not to lose my temper. Long ago, Ferris had memorized all the Jack Callahan buttons. "Fuck you," I said, perhaps too loudly.

"Leonard," Drac interrupted, "speaking for the firm, let me say we're monitoring this situation on a daily—no, hourly basis."

Ferris chuckled, having drawn blood. "Looks like you fellas have some things to discuss," he said, pushing between us out the door.

"So that's really him," Drac said, looking on as Ferris pranced in full coattails down the hall. "You've been dealing with Leonard Ferris personally on this? I thought he, I mean I read he—"

"They let him out last year."

"No wonder you've been getting your ass kicked. Better read this."

Drac handed me a fax envelope. Inside was a letter from Tatty.

"I don't believe this shit," I said, scanning the fax, which had been sent from a Western Union office in San Francisco three hours ago.

"What don't you believe?"

"Everything. That she wrote it. That she sent it. What it says. 'You are directed to instruct Ward Forrest IV not to contact me regarding the Raleigh *Criterion*.' Jesus, all that's missing is the phrase 'cease and desist.' She doesn't talk like that. She'd have to be up at four a.m. to send it. She'd never call Wardie by his full name, and how the hell does she know I'm here? Ferris is cooking this."

"Ask Forrest if that's her signature."

"I don't give a shit. Somebody wrote this and shoved a pen in her hand, and then waited until this morning to send it so they could screw us."

"Who'd do that, Jack?"

"Victor Broman."

Drac nodded at a passing team of lawyers and a banker from upstairs. "Morning, Quince—close today? Good. No problems. Attaboy."

"I'm telling you I don't believe this letter. It's Victor's bullshit."

Drac motioned me into an adjoining staff break room that emptied when we walked in. He closed the door. "I don't know what to say, Jack. A year ago you screwed your secretary—oh, and her mother?—in an RV, and the firm narrowly escaped. Then you covered up for Symmes, and I had to fix that. Somewhere along the way, you left your wife, which God knows is your business, but everybody in Charlotte thinks you're living in your car."

"I've got rooms at the Club."

"Wonderful. Now you're way over your head in a deal with Leonard Ferris himself. And I've got to tell you, Jack, watching your behavior, it's alarming. You're irrational, cursing, and this stuff about Victor Broman, it's paranoid, and obsessive. Compulsive. The Committee thinks you need help."

Drac had made up his mind about one thing. After this deal, they'd drive me straight to the Center.

I snatched Tatty's letter from his hand. "You and the Committee can kiss my ass," I said, and jogged down the hall, where Wardie was on a phone call in the gents'.

"Tatty, Tatty, Tatty," Wardie said, resigned, address book in his hand, leaning on a stall. "It's too early for that place she goes in Maine. I tried that number, too. She said Tuesday she was in."

I ran a faucet to drown out our conversation. "It's not her fault."

"What do you mean?"

I held the fax in front of him. "They got to her."

He read and reread the stilted language, turning the paper over and back. "Damn. Doesn't sound like Tatty. And writing a letter to you? Here?"

"Does it look like her signature?"

He rubbed his finger over the fax. "It does look like her signature."

"They drafted it."

"But how—"

"I don't know. He does things like that."

The bathroom phone rang and Wardie jumped for it; maybe it was Tatty after all, or the governor, whom we'd seen the night before, and Wardie had helped elect, sending in the Highway Patrol.

"For you," he said with a woebegone smile, handing me the receiver.

"Yes, Cherry. Thanks. Tell them we'll be right down."

"Who was that?"

"Cherry. The receptionist. Time for the show."

"What're we going to do?"

I put the fax in my pocket. "We're going to turn their evil energy against them."

We walked shoulder to shoulder back to the conference room. I checked out shoes for trailing TP. Inside, Ferris sat flanked by mounds of paper and junior wise guys. We took our seats across the table.

"You want to get started?" he said.

"Sure, whatever you got."

Ferris squinted at Wardie and shook his head. "Mr. Forrest," he began, as the room stilled to a hush. "Are you prepared to pay Mr. Broman what you owe?"

I kicked Wardie's ankle to remind him he wasn't to speak.

"Just give us the letter," I said.

Ferris grinned at me and passed it over.

"Dear Mr. Forrest," I read, "BFD Ventures, holders of twenty-one point eight million dollar senior debt of Raleigh Criterion, Inc..." I skipped the rest.

"Very simple, Jack," Ferris said, leaning over the table. "Pay the money, we're on a plane. Don't pay the money, we go to bankruptcy." He handed over another stack. "We've prepared Mr. Forrest's resignation, and then there's the general release."

"Wow, a release. Really? What are you doing that he has to release you from?"

"It's routine, Jack."

"Not routine. You've got eight armed men in unmarked vans outside the newspaper in Raleigh. What are you, mounting a military operation?"

"That's absurd."

"Listen up. That newspaper is a public trust. You enter the grounds, you're trespassing on the people's property. We've called the police, and we're prepared to defend ourselves."

Wardie slapped the table. "Absolutely," he said. "To the last man." I kicked him again.

"You people are nuts," Ferris said, sitting back.

"You're the one who put a paramilitary force on the ground!"

"Jack, you owe us."

"Yeah. We have twenty-four hours to pay."

Ferris flipped to the page where it said that.

"You're dead wrong. You absolutely owe us right now, in this time zone," Ferris said with mock exasperation. He flung pages to the table, standing and rocking on his feet, face reddening.

But it was all for show. I knew what he was up to. Ferris just wanted to see if we had the money. Now he knew.

"Why don't you ask a judge what the contract says?"

He shrugged. "You own them all down here. Doesn't matter. We'll finish tomorrow, once and for all."

I kicked Wardie a third time, and we hustled out, having done the first meeting in eight minutes.

A Marine Trusts a Marine

I EXPLAINED TO WARDIE that we'd gotten another day. He made calls back at the hotel to "get the story on Tatty." That didn't happen. At dinner, he talked basketball recruiting while eating a steak. He seemed less nervous than he should be. Maybe he'd resigned himself to whatever came.

"I'm going to bed," he said, yawning over his last Heineken. "You can fix this thing, I know it —use some of that old Symmes magic."

Which meant confronting Griffiths and making him do something he didn't want to do, plus violating a few laws. Piece of cake. And Elaine still thought we could get the Charlotte paper to do in the bad guys with a banner headline.

"Jack, have you called the *Observer*?"

She'd phoned on the hour until midnight, leaving that question in the message box. One thirty in the morning is normally too late to return calls, but I made an exception.

"I'm going to handle this my own way," I said when she picked up.

I could hear the television in the background, and a guy's voice. I imagined she was in some stage of sex with Senator Sid.

"Tell me you're not doing anything crazy."

"I'm going to try to make Griffiths do the right thing. It's what we've got left."

I could feel her getting mad. "Jack, this is what I was afraid of. You can't—"

"What?"

"Listen to me," she whispered fiercely. "Think about yourself. If you leak to the *Observer*, at least you'll be safe."

In my sleep-deprived stupor, I finally got it. She still cared, a little. If I leaked, I'd be a source, and the reporters would never rat me out. Mano a mano with Griffiths, only honor protected me.

◆◆◆

Near dawn, I set out walking to Griffiths' house, passing the bleary-eyed hotel night clerk reading the early edition of *USA Today*. Steam rose at the tops of uptown towers, spiraling from compressors and disappearing in a snappish wind. A pair of dump trucks rumbled toward floodlights where Charlotte's new NFL stadium emerged from steel beams by the railroad tracks.

It was a long walk, and I had overestimated my sense of direction. But I got it right in the end, remembering the house from a charity cocktail party my partners and I attended at Glock-point.

The sun had poked over the oak-lined street; sprinklers erupted from the grass, and dogs barked from house to house. An oncoming jogger crossed to the other sidewalk. I must have looked loopy in suit pants and a two-day old shirt. I knotted my tie.

Griffiths' gabled bungalow sat behind a brick wall. A wide porch led from the driveway to an ample backyard and a rear wing behind. I checked my watch: nearly seven fifteen, a decent hour.

Mrs. Griffiths answered the doorbell.

"Jack Callahan," she said immediately, standing before me in a plum-colored jogging suit, holding the leash to a barking Westie. "Have you been up all night?"

"I have. I'm sorry to call early."

"Oh well," she said brightly, "you're here. I'm taking Cece for her walk. Dalt's in the back."

She led me through the foyer to the living room. Brightly patterned armchairs and a Williamsburg coffee table caught the light through a bay window.

"It's quiet in the mornings now," she said. "With the boys gone. How's your mother?"

"Still not herself, I'm afraid."

She patted me on the arm. "Things will get better. Nora's a very strong woman." She paused to shush Cece. "I heard about you and Pren. Seems like all the young people I know get divorced. Chamomile tea helps, and you might read a novel before bed. Never television—it's awful for your nervous system."

"Thanks." I hadn't tried chamomile tea.

She smiled. "Come by any time you're in Charlotte. I know some nice young women who'll want to meet you. I'll go tell Dalt you're here. He's having his breakfast in the Florida room."

After a moment, she motioned me onward, into the library. She stood by a bust of Thomas Jefferson.

"Should be Alexander Hamilton."

"What'd you say, dear?"

"Oh, nothing. Role confusion."

She led me through the dining room to the kitchen and the edge of a glassed-in porch, where Griffiths sat at a wrought-iron table.

"Talk some sense into him," she said. "His advisors are all numbers people, they don't understand family. Poor Tatty and young Ward. I was at St. Elizabeth's with their mother, Anna Blanche. She called so excited when the Major proposed. Coffee?"

"Thanks."

"Honey, Jack Callahan is here."

Griffiths sat erect, half-lens reading glasses resting low, the remains of a poached egg and dark toast on his plate. He acknowledged my presence with a brief, pained look, and continued to read the editorial page of the *Wall Street Journal*, which he creased in half again to the fold like a subway rider. After some time of him reading and me standing, he put the paper down.

"You haven't solved the problem."

"Sir, I'm sorry to come to your home—"

"No, you're not."

302

"Sir, I—well, I mean, you've got to reconsider—"

"Start over, Callahan. When people say I've got to do something, it gives me a headache."

"Sorry, sir."

He wrinkled his nose and looked around the room. "Dolly?"

"What, honey," Mrs. Griffiths said, appearing from the kitchen with my coffee. She motioned that I sit down.

"Where the hell's that thing?"

"Overnight bag? I'll get it."

He checked his watch. "You have two minutes."

I'd made it to the Florida room, but time was short.

"I'm appealing to you personally to buy out Victor Broman's loan. You have the power to do it; you can end this problem in a second. It's in the best interests of the Bank."

He winced. "So that's your pitch? The best interests of the Bank? What the hell does that mean? Look, Callahan, lending money is an easy business. You lend a man money, he pays it back. Ward Forrest hasn't paid."

Couldn't argue. I took a sip of coffee.

"But, Mr. Griffiths, that's not really what's happening here."

"You mean Forrest paid the money, and nobody knows?"

The *Criterion* sat before me like a purple Braniff plane, ready to be painted. "No sir. There's a deal behind the deal."

"What the hell does that mean?"

"Broman represents partners acquiring newspapers across the country. They seek political control of the United States."

"Ridiculous! I'm sitting here for this? I could have you arrested."

"There's more, sir."

"You've had a great run, Callahan. Leave your family. Turn on Hugh Symmes. Make up time zones. Some damn conspiracy theory. Don't talk to me about the best interests of the Bank. You're a dangerous man."

"Victor Broman is way more dangerous than I am."

"I know Broman has partners. But this deal is small potatoes, and you need to move on. That's personal advice from an old pro. Now I'm going to tell you something truly important: this morning, I have to go to New York and give my quarterly speech to the analysts. Not one of 'em thirty years old, and they trade my stock like marbles."

I stood as he picked up his briefcase. "Sir, you can't leave yet."

He turned, his face reddening. "There you go again, Callahan, telling me what to do."

He moved toward the door and I blocked his way.

"Goddammit, Callahan, I don't know who's crazier, you or Ward Forrest."

"Sit down and listen to me for one more minute, or you'll regret it forever."

"Why the hell should I listen to you at all?"

"Because your employees kiss your ass, and Broman lies every time he opens his mouth, but I have no motive other than to tell you the truth. So, sit down, please."

A wild-eyed grin crossed his face, and he sat down again. "All right," he said, looking at his watch. "You have another two minutes. Then I'll have you arrested."

"Thank you. What I should have said before is that helping the Forrests is the right thing to do."

"Now you're finally sounding like Hugh."

"Yes, I am. That newspaper is part of history, a public trust. It needs to remain in the family."

He paused, stroking his chin, seeming to consider something he'd once dismissed. Maybe I'd hit the honor button.

"What's your proof of this conspiracy?"

He leaned back, waiting for whatever else I had. I retrieved from my pocket the folded sheets and smoothed them out.

"I've got to show you some signatures," I began again, my voice higher than I wanted it. "It's not illegal for you to look at them, but it's illegal for me to show them to you. Do you understand?"

He held up one hand. "Whoa, son, slow down. You don't want to do anything rash here. This is just a deal. There'll be another deal tomorrow."

"Not for Ward Forrest."

He got up and started to pace. "All right," he said finally. "My curiosity's up."

I set the wrinkled page in front of us on the table. "You see here Victor Broman's signature." I tried to meet his cock-eyed smile with one of my own.

"Yes, I do."

"Now look below. Recognize the names?"

"Sure. Investors who put money with Broman. So?"

"Sir, you see the Volt brothers there."

He squinted and held the paper closer. "Yep, Ronald and Donald, met them in Aspen. They're Republicans. Most people are Republicans."

"Sir, the Volt brothers aren't Republicans like down at the Charlotte City Club. They're moving on Big Data."

"So?"

"They aim for political control. They want to take over the country. It wouldn't be pretty."

"Look, Victor Broman is a terrific money manager. Maybe they just want to invest in media properties."

"Victor Broman is a power-hungry manipulator who has taken up right-wing politics. You think I'm dangerous? He's a nuclear bomb."

"This is way over the top."

"He's using the Bank for cover. He never planned on getting paid, by the way."

"Come on."

"The plan all along was to engineer defaults and take over the *Criterion* through bankruptcy. In California, they're doing the same thing."

"Callahan, Callahan." He shook his head. "All these conspiracies."

"Sir, there's something else. I haven't been able to confirm it, but—the Volt brothers—well, they apparently want to go back on the gold standard."

Hugh had taught me that about dealing with Griffiths. When you've run through Presbyterian destiny, invoked honor, and exhausted facts, throw down the gold standard.

His eyes narrowed. "Did Ronald Volt say that?"

"In so many words."

That did give him pause, and he stepped back, mumbling Volt's name. But the old lines weren't working today. It was the day of the analysts. He tapped at his watch. "Why should I trust you, Callahan? I trusted Hugh. But hell, you made up a time zone."

"Fine. Don't trust me, but then don't trust anybody, least of all Broman. Do one thing—even if you have to do it from your plane. Get your private banking people to track down Tatty Forrest and ask her what Victor Broman did. She's disappeared."

Griffiths looked at me quizzically and clicked shut his briefcase. "I don't know what you're talking about."

"Sir, please make the call. One call."

He sighed. "This isn't like the old days. I can't muck into every decision, even if my wife loves Anna Blanche Forrest, and Tatty and our kids went to camp together. See, you're not the only one lobbying."

"Yes, sir."

"Now, what I'm going to do, if you'll stand aside, is fly to New York and talk about our quarter. That's my job, and my car is waiting."

Mrs. Griffiths appeared with his overnight bag and followed him to the door. They stood outside speaking briskly, she with her hands on her hips, and he pointing to the air, until he shook his head and walked off. She stood on her tiptoes, staring as he disappeared down the sidewalk to a waiting black Lincoln, and then walked up the stairs slowly and held the front door open for me.

"I'm sorry," she said. "He's a stubborn man."

Thumpeta-Thumpeta-Thumpeta

WE GOT TO THE conference room at eleven, Wardie having dosed himself with coffee, me having donned a new shirt. I reported my breakfast meeting with Griffiths.

"What did he say?"

"He said he had to talk to the analysts."

"But not save our little newspaper."

"He's gone to New York. I'm sorry."

Wardie shrugged. "You gave it your best shot."

I didn't think it was my best shot. Hugh would have done better.

Cherry handed me a phone message from Elaine. "Big Mama at ten. Hell's Angels gassing up," it said. "Nice angels, too." I didn't quite get the last part.

Cherry tapped her foot and looked at the ceiling as I read. I don't think she approved of Elaine.

"Wardie, something's happening in Raleigh."

"Something's always happening in Raleigh." He seemed too calm.

"No, I'm serious. Elaine's trying to tell me something. I need to check in."

"TV there yet?"

"What? What? Did you do something? Wardie—did you do something? Answer me—Broman has men out front. It's dangerous."

"All I did was send the staff home."

"They've got guns and they're going to try to occupy. This is a situation."

"You mean they want to sit at my desk, smoke cigars and stuff, like Che Guevara?"

"You need to stop thinking this is funny. They're going to put out their own paper. They may have pages for tomorrow." I pictured an eagle in each corner and the mustachioed Volt brothers leering from the masthead.

"Look at him," Wardie said, studying Ferris as he set up his noxious stacks. "Everything going his way and his butthole's like a roll-up toy. No way to live, man."

Ferris recounted already-counted pages. His voice rose and fell on the flip phone, and he gestured with a Diet Coke can.

Wardie was right. Ferris had a case of nerves. He never got nervous.

"Is that your cell?" Wardie said, hearing my ring tone.

"Yeah, I'll be right back."

Elaine was on the line.

"Where are you?" I asked, clicking on.

"Standing beside Sheriff Moore." She had to yell over background chants. "There's been a development."

"Let me guess. The Volt brothers came with a marching band."

"No, way better. Your friend Lowry just brought me and the sheriff coffee, and we're all watching Reverend Sweeney march on the *Criterion* offices."

"What?"

"Somebody must have gotten to him. Protestors are chanting 'Wall Street Out.'"

"Jesus—who—"

"Oops, gotta go. There's Brenda Bobelink."

I passed a note to Wardie about the protestors.

"How about that Reverend Sweeney? Johnny on the spot."

"You tipped him off, you son of a bitch."

"It's 'sumbitch' when you're friends, right? We needed backup."

"Just couldn't help yourself."

He shrugged. "They're fucking with my paper. I'm a journalist, man."

It was the first time I'd heard him say that in a long time.

Ferris got very animated on his phone. He no doubt had reports about Reverend Sweeney and Brenda Bobelink, not to mention Sheriff Moore, who owed his election to the *Criterion,* barring the door in full Sam Browne-belted grandeur.

Ferris hated home cooking, and he was sure getting it now. But, despite the show, we still didn't have money, and he knew it.

"Are you ready, Mr. Callahan?" Ferris said, gathering his papers.

"Ready for what?"

Ferris handed me another letter.

"We got one yesterday," I said without reading. "But I guess you need to send a lot of letters when you're committing a war crime."

Ferris reddened. "Jack, if you read it, you'd see there's a new offer."

"What?"

"One hundred million cash."

It took a lot of willpower to stay stone-faced at that.

"Seems like a lot for a bankrupt business."

"Indeed, but there are...developments."

"Yes, the people have risen."

"We're aware of the mob in Raleigh. You have ten minutes."

"I'll talk with my client."

Would Victor Broman really pay a cool one hundred million in cash to have Wardie cut off the lights at the *Criterion* himself? Apparently so. Call it the Reverend Sweeney premium.

Wardie laughed out loud when I told him.

"Go tell Ferris to fuck himself."

"Hold on. It's a hundred million dollars you're turning down. You could buy a fleet of jet planes."

"But my newspaper would be owned by the Volt brothers."

"Yeah, that's true."

"Go tell him to fuck himself."

"Okay, but he can still foreclose, and then you've got nothing."

"I'm betting now he won't do it. Not worth the headline on the CBS Evening News."

"Victor Broman foreclosed on Braniff. You think that's good PR? They had dudes with Uzis towing planes away."

"You have my decision. I'm going with my gut. Tell him to fuck himself."

Wardie followed me back to the now-packed conference room. Ameribank brass had materialized, and security circled press in the hall. Silence fell as we sat down. Ferris tapped his Rolex. "Less than ten minutes. I'm glad it was an easy decision, Mr. Forrest. Now we can proceed in an orderly way—"

"There's no deal," I said.

"What?"

"Mr. Forrest has instructed me to tell you to, uh, do something nasty to yourself."

A bank officer guffawed and Wardie laughed, and then the rest of the room.

"Look, Jack," Ferris said smoothly, ignoring the commotion, "I'm shocked. That's an extraordinary, no, unprecedented, offer. If you don't take it—"

"Fifty paid thugs will pound down the doors of the Raleigh *Criterion* on national TV?"

"Are you going to let me finish?"

"No."

"We can continue the proceedings into next week, next month, if necessary."

Wardie turned to me. "What the hell's he talking about?"

"He means he'll wait until the Reverend Sweeney's gone to send in the goons."

"Unless you take this very generous offer, Mr. Forrest."

"No chance," Wardie said.

Ferris suddenly looked beleaguered. He'd miscalculated. He thought the Volt brothers wouldn't mean more than one hundred million dollars.

"We're not going to bargain," I said. "You're going to have to seize your assets."

"We have full authority, you know that."

"I'm not talking authority, Ferris. I'm talking about doing the deed. Breaking down the front door. Being on television with Brenda Bobelink. I've had the pleasure, it's not cool."

Ferris made a motion to his team, and then pulled back, fixing his gaze on me with an open-eyed, almost pleading look, like you'd give a loud kid misbehaving in class.

He'd expected me to make an outrageous counteroffer. Money solves everything in Broman-world. What about a little more?

"Look, Ferris, I've told you we're not taking your money. Full stop."

"But we can foreclose at any time, you get that, right?"

"Then stop talking about it and do it, you chickenshit!"

Ferris stood up and leaned over the mahogany table, his hands caressing the shockingly spurned papers. "This is embarrassing, Jack. It's—"

"Unprofessional?" I laughed heartily for the crowd, grown now to standing room. "Listen, we've gone way beyond unprofessional. We're telling the truth! Are you embarrassed, Wardie?"

"Nope."

"I think the only one embarrassed here is you, Ferris."

Ferris started to reply, but stopped as a stir rose in the foyer. His eyes grew wide and I turned to see what he saw: a single figure in a gray herringbone suit asking directions of Cherry, a battered Redweld under his arm. With a wink, he pushed open the glass doors to our conference room and walked in.

"I'm Dalton Griffiths, representing Ameribank," he said to the dumbstruck room, as a covey of vice presidents made room for him at the table. He nodded first at Wardie and me, and then at Ferris.

"Mr. Griffiths. I had no idea," Ferris said, rising from his chair.

"And you are?"

"Leonard Ferris."

"Really? Aren't you—"

"In jail? No sir, I'm out."

"Congratulations. I don't have much time. I'm supposed to be in New York. Somebody catch me up."

Ferris weighed in, gesturing to the stack of documents. "The loan's defaulted, but we've made another good-faith offer. So far," he continued, nodding at me, "Mr. Forrest and his counsel have refused to work with us. We have men on the ground to take control in Raleigh, but we haven't pulled the trigger—"

Griffiths blanched. "Thank God for that. Why the hell did you send a team to Raleigh? Do you realize what a damn media circus you've caused? The Reverend Sweeney, good God, man!"

"We, we didn't think it would get this far. We were simply protecting—"

"Mr. Ferris, the Raleigh *Criterion* is not some batch of rental cars you can tow away. You're way exposed on this."

"Do you want us to leave the room?" I asked, scarcely believing our good luck.

"Where is Victor Broman?" Griffiths said, ignoring me. "Are you running this operation, Mr. Ferris?"

"He's with another transaction on the Coast. I have authority here."

"So, I've finally found the man in charge. Good. Maybe you can answer a question."

"I'm sorry?"

"My people don't understand the ownership."

"It's fairly—"

"Does Broman own the *Criterion*?"

Ferris shifted in his seat. "I think, Mr. Griffiths, that Mr. Forrest and Jack here should leave the room."

"No, dammit. We're out of time. You damn lawyers have complicated this thing so nobody can understand it. I want this resolved. Does Broman own the *Criterion* or not?"

Ferris took a deep breath. "A Broman partnership will take control."

Griffiths turned to Wardie. "Did you talk to your sister Tatty today?"

"No, sir."

Griffiths fixed a drill sergeant gaze on Ferris. "I talked to Tatty Forrest, and she said your people made her sign a letter." He held up a copy of Tatty's predawn fax. "Tatty Forrest is a very good client of this Bank. She was so scared she had to leave her house. My people tracked her down at a yoga club in San Francisco where she was…meditating."

Ferris feigned outrage, mastered long ago for moments like this—not that there'd been many like this exactly. "Mr. Griffiths, I can assure you—"

"Stow it, Mr. Ferris. I want a straight answer."

"There's a partnership, as I said—"

Griffiths slammed his fist on the burnished tabletop. "No more double talk! You bullied a kind-hearted woman! Made her go—meditate! What kind of man does that?"

"It's not what you think, sir."

"Bull crap. Who's in your partnership?"

"I can't say."

"You mean you won't say."

"It's a complicated structure."

"Complicated." Griffiths nodded in my direction. "I run into that word a lot these days." He shoved my handwritten page at Ferris. "Is it these men? Yes or no."

Ferris read the names slowly, folded the paper, and put it in his breast pocket while Griffiths glared. He looked in that moment as though he'd rather be back in jail.

"These men have requested privacy. I can't say more."

Griffiths rose to his full height, while Ferris stood as tall as he could. Silence held the room. Griffiths looked the Broman team up and down, as though measuring them all for horrible duty in the brig.

"What's your payoff," Griffiths said finally.

"Excuse me?"

"What is the payoff on your note?"

Ferris punched at his calculator.

"With today's interest, twenty-one million, six hundred and forty-seven thousand, eight hundred and fifty-seven dollars and twenty-eight cents."

Griffiths unscrewed his Mount Blanc and wrote the number down carefully on a legal pad. "We'll pay you out."

Wardie began humming the Marine Corps hymn. I kicked him under the table.

Ferris shook his head, holding one hand up as though to stop air itself. "You can't," he said slowly.

Griffiths scowled, and a bank officer down the table looked away. "I didn't quite catch that, Mr. Ferris?"

"It's our option," Ferris replied, leaning in. But then, he was a rookie with Griffiths. "We choose the business. We won't take a payout."

Griffiths stared at Ferris, his eyes growing narrower. He seemed to be exercising an athletic dominion over the muscles of his body that let him stand perfectly, unnaturally still.

"People don't tell Ameribank what to do, Mr. Ferris," he said, smiling. "I'm going to pay you out, whether you like it or not. Get Victor Broman on the line."

"Mr. Griffiths, our agreement—"

"Listen to me. I'm paying out Victor Broman one hundred cents on the dollar. He's going to take it if he wants to do business with Ameribank ever again. And if there's any trouble in Raleigh, I'll put it right on your head, personally—to the police, and to the FBI, if this deal is as dirty as I think it is. Now get him on the line."

Ferris unholstered his flip phone and uncorked a cockamamie grin, as though he had met the immovable object that finally, and mercifully, stopped the unstoppable force. "Okay, I get it," he said coolly. "Let me explain it myself, Mr. Griffiths. I can put things in context."

Ferris retreated through the crowd to the telephone room in the back, and we sat for several minutes saying nothing while Griffiths muttered and looked at his watch. I could hear Ferris's voice rise and fall as he channeled Victor's rage. He sounded calm, matter-of-fact even, finally saying that he'd call the Volts himself, a task I suspected he might even relish.

"Mr. Broman accepts the cash-out," Ferris reported, reappearing at the door. He slid the phone back into its holster.

"Good," Griffiths said, having never doubted that he would. "You'll have the funds within the hour." He turned in my direction. "Jack, your firm can do the paperwork?"

"Yes, sir."

"Ward, I want you to ride with me to New York."

"Yes, sir."

"Call Tatty and tell her we're squared away. She's all shook up."

"I'm dialing her now."

Blue-suited handlers held the glass doors as Griffiths sprinted from the conference room with Wardie trying to keep up. Elevator doors closed around them, and scarcely a minute passed before I heard the *thumpeta-thumpeta-thumpeta* of a helicopter. The copter sailed up and tacked past our window, heading for Griffiths' plane and the flight north.

I sat staring at Ferris across the table while his shell-shocked posse packed up the papers and left the room. Ferris shook his head at the trail of the departing copter.

"Did you really call me chickenshit in there?"

"Heat of the moment. Sorry."

He cocked his head as though we'd finished an especially tough tennis match. "That didn't turn out the way I thought."

"Victor mad?"

"Oh yeah."

"At least you talked him down."

He shrugged. "I told him he had just saved a ridiculous amount of money and should feel good about it. You think I can make a two o'clock?"

"Sure. I'll get you a cab."

"Another deal on the Coast."

"So I hear."

"Overall, nice piece of legal work," he said.

"Thanks."

"One thing, though."

"What's that?"

"Your career is over. I hope it was worth it."

"What do you mean?"

"You know fucking well what I mean," he snapped, all banter gone. He pulled my hand-scrawled page from his pocket, with Ronald and Donald

Volt's names underlined, and tossed it onto the table between us. "You gave Griffiths the names."

"Griffiths runs the biggest bank in the world. He finds shit out."

"No footprints, man. He couldn't have figured this out in a million years. You stole it."

"Griffiths will protect the firm."

"But your partners will ditch you. I could tell from one look at Drac. He ought to be selling cars. In the old firm, we'd run him out before lunch."

In the old firm, in the old days, when men were strong and true. Ferris waxed nostalgic. I realized he missed it.

"You're giving career advice? That's a good one."

He clicked his briefcase shut. "I never did anything as bad as you. Didn't steal from a Federal courthouse."

"So, what did you do? I've never asked."

He shrugged. "Made some signatures appear."

"Practicing for Tatty?"

"Victor put twenty-nine million dollars in a Swiss bank account. I did four months. What's your price?"

"Don't seem to have one."

"Weird. What's the matter with you?"

He tossed the last documents into the shredder and whistled for the wise guys, who appeared, running like a pack of Dobermans.

"Today's my bad," he said, motioning them to carry off boxes. "I thought I knew you, but I was wrong."

"I'm retiring, did you hear? Going to Mexico."

He laughed. "Isn't that where all the ex-Confederates go? Except, wait a minute, you won. Or did I miss something."

Cherry appeared at the door. "Mr. Ferris, your cab's downstairs."

"Okay, Jack. Off I go." He saluted from the doorway. "It's been a little slice of heaven. I especially liked that part where Griffiths was going to turn me in to the FBI."

Privileges

RAIN BEGAN HARD NORTH of Statesville and lasted all the way to Raleigh, which was okay since the sound kept me awake. The end of the deal washed over me, like a nasty wave that I needed to rinse off, and I wanted to stop for a sink shower, except every gas station I passed looked even dirtier than I felt. We beat them, I reminded myself—Wardie was off to New York with Griffiths, Ferris scattered to the other coast, his San Diego deal likely dead, too, and the Reverend Sweeney was giving network interviews. It was a grand day for hero-ing, the good guys winning all around. Still, it felt like somebody else's victory, and I was happy to disappear.

Elaine called on the car phone. I didn't feel like high-fiving it up, but I whooped and hollered and went over the postgame anyway. She said it was foolish to drive back to the office without a couple of hours' sleep, advice I disregarded. I'd packed up and left as soon as I could, with Wardie's stuff and mine in the car. The last thing I did before leaving town was send two dozen roses to Dolly Griffiths.

I made it up Interstate 85 in one piece, and trudged up the steps from the parking deck for exercise. Really, all I needed to do was drop off my gear, and I could go home to the Club. But, alas, it was not to be. Huffing and puffing to the top, I sensed a celebration. New Year's Eve noisemakers sounded as Elaine opened the door to the Mussolini Room.

"Welcome home, champ," she said, flipping on the lights, which blinded me for a moment. She handed me a plastic cup of champagne, as applause and war whoops rolled on. I guess the reason she'd called was to be sure I'd make the party.

"You the man," Ballard yelled, brandishing a bottle of bubbly.

"You heard what happened?"

"Everybody heard, Jack. Griffiths called from the plane."

"He was fuzzy on his facts," Elaine added. "But the Bank is very pleased."

"Great. That's all that matters, right?" I traded champagne for water.

"Yep, it's all good," Ballard said flatly. He looked disoriented, crimson red tie akimbo, moisture gathering at his crown. A goofy smile crossed his face. I imagined his confusion: relieved we won, guilty he bet against me, jealous I got to play the hero. "You're the frigging man," he roused himself to say again over the din. "Any idea when we'll get paid?"

"Excuse me," I said, pushing past. "Got to take care of something."

Elaine followed me down the hall. "What's wrong?"

"Nothing. Everything is great."

"Something's wrong," she said, as we went into my office.

"Do you have any scissors?"

"Jack, no—don't do it, Jack!"

"Hey, calm down. Do you think I'm going to off myself with a pair of scissors?"

"On edge, sorry. Big morning with Reverend Sweeney, you remember."

She found scissors at the secretary's station. I opened my top desk drawer, removing a box of paper clips and ink cartridges covering my taped-over privilege license, evidence that I was a dues-paying lawyer.

"What are you doing?" she asked.

"Here, hold this envelope open."

I pried the gummy license from the drawer and cut it into pieces that I poured into the envelope Elaine held, aghast. Then I wrote a letter in longhand to the Bar on Butler and Symmes stationery: *Ladies and gentlemen, I quit. Please find herewith my privilege license, destroyed. Very truly yours, Jacob Callahan Gold.*

"Jack, what are you doing?"

"Should be obvious."

"Okay. You just cut up your privilege license. Doesn't matter, they'll send you another one."

"Then I'll cut that one up, too."

"What is the matter with you?"

"Nothing, I told you."

"Then why are you acting crazy in your moment of glory?"

"Ask Drac. He's packing me up for the Center, right?"

"Nope. You're totally bulletproof now."

"Good. Then it's a perfect time to quit."

She tossed the privilege license remnants in the trash. "Oh, now I get it. The moment I've always feared. You're quitting."

"What the hell's that supposed to mean?"

"It means—it means," she started again, her lower lip quivering, "what am I supposed to do now?"

I was tired and didn't want to get into an argument with Elaine about my quest for a new start. I had thought, naïvely, that whether I quit the law or not was about my own screwed-up life, but apparently it was about hers.

Voices down the hall called my name. She waved from the door. "He's coming," she said brightly, holding up her champagne go-cup.

We went back to the conference room and somebody flipped on the radio and somebody else began to dance, and then the rest of the staff drifted in and we had a real live office party, the kind HR says you're not supposed to have. I took advantage of the situation to nap on the floor in the corner, and Elaine brought me the old lady half-blanket she kept on her chair for when the air conditioning was on overkill. When I woke up, the music was off, the food and drink had been taken away, and Elaine sat beside me on the floor, reading a brief.

"I'm worried about you," she said. "Let's go back to my place. I'll make you some food. We need to talk anyway."

"Where's Senator Sid?"

"I'll make you some food."

Back at her condo, I dozed on the sofa while she cooked spaghetti.

"I've got something I've been needing to talk to you about," she repeated, ladling pasta. "I've been holding off, but since you're quitting it seems like the right time."

"Uh-oh, this sounds bad."

"Sid asked me to marry him."

"What? When?" I sat up, suddenly revived.

"Last month. I've been thinking about it. I told him you and I had to get through this Wardie thing first."

"Are you in love with him?"

She put down the ladle and shook her head, yes, no, no, yes. "I think I am."

"Oh shit."

She tossed the ladle into the sauce and gave me a teary hug. Then she stepped back and started crying, and I gave her a dish towel. "So, when are you two going to tie the knot?" I thought that's what people usually asked.

"Soon." She folded the dish towel neatly and put it aside. "The campaign is gearing up."

At least she said these things while feeding me. I didn't wonder about the timing. The flashy liberal candidate didn't need to have a flashy liberal girlfriend as he hit the hustings. He needed a wife, a hard-working career mom who had raised a son by herself, spoke well on camera, and liked putting on lipstick in private jets. Elaine was perfect.

◆◆◆

THE NEXT MORNING, I went to see Nora at Harmony Hall, to tell her I'd cut up my privilege license, and about Elaine marrying Sid Wheeless. She inhaled deeply and stubbed out her cigarette in a clamshell. "I'm not saying a word."

"About which thing?"

"Elaine Marchetti. What's to say, except bravo? He's handsome, he's rich, he's going to be a senator. She's no spring chicken. My hat's off to her."

How could I disagree? Nora had no equal in assessing a conquest.

"But for you to throw away a brilliant career?"

"Lawyers don't have brilliant careers, Nora. Nobel Prize-winning scientists have brilliant careers."

"Don't tell me it's nothing. You just saved the Forrest family."

"It's nothing."

She lit another cigarette, prompting me to preemptively spray the aerosol freshener. "I'm sorry for you, that's all."

"I think you're sorry for yourself."

"Maybe a little. I invested a lot in your career."

"You didn't pay a dime."

"I'm not talking about money, honey."

Thus, she called out our struggle. Together, the Callahans, mother and son, had bested the fancy people, one way or another. So, how fare the victors? Matriarch in a nut house; quasi-heir without marriage or job.

"How did we get here?" she asked.

"You changed our names."

She tipped her ash into the clamshell and looked around sadly for a nonexistent glass of bourbon. "I had a lot to explain when we arrived, honey. Didn't need questions about being Jews."

"Whatever you say."

"I raised you to be a Trotskyite rather than a socialite."

"Still got a chance to make you proud."

She stood up on her tiptoes and hugged me. "I'm always proud of you." Then she began to cry. I would have given her my pocket handkerchief, but I wasn't wearing a jacket. "It's going to be okay, Nora," I said. She cried harder.

I stood up and brushed the wrinkles from her blanket, mad at myself. I hadn't wanted to make a scene. She needed to stay collected so she could get out. Her clothes lay arranged on velvet hangers and her powders and rouge sat in practical rows on the hospital dresser, a good sign.

I adopted a forward-looking, cheerful affect. "There's good news. I've spoken to Dr. Gardiner, who's agreed to a two-week plan for you to leave. The pool's about finished, and it's beautiful, just what you wanted."

She sat down. "I can't leave! I'm on Level Three."

"You're off Level Three, Nora. I see shampoo in the bathroom."

She sighed and reached for a fresh tissue. She always folded them twice, for economy. "Okay, look. Here's the thing. I'm writing so well now. I'm almost through the rough draft." She pointed at typescripts tied bundle-like at the foot of the bed. It was the way she arranged chapters.

"You can write well at home."

"I don't think so."

"I'll move my stuff in with Robin. We'll be a great little family."

"You can't do this."

I didn't know which thing she was talking about: quitting the firm, fixing her house, or moving in with her. I actually could do each of those things. "It's time for us all to come home, Nora."

She started crying again, and turned her back to face the placid green wall of her room, nodding slightly, resignedly. On her bureau sat cleanly arranged action soccer photos of Robin, and a white orchid still opening from Lowry. Then I saw Hugh's car keys beside a curled pile of the Sunday *Times*, and I understood why she didn't want to leave, just now, or maybe ever, no matter what I did. Hugh was out there, and she'd have to face him.

I walked down the hall to the waiting room, where I found Hugh sitting in a kid's chair working the crossword, horn-rims perched on his nose. Children's games of ring toss and Candyland lay scattered on the soiled beige rug at his feet, and a television on the wall soundlessly played the Braves game in an empty stadium.

"Jocko," he said without looking up. "Is that you?"

It occurred to me I'd spent a lot of my life standing while Hugh sat. So I sat down in a folding chair and faced him. "Why are you here? Shouldn't you be at home with Mary?"

"Where is here?" He looked around the room.

"Harmony Hall."

"I thought we were watching the Braves game."

I stood up and turned off the television, kicking over a Tinker Toy fort in the process. He looked at me blankly, as though I were a Martian landed in Raleigh, without the least idea of how to act.

"Jocko, no need to be upset." He put his hand on my shoulder. "Jocko—"

"Don't touch me."

It was the touch I remembered from boyhood: half comforting, half controlling.

"You've done a good thing with the Bank—"

"You're changing the subject. I asked you a question. Why are you here?"

"Nora needs me," he said, stepping back and speaking in his teaching tone.

"I'm trying not to hit you right now."

"Jocko, what on Earth's gotten into you?" he asked, backing fully out of range.

"Take your keys." I dropped them at his feet. "And get the hell out."

"Now look."

"Don't come back. If you do, I'm calling the cops."

I said those things to Hugh without going over them first in my mind, and it occurred to me only afterward that I should have said it all years ago, except I didn't think it was my business. Maybe I felt the urgency now because Lowry had fixed up the house, and I wanted us all to move in and be a family. Later, Gardiner said after our talk in the kiddie room Hugh stopped coming around. Maybe all he needed was somebody to say get the hell out and go back to Mary who, miraculously, was still waiting for him. Shouldn't that person be me? I was the quasi-heir, after all.

The next night, I had a dream about Hugh. I don't usually remember dreams, but this one stuck. We were in a house with rooms that flowed together, filled with fancy guys and blonde sirens in red gowns, and debutantes in virginal white gowns. We wore matching black tuxedos, notched, with emblems and ribbons of military meaning. A crowd surrounded us, but I felt alone. Hugh left. I panicked, but he came back holding martinis. His face turned pink before my eyes.

"Here Jocko," he said. "You tried to poison me. Drink this."

He rocked on his heels, grinning as I drank the martini down like a soda. Dancing people whirled around us, and he motioned to an open room. He put his arm around me and whispered, "It's all right that you tried the poison. It didn't work."

The next morning, I called Elaine to talk about the dream. We had made up about me leaving the firm and her marrying Sid, although we were being unnaturally cordial. Elaine was good with dreams; she said she enjoyed her weekly shrink sessions mostly because of them.

I felt uncomfortable with the vividness, especially Hugh turning pink. Elaine loved that. "It's a humdinger," she said. "Wait a minute. I'm getting on the Beltline."

"Do you want me to call back?"

"No."

"What do you think it means?"

"Hugh turning pink? It's not really Hugh. It's you seeing yourself, pink."

Wow, that was brilliant. I looked at somebody else, Hugh, and saw myself. The rest still bewildered me—a house of many rooms, fancy guys in tuxedos, sirens, debutantes, martinis. "What about the poison thing?"

"He was inviting you back."

"What?"

"The party is your old life. You're leaving, and feeling what leaving means."

"You're really great at this."

"I've had lots of practice. He gives you a martini, a kind of poison, and then says you're the one trying to poison him."

"Right. So since I'm pink Hugh, am I doing it to myself?"

"Everybody's always doing it to themselves."

"I get it. So, is the dream good or bad?"

"Dreams aren't good or bad. They're jokes played by your subconscious. The Marx brothers couldn't do better than this one. Congratulations."

"Beginner's luck."

We rang off before I could tell her about the other dream I'd been having. It came in parts, and then the whole, like a symphony building. She and I start walking in the desert, burned-out bushes, cattle skulls, holey snakeskins. Suddenly an oasis appears, and we sit down for a picnic.

I have some bread, cheese, and wine in an old-fashioned wicker basket, like in the famous painting of naked people picnicking. Sure enough, naked people sit down near us, Suddenly, I turn around, and I'm not with Elaine, but Tessie, and we're back at the sandspit island. She wears a flowing skirt that blows in the wind, and her hair is down. Then something catches fire on shore, a large red flame that envelopes the horizon, rolling above the water, heading toward the sandspit. We escape in the Chris-Craft, heading out to sea, toward another horizon. "It's everywhere!" she says joyously, throwing her hands up toward the lighted sky, as the fire retreats behind us.

"No, it's nowhere," I say, and she laughs.

"Everywhere!" she shouts.

"Nowhere!" I shout back, again and again, while the sea washes over us.

Grant's Tomb

I ALSO HAD A dream about Teri Lynn. She appeared before me as in a slideshow, younger and younger, until she eventually presented in a pixie haircut, jeans, and a Peter Pan shirt, like Scout in *To Kill a Mockingbird*. But then we ran into each other at the Whole Foods, a brand-new grocery store with mostly vegetables grown without fertilizer. I was eating oatmeal with additional, healthy nuts when she approached briskly, carrying a cloth bag of vegetables and wearing scrubs.

"Jack!" she said, sprawling across from me in the booth I had occupied for my breakfast with the *Wall Street Journal*. "I moved to Raleigh! You live around here?"

"Sort of. Are you nursing? I mean, not that, but working, you know."

She flicked her hair out of a headband, and strands fell in a brown tumbrel to her shoulders. I'd never seen it brown. Maybe that was her natural color.

"Still awkward, huh?"

"Sorry?"

"I've got another semester at Chapel Hill," she said. "But they hired me already at Rex. Oncology, you know, people with real problems."

"I remember you liked the challenge of that."

I imagine she paid her tuition with the money from our lawsuit—that is, from me. I ended up paying for nursing school after all.

"I heard you quit the firm and you're going to Mexico with Lowry."

"Where'd you hear that?"

"Ran into Robin at Lowry's church. I go there now."

"Really? Mighty Lamb? Well, okay, you heard right. I'm done with the law."

She crunched on an apple. "Good thing if you ask me. That firm's a sorry place."

"Yeah. And I want to say, if I haven't before, that I'm sorry about what happened."

I hadn't planned to apologize; it just came out. She held up her hand to block either more words or the sunlight through the windows. "Oh Jack, that's sweet, but you weren't the only one in the room. I was a Pure-T mess back then."

"I'm really glad. I wanted to say I'm sorry, though, because you're a young woman, and I shouldn't have, you know, imposed on you, as the older man."

She leaned forward, squinting. "You have no idea how old I am, do you?"

"No, come to think of it."

"Let's just say age wasn't the problem." She deposited her apple core daintily in a napkin. "Got to go to work."

"Could I...would you like to have coffee? You know, for old times' sake?"

She laughed. "Bad idea. But hey, listen, catch me at the Mighty Lamb—with Robin! You're really lucky, getting to go to Mexico with Lowry."

◆◆◆

WHAT A SCHMUCK! HAD I no shame? Thankfully Teri Lynn said no to coffee. No was a useful word, one I—not to mention the president, now in trouble with a woman named Paula Jones—should have employed more often in the past.

How old was Teri Lynn? It was a puzzlement, like the room of curios that I never saw in her old double-wide, apparently now traded for a city condo. And what went on at the Mighty Lamb? Looked like everybody I knew was ending up there, treating Lowry like some kind of spiritual leader. Maybe it *was* special for me to get invited on a road trip to Mexico.

Teri Lynn seemed so together, too, with a clear career plan. Was she pitying me, being at loose ends, or was that my imagination?

Needing a break from all the Raleigh excitement, I flew to New York and took a room in a cheap hotel on the Upper West Side. Robin was with Pren for the duration, and not happy, as I'd learned picking her up from Bingham the day before I left. We were still negotiating the Enright deal.

"Mom's so mean, she doesn't get my substance issues at all," Robin said, easing into the front seat of the Mercedes with a grimace, her back still on the mend. I snaked carefully out of the parent pick-up line while she settled in.

Robin likely meant something else, that Pren had refused to lift grounding so she could go to Bingham's big dance, the Hearts and Aces Ball. I had argued that she trade the big night for excising the belly ring, especially since she had an invitation from a suitably polite pre-SEM sophomore boy on the tennis team. But, no going, according to Pren. "Jack, you're such a marshmallow," were her exact words.

"Honey, your mother takes your issues very seriously, and so do I. One of us picks you up from school and drives you to Duke every day for life skills. I'm very proud of you for sticking with it. You're working much harder than you did in anger management."

She started to tear up. "It's hard, Daddy. It would be so much easier for me to stop drinking if I could have fun—like going to Hearts and Aces. It wouldn't even cost a dress, Melissa can give me hers from last year."

"I'm sorry, honey—if you do the crime, you've got to do the time…"

I didn't know how long I would stay in New York. I didn't even buy a return ticket. For two days, I wandered up and down Broadway past the old apartment on Morningside Heights, drinking coffee at a Cuban restaurant I thought I remembered as a kid, trying to connect with something familiar. On the third day, I took a taxi to the graveyard in Queens, flowers from the neighborhood Korean grocery in hand, and put them on Dad's grave, while the cabbie waited. That night I'd booked dinner in Red Bank with Aunt Judith and my stepsister Rachel at Dad's house, which was hers now, since Laura, my stepmother, had moved to California.

I took the PATH train and then a taxi that deposited me in front of the two-story brick Tudor now enveloped by oaks, pines, and smaller cherries planted decades ago. Rachel met me at the door. "The kids are out for the night," she said, kissing me routinely on the cheek, as though I'd just been on a business trip rather than having only visited twice in the last twenty years. "And Blair's in Kansas City."

Blair was her husband. He wouldn't mind having dinner with me, but maybe I needed to be fed the fatted calf alone before I could be unleashed on the kids, now teenagers. "I guess Aunt Judith's cooking."

"Your favorite, chicken paprikash."

Actually, that was Dad's favorite.

We ate as a jolly threesome, showing photos of the cousins around. Rachel had also raised soccer players, so we had plenty of North Carolina–New Jersey action shot comparisons. While admiring team photos, I searched for kinship in her face. She did look like Aunt Judith, a trimmer and more stylish version, with a Soho-short haircut and scarlet lipstick and jeans that cost about a thousand bucks. She'd been too young for style back in the day, when we ran around chasing lightning bugs.

"You look like him," she whispered while we were drying dishes. Judith was holding forth on multi-store plans for Presscort Flooring.

"That's what Judith says."

"But that's not how I know it's really you."

"How do you know?"

"Because you're a sentimental slob like he was."

Nobody had ever referred to me that way before, but I guess I did get weepy over the soccer pictures. I mean, our kids did the same thing, totally defensible.

She took my arm and led me to a highboy, and then opened a drawer and handed me a portrait of Dad. It was one of those backlit, big-eyed studio shots taken in a business suit, where the subject sported a serious yet jaunty expression. I turned it over in my hands and they shook a bit, but I managed a good, long look. Rachel and Judith were right, he did look like me: same wire hair, Caesar-like nose, high forehead, but jowlier.

"Take it," she said.

"Thanks."

"There's something else."

She led me downstairs to the den Dad had fixed up for himself. They hadn't done much down there in all the years since he died, and I could see the way he left it. A good Brunswick pool table, a custom bar with a Schaefer sign, Yankee pennants from the sixties. His desk stood to the side, a roll-top number still laden with account ledgers and a worn leather sample book resting by the claw feet of his ersatz leather chair. A couple more good years and he would have bought a real one. Golf clubs—Wilson all-steel blades and Wilson Persimmon woods in a Wilson bag big enough for Nicklaus—stood in the corner with framed scorecards: 82 at National, 77 at Shinnecock. I'd frame that last one, too.

"Take them," she said, pointing to the clubs.

"For real?"

"Yes. I don't know what to do with them. Are they good clubs?"

"Vintage. I don't know what to say."

"Oh, Jack, just take them—you're doing me a favor. I don't want to give Dad's clubs away."

What unbelievable good luck!

"Bring Robin when you come back," Aunt Judith commanded, following me out the door to the honk of my taxi. "We'll plan a barbecue."

"You're on—if she's talking to me that week."

Rachel handed me my coat, and they both kissed me goodbye. I only felt a little foolish lugging those clubs to the PATH station.

◆◆◆

CHECKING IN WITH AUNT Judith and Rachel and scoring Dad's clubs felt good, but it didn't complete my mission. It wasn't even the biggest reason for my escape to the city. Tessie had moved to an outpost in Brooklyn— formerly a ghetto, currently favored by trendy white people. Now that she was on the East Coast, why not have lunch?

She had written me a letter at the old firm address when she heard Pren and I were separated. She said she was sorry; she'd gotten divorced two years ago, which I'd heard from Mary. After that, we started trading emails, sometimes a letter, which felt more natural. She didn't have kids, which she said made her divorce easier, but I knew from the way she wrote that it made her sad. She'd beaten me to quitting the law, too, five years before in fact, and she'd gone back to history grad school. When I asked, she sent a picture, but even so, I wasn't sure I'd recognize her. Yet there she sat, at a window table in the West Village café she picked for us, halfway between her Brooklyn apartment and my hotel. She was flipping through notebook paper, and I gathered she was grading. After getting a Masters at UCLA, she'd started teaching high school in LA and now had a job in New York.

"Tessie?"

"Jack?" She stood up, and we did an awkward cheek-to-cheek kiss, then a better hug.

"You look great," I said, cliché though it was. She did: shortish blonde hair, earth-tone sweater and jeans, stylish black city boots. She'd ordered up carrot juice for two. Healthy food had become an epistolary joke between us.

"Oh, thanks," she said, in her husky southern alto. "I had to change everything for the East Coast, so all new stuff."

"It's working."

She smiled and zipped her student papers into a leather satchel. "You caught me grading. We're into the 1890s at Marcus Garvey High School."

"Isn't that in Harlem? Is it safe? What train do you take?"

She sighed. "Drink your carrot juice."

I got that I was fussing too much. "Thanks. Love me some carrot juice. Yum."

She rounded up a stray Xerox from the floor and folded it in the satchel. "We're talking Manifest Destiny tomorrow."

"There are so many jokes I could make about that."

"That's my Jack, making jokes about Manifest Destiny."

"I guess you could go on to the Wilmington Riots, if they tire of the rape of the West. Centennial's around the corner."

Tessie, who read the *Criterion* in exile, had been most curious about the Wilmington Centennial in her letters, an event the paper had announced in sponsorship with the city. A century passed with the new year, 1898 to 1998. Wardie decided it was time to come clean. Actually, it was Lowry's idea, but he was happy to give up authorship. Reconciliation, that was the thing, talking it out with white people and black people together where the outrages all happened. Wardie and I had been going back and forth on some project ideas—placing statuary, seating arrangements, order of speakers; whether there should be games and prizes, a festival atmosphere, or whether it was solemn stuff gavel to gavel. Wardie said he wanted to work on the grand design all by himself, but I expected to be pressed into service any moment. I figured Tessie's interest was less in ginning up the pageantry and more in settling scores.

"This is really happening?"

"Yeah. It was Wardie's idea, or really Lowry's."

"I remember Lowry—not surprised he's behind it. The only original idea Wardie ever had was running his boat aground at Shell Island on the Fourth of July because he had to park it and there weren't any slips. He'd been drinking, what a shocker."

I'd forgotten that when she was younger she'd sometimes found herself on Wardie's boat. I hadn't asked any questions.

"Your dad's making a speech."

"I know. He's confessing, right?"

"I have no idea what he'll say. Stopped predicting that years ago."

She laughed. "Do you think he actually feels shame?"

I'd thought about that myself. "Guilt yes, shame no. It's complicated."

"Bet you go for both guilt and shame."

"End Times."

"What? You mean like in the Bible?"

"I just say that when it comes in my head."

Left unsaid were the effects of Hugh's wandering mind. Mary had guarded the secret artfully, even through the night of Kai-Jana's fundraiser, but at the Center Dr. Wishener had mapped Hugh's TIAs, small strokes that over time had claimed parts of his short-term memory, and which perhaps explained the lapses I'd noticed during the past couple of years, including, interestingly, his inability to remember meetings, or follow in detail when I took him. I'd attributed his lapses to alcohol—so had Ballard and Drac—but drink wasn't the diagnosis after all. While in treatment, a larger TIA had caused him to fall, and they called that a full-on stroke at the hospital. He was in for two weeks, and then went to Atlanta for a month of rehab. He left with some gaps in his speech, sometimes a shaky gait, and some evidence of paralysis on his face. He'd been recovering with Mary, and at the Landing since.

But he was set on making a speech at the Centennial. There would be no debate.

"I do need to ask something else," she said. "And you're literally the only person on Earth I can ask."

"What?"

"Are Nora and Dad really over?"

The non-secret secret lived on, even when it didn't. "Yep. What, you didn't believe it?" I'd assumed Mary had said that Nora was out of the picture, and she and Hugh were back together, and it was all right with her. This hadn't been a topic of our correspondence. Probably Tessie said something back like, "You're crazy, Mom!" And then Mary had said, "He makes me laugh, dear, and he's handy around the house." Then they both wondered about the craziness of life, and what Thanksgiving would be like, now that the non-secret secret was out, and over.

That was the other thing Tessie had announced in her last letter: that if the Centennial happened, and Hugh apologized, she was coming home, going against decades of decrees. I imagined the demise of the non-secret secret had something to do with it, too.

"That settles it, I'm moving back," she said, affirming the earlier epistolary promise, and plunking down her carrot juice for emphasis. "After the semester is over."

"You can come back, just like that?" I snapped my fingers for emphasis.

"Love my kids, but I can teach history in Wilmington."

So, Wilmington was where she'd settle. Good choice. Raleigh seemed crowded these days. "Terrific that you're coming back."

"Really?" She peered at me, squinting and smiling, like a skeptical female Hugh. "You don't sound thrilled."

"No, really. And Wilmington's great. They make that TV show there, with the teenagers."

"*Dawson's Creek.*"

"That's the one. If I seem weird, it's just that a lot has changed, and I don't know really what to do with you coming home."

She sat impassively and smiled, as though she'd already decided not to engage in personal history; and why, when there was so much dress-up history to occupy us? "You don't have to do anything, Jack."

"Your dad's got plenty of care, if that's part of it. I go see him."

"I know, Mom tells me. And that's part of it. Mom can't handle him by herself. It's not just the strokes."

"What do you mean?"

"Nora always kept him out of that place in his mind. Mom never had to worry about it."

"You mean that place by the mad river."

"Yes. Turns out Nora made Dad possible all these years. Guess the joke's on us."

She stood up to leave, and I stood up, too, not knowing what to do to say goodbye. So I kissed her straight on, and she dropped her satchel with the papers in it and kissed me back, and we stood there, kissing each other like dopey kids in front of a restaurant full of New Yorkers who couldn't care less.

"So—guess I'll see you back home," she whispered, smoothing her lipstick and pulling away.

◆◆◆

ANOTHER JOKE, AN OLD vaudeville riddle, kept going around in my head on the flight back to Raleigh. *Who's buried in Grant's tomb?* You're tempted to say Grant, as though the whole thing is a play on words. But the comic just stands there—Jack Benny, Henny Youngman, Groucho Marx, doesn't matter. *Who's buried in Grant's tomb?* he says again, and everybody laughs.

My jammed American Eagle flight banked west and then south over the Hudson, with Grant's tomb in fleeting sight on Riverside Drive below. I got out my old photograph of Nora and me, with Dad behind the camera, and I thought this: *You don't know until you open it up and look inside.*

More than that, maybe you don't know until you air it out, poke around, and clean stem to stern. Old soldiers lay wreaths, a brass band plays on Memorial Day, and the park guys in the natty green uniforms buff the names of battles, but nobody really knows if the old drunk's in there or not, and, if he is, who's in there with him.

Who's buried in Grant's tomb? Who isn't?

I puzzled over Tessie, about her coming back, and that goodbye kiss in the restaurant. I also puzzled over what she said about Nora making Hugh possible. What did that mean? Did I need a woman to make me possible? I didn't think one had ever done that. I think Pren tried, and got tired of it. Teri Lynn did, for a brief and shining moment. I guess the longest enabler was Elaine, grudgingly, but now she was off to bigger and better things.

For the future, I resolved to make my own self possible, if for no other reason than to conserve precious female resources.

◆◆◆

BACK IN RALEIGH, I got a surprise invitation: Wardie asked me to move in at the mansion. I think he figured I was a shiftless knockabout, rudderless and in trouble. Lowry's renovation at the ranch-palace was way behind schedule, and there'd been grumbling about my long tenure in the spare room at the Club. Wardie said he wanted me to be a consultant for the paper, figuring, I guess, that I could do some of the work he wasn't doing. What he really wanted me for, as I'd predicted, was to look after plans for the Centennial, since I was a Symmes, and he was a Forrest, and he didn't bother with details. Besides, he was busy with the Engine. In California, they'd done beta tests and started packing the thing with Big Data, and all systems were go.

Dutifully, I started making lists. I asked Kai-Jana what she'd suggest for the agenda. "Truth and reconciliation," she said, on her cell at RDU getting set to fly out for money. "The South African model. But then you'd need Bishop Tutu. And all you've got is Bobby."

Bobby was what she called the Reverend Sweeney, which was his name when he worked for her grandfather. I'd detected from her some downrating for the Reverend, despite his victory in the street against Broman. Maybe nobody could run a protest movement like Grandpa.

So I asked Lowry what to do. "Easy," he said, "but hard." He was shoveling in azaleas. "You start by being sorry."

"Confessing?"

"You can look at it that way."

He'd been to see Hugh, at Mary's request, and the two of them had made up. I had the feeling Lowry was helping Hugh with the being sorry part. I decided my consultant's role was to take care of the ordinary things that kept piling up: seating charts, high school bands, and golf carts were the latest. I wondered whether it was petty to misplace Brenda Bobelink's press pass.

Wardie got Griffiths to underwrite—good stroke there—and I penciled over budgets with the head of Ameribank community relations. She focused on placement of the corporate logo for TV shots. I sat daily on a city committee exquisitely balanced in race and gender to set agendas and speeches. Hugh would go at the end, before Tatty, in a draped gown that made her look like a goddess, unveiled the monument.

Wardie guarded the monument design. He'd been working on it in secret for months, down to the casting in bronze. I had to pester him for the model, and finally he showed me: dolphins, leaping.

"They swim upriver," he said. "Thirty miles. On a good day, there's four or five in the harbor."

"That's amazing, Wardie," I said.

The Committee had gone for a martial theme, heroic figures of all races straining into the future. But, they fell into dispute, and got dolphins instead.

When I described the monument to Nora, she wrote a line of poetry on her scratch pad.

"Try this," she said. "For the inscription."

"'Came Neptunus, his mind leaping like dolphins,'" I read aloud.

"Ezra Pound. 'Canto 116.' Must have been what Wardie was thinking."

"I don't think people will get the allusion, I mean some will, but generally."

She patted me on the arm. "You know better than I do."

I believed, alternatively, that Wardie was not thinking about Ezra Pound, but about dolphins swimming by his power boat as he careened downriver into Shell Island, drunk. But, then again, he did read.

"Pound was a fascist," I said. "We can't have that mucking up the media coverage."

She shrugged. "Poor Ezra. He just wanted to get free of history, like you boys."

On weekends, I worked with Lowry to finish the ranch-palace. Getting the pool done meant we were nearing the end. The plans called for a well to hook up Lowry's spring, so we wouldn't have to pay for city water. We'd pump our own strange stuff, mercury and all.

◆◆◆

BUNKING WITH WARDIE GAVE me a chance to stay in the only house I knew where real people lived that had an historical marker in the front yard. Wardie didn't think anything of it, and his patience ran thin as I slowed the car down yet again at the driveway to recite the inscribed homage to his grandfather, the Old Man.

"Colonel Ward Prestwick Forrest, 1862–1948, Philanthropist, Publisher, Advisor to Presidents."

"Don't know where they got the colonel part. The sign just appeared one day—had to move a two-hundred-year-old boxwood."

"Maybe we need to get our facts straight before the event."

"What do you mean?"

It had been a ticklish subject, the facts. "Well, the Committee kind of tiptoes about exactly what happened, who did what, you know. Who was in the Group of Nine, who burned the newspaper, who chased out the families, who rousted the city councilmen, who put the so-called troublemakers on the trains north. Most of all, who did the killing, and was it eight dead, like the Old Man reported, or the two hundred who never got accounted for? The Committee wants to get it all straight."

"It's a lot of facts nobody knows," Wardie said. "Waddell took over and wouldn't investigate himself."

"What about the US Attorney?"

"Wouldn't do a thing. They sat on it in Washington."

"All I knew going in is what I was told: Big Hugh reported the killings, and the Old Man buried the story. It's the eight-hundred-pound gorilla in the room."

Wardie slammed the car door and shook his head. "Is that what Hugh said?"

"He said the Old Man buried the story about the Gatling gun."

"Son of a bitch," he snorted. "That's just like him. It's not what happened."

"Okay, so what happened?"

Wardie walked into the kitchen and opened a Heineken for himself, and one for me. "What happened is this. Big Hugh was going down there to calm down Waddell, because Waddell had gone nuts, getting all those people in the street. But somehow he turns up—" He took a long draught.

"What?"

"He turns up on the wagon shooting the Gatling gun."

"Wow." I sat down at the kitchen table and tried to take in the obvious. I hadn't ever thought about the simplest answer of all—that everything horrible Hugh saw by the mad river was real. "So all those visions—they happened. The ones I told you about."

"My theory is PTSD. Instead of dialing back Waddell, Big Hugh saw the Gatling gun and got mesmerized. So it was like a trance, and he was there, but he wasn't really there, and he started shooting people down, awful, awful stuff. He'd just come back from Cuba."

I could have questioned the retelling, but as Wardie went through the scenario, and I figured in the meaning of the Symmes delirium, PTSD made a soft landing for murder.

"So, the first Symmes-Forrest deal was the Old Man lying to protect Big Hugh?"

Wardie shrugged. "What else could he do?"

I was about to say report the crime, but I didn't. What was the point? Their lie stretched across a century. "What we really have here is an unsolved mass murder," I said. "It's hard to get closure with that."

"It's not unsolved, just uninvestigated. Waddell grabbed all the headlines, giving speeches about the glory of the Anglo-Saxon race. The

United Daughters of the Confederacy put up a bunch of statues, and everybody forgot about it."

"They all figured they were doing the right thing."

Wardie beckoned into the library. "Yeah, for themselves. Look at this."

He held up a well-thumbed copy of Kipling from the poetry collection. It fell open to "White Man's Burden."

"No way," I said.

"Every now and then, you find a gem or two here in the family library. 'Bear the White Man's Burden,'" he began, and then his voice trailed off.

Do it, lie about it, enjoy the spoils, and live with the crimes. They had plenty of company.

Wardie put Kipling back and removed an old King James Bible. "Look at what the Old Man read at bedtime."

I opened to the Old Testament, bookmarked with a leather cross. Underlined was a passage even I recognized, King Nebuchadnezzar at dinner. "'The moving finger writes, and having writ moves on.' Looks like the Old Man thought about what they were doing."

Wardie closed the Bible and pointed it at me. "No, wrong. There wasn't a 'they.' This is Hugh's problem, why he's crazy with this shit. Hugh's grandfather is the one who shot those men. My grandfather didn't kill anybody. He put out a newspaper. There's a difference."

I held back from defending the Symmes men, all of them dying, or soon enough to die, with the killing on their heads. As the quasi-heir, I felt the tribal call to arms. But I said nothing, and instead took the old Bible and opened to the next passage. I recalled it from my limited Sunday school days: "Ye have been judged in the balance and found wanting." That part wasn't underlined.

"I've never had this conversation with anybody," Wardie said. "But it's been going on in my head all my life. Boy, I feel better. You can ignore the past to death. Almost."

"That's why we're having this Centennial, right? You know, some truth-telling."

He smiled ruefully. "Hope so."

Relieved for the moment, Wardie bounded upstairs to prepare for his afternoon run. Presently, he appeared carrying his shoes and a Walkman.

"You making dinner?" he shouted, pointing to his earphones. It was my turn.

I nodded. I moved to sit in the study with the rest of my beer. As in the Symmes house, up and down the paneled walls hung reflections of past glory: inscribed photographs of flash-bulbed luminaries, gold-flecked honorary degrees, a Pulitzer citation. Family vacation scenes at Victorian mountain houses during spells of public service, daughters holding croquet mallets, mothers in white hose beside high-collared men, bored boys to the side, horseshoes in hand. Through double doors, the dining room sat bare except for a dark mahogany table, twelve chairs still arranged, and a linen center cloth and ornate crystal bowl awaited the morning's cut flowers.

◆◆◆

I DIALED KAI-JANA ON the rotary phone. She'd called when Wardie and I were having our history-and-guilt chat.

"Jack," she said firmly. "I need you to go with me to church."

"Hello, Kai-Jana, how was your day? Mine sucked. Having a beer now."

I heard cocktail party racket in the background, and finance man Chip telling her to meet somebody named Anderson. "Jack," she said, coming back on, "you've got to help me!"

"Okay, okay. What's going on?"

"I'm stepping away. You still there? Winston won't go with me, and it's a problem. You did great at the Symmes event, and you're—"

"A white guy in a suit."

"There is that."

"Sort of reverse diversity?"

"Reverse diversity is not a thing. It's all diversity."

"Well, I'm working on Wardie's Centennial, and paying for my mother's pool, and trying to keep Robin off the sauce, and then I'm booked to go to Mexico with Lowry, so—"

"Jack, help!"

Church wasn't the whole deal, there was another hard ask for Kai-Jana, always self-sufficient. I just guessed what else she wanted me to do.

"You want me to talk to Winston?"

"Everything I say is wrong," she whispered.

"Let me try."

"Bless you," she said. "You'll love church in Rocky Mount on Sunday. The ladies will make a covered dish…"

◆◆◆

WARDIE OPENED THE FRONT door with a gust of wind and waved on his way to the kitchen, where he retrieved more beer to nullify the effects of his run.

"Seen the mail?" he said.

We were past murder, or at least he was, and back to the day-to-day.

"Shit," he said tearing into an envelope.

"What?"

"Invitation from Griffiths. Black tie dinner in Charlotte. Here's yours."

"Not going."

"We have to go."

"Why?"

"You know why." He rubbed his fingers together in the universal money sign. "You need a date. I vote for Angie, that'll cause a buzz."

"I'm staying away from Angie."

"What the hell's the matter with you? Huge tits, rich as hell."

"Broman's money."

"Is he in the bed when you're doing her?"

"I don't want to talk about it."

"What about Tessie?" he asked, trying not to crack himself up. I'd made the mistake of telling him about our long-ago summer. I hadn't mentioned the hello/goodbye kiss in New York.

"My suspicion is that she'd rather have a sharp stick stuck in her eye than go to something like that."

"Yeah, and screwing her in the hotel after would be kind of like doing it with the field hockey coach."

"Whatever, man."

341

"Elaine's going to be there with glamour boy."

Since their engagement, Elaine and Wheeless had become quite the social as well as political item. Sid had called me after Elaine spilled the beans, and we had a retro gentlemanly chat, as though we owned neighboring mineral rights.

"You don't mind, do you?" he said. "If you'd been involved with her…"

Later, I got to read about them in the social column of the *Criterion*, "Senate candidate Sidney Wheeless appeared at the Heart Campaign Ball escorting his fiancée, Elaine Marchetti, a prominent Raleigh lawyer. Ms. Marchetti wore an off-the-shoulder magenta gown by Ann Wang…"

Wardie stood up and stretched. "If you don't get your own date, Dolly's going to fix you up. She's got a list."

I thought about stopping by Rex and asking Terri Lynn. That would cause a buzz. But then, my past behavior had been shameful, and she'd said no to coffee. If not too young, she was too well-adjusted for me now.

◆◆◆

THE NEXT MORNING, I met Winston for breakfast at his club in Durham. "This is my free time," he said, "after I drop the girls at school. Been playing any golf?"

"No," I said, buttering wheat toast and sampling an egg from the hot plate that was poached too hard. "Got too much on the calendar. Going with your wife to church in Rocky Mount, for instance."

"When? She didn't tell me."

"This Sunday. She said you wouldn't go with her."

He frowned. I was wading into turbulent waters.

"Look, man," I pressed on, "I have some experience here. You don't want to mess up your marriage."

"Callahan, my marriage is fine, and it's not your business."

"I think it is, because, see, your wife calls me all upset, and she's on a mission, and I can see you don't like it."

He tossed his napkin to the table. "Yeah, well, I'm soldiering on, making excuses at the office for all kinds of bullshit."

"Because your wife is going to be attorney general."

"Which I want her to be—"

"And you're not."

He shook his head. "What's your point?"

"Try this. Swallow your pride and call up her mother and say you need help with the girls. Do a deal at work, and stop trying to cover it all. I don't think North Carolina Associated is going to be pissed off when Kai-Jana gets to be AG. I think they're going to like it. Then show up for a couple of events with a smile on your face and let some lobbyists kiss your ass. It's actually not so bad."

He sat nodding, his arms crossed in front of him. Finally he laughed. "You've been thinking about this little speech, haven't you?"

"Yep. And it's my speech, not hers. We can play golf every day after she's elected. You get a car and a driver, I'm not kidding."

Raleighwood Ranch

I HADN'T MADE ANY progress on a date to the Griffiths soiree, but it turned out not to matter. Friday morning, as I came in from my morning run, I tripped over Wardie's beaten-up camel-colored Hartman suit bag packed at the bottom of stairs, propped against a brace of tennis rackets. He sat in the kitchen, his blue blazer draped over a chair, drinking coffee.

"Sorry. Been meaning to tell you. I'm leaving for San Francisco," he said, tossing the paper aside.

"Visit with Tatty?"

"Truth is, I won't be back for a while. I—well, Griffiths—I mean, I've decided…I don't know what to say. I've decided to sell the paper."

"What the fuck?" I realized I had barked that loudly enough for the whole block to hear.

He winced. "It all came down this week, had to be decided."

"And I was doing something else? Oh, of course—planning the white-guys-get-out-of-guilt-jail Centennial."

"I'm really sorry, Jack."

Of course he could sell the paper. In fact, several times during the Broman wars, I told him he could myself. So why did it feel like he was breaking up with me? And why did he act like he was?

Wardie massaged the old oak breakfast tabletop, as though to rub out the bad feelings. "These people in California," he began again, taking a deep breath. "Griffiths put it together. They do things the way we do."

"Sounds like something Griffiths would say."

"Yeah, fair point."

"Who are these wonderful people? Do they have names?" I tried not to sound bitchy. He chose not to involve me, and nothing was going to change that. I stood up to pour my coffee but sat down again, disoriented by the sudden end of our struggle for—what was that grand cause again?

Wardie reached into his shirt pocket for his lone cigarette of the day. Retrieving a wrinkled Marlboro, he fired up with an unsteady hand, and I heard distant trumpets across Monument Valley summoning a Raleigh cowboy west, our own entrepreneur hero answering the time-honored American call to cash out.

"You wouldn't know the company," he went on. "It's family-owned. Like I said, Griffiths' people set it up."

"Guess they're hot for that old Engine. Now that the beta test is in."

"I'm grateful for all you did, Jack. You saved the paper, you really did."

"Can you at least tell me why?"

He stubbed out the smoke after a puff, then stood up. "I want a new start. I'm tired of the past. Putting together Wilmington closes things out."

"Nothing ever gets closed out, man."

"I figured you'd say something like that. You're the last Symmes standing."

I guess he was right about that, if I was indeed standing. "Never thought of it that way."

"There's something else."

"What?"

"Griffiths got a retention bonus for you."

"Nobody owes me anything."

He looked a little hurt. "Jack, after all you've done? It's two hundred and fifty thousand dollars."

I laughed, and tried to stop, but then laughed some more, finally sitting down at the breakfast table, noticing for the first time how the yellow-flowered chicken porcelains went with the wallpaper, the Other Room prayer books stopped in 1967, and the Gatlinburg cuckoo clock ticked away nowhere close to time.

"I'm retained for a job I'm not doing?"

"You just get the money. They do it all the time, Griffiths said."

"I understand the concept."

"Is it enough? I could probably get more."

"The number's not a problem."

He scratched his head and sat down on the steps by the Hartman. "Jack," he began again, in a tone of concern. "I thought you'd be happy. It's the least we can do. I'm selling the paper and giving you two hundred anf fifty thousand dollars."

"Appreciate it. Thank you."

A car horn sounded outside, and he stood up again and put on his blazer. "I also owe you some truth, man," he said, pocketing his plane ticket. "Sometimes it's easier to just write a check, but we go back. I've tried to help, but being around you, there's lots of issues. You're not a happy person. You're working through your divorce, your mother's depressed, Robin nearly killed herself, and you have, I don't know, not much career direction. You tore up your law license, and you know, it wasn't cool that I didn't have my own lawyer for the biggest deal of my life. It's taken me time to get my shit together, but now, I've kind of done it. I've put together the Wilmington thing, I've sold the business, and I'm happy. My advice is you work on getting your own shit together, man."

He offered his sailor-brown hand and I shook it. I held the door open as he lumbered forth, loaded up.

"Stay in the house as long as you want." He waved grandly from the curb. "Somebody should."

◆◆◆

"You need help," Lowry said as he dumped the topsoil laced with manure in a grand mound at the end of the driveway. He looked at the middling trees that intruded on the grassy vista around the new pool, then quickly marked with red tape a score of oak and maple saplings, pine

346

wastrels, errant acanthus and holly and attending ground-rooted vines and miscellaneous noxious invaders for extraction. Satisfied, he ambled back to his truck and produced from the back a well-oiled Briggs and Stratton chainsaw big enough to have slain the Philistines.

"This, for instance," he said, checking the gas mix. "I'll put it on your tab."

"You think I'm crazy, don't you?" I said, priming and revving like he showed me.

"Nope. I think you need some help with the landscaping."

Lowry and Juan had been working on the house punch list, after putting in the pool. I wanted some part to be my labor and thought I'd tackle landscaping. It would take my mind off Wardie selling the paper, and me pocketing a quarter million dollars for doing nothing.

I'd told Lowry about the goings-on, and he wasn't surprised or even opposed. "I think Ward should leave," he said. "He's finished his work here."

"Well shit, Lowry—what did I do all that for, keeping the paper? Hell, I cut up my privilege license! Now I get stupid money. None of it makes sense."

Lowry squinted at some uncooperative roots, and motioned to Juan and the guys to come over with a pickax. "Why do you think it should make sense?"

"There you go. I know you're going to tell me about God's plan. You and Griffiths should hang out."

He nodded as though the idea of talking with Griffiths about God's plan had occurred to him. "You kept the newspaper away from evil men. The money appeared because your family has needs. If you don't use all of it, you can give the rest to the poor."

He didn't go into the privilege license, because we'd had words over that already. That part made him angry. "You have great gifts!" he'd said. "Do you think you can bury that part of yourself? There are others in need of your talents, many people."

I hadn't seen Lowry so worked up before. Juan stood beside him, nodding. Nothing got Lowry going like somebody burying their talents. I knew he wanted me to take on more immigration work, but sitting in

Charlotte at INS twiddling my thumbs didn't sound like a glittering future. There'd be no helicopters going *thumpeta-thumpeta*, no pinging satellites. On the plus side, I'd be helping real people, and I'd get hot meals and road trips to Mexico.

I continued on with the landscaping, putting down the chain saw and looking for my old Boy Scout hatchet in the garage. For the rest of the afternoon, I busied myself felling saplings. Resigned to me doing the yard work, Lowry returned toward the end of the day, and unloaded more mulch.

"I hired Adam Marchetti for you," he said.

"Really? Just now?"

"If you're set on clearing the brush, you'll need help. He has a strong back."

Lowry had played me like a fiddle. He knew I wouldn't object to Adam. He'd saved Robin's life the night of the frat party, and he did have a strong back from all that soccer. Also, Elaine wasn't around much to supervise him, what with Sid's campaign and all, and I figured Lowry thought he needed looking after.

On that point, I'd stopped for a beer at Riley's the week before and noticed Adam's red Fiat. He sat at the end of the bar with a couple of young fancy guys.

"You gave that bunch beer by mistake," I said to Hank, the bartender. "Must have got the orders mixed up. I'll bet they could use some Cokes on the house."

I claimed the stool next to Adam as his friends scattered. He was wearing a regulation team rugby shirt, chinos, and deck shoes, and had perfected the relaxed, somewhat bored, and presumably untouchable look of the entitled friends who wouldn't quite befriend him, a look that hadn't changed much in a generation.

"So, Adam," I said, "come to Riley's often?"

"Sorry, Mr. C—you shouldn't have to deal with that."

Some of Robin's other friends had started calling me Mr. C, and maybe Adam was the source. "It's not a problem for me, son, but here's the thing: you can keep your nose clean, go to Duke, have a leg up—or you can go down the wrong path with these society clowns and ruin your chances."

"Yessir, you're right, I get that." He cocked his head at me the way his father Roger might have in Cambridge twenty-five years ago; as Adam matured, he favored Roger's dark, intense look more, with a slight eagerness around the mouth I knew from our twenties. Becoming Roger seemed unfair, since Elaine had raised him.

"One underage drinking citation, and Duke's down the drain. Right out there behind that pine tree sits an unmarked police cruiser, just waiting for kids like you to pull out of the parking lot."

"Mr. C, you're not going to tell my mom about this, are you?" he asked, in a tone between demand and question.

"Nope, I'm not, it would break her heart."

"She goes off on things, is all."

"She's a complicated woman, Adam. Sometimes, it's our fate as men to find ourselves in the company of complicated women. We have to cherish them."

"Uh—yessir."

"On that score, I haven't thanked you properly for looking after Robin that night. You stepped up like a man, and I want to thank you, man to man."

I held out my hand and he shook it. "Um—Mr. C?"

"Yes, Adam."

"Is it okay if I go now?"

"Sure," I said, waving expansively. He walked briskly into the parking lot and guided the Fiat carefully past the heretofore camouflaged police cruiser, soon to be known to every inside-the-Beltline boy.

◆◆◆

THE NEXT DAY, WE cleared enough to start spreading the mulch. By the weekend, Adam and I had moved on to sod. The arrangement over time helped close another deal: Robin moving in. She had wanted to live at Raleighwood Ranch, as she and her friends called our fixer-upper, but she held back. To redo the ranch-palace and christen it with a swanky new name, maybe live there outside the Beltline, these were large events. Wasn't going to Enright enough? Somehow seeing Adam flail away at the brush and till the soil made it all click.

As predicted, Enright meant serious studying. I had to beg at City Hall to enroll her in AP courses mid-year. Begging worked: they classified her overnight stay at Rex as a trauma event eligible for a substance-abuse-mental-health-special-deal-pass. Sometimes, you have to love the bureaucracy.

"Let's look at the alternatives," I'd said to Robin, putting forth the deal. "You can continue your present path, become an alcoholic, and flunk out of hairstyling at Wake Tech. Or, you can give up your hell-raising friends, go to Enright, and who knows—end up at college somewhere in the ACC."

"Dad, they have tons of Asians there."

"Yes, this is America."

She shook her head. "Dad, I'm never going to make good grades. Asians destroy the curve."

I shrugged. "You've said this before. But you're going to have to rise to the challenge, honey. Befriend them. Teach them our ways. Soon, they'll be mediocre, too."

"I can't do this. My GPA already sucks. I'm hopeless."

"Never hopeless! This is America! Land of many chances! Now is the time. Look at Enright like a giant road trip."

"The kids there are geeks."

"Geeks rule in the end. Besides, Adam Marchetti's there. He's not a geek, is he?"

"He's the only cool guy in the whole school."

"What could be more perfect? You already know the one cool guy."

◆◆◆

PREN HAD FINALLY AGREED to the Enright plan. She'd also come around to Robin living with me for a while. But it hadn't occurred to her we'd be bunking at the newly dubbed Raleighwood Ranch. It was unthinkable for Robin to live outside the Beltline.

Living at Nora's was worth a try, I tried to convince Pren over a dozen telephone calls. After all, Enright had turned out to be a way better choice than the Duke therapist's alternative: boot camp in Utah.

"I can't believe you're going through with it, moving into Nora's house," she repeated incredulously. She spoke from her car phone, on the way to meet a couple relocating from Connecticut.

"Nora's coming back in two weeks." It was the moving two-week target. Thankfully, there'd been no more Allegra overdoses, and we were ginning up the willpower.

I could hear doors slamming and Bingo's loud voice. "Hold on," Pren said. "Need to move the car."

"We can talk another time."

"No, now. You really want to take Robin and move in with your mother? I get to decide that."

Pren and I employed a hard-earned, respectful joint parenting style, but she hadn't internalized the notion that Robin, at sixteen, could choose where she lived, even if it was with me and Nora—and, even outside the Beltline.

"Robin's decision, remember?"

"That's not what my lawyer says."

"You haven't talked to your lawyer, because no lawyer would say that. Why don't you ask Bingo. He's got kids scattered around."

She laughed self-consciously. As I progressed in conquering my fear of arguing with her, I'd learned that playing the Bingo card made Pren step back. I think she fancied me jealous.

"Jack, you can't manage her."

"Hah. I believe you were AWOL the night she had her stomach pumped."

"You shit!" she shouted into the phone. "I can't believe you said that! Robin hates you for leaving us. She'd never move in there."

I counted to ten and remembered not to get angry, but be constructive, as our last counselor had counseled. *Empathize with the anger and flow into it* was her exact advice.

"I understand your feelings, and you have a right to them. Putting our differences aside, we both agree Enright's been good for Robin—less ITB, more academics. The fact we're now talking about Nora's house—"

"Nora's crazy. And an alcoholic."

351

"Robin's an alcoholic."

"That's stupid. You're just repeating—"

"What they said at Duke? She binge drinks."

Pren muttered a command to Bingo, and I heard his staccato sales refrain in the background.

"Nora's a big plus when you think about it," I pressed on. "She's gone through treatment, and she's sober."

"Listen up, Jack. You're not taking my daughter outside the Beltline to a crazy drunk house with an insane old woman of…of loose morals."

"That was really below the belt."

"No, it wasn't. No sane person would allow Nora to raise a child! She raised you, and look what happened."

That was actually funny. I counted to ten again. "I'm making the commitment to be principal caregiver. I'm around more than you. Phasing out at the paper."

"Great, so you lost another job."

"No, I haven't lost my job. I'm working at home now. You're still getting checks, aren't you? In fact, I just got a bonus."

"Wow, working from home? Jack Callahan? I didn't see you at home for fifteen years."

"I was earning a living."

"You were fucking every woman in sight."

Seems she'd learned to say the word. In fact, she used it routinely now, with Anglo-Saxon crispness.

"I'm trying to help with our daughter. You've got battle fatigue."

"You have no right to say that."

"Okay, let me say this in a different way. It's time for me to step up."

We spoke again over the weekend, and then Pren talked to Robin one last time, and it was a done deal.

We agreed to make the house switch at the semester break. By that time, Raleighwood Ranch would be up and running. Robin began spending weekends working with me and Adam, painting the rooms a sunny yellow. Without telling me, she also cleaned out the back seat of the Mercedes, excavating two old Blockbuster rentals, a golf glove, a laundry bag of white shirts for the cleaners, half of an onion bagel, and a sun-yellowed page from the *Wall Street Journal* I'd saved for a forgotten reason. Finally, I felt organized.

Nora stayed on plan. She attended her own life-skill sessions, led by a man with a megaphone. In addition to AA, she met daily with a group of rough-and-tumble women who forged female solidarity to resist what Nora now called addictive behavior. In the past, she had called it the stuff of life.

Somewhere on this journey, Hugh had become her addiction, and I her "enabler," a new word for me. Apparently, I was also a "codependent," a word I'd heard before but never understood. What it meant was that I got perverse pleasure from cleaning up Nora's messes.

Although I generally resisted therapeutic explanations for bad deeds, the idea of Hugh as an addiction had appeal. It shifted the sadness of life from fate to something manageable, like a bad habit. Swearing off Hugh became another box to check. On that score, it seemed she had abused most every drug available, even Affrin, the lowly decongestant, and finally nicotine, the last frontier.

She'd invited me to an event commemorating her victories, a celebration at Mighty Lamb. Lowry attended, as well as Dr. Gardiner, caregivers from Harmony Hall, and a table of women from the solidarity group. They all seemed to know a lot about me.

Lowry officiated, praying over an old-fashioned spaghetti dinner ladled out of fellowship-hall pots onto paper plates, with lettuce salad, and garlic bread from the church oven. The guests told inside treatment jokes and used only first names. One by one, they toasted Nora with ice water on the occasion of her one-year anniversary of sobriety. She rose and gave a speech so modest, without literary allusion or political blame, that I thought she'd been possessed by Mother Teresa.

"Thank you," she said simply, "for letting me go."

Murmurs of approval, tears, and a remote shout out "You be you, girl!" greeted her. She had shed a decade of worry lines, and stood peaceful and pretty.

After she spoke, Lowry, whom everyone knew, praised Nora as a "sister to us and a daughter of God." Others witnessed to their struggles and Jesus, announcing themselves from meeting halls at country churches named Corinth and Ephesus, speaking ancient invocations: "My name is Harry… My name is Jane, it's been 1,078 days, praise God."

I looked across the room at Gardiner and he shrugged, pointing to Lowry, whom he'd learned to trust. All this time we thought the good doctor was the one practicing medicine.

Outside, I offered Nora a smoke, and she refused. "Haven't had one for three weeks and a day," she said, counting on her hand.

I felt lost, unable to enable. "No cigarettes?"

"Don't get in a state, dear. The craving for nicotine lasts chemically for five minutes. Time me while I say no."

"What happens if you break down and smoke one?"

"I start over."

"You get a do-over?"

"Everybody gets a do-over."

"Wow."

"I won't need one. Nicotine is a strong addiction, but once you've done alcohol, barbiturates, cocaine—"

"Cocaine, really?"

She sighed. "Nasty stuff."

Swearing off Hugh was the final hurdle. The Big Enchilada, as Nora put it. "Like Nixon," she added for those needing a prompt, thus making a perfect Nora allusion. To get the meaning, you had to remember John Ehrlichman's name for the boss, associate Nixon's obsessions with her own, and appreciate the kitschy evil of Watergate, plus the thrill of watching the resigned president whirl away in a Navy helicopter, having declared his mother a saint. A grand passion, or a grand poison, or maybe just a need; you think it will never end, then it flies away, a speck in space.

"Ehrlichman," I responded on cue. "Soon our long national nightmare will be over."

"You're back," she said, laughing.

"From where?"

She raised her arms upward, breathing in luxurious breaths. "Exile. Your mind is free again."

"I didn't know I'd been in exile."

"You have, dear. But now I see you rising, like a splendid, many-colored bird."

I didn't feel like a splendid, many-colored bird. I felt ordinary in jeans and a work shirt, away from over-decorated conference rooms. We turned to the last change orders on the house. She had marked next week to move in.

"I think the screen porch should come to here," I said, pointing to Juan's revised plan. "We originally had it three feet back, but you couldn't put in the breakfast table. We'll have to cut a smidge off the hardscape."

She put her glasses on—they dangled now from a rhinestone chain—and squinted at the fine blue sheets. After a moment, she waved her hand over the scribbles. "You decide," she said. "You have the vision."

I rolled up the plans. "It's your house."

"A technicality. You're the alpha dog now."

She used this phrase often, pleased with new meaning. She'd become fond of a television program where a dog trainer explained the sociology of packs. In the manner of canines, I had succeeded to a higher station, which released her to follow. We now had better boundaries about who was in charge of what. She had stepped in with advice on Robin, which amounted to patient patrolling of my tendency to micromanage. "Save yourself for big things," she counseled. "You weren't so easy yourself." Apparently, in the authority exchange, I was firmly in charge of her home design, less in charge of my own daughter.

I was also on bad boyfriend patrol. "Okay, as the alpha dog, I need to know whether you've kept your word and not called Hugh back."

She sighed. The Big Enchilada.

Pride of the Yankees

FERRIS CALLED AGAIN. I decided this time to call back. I'd kept up with him through Nora; their literary correspondence had grown to a flurry. She'd begun referring to him as her editor for the Death of England project.

"He's freeing for me," Nora said, when I asked why. "He sees how bad things negate each other."

Suddenly, Forster's contradictions made sense. "He could reveal a world, but not himself," she said, having made a pot of tea in her new, almost-finished kitchen. "Loving is not weakness, for a person or a country."

Apparently, there was hope for love, and England, after all.

"Ferris encourages this line of thinking?"

"Oh yes, a very facile mind. You remember, he studied with Paul de Man."

"The Nazi?"

"He was so much more, dear. Tea?"

She poured, but withheld milk and sugar. These days she looked after my calories, quietly.

"Thank you. Feels like I'm with you there, in England."

"You are. Over twelve centuries, since *Beowulf*, mothers and sons have been doom-laden. Well, no more. Not us."

"On that point, I've put in a chlorine shock to the pool. Grendel lurked at the bottom."

Ferris had gone to visit his own mother in New York. He had recently installed her in a retirement village not far from the family's ancestral, many-gabled manse in Oyster Bay, just down from the Roosevelts, he mentioned. A rock and roll band now occupied Ferris's family home. He enjoyed showing photos of an album cover featuring slovenly millionaires and their girlfriends posed by the front door, and pointing out his second-story bedroom window.

"I think Ferris should stay with us when he comes," I said. "That is, when he's finished seeing his mother in New York. It's better for the work."

"If that's what you think. He offered to stay in a hotel."

"You're writing steadily, and we have a guest room."

"Will it be too strange?"

"No. But I do think something's up with him. It'll come out soon enough."

I suspected what it was, and he confirmed when we spoke the next day. "I've quit Victor," he said simply.

"Called it. Was it the Mesoamerican Exhibit?"

"Oh God, no. The Volt brothers. They're screwing up everything."

"You weren't exactly feeling the love in Charlotte."

"Victor's their little disciple now. I told him it was them or me. He said he'd find another lawyer."

"Best thing that's ever happened to you."

"He thinks the Volt brothers know the secret to politics."

"Yeah, screw up the government and hide the money."

"That works until the peasants come after you with pitchforks, but you can't tell Victor anything."

I wanted to ask about Angie, and how she would take being left alone. She hadn't been well. Apparently, the depression she'd managed so long and so quietly had pounced. Who knows what, if anything, triggered her? Realizing that her future could be travelling the world truly alone on the plane with Victor might have done it. Whatever it was, something took over her funny, warm, art-loving mind, and one day going for a jog, she ended up floating in the East River. A tugboat captain pulled her out, and paramedics revived her. She spent twenty-eight days in Bellevue.

"How's Angie doing," I ventured.

"She's out," he said simply. "Back with Victor."

"Administering lithium?"

"Yeah, all that. She got off track."

"She always said she'd end up in the East River. But she said Victor would throw her in."

"Really? She said that?"

"Years ago, when she was grilling me steaks."

"Well, she's getting better. I talked to her yesterday. Should I invite her down?"

"Great idea—later, when I get back from Mexico. Let's keep an eye out for her. I'm trying to get organized with Nora and Robin now, and you're coming to work on the book, and then I've got the Mexico thing. It's a full calendar."

◆◆◆

After Ferris arrived, Lowry brought by a Corona electric portable for the guest room.

"She's a beaut," Lowry said. "Picked her up at the Goodwill. Just needed some oil and a ribbon. Ready for book work."

"Gosh Lowry, thanks," Ferris said. "I'm touched." He rubbed his fingers gently over the chipped blue paint. Nora had introduced Lowry and Ferris by phone, and they'd gotten better acquainted over Nora's meat loaf. She'd taken up cooking again. "Let me pay you for this."

"Don't owe me a thing. Maybe take some clothes down to Goodwill?"

"Great. I've got a hundred suits I'll never wear again. Are we on for the pre-meeting?"

"Sure, I'll pick you up at five thirty."

I thought about suggesting that Ferris keep a suit around, since he might end up helping me on the INS cases Lowry kept sending my way, but that would be down the road. Lowry had other plans for Ferris. Recognizing a new civic resource right off the bat, Lowry had introduced him to the organizers of Raleigh's Gay Pride parade, and, after one meeting, they'd asked Ferris to take over. He was already lining up a bus for friends from New York and getting together a speakers' bureau.

"Men are coming out here daily, young men, older, it's great. Everyone works together in this town, no factions. It's amazing."

"Are there usually factions?"

"Oh yes. But the lesbians are fully integrated down here. Even the vegans get along."

Nora and Robin sat knitting in a corner of the family room. Lowry had bought Nora a second-hand rocking chair—from Goodwill—and she was teaching Robin to stitch from what she'd learned at Harmony Hall. Knitting, I'd come to understand, was good for anxiety, and also a companion activity to eavesdropping. No one minds a knitter.

"Leonard, tell Jack who you met yesterday," she said.

"Oh yeah. Your friend Billy Arnold. He's on the Steering Committee."

"Oh my God."

"Yeah, he came out a couple of months ago. He's in with these other guys starting this new community bank. Happy as a clam not to be in that Charlotte thing. Apparently, Griffiths kicked him out."

"That was my bad. It was over the time zones."

"What? I thought that was funny. He got fired over it?"

Nora looked at me over her glasses. "Jack, you need to plan to go to the parade. Your friends Leonard and Billy are working so hard."

"Yeah, Dad," Robin chimed in. "You need to support Leonard and Mr. Arnold. Gina's marching with us."

Gina was Billy's younger daughter. "I didn't know you were marching, honey."

"Enright has a group going."

"Of course it does." Robin had thrown herself into causes at Enright, with Nora's encouragement.

"Gina's joining even though she goes to Bingham. To support her Dad."

"Listen, let me say something to all of you, please. I'm not gay. I don't want to go to the Gay Pride Parade. Nothing against it, I just don't want to go. Everybody clear?"

"Dad, why are you being such a jerk?" Robin said. "I think you're uncomfortable in your masculinity."

Silence gripped the room. "Robin," Ferris said finally, "your father needs his space right now. I understand that. There will be other times."

"Really, Jack?" Nora said, rising from her rocker and rolling up her stitching. "I'm going for some air."

"Yeah, Dad, really?" Robin said, following her out.

◆◆◆

LOWRY PICKED US UP on Saturday for the parade. It was full-on first spring, not a cloud over Raleigh. Thousands arrived festively by bus and car, and the Capitol Police were all smiles. Lowry had arranged for me and the other straight men to hand out water bottles from tables on the Capitol grounds below the Confederate monument. I got dispatched from there to serve the head group at the terminus of Fayetteville Street, where the marchers formed up.

Ferris and Billy each wore sashes, denoting event leadership. "Jack!" Billy said, taking the offered bottle. "Thanks for coming! Leonard said you'd volunteered. Remember Jimmy Greene from Indian Guides? He's right over there."

I waved at Jimmy, holding up water bottles to let him know my status.

"Billy's invited us for a drink after," Ferris said.

"I tell you what. Why don't you and Billy get a drink, I'll catch up later."

"Oh, okay. But you're welcome to join. He's also said we need to go play golf at Pinehurst this week."

"The usual Wednesday game."

"Yeah, I think that's what he said."

"Hey, Billy," I yelled to get his attention. He was directing baton twirlers of uncertain gender. "If Ferris and I both come for the Wednesday game, won't that screw up Sam?"

"I'll call him. By the way, Number Two's in top shape. All the rain, and it's not even April."

April was Pinehurst's zenith.

"Who's Sam?" Ferris asked.

"Our usual caddy."

"We're going to Pinehurst?"

"Number Two."

"And we get caddies?"

"Yep."

"I love it down here."

"Run your parade, big shot."

After Enright's Rainbow Club passed, and the Progressive Lesbians of the Piedmont, and a group wearing fezzes, who may or may not have been Shriners, wound up the processional, Lowry gave us all a ride home in his truck. He'd been resplendent himself in full headdress and buckskins, leading the Lumbee delegation.

"It's appropriated authenticity," Robin explained. "Some of the Eastern tribes now use Western dress, like the Lumbees. They're way out on the authenticity scale."

"Where did you learn this?" I asked.

"History class."

"Is there any time in your history class at this public school that I pay taxes for where you actually learn real history?"

"You mean white male European-American history?"

"I have no idea what you're talking about."

"Do you know how racist and gendered you sound sometimes?"

Though I did the curmudgeon bit, I was delighted at Robin's radical turn. It was a good trade. I could take becoming an object of political abuse, as long as we left behind the late-night trips to Rex Hospital.

Ferris came back late himself from his drink with Billy. I waited up.

"Successful day," I said, pouring us a bourbon nightcap. "Congratulations."

"Thanks for coming."

"Not a problem, enjoyed it."

"Hmm," he said, nursing his drink.

"Something on your mind?"

"Yes, actually. Lowry."

I was relieved he didn't say Billy.

"Nora said to me, and I don't want you to take this any particular way, but she said he was a time traveler."

"Nora says lots of shit. Doesn't mean she's crazy—anymore."

"I don't think she's crazy."

"What, then? It's just her way of talking. Forget about it."

"No, she was absolutely serious. She said that he met Sir Walter Raleigh at Roanoke Island with, I guess it's called the Lost Colony, and kind of took care of those people, who didn't really know the lay of the land; and when they got left without food that year the Spanish Armada came, he organized the Lumbees to take them all into the tribe. Saved the whole bunch. Made a particular point to mentor that young girl—"

"Virginia Dare."

"You know the story?"

"It's pretty famous around here. It's not true."

"That's the thing. I'm not sure."

"Not sure about Lowry being a time traveler? Or the Lost Colony getting saved by Lumbees? A tribe of superheroes emerging from the swamp to do battle for freedom?"

"I think it's all possible. I had a dream about Lowry leading them out."

"In his headdress and all, like at the Gay Pride Parade?"

"Make fun all you want. It was a powerful dream."

"Looks like you're going for a month at Harmony Hall, too."

He yawned. "It's late. I'm the new guy, looking at things fresh. You might try it sometime."

◆◆◆

ON ROAD-TRIPPING TO MEXICO, I had second thoughts. There was so much to do here, and Robin needed me around. I took it up with Nora.

"Do you think Lowry would be disappointed if I didn't go to Mexico on this trip?" I asked. She was digging up zinnias.

"Jack, you're going to Mexico. It's all planned. Lowry and I discussed it yesterday."

"You and Lowry."

"Yes. He figured you'd get cold feet and predicted it would be over scheduling."

"It's not scheduling. I think things are a bit—fragile."

Ferris arrived with a wheelbarrow of topsoil.

"Leonard," she said, as he artfully dumped dirt in the holes she specified. "Do you think we're fragile? Jack does."

"Not a bit. We have chapter seventeen to go over. England and the Lumbees at the Time of the Armada. Just working that in."

Ferris had bought some appropriate SEM clothes, as his stay extended. He flicked a fleck of leaf mulch from a pair of burnt-orange cargo shorts, acquired for gardening.

"Jack, I'll be here through Easter, and another month at least with the manuscript. You're fine to go. Nora's occupied."

"Yes, I'm occupied."

"Are you going to look after Robin, too?"

Ferris handed me his shovel. "Here, shovel while you talk." He looked at Nora, who shrugged and poked away with her trowel. "Jack, Nora and I think you're hovering," he said.

"What are you talking about?"

"You're hovering all around Robin. You used to helicopter, and now you hover."

"So, you're an expert on teenage girls? You never raised one."

"You're right. But sometimes it's better to be the uncle figure. That's what I am here."

"Being an uncle figure is not a thing. You're either an uncle or you're not."

"Jack," Nora said, "my dear son. You have been a wonderful father to Robin since she had her accident, and she's needed you as she recovered, but now she's—recovered—and you're hovering. It'll be good for her if you leave for a while, and it will be good for you to go. Just go to Mexico. We'll all still be here when you get back."

Nora's speech sounded heartfelt. "Have you been cooking this up with Lowry?"

"No," she said firmly. "The hovering is all around us. There've been other incidents."

I did another ten count, and weighed whether Nora was really going to blame me for the Jack Daniel's argument. Last week, I saw Nora taking a fifth of Jack Daniels out of her room to the patio. I intercepted her. "Dammit, Nora, give me that," I said. "After all you've put this family through, no fucking way!"

"Jack, calm down—"

"I'm not going to calm down, you hand over that bottle! Now!"

She retreated and held onto it, eyes narrowing for a fight. "I've overlooked your tirades," she said, "Giving you deference as the alpha dog, but you go too far, lording it over everybody."

"Give me that damn bottle."

"I will not."

We tussled, and then somehow the bottle escaped my grasp, and flew disastrously toward the pool. It shattered at the edge, and fine brown Tennessee liquor spread over the surface of the water. A multitude of glass shards settled to the bottom.

I knew enough to cut off the filter, and then I called Lowry, who asked no questions. He and Juan drained the pool, and refilled it with more strange mercury water.

Turned out the bottle was a party gift from Ferris to Billy Arnold. Nora had offered to wrap it.

My mistakes with the bourbon fleshed out some lingering anger I held toward Nora. Getting ourselves settled, the incidents with Robin, and the drama of the last days at the firm had kept me busy, kept me from going after the real story about why we came down here all those years ago, finding out whether she'd lied to me from the start. It was that day with Aunt Judith I couldn't get past, the truth about how everything Nora had said about Dad and why we left New York was wrong, and not only wrong, but backward. Her fault, not his; her leaving, not him.

"I need to talk to you about something," I said, bourbon and shards finally cleared from the pool.

"What's that, dear? Searching for more whiskey bottles?"

"Did you ever love Dad?"

"What?"

"You heard me, I want to know."

She took a deep breath. "Well, yes I did. I loved him."

"Why'd you get married? You were young."

"We got married because I got pregnant with you. That's what happened in those days. I was twenty-four, and wanted my career, and we were graduate students together."

"But you wouldn't have married him otherwise?"

She looked over the pool, brow furrowing. "I don't know."

"Really?"

"That's not meant to be evasive. I don't know because I just don't. I did love him."

That seemed enough for her, and I figured she was the one who counted.

I decided on the spot not to quiz her further about the part of Judith's story where she'd had an affair with her professor. It wasn't really my business, and, without knowing one way or another, I could indulge the fantasy that Lionel Trilling was my biological father.

What did it matter, anyway?

"Why didn't we move somewhere else? I didn't think you liked Raleigh. You complained all the time."

She'd had offers. We flew once to Houston, to see Rice. I thought it had a funny name.

She shrugged. "I liked it well enough. At first I thought we'd have to visit every Sunday with Grandma and Grandpa Callahan, and I couldn't have taken that. But they didn't ask."

"Did Dad ever meet them?"

"Ma came to New York once. Pa wouldn't get on the train. He was a Jew."

"Oh."

"And then we ran out of time."

"Why?"

"Well, we got divorced, and then they died."

I reflected on that: the death of Nora's parents, my grandparents, making Nora an orphan, and how little we made of that—funerals, flowers, and then, nothing. We hadn't seen them much before, once or twice for Sunday lunch in their row house, with the gardenias and green pickup in the front. It was tense, argumentative, with Nora dropping g's all over the place. "Not goin' to cousin Roxanne's, Ma, she hates me."

It occurred to me at that moment that Nora didn't go more not because they didn't read her articles, or care for her Jewish husband, or her divorce from her Jewish husband, but because she was afraid she was like them. Then, they died.

"But we could have left any time. You got more offers when Volume One came." She kept framed a notice from *New York Review of Books*. They had used the word *masterful*. "So, why not?"

"You were doing well in school, and then there was..."

Her voice trailed off, and I knew what there was: Hugh. We stayed because she couldn't bear to leave the Big Enchilada.

Camerado

I'D RUN OUT OF time to back out on Mexico. Resigned, I decided to
learn Spanish phrases, me llamo Jack, etc. I also began to wonder what
I was supposed to do with the Fathers, as Lowry called them. I bought a
guidebook and found the Benedictine Monastery near Dolores Hidalgo.
Pictures showed them leading marchers bearing a bloody statue of Christ.
Folks flagellated themselves with ropes bought at street stalls. I didn't think
I qualified for those activities.

"Lowry, this stopover at the Monastery. What exactly will I be doing
there?"

"Nothing." Lowry was edging around our new sidewalk. We prepared
for a cookout to formally inaugurate the new digs.

"Surely there's an agenda. Do I bring my clubs?"

"No. At the Sanctoria you'll have a room with a bed, and a chair, and
a table, and you'll have all day to reflect. The Fathers are up at four, with
prayer every three hours, and they'll make a place at meals. Oh, and you
can walk in the vineyard. The weather is beautiful."

"No activities? No hiking, no books, no golf? Maybe I could work in
the garden. They must sell jelly or something."

"Your discipline is to do nothing."

"For how long?"

"An undetermined amount of time."

"How will I know when I'm finished?"

"You'll know."

It occurred to me that Lowry had fashioned for me a personalized program, or nonprogram. All along, I'd thought I was going on a touristy road trip with local entertainment, parties, fiestas. Now you see it, now you don't.

This is how Lowry got things done. For a while you don't know at all what you're looking at, and then you see it. All the while, it appears you've been doing a lot of nothing, and then you start doing something, which is what Lowry had planned all along.

Elaine called. We hadn't spoken for a month, except when she called to ask where Adam was. She should know, because he was always here working around the house. But Elaine stayed busy, campaigning with Sid, who trended ahead in the polls. Some days they short-hopped from Morehead to Fayetteville to Charlotte. Some days they flew to New York or California for fundraisers. Complicating the schedule further, she'd also taken a role as the first woman on the firm's Management Committee. Drac had seen to it, because of her leadership, he said. He also noted she controlled our old accounts, and thus lots of money for the firm. There was talk of her opening a Washington office, provided Wheeless won. *Enterprise North Carolina* featured her as a "fast-track female performer."

Ballard hadn't taken these developments well. Before I left the firm, I was his dueling buddy and Drac's natural target, and they both could blame me for things. Now that I was gone, Elaine had become the golden girl, and Drac's full fury, not to mention his Glock, was trained on Ballard. He was in week two at the Center.

"Not going to be able to make it to Wilmington," Elaine announced. "Sorry, Sid asked me to call you."

"I guess I'm surprised."

She yawned. "Sorry, I'm just sleepy, all night on the plane. Wilmington's a downer with the polling, not the right photo ops, according to the consultants."

◆◆◆

FERRIS POURED HIMSELF A beer and sat down on a lounge chair. I had been cleaning leaves out of the pool, and was now staring at it, watching more leaves go in.

"Could be wrong, Jack, but I have this feeling you have a problem with your old friends doing so well."

"Kai-Jana and Elaine?"

"Those would be the ones."

"Maybe, I don't know. I don't think about it."

"It could be that we screwed things up, guys like us, and some other people need to come off the bench and help the team, that's what's going on. See, it's nothing personal. It's just hard to be sitting on the bench when you've been a starter."

I considered what Ferris said. Was he right? Did I resent Kai-Jana and Elaine? It was true that the Party had asked Kai-Jana to run for Attorney General, and she'd been picked up by lists of national contributors who specialized in advancing women, and nobody ever asked me to run for anything. Come to think of it, I did have a sex scandal to deal with, and a recent, messy divorce, and they probably all figured as the Symmes quasi-heir I wouldn't be interested anyway. So why should I resent Kai-Jana running? She actually wanted the job, and would be good at it.

"Don't have a problem with Kai-Jana running for AG. She saved my ass a couple of times."

"I remember."

"It's hard for her to raise money. Tougher for chicks, not to mention black chicks. I was glad to hook her up."

I walked to the pool edge and popped up the skimmer basket. It was full of mangy wet leaves.

"Here, let me help," Ferris said. He picked up the net and scooped some more.

"You don't need to do that."

He dropped the net. "Do you want me to help around here or not?"

"Yes, help, help, thank you."

"No use skirting it. The problem's not Kai-Jana. It's Elaine. You need to get over her."

"What?"

"You need to accept the fact that Elaine's sleeping with Wheeless, who's going to be a US Senator, and she's going to marry him, move to DC, and get famous. She took over all your clients. You're stuck looking after her kid. Oh, and she gets great press."

"None of that matters."

"Really? Not even that you broke up with her, and now she's with Wheeless?"

"There was no breaking up. We weren't sleeping together—not recently, anyway."

"Not the point, idiot. You left her. It was the Jack and Elaine show for years. You had 'em laughing in the aisles. And then you walked away from the firm. What did you think would happen?"

He was right. "Shit. I guess I didn't think. I always figured we'd end up together somehow."

"You're still in love with her. You need to move on."

"I've moved on. I'm sitting by the pool."

"Jack, here's the thing. She was never in love with you. Not even in New York."

"Sorry?"

"I was there, remember? She was never into you. Not one minute. Not one nanosecond."

Now I understood the benefit of having a gay friend: total emotional clarity. "I think you're right. She's never been into me."

"Bless your heart," he said. Then, when I looked at him funny: "Isn't that what you're supposed to say to people down here?"

◆◆◆

IT WAS PALM SUNDAY, and Robin and Adam were helping Lowry up at Mighty Lamb. They had been going with him to services, and then sometimes to the youth group during the week. I didn't think anything of it, figured if they got in too deep, at least it was religion and not drugs.

I'd been reading the Bible some, getting Lowry to give me assignments in order to bone up before getting to the monastery. He gave me little snippets of things to read from the Old Testament, stories about Job, and Esther with the Persians, and Daniel, which was kind of like the end of the world, and then the New Testament, the apostles going all over the place, and the parables of Jesus—stuff I'd heard about, since I was in Sunday School as a kid. We'd talk about what I'd read while doing yard work, but he always ended up asking me questions. Finally, I asked him what his favorite parable was.

"What's yours?" he said, mulching around a hydrangea. "I think we should have taken this down a little farther."

"Sorry?"

"The hydrangea."

"Oh. I guess the one about the Rich Young Ruler. Can't really figure that out."

"Why?"

"Well, I feel sorry for him, all he's trying to do is get Jesus networked with the progressive Roman crowd, you know, business types in Jerusalem, the cool Centurions—something I'd do, I guess, if I met Jesus, to be helpful. And Jesus blows him off. I don't get it."

"Actually, the gospels say that Jesus loved him. Then Jesus said to him, give up all your possessions and follow me."

"Which was a nonstarter! He asked him to do something he couldn't do, not a win-win. I don't understand."

"Oh, you understand plenty. Need your shovel right here."

I dug out the hydrangea, and we sunk a deeper hole. "I feel really bad for the guy. It says, 'Sadly, he turned and walked away.'"

"Don't feel bad for him," Lowry said, straightening and taking a drink of strange water. "It turns out in the end."

I didn't know what to make of that last comment, since the Bible didn't go on with the story. But then, Lowry had said some strange things lately. On my own I decided to go to the Mighty Lamb on Palm Sunday to check out services. Robin and Adam were going, but I preferred to sit by myself the first time. I'd never been to a proper service there, only shuttling back and forth sometimes for AA or dropping Nora for meetings with her women's group after hours. Contrary to my experience as a kid with the Methodists, and my sometimes attendance in the Episcopal world, at the Mighty Lamb no one wore a suit. I parked in a lot about the size of a minor league ballpark, and somebody handed me a palm frond. "Just looking for my daughter," I said to the usher inside, and he smiled and led me to the balcony.

Jesus came in at the back on a donkey, as I remember actually happened. To my surprise, Robin and Adam followed, eyes ahead, hands clasped together, both of them dressed in white altar robes. Then the choir walked in, and Lowry himself brought up the rear. The preacher, far away on the rostrum, broadcast the sermon about a joyful entry to Jerusalem spoiled by sin, but redeemed by blood, on a screen behind, and the choir, with electrified help, sang a jazzed-up invitation. A scattering of the audience came down for the altar call and got conducted behind the screen for what I took to be a dunking. The crowd waved the palm fronds and said Amen; wanting to fit in, I waved my palm frond and said Amen, too. What was the harm?

As Jesus marched out, waving solemnly on the donkey, I tried to catch Robin's eye. I'd given her a heads up I might come, and she had spotted me from her perch at the front, motioning me to follow the processional outside. I gave the large throng following them a wide berth. They were singing a rock-and-roll version of "The Old Rugged Cross." I scooted through the doorway amid Hallelujahs and an occasional Praise the Lord, and many resounding Amens.

"Is there an after-party?" I asked Robin as a line formed up by the portico. She and Adam had put on different robes and were heading up a hill behind the church, following Lowry, who was leading a group of Mexicans.

"Very funny," she said. "Didn't you think the service was nice?"

"Yeah. Does Jesus come in on a donkey every week?"

"Dad. It's Palm Sunday."

"I get it."

She motioned up the hill. "We're going to help Lowry."

"So there really is an after party?"

"Some of the Mexicans who don't go to Catholic church come here because of Lowry, but they don't understand the service. So he says one in Spanish and they have communion, like they do at home."

Sixty, maybe seventy kneeled as Lowry, with Juan beside him holding a Bible, recited a Catholic liturgy in Spanish. At points they chanted together. Adam came forward, holding the box. Lowry took out pieces of bread and wine and held them up and gave a blessing, and then Adam and Robin helped him hand it out as the congregants came forward. Some of them kneeled before Lowry, and he made the sign of the cross on their foreheads.

After they had all taken communion, Lowry went on in Spanish, softly, gesturing upward. Some began to cry, including Juan, who kneeled in the front. Lowry held out his arms, as though to quiet them.

"What's he saying?" I whispered to Robin.

"He said that if your mother is far away, you have a mother in Heaven, Mary, who will take care of you."

"Oh."

Lowry led the group down the hill, with Adam carrying away the bread and the wine and Juan carrying the Bible. I waited while they took off their robes to give them all a ride back to the house.

"That explains a lot," I said to Robin, as we started back down Six Forks Road past the mall.

"What?"

"Lowry's a priest."

Robin looked at Adam, who had gone to Catholic school and knew priests. He shrugged. "Lowry's not a priest, Mr. C," Adam said.

"So, what is he then?"

They both laughed.

Hamburgers for the Road

"IT'S ALL UNDER CONTROL, Mr. C," Adam said as he unloaded charcoal and citronella pots from my car. I'd let him take my used, dinged-up Explorer to the Harris Teeter. The other week, I'd made a profitable trade with a Ford dealer for the Mercedes.

"You get the drinks?"

He feigned shock. "Forgot. No, I got 'em. Just playing with you."

"Okay, okay." They could all tell I was nervous. It was our first hosting event. "Nora and Robin will be back from the mall any minute, and I want that fire ready to cook by six."

"It's all good, Mr. C. You chill out. Want me to get you a beer?"

"Nope. Just dump out that mess in the grill, lay out the fire in that chimney thing, and pat me out the burgers. Oh, and I started slicing those tomatoes and onions if anybody wants 'em, so finish that up. And take that potato salad out of the refrigerator."

"Yes, sir."

"Do you think your mother will want supper when she comes to pick you up?" Lowry and I had impounded Adam's Fiat. There'd been another night at Riley's Bar.

"She's not picking me up."

"Where is she?"

"She had a campaign thing, then she went to work."

"That's a long day."

He shrugged. "You know what her job's like. You used to be her boss."

I shook my head at this falsehood, and at the twenty years it abbreviated. Soon, she'd be headed to Washington, furnishing a ritzy Senator's house on Massachusetts Avenue, organizing civilized opinion. Tomorrow I was heading to Nowhere, Mexico.

"Your mother and I worked together. I wasn't her boss."

"Whatever." He paused to look over this week's project: a flagstone walkway from the driveway to a brick patio Lowry had just put in around back, which connected with the pool deck. I was sprucing it up with red garden gravel, having tamped in the black aluminum borders with a meandering S-curve for show. "You want me to help with that first?"

"No, you're on kitchen detail. And remember, Lowry, Juan, and the team's coming, so we have to add five."

He ran up the steps to the deck and into the house, and I set out the citronella pots myself. We'd had a wet, warm spring, splendid balmy days followed by deluges, and our reward was mosquitoes in April. "Mosquitoes in April! The cruelest month, indeed," Nora said, as she slapped at one lighting in a mound of dough.

She and Robin now baked together. This morning they'd made pies for the cookout.

"This place looks like the surface of the moon," I'd said, when I came into the kitchen looking for some breakfast. The two of them stood covered in white.

"Dad. It's what happens when you make pies." Robin said.

"Are you making them for an army?"

"One's just for you, Jack," Nora said, smiling, wiping her brow with the outside of her hand. "No sugar, peaches and cherries, very healthy. Got to watch your cholesterol, given your unfortunate gene structure. God knows what you'll be eating in Mexico."

"Handfuls of rice, according to Lowry."

◆◆◆

ELAINE CALLED LATER TO say she didn't have time to pick Adam up after all and asked if he could spend the night, which was fine, optimum really, since Pren decided to drop by, and I still couldn't deal with her and Elaine in the same place.

Pren walked to the edge of the deck and waved. She wore jeans and a white blouse and flipped her hair back as though she was growing it to go behind her ears. She'd brought a flower arrangement for the party, very classy.

"Sit down," I offered, motioning to the new Adirondack chairs. "You look great."

"No, I don't." She wrinkled her nose in rebuttal. "I've been showing all day, and I've got these awful bags under my eyes."

"Hmm. But you've got a great new stylish haircut. Looks terrific."

"Actually, Jack, my hair is longer, but it is different, so you get an A for effort."

"Always take an A. Want a burger? I could put one on."

"No, but thank you. Shocking, really—Robin says you're doing the cooking?"

"Burgers on the grill. I can handle that."

"You made the fire yourself?"

"Hey, it's a turnkey job. Look around you, I'm a changed man. Simple, reliable, like a lawn mower."

"What?"

"Just an expression."

Pren fluffed her flowers on the kitchen table while taking in the new décor. She had become more familiar recently, ever since I confronted her with the Bingo rumor. She'd denied what Robin had reported, that Bingo had produced a ring and asked her to marry him. She didn't want to discuss it much. For my part, I'd been working up an apology, or series of them, for all of my bad behaviors, but I couldn't quite get it right, and so I hadn't said anything. It was hard for me to decide whether I should apologize for everything in detail, all the sex and sex-like acts, including, for example, with Ginger and some of her other friends, or apologize in general, and let it go at that. Lowry said I was on the right track, but suggested I take it to the Fathers, reflect, and have a go at saying sorry when I returned. Until then, we kept things on the light side.

"Where's everybody?" she asked.

"Well, Adam and I are getting set for the party, and after making pies Nora and Robin went shopping."

"Oh Lord."

"And Ferris is gone to Pinehurst with Billy Arnold."

She rolled her eyes at that. "Honestly, Jack, how do you permit Leonard Ferris to stay here? He's a criminal."

"Afraid he's going to give Robin insider trading tips?"

"It's the principle. He's a dangerous influence."

No one had told Pren that, in addition to being a convicted felon, Ferris had led, and Robin had marched in, the Gay Pride Parade, an event that blessedly escaped her attention. She'd probably heard from Robin that Ferris was gay, and knew about Billy Arnold, too, but wouldn't have gathered they were on a man-date. I wasn't going to enlighten her.

"Look, Ferris isn't dangerous. He's helping Nora finish her book. If he gets that done, it'll be well worth a couple of months at Raleighwood Ranch, believe me."

"What are his qualifications to help Nora with a book?"

"He studied with Paul de Man."

"Who's that?"

"A Nazi, but so much more."

She smiled. "You're a strange man, Jack Callahan. And you've got strange friends."

Apparently, strange wasn't a bad thing for Pren anymore. If memory served, she actually liked me strange. Along those lines, she had become a vocal supporter of my trip to see the Fathers in Mexico. Her only complaint, and a mild one, was that Lowry, whom she had hired since Ike retired, wouldn't be around at high season for her yard. She also insisted that Robin spend my time away with her, which I said I'd leave up to Robin. Maybe Pren realized that she'd be in the care of Nora and Ferris, and that could turn Robin totally to the dark side—that is, an embrace of bohemianism and homosexuality, leading to rejection of the ITB zip code. Maybe she just missed her daughter, fair enough.

"I do have something I want to discuss," Pren said, moving to the living room and sitting down on the sofa.

"Uh-oh," I said, sitting beside her. Usually that tone meant an argument over money, child-rearing, or the stalled character of our divorce.

She held up her hand to stem anxiety. "It's my decision, but it affects you. I've decided to sell the business."

"What? Is selling businesses some disease going around, like the Hong Kong flu?"

"Oh, relax, you worry too much. My lawyer says you own half, so when we divide things up, you'll get money."

"Why are you doing that? You've worked really hard."

She shrugged. "I saw a piece of land out near Wake Forest. I was going to put down a strip mall, but then I stopped to look at it. It's a nice little horse farm, about seventy acres. Turned out I'd taken riding lessons there when I was a girl. I got really emotional about it, like it was fate. The land has an old farmhouse on it—needs work, but, you know, I made an offer and they took it."

Her eyes danced, and she was excited, I could tell. But then there was the vast house she lived in now, which I had just deeded over. "What about—"

"Oh yeah, the Crimshaw house. I want to sell quickly. It'll go high in this market. It's a lot to keep up, and honestly, the ITB buzz, I just can't deal anymore."

"Wow." She'd said goodbye to years of gossip and house envy just like that.

"I know it's a lot to take in."

"No, no, do what you want."

She smiled and pulled back her new horsewoman hair. "I was hesitating because of Robin, but she doesn't care about the Club, and she said last week she doesn't want to do her debut. I think that's great."

"She hasn't said anything to me about it."

"She's afraid you'll be mad."

"I'm totally okay with it."

She patted me on the arm. "You know Daddy tried to bribe me with a trip to Europe if I didn't do mine. Big mistake, not taking that deal."

"No kidding." It was the first I'd heard that she turned down the Grand Tour for an evening with Kennell Whitfield. Youthful blunders, I'd had some myself. "Look, Pren, I won't stand in the way of any of this, if that's what's on your mind."

"Didn't think you would, but things aren't settled with us, are they? And now you're going off to Mexico."

"We're late," Nora said, entering behind us from the door to her prized new garage, which she called a "covered garage" as though there were another kind. For her shopping trip, she had chosen a buckskin outfit with a fringed jacket and skirt Dale Evans would die for. She hung her car keys by the door. "There were so many to choose from," Nora said ominously. "Hello, Pren."

"Hello, Nora."

"Hear you're buying a horse farm."

Pren stared daggers at Robin, who shrugged defensively. "She's my grandma, can't I tell her?"

"You're supposed to keep a secret when asked."

"Whatever."

Nora smiled prettily. "Robin, help with that potato salad before your father makes a mess."

"So many of what, Nora?" I said, as Robin moved purposefully toward potato-salad-in-preparation.

"Sorry?"

"You said there were so many to choose from?"

"Hats, of course, that's why we went to the mall. Robin and I can't go to Easter services at Mighty Lamb without new hats."

She motioned behind her to the open garage door, where seven hat boxes sat stacked. "We couldn't choose, could we, Robin?"

"No, Grandma, it was very hard."

"Your father will just have to pay for them all."

Pren and I sat paralyzed as Robin stacked boxes in the living room. Nora removed the hats one by one—here a green bonnet, there a draping chapeau of gold and blue, a smart sailor's cap, a hunting rig with a crest of feathers.

Nora held the green bonnet aloft.

"I think this one suits, don't you, dear?"

"I think it's great, Nora."

"Robin, give that white one with the spring flowers to Pren."

"Oh, no," Pren said helplessly. "I don't do hats."

"Nonsense. You'll look fabulous. No one at Christ Church will have this one."

"Nora, please."

"It's Easter, dear. Every girl needs a new hat."

◆◆◆

Two weeks before, we'd marked the Wilmington Centennial. The Committee of the Commemoration, as it ended up being styled—Wardie charmingly referred to it as "COC"—ended up using some of my ideas as *Criterion* liaison, and some they skipped. Community organizers went for a Truth and Reconciliation approach, but focus groups thought that was a downer, so everybody scaled back to a Chamber of Commerce-style two-day Celebrate Wilmington event. Everybody, that is, except the Reverend Sweeney, who said he'd watch on television. He didn't speak out against it, probably because Kai-Jana had already agreed to sit up front, and he was afraid of her, or the memory of her grandfather, according to Wardie. "Sometimes you get lucky," he said. "Everybody's got a ghost or two."

The Committee invited a full list of honorees, with color-coded tags for victims and coup leaders, drawing on research from the *Criterion* and scholars who knew the details of the massacre. Hundreds of descendants signed up—people descended from the African-American newspaper editor who fled for his life, the exiled black congressman, the tradesmen and artists run out of town, propelled to points north with railroad tickets courtesy of the coup leaders. Representing the diaspora of the black bourgeoisie, the Blounts had arrived early and in force, led by Kai-Jana, Winston, and the girls. On the dais, courtesy of Wardie's finagling with the seating chart, she and the family would sit photogenically in front. Onward and upward to Election Day.

As for the dead, thrown in the river by Big Hugh and his men, the Committee had found the names of as many of the poor souls as could be found. They had inscribed these on a simple tablet by the water, beside the spot picked for a monument, the design of which had proved so controversial. "Dammit, it's my event, we're going to put up the dolphins," Wardie said to the Committee's bi-racial cochairs, when they reported their deadlock. "I'll handle it myself." That's when he ordered the event crew to haul out his dolphin statue, and hide it dockside under a tarp.

Stress mounted as the hour grew near, and I got a voice message from Kai-Jana asking that I meet her at Café Quarto. She didn't sound happy.

"What's all this about Wardie's fish statue?" she said by way of greeting, as I pushed my way past a waiting line of latte lovers to the table at the back she'd claimed.

"I don't know—it's—"

"And you couldn't even tell me Elaine and what's his name aren't coming?"

"I'm sorry, there's just a lot of details –"

"These aren't details, Jack! I need to be at the table."

"I'm really sorry—"

"I had to learn all this second-hand from Bobby. Imagine that conversation."

"Not good." Bobby—the Reverend Sweeney—would enjoy tattling to her about our dysfunctional group.

"He thinks I'm being used and I'm way in over my head."

"Being used by me and Wardie? Is that what you think?"

She paused, gathering her short, gray jacket around her shoulders and nibbling at half of the bagel she'd ordered. She nodded and smiled at a table of three young mothers tending strollers who recognized her. "No," she whispered. "But I'm mad at you. Pick up the damn phone and call me and stop treating me like I'm some kind of stage prop."

"Ouch." I took out my date book. "Watch me while I write down a note to brief you every afternoon until Wilmington is over."

"That's a start." She pushed half of her bagel in my direction.

"Thanks, I didn't have breakfast." I found some condiments on the table and spread grape jelly with her plastic knife.

"Met your daughter yesterday," she said quietly, flashing a big smile past me to a table of star-struck State students.

"Robin?"

"She came by the office and volunteered. Chip put her to work on the phones."

"Gosh—she didn't say anything."

"What an impressive daughter you've raised—well spoken, self-assured. She also told me you'd built your mother a house."

"That's an exaggeration."

Kai-Jana stood up to leave, hands on hips. "Jack Callahan, how can you be so good with your daughter and your mother, and so bad with women your own age?"

"Hmm. Great question. I'm trying to do better."

She smiled and leaned over to give me a kiss goodbye, and then pirouetted back. "Can't do that," she said, smile still in place, cocking her head slightly toward an awkward-looking mustachioed man of some bulk in the corner, folding back pages of the *Criterion*. "Oppo research. He'd love to get me planting one on a white guy." She blew a kiss at him instead.

◆◆◆

I DID CALL KAI-JANA every day that week to report, leaving staccato voicemails recounting lurching progress toward the Saturday event. The Committee had planned to seat descendants of the coup leaders with descendants of the victims, as a gesture of conciliation, and they hoped no one would boycott. Actually, the opposite happened. So many descendants of black families chased north in 1898 to Brooklyn, or Washington, or Baltimore, or Cleveland, or Philadelphia responded yes that there wasn't a hotel room to be had in town. Descendants of the Group of Nine and other coup leaders proved less enthusiastic, but enough came to mark off a good reserved section. Hugh had been invited to apologize for all the coup leaders, but no one knew what he would say, because he wouldn't give out a draft of his speech, even to me. No one on the Committee knew about the strokes, and I had promised both Hugh and Mary I wouldn't tell. Mary had worked with him on his gait.

On Saturday morning, the city fathers led off events with a parade down Market Street, which ended up tracing roughly the route of the riot. The city's several high school bands led a procession of invitees toward an arena fashioned near the waterfront. So many people showed up that Ameribank paid for dual Jumbotrons to flank the stage, projecting the speakers to the outer rows. Surveying the packed seats, Wardie grinned at me from the dais—I sat below in front between Mary and Robin, who'd wanted to come since she now worked on the campaign. Kai-Jana led the Blounts in last to applause.

"Did you and Wardie really put this on?" Robin asked. "I thought all you guys did was shoot pool and drink beer." She looked smart in a black wrap dress and heels, and stood up to give Kai-Jana a raise-the-roof sign and whoof-whoof when the Blounts passed.

"Lots of people put this on, honey."

"Impressive."

Following a greeting by the mayor came carefully scripted reenactments: first, the march into town by Winchester-wielding Red Shirts, the paramilitary force armed by coup leaders; and, then the march out of town at gunpoint forced upon the Blounts and other black families of property, each known family name read aloud and accompanied to the beat of a single drum. Those were the only reenactments. After a sometimes tearful debate, the Committee declined to reenact the torching of the city's black-owned newspaper, posting instead near the entrance to the arena a billboard-size photo of Red Shirts posed proudly by the smoldering building. No one proposed portraying the scores of killings in the street.

After the final drumbeat for the banished families, Wardie rose to apologize. He made a speech in behalf of the Forrest descendants, stating he was regretful for the *Criterion* "blowing the story" of what he notably called "the massacre." He used the word *empathy* several times. I could tell his new PR team in California had drafted the text. They must have thought it a strange assignment. For good measure, he recanted the *Criterion's* role in black disenfranchisement and generations of Jim Crow. The crowd applauded politely, even drawing an Amen.

Hugh went last, speaking for the coup leaders. Wardie helped him walk to the podium, holding one elbow while Hugh gripped his rolled-up speech. The crowd watched in silence as the two of them made their way slowly forward. When they reached the edge of the stage, Hugh waved Wardie off, gripped the podium with one hand, and set down one wrinkled page for his speech with the other. He got right to the point.

"November tenth, 1898, was the worst day of our history, and my family was responsible for it. I am so sorry, so sorry. If I could say that word a thousand times and bring back the dead, I would. This river behind us carries a tragedy of such proportion. I say again to the families gathered, I am so sorry for it all. What I am horrified for, and sorriest about, is that my grandfather, armed and out of control, insane at that moment, is the only way I can make sense of it, mounted the wagon himself and turned that Gatling gun on the black men in his path and shot them dead on the street, in front of their homes, in front of their wives and children. He had gone to Wilmington to preserve the peace, but instead did murder." Hugh began to cry, shaking and wiping his eyes with a pocket handkerchief.

The crowd made no sound, and all eyes remained on Hugh at the dais, the dual Jumbotrons framing his face as he sobbed, closing and opening his eyes, finally stilling himself, and then muttering audibly, into the microphone: *rat-tat-tat, rat-tat-tat, rat-tat-tat.* He paused at the podium, gazing upward, as though searching for Big Hugh. "He was a good father, I want you all to know that," he said, gazing back on the crowd. "But it's the sound of it that stays." He put his hands over his ears and began to mutter again, and then repeat louder in crescendo: *rat-tat-tat, rat-tat-tat, rat-tat-tat, rat-tat-tat, rat-tat-tat, rat-tat-tat, RAT-TAT-TAT, RAT-TAT-TAT, RAT-TAT-TAT, RAT-TAT-TAT...*

From the dais, Wardie looked down at me, wide-eyed. "Go help him," I whispered loudly, pointing at Hugh, lost and now shouting his mantra, eyes closed in a daze. Wardie breathed deeply, grasped Hugh by the shoulders, wrested him from the podium, and led him back to his seat.

Beside me Mary sat staring at Hugh, and then his face contorted on the Jumbotrons, and then back at Hugh, stunned. Involuntarily she stood to go to him, but I held her back. "It's going to be okay," I said.

"Dad," Robin whispered, "Mr. Symmes has gone crazy."

Correct, but even she had to observe a non-secret secret or two. "Show some respect," I said, "that was hard for him."

As Wardie and Hugh reached their seats, I jumped up and began applauding, and a scattered few, then others followed. As more of the crowd rose, I sprinted down the front row to the band leader beside the podium. "Play something," I shouted. "What?" he yelled back. "Anything, as long as it's not *Dixie*."

He flicked his baton, and the assembled high schoolers in their marching band splendor swung into a half-time worthy *Sweet Caroline*, which, I figured, would have to do. Wardie helped Hugh stand, and held his hand high to wave. Hugh, confused, looked from side to side at the cheering crowd, and tried to move back to the podium, but Wardie held him back.

Mary recovered herself, and she applauded with the rest, crying with what seemed like relief. I hugged her and handed over my handkerchief. I realized I'd never heard Hugh really apologize to anyone for anything before.

Sweet Caroline ended, the cheers stopped, and Wardie walked alone to the edge of the podium, mike in hand, determined to resume the program. He motioned to Tatty, who walked from the platform toward the water. Tall, tan, and erect, she stopped and kicked off her shoes, standing barefoot by the river in a long white dress, with flowing blonde-and-gray hair, one hand resting on the soon-to-be-unveiled tribute. "We must free ourselves," she and Wardie said in unison as the tarp fell to the ground, and dropped into the lapping river, carried away as the morning tide pushed in.

A quartet of bronze dolphins leaped upward from the pediment, above the inscription: *In Memoriam, November 10, 1898.*

"That statue is weird," Robin said, too loudly.

"Hush, unless you want to give a speech, too."

I stood up again to lead scattered applause, which gradually grew. Per the script, Wardie brought Kai Jana and the Blount family to the podium and stepped back, himself applauding, while a full-scale ovation arose. I caught Kai-Jana's eye and she nodded slightly, perfectly composed, betraying no astonishment, or anger, or vindication, or thanks. Having mastered the moment, she flashed her big-event smile and leaned into the applause, turning at different angles to the clicking cameras. Winston stood stalwart beside her, holding the girls' hands. Win or lose, it would make a fine Christmas card.

◆◆◆

HUGH'S CONFESSION WENT NATIONAL that afternoon, but Wardie and Ameribank PR were able to issue a statement pleading ill health and hide him away in Raleigh. A couple of days later, Mary drove him to the Landing. She didn't stay. I came the next week, to say goodbye before Mexico and to help Tessie move in. After sorting through the first dozen boxes of her books, I took a break and went down to the dock to find Hugh at his favorite sitting spot. He sat in a beach chair, legs crossed jauntily, sweater thrown over his shoulders, reading the Sunday *Times*. I took that to be a good sign of his mental condition. He'd been staring for hours a lot at boats, according to Tessie.

"I did the best I could," he said, squinting into the afternoon sun. He'd never been one for sunglasses.

"You did great."

He pointed up the river, toward Wilmington. He was staring at a Chinese barge and a Cape Fear tug heading up the channel.

"No interest can vest, unless it must vest—how does it go?" he said, brow furrowed.

"Twenty-one years after a life in being," I said, completing the mantra.

"Useless rule."

Not useless, I was about to say, but I held back. Three generations is about all you get. Tessie appeared in a smart aqua-trimmed tennis skirt and sleeveless top, racket in hand. I'd managed to find work-out clothes. "Are we ready?" she said.

She and I were motoring the Chris-Craft back to the sandspit island. The boat trip was nostalgic and unnecessary, since for years a perfectly serviceable bridge made auto transport convenient and quick. Now, where we used to make out, sat million-dollar houses, in-ground pools, and tennis courts. Today, we were going to play tennis.

"Yeah, I think so. Hugh and I were checking out the barge traffic."

She kissed him on the forehead. "Jack and I will be back in a couple of hours."

He smiled. "Take your time. Just reading the paper."

Tessie's stuff was still arriving in boxes at the main house. She'd called the day after the Centennial to ask if "he'd really done it." I confirmed that he had, leaving out details of the speech, and she flew in the next afternoon. She'd already packed.

She beat me routinely in straight sets, and we took the Chris-Craft back across the river, and then drove her puttering Volvo to the highway to pick up chicken for me to grill. Two of her girlfriends were coming from Wilmington with their husbands for dinner, and it looked like I was going to be Tessie's date, brother, or both. Let Faulkner stew on that.

When I first drove up, she'd met me on the porch where she was sorting her first pile of boxes. I recalled the sensation of our café kiss in New York, and I think she did, too. She stepped back, held my hands in hers, and then kissed me—on the cheek. "Are you and Pren divorced yet?"

"No, not technically."

"Then you're not." She led me to one of the hall bedrooms. "Daddy's in the Big Hugh room, and my room is next to yours, but don't get any ideas."

"I didn't have any."

She smiled as though that wasn't really the right answer. On the drive from Raleigh, I'd thought about whether being the quasi-heir had spoiled romance for us. It was all too close, and family-like, and what would we all say to each other while Mary served Thanksgiving dinner? And then there was Pren—how would that conversation go? *I'm now sleeping with your camp counselor?* But when I came down the dirt drive and saw from a distance Tessie bending over her book boxes, I got the old thump-thump going big time. She stood up and stretched, and waved hello with a big easy smile, and, if anything, dressed in black tights and top, her hair pulled back, she was even more attractive than when we were kids: tawny and athletic, her bourbon voice commanding, and seductive in the bracing Symmes manner, and, on top of that—happy. It had taken her about five minutes to get a job teaching high school history in Wilmington, and she started in the fall. She was the first Symmes I'd seen in a long time, maybe ever, with actual smile wrinkles.

Still, as she bluntly reminded me, there was the matter of my non-divorce divorce, which meant a lot to her. She talked about taking communion again at Christ Church, and I deduced that meant having sex with me only when I was completely, and totally, and finally, single. That news meant a special torture, since everything around us, from beach to dock, to the varnished blue trim of the Chris-Craft, recalled unbridled teenage passion.

After we got back from tennis, Tessie went to the big house to cook, and I walked down to the dock to find Hugh where we'd left him. He'd fallen asleep over the paper. As gently as I could, I retrieved it from his lap, but he woke up, startled. He began to say something and shook his head, and then leaned over and touched my arm, beckoning me to lean close.

"Big Hugh said two things to me before he died," he whispered. "Over there." He turned away from the water and pointed a single crooked index finger toward the house, now in spreading shadows from the canopied oaks, and the front bedroom, its dappled windows reflecting the afternoon light.

"That's where they laid him out?"

Hugh nodded and smiled, his charmed, canine smile, now permanent. After the first strokes, he had been self-conscious, realizing he had a slight atrophy at the corners of his mouth, which made him always seem to be smiling. But lately, after the speech, he had made peace with always smiling.

"Big Hugh motioned to me, like this, with his finger. 'Come here, boy,' he said, and everyone got quiet. The room was full, all the family, but he had this important thing to say just to me."

"What was it?"

He leaned over and motioned again with his index finger. "Come here, boy. Big Hugh said it like I was little, but I was grown of course, I was back from the War. Still I leaned over, because he wanted to whisper."

"And?"

"Oh, he said—and everybody wanted to know, the Major was there, see. Big Hugh had his stroke when they were all up the river at a party, I remember they were all dressed up."

I didn't know whether he was going to tell the secret, or whether there was a secret, or whether the condition of his mind led him to go back and forth this way.

"Want me to get you a Coca-Cola?" I said, after waiting a while. "I thought I'd run back up to the house."

"He whispered two secrets."

"Well then, you better tell me."

He leaned forward and looked from side to side. "The first one—he said, 'I voted for Eisenhower.'"

"You're kidding. Did anybody hear?"

"No one spoke of it."

"And the second secret?"

He leaned closer, his face darkening. "Our family has Negative blood."

◆◆◆

PLOTTING OUT THE TRIP to Mexico was easy, really, straight lines all the way, south by southwest. I suspected Lowry didn't have much use for a map. I put one in my bag anyway.

Lowry was turning burgers at our bon voyage pool party. He had volunteered so I could greet the guests. There wasn't any need of that, since it was Raleigh, and they all knew me and each other. I'd asked Tessie to come, at the last minute, but she had tennis in Wilmington. She did say that Lowry had given Hugh communion on the dock, which he received in great peace. She'd taken the elements also, having successfully avoided sex. Of course, Lowry completely won her over. *A great guy!* she said. *Have fun in Mexico!*

We'd invited people from the firm, faculty from St. Elizabeth's, Nora's friends from Mighty Lamb. Pren had dropped by for the pregame, and Kai-Jana and Winston had phoned in regrets from the campaign trail. Robin and Adam's friends came, the Enright crowd huddling to discuss the latest capitalist outrage while the Bingham kids looked for beer.

Ferris and Billy had invited some new fellows, and they stood talking with Juan and the Lowry work team, all pressed and starched. It was a mild and humid night, marred only by mosquitoes, against which we had employed Tiki torches that sputtered on spikes with a yellow flame.

Ferris had told me earlier that when he finished helping Nora, he had to go to Zurich to wind up his last business with Victor. I took that to mean he was going to meet the Swiss banker who kept watch over his $29 million. I imagined Billy would enjoy the trip.

That set me to thinking about how lots of sex, and some non-sex, along with money had been my ruin. This quest for sex and money, and immoral things you had to do to live well, led me first into fatigue, and then into a paralysis that Ferris, who did so many more bad things than me, somehow didn't have. When he asked me if I were jealous of Elaine and Kai-Jana, I had said yes, a little; but what I really felt at that moment was envy for him. He could go to prison, and take that money, and date men, and be happy, and embark on a future—maybe here, maybe with Billy. Come to think of it, Pren and Teri Lynn and Tessie, all of them were embarking on a future, too, each off to new worlds: a horse farm, the oncology ward, a return home from exile.

As for me, I puttered around Raleighwood, undone by past battles, tied in knots by sin, mine and others. Why couldn't I get free like the rest? I wondered if Lowry had any thoughts.

"Satan loves the strong," he said ruefully, depositing rounds of sizzling meat on a tray Robin set out.

"I don't understand." Lowry sometimes referred to Satan as one would a rival NFL coach.

"Satan confuses the strong. He uses baubles."

"Are you saying sex and money are baubles? I'll give them up. Do I have to?"

"I don't know. What do you think?"

"That's not helpful."

"Okay, consider hamburgers." He deposited a fresh round of sizzling patties on the grill.

"What do you mean, 'consider hamburgers'?"

"Do you eat hamburgers?"

"I do eat hamburgers."

"Well, plenty of people don't. Hamburgers make them sick, and they eat something else."

"Yes, and so what?"

He pointed at me with the spatula. "If you can eat the meat, then eat it. If you can't eat the meat, then don't. It's not Harris Teeter's fault, see?"

"No."

"We'll have lots of time to talk about this on the way to see the Fathers."

The party lasted until midnight, and the next day we loaded up the cambio. Nora and Robin made buckwheat pancakes for breakfast and wrapped up their low-sugar pie. Ferris packed a lunch basket with green and yellow ribbons for Mexico, and Adam gave me his St. Christopher medal.

"I'll take good care of it, Adam. Thanks."

"Just be careful, Mr. C. Don't get kidnapped."

"That ship has sailed, my friend."

I thought I should ask Lowry for details, now that we were about to embark. "Lowry, what route are we going to take, you, me, and Juan? It's a good three days."

He looked at the sky, as though picking out a cloud to travel by. "I don't know exactly. I haven't thought about it."

Before I could worry, Juan motioned from the cambio. Nora and Robin, Ferris and Adam gathered to wave goodbye, and Lowry and I climbed into the front seat.

Lowry cranked the engine and left it to warm. I handed him the map I'd saved with the route I'd marked, black lines from Raleigh to the Mississippi, south to the Rio Grande, over the border into Mexico, a straight drop to Dolores Hidalgo, and the Fathers.

"Great, Jack, thanks for the map," he said, folding the crinkled pages. I figured he'd never look at it. He knew the way by heart.

The End